THE ROOM

By
Hannah Adkins

© 2020 Hannah Adkins

*To my husband. Thanks for enduring.
May you never need your own Room.
Yours forever, H. x*

Prologue

"...and then, in dreaming, / The clouds methought would open and show riches / Ready to drop upon me, that when I waked / I cried to dream again."

—William Shakespeare, <u>The Tempest</u>

At the end of the street, just far away enough from where the body of a woman lay like a discarded rag, and where a police cordon stemmed the tide of a curious crowd, a Birmingham News Today channel van was parked up. The back doors were wide open, giving way to the strain of stacked wires and cable spools. Burrowed deep in this mess of snaking technology, a makeshift desk was the only clear space; a laptop sat on the plywood, glowing white against the night's sky.

Michael Powers was sitting on the tailgate of the van, leaning forward in what was once a well-pressed suit, his elbows on the tops of his thighs as he adjusted the cuffs of his shirt to make them frustratingly even. He'd become so good at this he barely looked at them anymore. This time was no different as he stared down the busiest street in the suburbs; a frown trenched deep onto his face.

Busy for all the wrong reasons, Michael thought.

He allowed the haphazard flow of townhouses to direct his gaze and then thread through the other channel vans irreverently parked on the street thrown into excited confusion. Beyond the vans, all he could see was an unsettling mesh of bodies talking animatedly, and the punishing blue lights from the ambulance service.

He didn't need to take down any more than that visually. He'd seen all this before, and frankly, it bored him to bloody tears. While the Head Reporters were grabbing stories on murder mysteries and features on the entangled party system, he got the *fluff*. He got the traffic accidents, the idiotic animal stories, the potatoes that looked a little-like-Kim-Kardashian. And tonight, he should be oh-so-gracious that he got a *sodding suicide*. Admittedly, he thought, one that had caused quite a turnout. But, to Michael, it was still a fool throwing themselves off a building; someone who couldn't be arsed anymore and wanted to be slightly more dramatic than swilling down some pills and alcohol in the comfort of their own home.

There was a crash from inside the van and a loud 'Oh, bollocks'. Michael sighed audibly. As well as the "fluff" assignment from Jennifer, he'd been given a babysitting job for the clumsy intern.

The sound of a helicopter overhead cut through the night. He strained his neck to see it. 'Looks like they've called out the big guns,' he said.

'Say again?' Zach walked steadily around to the back of the van carrying the camera like it was a suitcase. He placed it gently on the floor and then crouched protectively around it.

'Never mind,' Michael replied, not bothering to look up from his cuffs. He was now intent on the natural matting of black hair on his tanned wrists. It splayed out from under the crispness of his white shirt; Michael thought it looked like spiders were creeping down his arms. He shuddered sharply.

'I'm sure I've visited this place in my nightmares,' he added as he laid one final tug on his cuffs and stretched to his full height. He stepped around to face Zach who, rather annoyingly in Michael's mind, sprang to his feet with the camera already perched on his shoulder. 'And you were there,' Michael continued, pointing to Zach, 'and you were there too.' He pressed a finger into his left ear.

'Very funny,' the voice in his ear retorted.

Zach sniffed loudly and looked quizzical until Michael met his gaze and motioned to his earpiece. 'And in my nightmares, I have voices in my head, too,' Michael continued.

'Trust me, Michael; I'd rather be in bed than in your ear right now.'

'Saucy bitch.'

'You can't see me, but I'm rolling my eyes.'

'Mr. Powers, shouldn't we be over there where the action is?' Zach asked.

'Did you hear that, Harriet?' Michael pressed his ear again and lowered his voice, 'the clumsy intern, who is so graciously my cameraman because the real ones are on the bloody important stories, actually used the phrase "where the action is".'

'And he called you 'Mr.',' Harriet said. 'You better hang onto him.'

'You take all the fun out of this job. Besides, I don't have to take this from you. You're only my assistant.' Michael reached into his front breast pocket and slid out a thin mirror. He immediately spread his thumb and index finger across the top of each eyebrow. He tilted his head back to check for stray hairs from his nose.

'Yes, until Jennifer says otherwise.'

Michael replaced the mirror and straightened his tie. He reached for a slim tablet he'd left just inside the van then returned to his mark. 'Of course. Where is our Commander-in-Chief anyway? Doesn't she know they have the helicopter darting about?'

'She left for the night. Probably in bed-'

'Probably fucking someone over.' Michael studied the writing on the tablet.

'I was going to say probably dreaming up new nightmares for you.'

'Same thing.'

'Wow! You really hate her, don't you? Are you ever going to tell me what she's got on you?'

'Maybe.' Michael coughed lightly. 'Harriet, I'm reading these notes. What do we have on 'The Room'?'

'Next to nothing. All you see there. Woman face-plants from the roof of what seems to be a café. Only three stories high, so she must've fell nastily, or really meant to do herself damage. No I.D. on the woman yet, but that shouldn't take long. In the meantime, get creative.'

'Gee, thanks, I can work with that.' Michael said, only half-smiling.

'No problem,' Harriet returned. 'Oh, and while you're there, if it's not too much trouble, can you ask Zach to turn his headset on?'

Michael mimed to Zach to turn his battery pack on, but eventually had to come off his mark and do it for him.

'You know they don't pay me well enough to work the useless twat circuit,' he whispered to Harriet on his way back to his mark.

'You do know he can hear you now, right?' Harriet said.

Michael turned back to face the camera. He gave Zach an awkward smile. 'How long?'

'Fifteen seconds,' Harriet replied efficiently. 'Zach, the reason Mr Powers is hanging back away from the action is that he wants an establishing shot first and then a slow approach towards the melee.'

'Yeah sure, that's what I thought you were doing, but at Uni they said you should start with a big pan and then go into the-' the intern's voice rang in Michael's ear, making him wince. He couldn't help thinking that the kid sounded so bloody *young*.

'Just leave it to the professionals, yeah?' Michael interrupted.

Harriet counted down to four then Zach silently took over the count with his fingers, leaving his middle finger last.

'I'm standing on the corner of Share Street, where earlier this evening, a woman fell to her death from the roof of one of the dwellings. Although it has not been confirmed at this time, the building is likely to have been a place of business known only as 'The Room'. Locals have stated it is a fashionable café hidden amongst the Share

Street townhouses. What is also not clear is the identity of the victim, although it is believed that the woman was local to the area.'

Michael was about to move towards the scene when he became distracted by the camera shifting up above his head. He stumbled over his words as he struggled to maintain his frame. But then, he followed the gaze of Zach and the camera.

Harriet's voice was loud, too loud, in his ear.

'Michael you stopped, is everything-'

Michael pulled the earpiece clear.

It was hard to see if it was a man or a woman, but the person silently jumped from the building. The sound of the impact was mercilessly loud. The life spilt out over the people below. Michael spotted Elena Edwards, or more specifically, *heard her*, first. She was the new woman from Channel 4 news; a mass of blonde hair and a skinny, overly tanned frame that was always squeezed into a dress on the verge of being obscene. Instead of doing her usual nasal broadcasting, she was screaming. Her eyes fixed on the floor, her arms bent at the elbows, hands stretched with the palms upwards. Her white dress was splattered crimson.

Zach was already on his way to the site of the drama; his camera was blazing with lights and gathering raw footage as he went. Michael followed him, running through the busy street and feeling his dinner, a burrito, bouncing proudly in his stomach. He noticed the intern getting down all he could through the camera. Michael wondered too if they would have the luxury to go through that unedited roll before the authorities could get hold of it. That specific joy was all too rare these days.

Zach was far in front, already partially engulfed by the forming crowd. Michael stopped; his black hair was flat and matted over his forehead; his breath was short and strained. He was close to the end of terrace house now, with a view to the grey metal front door, leading to this 'Room' place, to his right, and the gabbling crowd to the left.

'Film the roof, Zach' Michael shouted through the crowd. He lifted his gaze to where the jumper came from, but he could see no signs of movement, there wasn't even any lights coming from the building that he could see. It looked like the person had jumped out of the darkness.

Apart from the crowds who showed no signs of abating, Michael's eyes were drawn to the metal front door of the so-called 'Room'. A man cautiously opened the door and left the building. He didn't look at the crowds who were too busy screaming and capturing Elena Edward's frozen stance to see him, but the man bowed his long neck and walked quickly into the road.

In the thirty years that Michael had been in the business, he had come across all manners of people, but the way this man was acting was *unusual*. Michael motioned to Zach who was too busy filming the crowd, the body on the floor, and the screaming reporter from Channel 4 News, to notice. He shook his head and backed away from the crowd and towards the man.

The man who didn't want to be seen was thin; even wearing a large thick coat, he appeared to be almost painfully jagged. He was tall, perhaps 6ft 6 or 7, but with his bowed head, he looked more like a long shadow than a man. Michael could see how easily he could slip away into the darkness. He managed to follow the man for a few steps before reaching for his arm. He knew better than to find himself alone with the stranger, so he had to move quickly.

The tall man squeezed and contracted under his grasp and turned his head to Michael, eyes wide,

'What? What is it?' He stammered.

Michael, through the dim lighting of the streets and the attack of the police's blue glaring lights, saw a sharp terror spread across the man's sallow face. His long arms curled up, and he adjusted his oversized glasses and brushed thick black hair from his face. His eyes, almond in shape, flickered just once to the crowd behind them.

'You're not curious about that?' Michael gestured with a nod of his head.

'What? I don't know nothin' so…Look I'm sorry I've gotta go.'

The man's accent was soft, but still noticeably from South-East London. Alongside his sheer height, he would be even harder to miss in Birmingham now. Michael made no attempt to stop him as he turned away.

'I think the police will want to talk to you. After all, two people did just jump from your building,' Michael called after him.

The tall man stopped dead. Michael heard the man inhale deeply as he reached out to draw himself to a short piece of garden wall so he could sit. He turned his full, long body towards Michael. For a moment, the tall man looked at his questioner; he focused on his microphone, the channel's emblem across it, then his almond-shaped eyes poised on Michael's face. As the icy blue lights flashed across his thick hair and sliced shadows on his cheekbones, a grin, thin and wide, grew across his face.

'Jesus. They called you to report on this?' he asked in disbelief.

Michael coughed lightly, his heart beating faster. 'Yeah well, I've already done all the stories about cats up trees tonight.'

The man laughed, high pitched and coarse. The sound made Michael wince. 'I can't talk to the police, and I don't think you'd want me to talk to them either,' the man said.

'Now, why wouldn't I want you to talk to the police?'

There was that thin, wide grin again. 'Because I know who you are, mate, an' I know what you did.'

The tall man's breath returned and calmed. He continued, 'But there's a funny thing 'ere, Michael is it?' He paused. Michael nodded. 'That's not even the best bit, mate. When the police piece this together they're going to clam up, they'll have no choice. I won't be allowed to speak, and some things will be lost forever.'

Michael scanned the area; the confused mob of people, the building and the tall man who knew his name,

'Is this something to do with "The Room"?'

'Michael?' Zach was feeding back out of the crowd.

Michael turned to the tall man who was already on his feet. 'If I let you go, then what? You seriously owe me.'

The tall man was already back-stepping, building up momentum,

'I....I'll find ya in the next couple of days. I know where you work.'

'Wait!' Michael, reaching into his pocket, strode up to him. He pulled out his smartphone and took a picture. 'Insurance, find me - otherwise, I'll print this on the front page-'

'I don't think you have any stories on the front-page mate, not anymore. I'll be seeing you.'

Michael felt a hand on his shoulder that brought him back to reality. He had been staring into the dark where the tall man had drifted.

'Harriet's sending me deaf with this thing. You're needed on the front line.' Zach still had the camera mounted on his shoulder. 'I can get us in close, but we have to move now.'

Michael nodded slowly, consciousness building up again. 'Lead the way.'

The two men fought through the jostling limbs until they couldn't fight anymore. This was their patch now, so they cleared a space. Michael was close enough to see the bodies in the shot. He also knew the police were frantically trying to get the crowd back and cover over the freshly decorated street, so they needed to move fast.

'You ready?' Michael asked.

Zach made a few checks on the camera and with Harriet. 'Under a minute,' he confirmed.

Michael strode over to Zach, arms wide to stop the journalists getting into their self-made filming spot and whispered into his ear, 'Don't film the bodies directly. If they see you filming the bodies we've lost.' Michael returned to his mark. 'How long?'

Zach seemed to respond to something in his ear. '50 seconds.'

'Hold your position, Zach,' Michael said as he turned towards the scene. The only people left to fight to get to the real crux were around twenty journalists, clamouring for the moment that would give them the edge in the great ratings war. Michael recognised Eric, an old runner he used to piggyback when they both worked on the Echo. He reached out through the living bodies to grab the back of Eric's coat.

'Michael.' Eric turned and instinctively grabbed him, pulling him to the cordon tape. He was bigger than Michael and always wore the puffiest winter coat you ever saw, which made him look even more substantial, like a thick oak tree.

He didn't have much time. 'What you got?' Michael winced at the sound of his voice; he wanted to give an air of knowing more than he did, which was absolutely nothing. He might well have said 'what the hell is going on here?'

'Well, I think we missed the money shot.' Eric pulled on Michael's lapel to direct his attention to Elena Edwards. She was crouched low, blonde ashy extensions slick with a red liquid, her overly tanned limbs quivering in the arms of an Ambulance staff member.

'I'm not sure that's the proper use of that phrase, Eric,' Michael said, unable to contain his smile. 'But I'm sorry I missed it.'

'Mr. Powers, Michael!' Zach shouted above the crowd, 'It's nearly time!'

'Is that your boy?' Eric asked.

Michael nodded. 'Yeah, first gig.'

'Well, hate to say it Powers, but I think you've shit it.' Eric motioned out down the cordon. A group of Uniformed Police Officers had started to wave the cameras down. 'It's started.'

Michael watched as scuffles broke out across the police tape. Cameras were snatched out of hands and allowed to fall to the floor, adding to the already messy street with splintered black plastic and shards of glass.

Something was wrong.

Michael moved past Eric to get closer to the bodies. He caught Zach's eye and quickly shook his head, motioning him to stay back. He couldn't risk Jennifer's wrath if the intern's camera was smashed up in the mayhem.

Michael found himself opposite the bodies and at the front of the line; the cordon tape relaxed and hung in a limp 'u' as the cameramen who had stretched against it retired to their vans, half smashed cameras cradled in their arms. He looked at the scene, in all its horror in front of him. The man, the second faller, was shrouded in the bonnet of a car; he formed a mass of blood and pulp. The window had collapsed, half inside the vehicle and half inside the man. Blood had risen above the crumpled metal and fell like mascara tears down the front of the headlights. The man's face was distorted, but despite this, there was a familiarity about him.

And then Michael turned to the first faller. The woman was bent unnaturally across the pavement, spilling out onto the road. It wasn't pleasant to follow the contour of her once slender body. Her beach blonde hair was still changing crimson colour, and its disarray threatened to cover her face completely, except for her wide staring eyes. He had to crouch to see her face.

Michael froze. The night's coldness pressed upon his chest. His breath became short and painful. He had a desperate desire to throw up. After what felt like hours of staring at the woman's glassy eyes, he flung himself backwards.

For the second time that night, Zach's hand on his shoulder shook him into life. Slowly and awkwardly, Zach got Michael to his feet. Michael still stood facing the bodies as though it were some grotesque installation in a museum. He knew Zach was talking to him, but he no longer heard the words.

You get one, and you have the other.

Michael recognised the woman straight away, and that meant he'd already pieced the distorted images of the dead man on the car together. He knew them both.

Because I know who you are, mate, and I know what you did.

Michael turned and grabbed Zach by the arm, flinging him around. 'It's over kid.'

'Bu, Mr Powers-'

'It's a fucking lockdown. We have to go,' he snapped.

Michael pushed through the crowd and ran back to the end of Share Street and the waiting van. He almost got to it before he had to duck down and, slamming his back against the brick wall of the nearest house, he threw up. When he was sure it was over, he allowed himself to fall on his backside and enjoy the cooling bricks on his back, cradling his head against the stabbing pain.

Zach carefully placed the camera down and found a spot next to him. A few moments passed before Michael broke the silence.

'So, Zach. How was your first assignment?'

They both smiled.

Zach began nervously playing with his headset before reaching across to re-attach Michael's earpiece. Michael turned to him briefly.

'Oh, no. Why?'

'Harriet wants you. Sorry, Mr Powers,' Zach said.

'Oh, hello, Harriet. How has your night been?' Michael began.

'Michael I'm not sure I know what's going on-'

'Me neither,' he interrupted.

'-but I've got Jennifer on the connect.'

'Of course you have. A perfect end to a perfect night.' There was an audible click. 'Jennifer.'

Her voice came on the line. Sharp and fast. 'Powers, it seems like you have a few answers about what's going on down there, but for now I'm not interested. What does bother me is why I've been woken up in the middle of the night with a countrywide slap down on a double suicide.'

'Sorry, Jennifer. Just to be clear - are you bothered about the slap down or being awoken in the middle of the night?' Michael thought he heard Harriet snorting through the earpiece.

'First thing in the morning. That means eight. You better have some answers, Powers, because as sure as shit I've got some questions.' There was an audible click.

Michael pulled the earpiece free.

I've got a few questions of my own, he thought.

He sat for a while as Zach started to pack away the gear in the van. The two men didn't speak at all on the ride back, but Michael's head was filled with the image of the dead woman laid out across the gutter and the dead man who shouldn't have been there at all.

Chapter 1

Then

Everything was new to the little girl. The sounds and colours, picked out and tossed around the park as they bounced from shoulder to shoulder. Bodies twitched and sprang in all directions, following no discernible patterns, other than the loudest noises and the strongest, sweetest odours.

The little girl was entirely shaded from the sun amidst the crowd circling her. She noticed that the grass beneath her feet was hard; not the soft lush green she remembered before the fair had arrived. In fact, nothing looked the same to her. As she strained to look beyond the faces and heads that bobbed like puppets, all she could see was the deepest blue sky, unbothered by cloud. Every so often she would catch sight of a castle turret reaching far beyond the busy crowd. Or the blurring whir of spinning metal buckets filled with older children as they screamed in delight.

It was the screaming that the little girl didn't like. She squeezed her fingers tight around her father's hand, a vain attempt to cover every inch somehow. It was a frustrating game she had been playing ever since she first discovered her fingers and how useful they could be to her. She looked up into her father's face as it tilted down to meet her stare. He guided her hand to his chest such that her arm was at full stretch. She knew what that meant. The little girl jumped high into his gathering arms, and they squeezed each other before she settled into the nook created by her father. Her brown eyes were wide as she struggled to take in the fair bubbling away in front of her.

Her father joked with her about her hair, pretending to get lost in the thick black curls as they watched the rides. When she knew she was safe, she fixed her attention on the carousel over by the great oak tree and on the edge of the largest crowd. She found the carousel almost straight away because the oak tree was the only part of the park she recognised from her new vantage point; the only familiar thing that had escaped the fair's clutches.

Together, they watched the carousel. The wooden horses glistened in the dappled sun from the great oak tree and, with fixed toothy smiles, they went around and around to the sound of a pregnant pipe organ. Some of the better-painted horses had children hanging from them, pulling their straggly manes, pretending to kick their swollen bellies.

She picked out one of the empty horses and followed it around with her eyes. Transfixed, she hadn't noticed her father crouch down beside her. With splayed fingers, he swept back his black hair and scratched at his cheek.

'You know,' he began, 'I like the look of the one with the orange face and the purple bum.'

The little girl narrowed her eyes and looked at the horses circulating. 'Daddy. There isn't a horse with an orange face and a purple bum,' she said after a few moments.

'Who said anything about horses? I'm talking about the old lady in the middle, making it go around.'

She giggled and placed her hand into her father's once more. He stood up and made towards the carousel, held back only by the gentle pull of the little girl's stiffened arm. Her mop of hair shivered as she shook her head.

'Jasmine, don't you want to go on the carousel?'

'Don't know,' she whispered, barely audible over the pipes and screams. 'Will you come with me?'

'I don't think those horses will be able to take my weight, especially after those hotdogs we just demolished. But you,' he pinched her tummy, 'you are just about right for this race. I'll be here, though. Got to get some pictures of my girl coming first.'

'I don't think it's a race, Daddy. It just goes around and around.'

'Yeah? Well, maybe you're right. Still, looks fun though, don't you think?'

The air around them was close and full of that gasping pipe music that rolled out in waves. Closer still, and the horses seemed more pleased with themselves, flaky painted smiles unmoved, as they completed yet another lap.

'You know...' he said, watching a little smile percolate from the corner of her mouth. Jasmine knew that whenever he started a sentence off with "You know" that she would end up giggling over something he had said. In those moments, she couldn't help but smile. No matter how hard she would try to resist, even to the point of holding her breath, eventually she would just explode into a fit of laughter.

'I've always loved your hair,' he continued. 'It's so thick; it must be an adventure in there. Do you think there's an explorer lost in here, somewhere, in the forest of your head?' He gently ruffled her hair until she burst out laughing. He buried his face in her curls, and as it disappeared, he said in a high-pitched voice, 'Over here. Go towards the light you fool. No, no. Leave the snake where it is!'

She giggled, pushing his face out of her hair.

'Another reason I love your hair,' he continued, blowing her curls from his face, 'is because at your age there are so many different and exciting ways to let it fly in the wind. I think it would be a shame not to take your hair for a spin on one of those horses.'

Another scream came from somewhere behind them, and Jasmine tensed her body.

'Not all screams are bad,' he said to her after a moment. 'At the end of some screams lives uncontrollable laughter.'

The carousel had slowed and come to a stop. Jasmine found a horse she liked; it was brown with a green saddle and a candy cane right through its middle. Despite being spiked with a sugary treat, its smile was big. Her father swung her high until she landed firmly on the saddle. She gripped the candy cane bar desperately with both hands. Jasmine's father knew she wasn't going to let go, so he pushed a pound coin into her fingers. 'This is for old purple bum when she comes and collects it.'

He turned away and started to take up his position against the oak tree. He fumbled, getting his phone out of his pocket and swiped through to the camera. He looked up and mouthed, 'I'll be right here.'

Jasmine never took her eyes off her father, except of course when her horse took her round, literally out of sight. Each time the carousel came full circle, Jasmine would pick her way through the horses in front and the swinging limbs of the other children to see if he was still standing there like he'd promised. The horse beneath her shuddered into life at certain points on their journey, lifting Jasmine clear off her seat. She screamed and laughed and was relieved to see the other boys and girls doing the same. She became lost in the noises of the carousel which had now become soft and seamless. The carousel was her new *favourite thing*. She could feel her hair lifting from her shoulders, tugging her head back and tickling her face as it flapped for its freedom. She looked across to see if he'd noticed.

Something flickered over by the oak tree. It was like an incomplete picture that came in and out of itself. She looked for the familiar figure, his blue t-shirt, his black hair. But he wasn't there. Her eyes were wide, and her body went cold as she strained against the agony of having to go around once again, hoping that by the time the oak tree came along, that he would be there, that he had always been there and that she had imagined the whole thing.

Coming around once more, her eyes swam with tears as she saw her father standing where he should have been all along. She found the courage to let go with one hand of the candy cane bar and mop handfuls of tears from her eyes. She didn't want to lose him again in a wet kaleidoscope of summer fairground colours.

As the two of them strolled away from the carousel and towards the park entrance, Jasmine stopped abruptly and looked up at her dad.

'Where did you go?' she asked.

'Go?' He squeezed her hand gently. 'I didn't go anywhere. What do you mean?'

'I couldn't see you and then I could. It was like magic, but scary magic because you weren't there and then you were.' Jasmine's eyes started to shine with fresh tears that threatened to overflow and spill down her cheeks.

He knelt and grabbed his daughter, taking her in his arms. 'Well, I'm here now.' He paused before saying, 'It does sound like a magical thing though, and what better place for it to happen than the magical fair.'

Jasmine looked back at the fair and the bubbling crowd and then finally at the carousel where already she noticed her horse was throwing around another little girl. She looked back at her father and said, 'I think I like the park better.'

*

Catch the wind in your curls, Jasmine.

Jasmine remembered the wind in her hair, way back when she was a little girl. But this time, her father wasn't there to see it, and she was thankful for that. She felt the air rushing against her face, pushing back the black curls away from her ears and having the force of that wind fill them with harsh white noise that drowned out her heartbeat.

The space between life and death was far smaller than Jasmine had pictured; it was a hands-width at the most. She scratched the concrete slabs with her foot, and a tiny piece of gravel loosened, flinging itself valiantly ten centimetres away and then slipping over the edge of the building, as easily as oil over water. The skin prickled on the back of her neck as she imagined the gravel falling to the ground, soundless and unnoticed, blending into the pavement like a heavy, dark raindrop into a puddle. She dug her nails into her arm, feeling the heat rise as she scratched.

Jasmine squinted at the harsh sun, just peeking out of thin clouds overhead, the type of clouds that bounced the sunlight around them like bright glass mirrors instead of hiding it within their greying bellies. She wiped at her eyes. She couldn't work out if they were wet from the wind whipping the top of the Radisson Blu Hotel, or because of the moments that had brought her to the edge, overlooking Birmingham, thirty-six stories up. Her sleeves were patched with black mascara. Jasmine hurried to wipe away fresh tears in case anyone would see.

But of course, no one would. She was alone, and she had contrived it that way; the lift from reception had taken her straight up to the 35th floor of the hotel. When she left the elevator, the door opposite was propped open with a bright red fire extinguisher, the padlock and keys hanging sulkily next to the opened bolt. She spotted the staircase leading to her final destination. She then climbed up a last set of stairs before opening the door to the roof with a single push.

It had been easy to remain anonymous. No one had said anything to Jasmine as she'd walked past, busily looking at their phones, shouting into ear-pieces. They had all missed the woman with the thick black curly hair and tired, puffy eyes. That must mean that no one cared, Jasmine had assured herself as she walked past the whirring fans and pipework, towards the front of the building. She had lifted herself onto the edge of the blue sugar-coated building. And there she was, her eyes streaming, because she wanted to die with her father's words fresh in her mind.

Catch the wind in your curls, Jasmine.

Her chest was tight with the stabbing cold November wind, making her breathless. She hadn't thought to bring her old parka coat that still hung on her peg at work; why would she? Besides, since she'd made her mind up that today was *the* day, she couldn't wait to get away from the café and Martin's indifference to all but his precious son and business. She could have stood up on one of the little wooden tables and announced with a certain fraction of pride what she was going to do, and she imagined the only response from him would have been, "Okay then bab, but I want you back for the afternoon rush".

Jasmine eyes drifted towards the ground. The streets below fidgeted to their own brand of music; the tapping of feet on the pavement, honking of horns around the roundabout, while the office blocks ahead of her heaved with bankers and brokers, white collared men and women in shift dresses. Their buildings rose high above the hotel where Jasmine stood. She was like a Shakespearean actor in the round, waiting for her cue.

It was hard to discern the scenes in the busy buildings opposite, but she found her eyes focusing on them instead of the road, so very far below. Right ahead was the ugliest building of them all; a leftover from the Brutalism period. The grey rendering of the building was puckered with square white windows. Jasmine could just about make out figures moving about. Her gaze shifted from window to window, catching glimpses of life - a pot plant on the windowsill, men talking animatedly to another. Her eyes rested on a lone figure looking out of the window on what would be the thirtieth—no - thirty-first floor.

It was challenging to pick out any of his features; she'd assumed it was a man from the cut of his figure despite floating reflections of clouds from the turbulent sky. But the face - his face - was as indistinct as a thumbprint in mud. She scorned herself for not going to that optician's appointment, another failed attempt at life's precious admin. She could just about make out his dark brown or black hair, a white shirt, harshly pale skin. But the face itself looked *blank*.

She shook her head, feeling her curly dark hair shivering down her back, and squinted harder. Perhaps, the person was looking at the road, surveying the cars and hoping to spot someone they knew driving past. Maybe it was an office worker, looking for entertainment and light-headed from the realisation that their daily destitute life revolved around four office walls. Perhaps, the face was looking at Jasmine. Perhaps it was the wind, pushing her away from the edge, but she felt much colder—vulnerable. She simply hadn't thought that throwing herself off a building would be so *public*.

Jasmine dug her nails into her arm, feeling the warm sting of blood under her fingernails. Her legs folded under her, dropping onto the ledge as she vomited across the roof.

Such a pussy. Jasmine muttered to herself, wiping her mouth. Panting, she looked up, across to the glass stairwell that snaked up the side of the office building, expecting to see the faceless man, but he was already turning away from the window. He descended the stairs and disappeared from view.

She crawled away from the ledge and towards a large concrete block, hiding behind it to stop some of the relentless wind. She pressed the side of her face to the concrete to feel the fresh cooling of the stone against her sweating temples, and began to knock her head against the wall, each time more forceful than the last.

Jasmine felt a trembling start in her right pocket. She closed her eyes and tried to ignore the feeling; it would be her body shaking, the fear of the jump, causing her legs to go weak. But the sensation was buzzing and pausing methodically; her phone was ringing. Jasmine opened her eyes. Before she knew what she was doing, she'd got up and walked further away from the edge and put her hand in her pocket. Martin's name flashed up on the four-year-old iPhone, scratched and sore from multiple crashes with the floor.

Jasmine, Betty's turned up at the café. She's playing up again. She won't let anyone else take her home. We need you. M.

'We need you,' Jasmine said the words back slowly. She threw her phone across the roof, barely missing the pile of sick. For the second time that day, she climbed on the ledge and faced the towering buildings. With the wind caught in her curls, she took in a deep breath, pulling in so much air that it started to hurt her chest. She screamed at the building opposite.

Chapter 2

The Fly by Night Café pulsed with a fluorescent tinge that peeked from behind the special offer boards tacked to its windows. The mid-afternoon gloom painted the café a wintery grey between the tattoo removal place and a t-shirt printing business; a faceless space that always appeared to be empty except for its backroom. It had taken to cover its windows with lude t-shirt designs that were reminiscent of family seaside holidays some thirty years ago. Jasmine had often wondered if anyone even went on those types of holidays anymore.

While the T-shirt shop was eerily quiet, the Fly by Night Café was always busy with those who wanted a cup of coffee for less than £4. Martin had been one of the last to invest in a Life Enhance Chip scanner, which suited the clientele just fine. But when cash became a thing of the past, even for pensioners who made up most of the regulars, Martin had resentfully ordered one and had his chip put in himself, brandishing the NHS scar on his forearm. Jasmine could barely see her scar anymore. It was a pinprick at most, between her wrist and her elbow. She still remembered squeezing her Dad's hand as the nurse inserted the micro-chip into her arm, though.

She stood in front of the café, willing to brace herself against the cold for a few more moments before going inside. The tables and chairs that usually dressed the pavement were folded and shackled to the front. Under some deep intakes of breath, she had a quiet word with herself, enough to move her forward towards the recessed door. As she did, she felt her phone vibrating at regular intervals in the back pocket of her jeans. Someone was trying to call her. Ignoring the slight intrusion to what she hoped would not be a dramatic entrance, she opened the door slightly and slipped in through the narrow crack.

The tables strained under unsympathetic diners hunched over cups and discarded plates, pushed aside for a crossword or a glowing tablet. In one of the windows, a woman fought with two children and an empty pram that one of the children repeatedly pushed against a neighbouring table.

The constant rise and fall of traffic on the ring road was replaced with café noises when she finally closed the door behind her. Chatter went in all directions. Even the man in the suit, his back against the black and white tiled wall, idly fingering a menu, seemed to be talking to himself, quickly swapping one conversation for another by just pressing his ear.

Martin was standing on a chair, reaching with a cloth in one hand and a mobile phone pressed to his ear. The cloth was drunkenly threatening the *Lemon Meringue*, in chalk form on the blackboard behind the counter. With one stretch to his full height, which wasn't much more than five feet, he swiped the dessert out of existence. Almost losing his balance, he turned and saw Jasmine just inside the door. He brought his phone down from his ear and clumsily pressed buttons. At the same time, the vibration in the back of Jasmine's jeans stopped.

'Where the hell have you been?' he grunted loudly, stepping awkwardly off the chair.

A few heads turned in Jasmine's direction, overcome with curiosity.

Martin discarded the chalk, and with two hands, he pulled his overweight frame around the counter and neatly through its gap. 'I've been ringing you. Don't you answer your phone anymore?' He raised his hand and with a determined flick of his index finger, he beckoned her closer.

He took the cloth he used to wipe away the lemon meringue and mopped his neck. Strands of hair, shining silver with grease against the fluorescents lighting, curled and stuck to his already beaded forehead. An oversized moustache covered his top lip.

'Well?' he said, distracting Jasmine from looking at the sweat beads dribbling down his neckline.

'Yeah, sorry, Martin. Where is she?' Jasmine took a few more steps closer as he flicked his chef's hat to his right.

Jasmine hadn't seen Betty at first. An impressive supporting column that rose from the middle of the floor to the ceiling split the café, causing parts of it to remain unseen depending on where you sat. Jasmine rounded the column and saw her friend sitting in a corner, just under the far end of the counter. She'd been given her own chair and a borrowed table from the suite of furniture in the dining area. On the table was a bowl with sweet-smelling steam drifting up from the butterscotch surface, catching Jasmine off guard and reminding her that she hadn't eaten. Betty was sat at a right angle to the bowl, her knees facing away from the table. Her chin rested on her chest, which served to highlight her steady breathing. She had both hands on her lap but together around a half cup of tea. Jasmine knelt before her friend. She cupped her own hands around Betty's, and the older woman raised her eyes to meet Jasmine's.

The sharp, powdery blue of Betty's eyes was strikingly vibrant against her olive skin and the aged creases. Betty took in a deep breath and allowed herself to smile slowly. She leaned in to whisper. 'They think I'm mad, Jas.'

Feeling that the cup in her hands was cold, Jasmine gently prised it from Betty's firm grip and put it on the table. 'Well you are, aren't you?'

'Yes, but we're not supposed to let on to the likes of them.'

'Who's 'them', Betty?' Jasmine asked. Martin shuffled from foot to foot behind her. His presence caused unease to spread like thick oil across Betty's face.

Betty's eyes darted from over Jasmine's shoulder and then back to her. 'He tried to touch me, Jas. I don't want to be touched.'

'Who tried to touch you?'

'That fat bastard.' Betty raised a shaky finger at Martin.

'Now, come on, there's no need for that. All I wanted to-' Martin said from behind them.

'He tried to scan my arm for that soup. I didn't even want it.'

Jasmine shook her head then turned to see Martin standing over her. He was wiping something red from his hands onto his apron. 'Martin, really?' Jasmine sighed. She rolled up her sleeve and gave him her outstretched arm. 'I'll pay for the soup.'

'Oh, now c'mon Jasmine. It wasn't like that at all. I…' Martin's voice faded to nothing as he went back behind the counter.

Jasmine put her arm down and took Betty's hands in hers again. 'Maybe it's not a bad idea. A bit of soup might do you some good. Get your insides warmed up,' she said, just before she felt Martin reaching over with the scanner. He placed the horseshoe-shaped reader around her right forearm. She looked up.

'Come on, Jas, I need you to activate.'

She let out a long-drawn breath and closed her eyes briefly. The underside of her forearm flashed a soft purple colour, and Martin's horseshoe pinged.

'Right,' he said, 'do you want a -'

'I think you know what you can do with your receipt,' she said, cutting him off. She stood upright and stretched out the aches from bending down so long. She draped an arm across Betty's shoulder. 'I'm going to take you home. Deal?'

The old woman smiled and nodded.

Jasmine followed Martin behind the counter and waited for him to serve a man in a dark suit. He asked Martin for 'tea for one'. What a strange way to ask for a cup of tea, *tea for one,* Jasmine thought, as she observed Martin clearing away the scanner and cleaning the surface. He swung around and searched under the counter to find a clean tea towel. This was whipped across his left shoulder where it would stay, like a gun in a holster, cocked and ready.

At the end of the counter, Martin kept an old cash register he'd rescued from the days when his grandfather owned the café. The old machine, no longer in use, sat stoically in the same place it had always been. It was a deep olive green with rounded corners and two display windows. It was decorated with old receipts deliberately slid between the long tentacle-like keys that no longer pushed down and produced the heavy, clunky mechanical thuds. Jasmine waited patiently for Martin to perform his ritual; the same routine he always did every time he made a sale. He reached out and patted the old register as though it were a child with an excellent school report.

With one thick hairy arm leant on the counter, Martin spoke quietly. 'It wasn't just the soup, Jasmine,' He scratched the top of his head through the fallen chef's hat, unable to make eye contact with her, he continued, 'I admit I did try and get her out.' Martin saw Jasmine raise her hands and shrug her shoulders. 'But I hardly touched her,' he added. 'It's just that—'

'Just what?'

'She started on with Freddie.' Martin met Jasmine's gaze, and together they held each other with a knowing look.

'Again?' Jasmine broke eye contact with Martin and turned to look at Betty, still sat there, her hands neatly folded in her lap on her unseasonal flowered dress.

'Jas, she thinks he's coming here to meet her, and she was shouting the place down, thinking I was hiding him from her,' Martin added.

'What did you say to that?'

'I told her that he'd probably be waiting for her at home and-'

'Jesus, Martin. So, you wanted her out because she's bad for business?'

'You shouldn't talk to me like that - I'm your bloody boss.' Martin cut himself off abruptly as a few heads turned in their direction.

Jasmine slipped through the counter and knelt before Betty a second time. 'What's all this about Freddie?'

Betty's pale blue eyes brightened and became full and hopeful. 'I told you they think I'm mad, but he *is* coming to see me. He brought me some cakes yesterday, the chocolate kind that I like, and he promised to come back, and we'd settle down with a cuppa and eat them together, that's what he said.' Betty had both her hands on Jasmine's cheeks, her thumbs wiping away imaginary tears from her face as she started rocking back and forth in her chair. Real tears had started flowing down Betty's face, cruelly spreading across her cheeks, following the lines that had formed throughout the years.

Martin had come around to the front of the counter and took up his spot behind Jasmine again. 'Betty, do you remember, it was me that brought you those cakes yesterday. I dropped them off.'

'Were they fresh?' Jasmine quipped.

Betty scowled at Martin and turned up her top lip, mouthing a silent expletive that Jasmine enjoyed. She looked at Jasmine, 'He's trying to trick me, Jas. They all are. They want me to leave, and I'll miss Freddie If I go now. He'll come, and I won't be here. He'll be lost.' Betty's voice fractured and splintered. Her breath quickened, and all her words became interspersed with short stabbing breaths. Jasmine caressed her cheek.

'They want to tell me he's gone, but he's not gone. He's coming for chocolate cake. He's not gone.'

She wiped the tears from Betty's cheek and kissed her. 'Come on, let's get you home,' Jasmine said and was relieved when Betty gave her a small nod.

Chapter 3

The mirror in the Cafe's staff toilets was tiny and cracked like a Christmas bauble. Jasmine sighed when she looked at her reflection. Thin, wiry strands of dark hair clung to her cheeks and the sides of her head, making her skin look sickly yellow. She ran her hand over the strands, pulling them away from her cheeks. Her lips were bitten and flaky like slate tiles, and there was a cut there, fresh and pink as a baby, running from her uneven and sparsely plucked brow to her cheekbone. She couldn't even remember how she'd got the cut now. She splashed water on her face and pulled down her tight polyester shirt, greying under the belly of her armpits with a dank smell of sweat.

'Jas?' Martin tapped the door.

'I'm on my way, Martin. Just needed to get my things,' Jasmine replied.

'I need to talk to you about something,' he said as she opened the door. He grabbed her arm tightly. She winced at the touch, pinching at her forearm. 'I'm sorry I,' he paused, letting go. 'I don't know my own strength.'

They both stood in the light offered by the open doorway, and Martin saw her face for the first time since she'd gone into the cloakroom. She could see a nervousness creeping into his eyes.

'Have you been crying, Jas?' he asked, visibly tracing the dark stains under her eyes.

Jasmine glanced over his shoulder to see if Betty had overheard. She hadn't, as far as she knew. She had remained where Jasmine had left her, perched on the edge of a chair but was now wrapped up for the walk home, clutching her shopping bag, still ignoring the long-dead bowl of vegetable soup.

'Listen,' Jasmine said. 'Can it wait, Martin? I should get the old girl home.' She started to move away, but Martin stopped her for a second time.

'No, it can't wait,' he said. 'I should have had this conversation with you a long time ago.'

'You sound like my dad trying to give me the "Talk",' she tapped him on the shoulder with her hand and, confident that he wouldn't try to stop her again, moved out of the staff area and behind the counter in the full glare of the café. 'But not to worry, I already know about the birds and the…'

Jasmine stopped. She knew he was there before she'd laid eyes on him. Despite three months of her heart hurting, she felt a pull of excitement in her stomach, like a rollercoaster, or a carousel. She watched Paolo from behind the counter while he stood over a bay table. The two ladies at the table were hanging onto his every word, their heads eagerly nodding.

It was no surprise to Jasmine that her heart was beating a little too fast, and her breath had shortened in response. She took the bag off her shoulder and together with the coat, slammed them both onto the counter. It was enough of a noise that everyone turned to see, including Paolo.

'What…what is he doing here?' she stammered.

Martin lowered his voice. 'Jas, it's part of why I needed to talk to you,'

'I thought he was at Uni?'

'Yes, Business Studies. Doing well by all accounts, he got a first in his last exam.'

'Great. Just *great*. But why is he here?'

'As you know this will be his third year-'

Jasmine had already started to piece it together. 'His placement year?' She paused. 'He's going to be working here? Do you think that's a good idea?'

'No. It's not, what with the both of you and,' he paused, 'what happened. That's why I'm going to have to let you go.'

'What?' Jasmine snorted. She turned to face Martin, expecting this to be another exaggeration from her boss. He was so quick-tempered; he'd snap and apologise in the same breath. It was one of his many features, as intrinsic to his personality as his moustache was to his face. But his look was calm this time, apologetic. Cold slivers of understanding cut into her supporting limbs.

Jasmine reached out to take Martin's hands, but she flinched when he pulled away.

'No, Martin, you can't, please.' Her hands went to her head to stop a pounding of thoughts turning into panic. 'I need this job. If it's about Paolo and me working together, I-'

'It won't work. I was sorry that it didn't pan out for you two, but you must have guessed that he would come and run things eventually. He's my son, family. And frankly, you've been a bit of a shit to work with recently. You only have a twenty-minute break and you were gone for bloody hours today. God knows where...'

Jasmine's head sank to her chest. Those two words he used to describe her and Paolo's three-year relationship, "pan out". Jasmine looked up slowly and caught Paolo's eye from across the café. She tasted blood in her mouth and guessed she had bitten into the inside of her cheek.

Once again, she turned to Martin, ushering him into the small corridor behind the counter space, away from sight. This time, she took his round cheeks in her hands, forcing eye contact.

'Martin please; it's not about Paolo. You know what I'm going through with my mum. I can barely pay for the help she needs. I have to keep this job.'

Martin's hands went to meet hers, and for a brief moment, he stroked them. He gently peeled away her hands from his face and, taking a step back; he plunged his hand into his pocket and brought out his phone. He opened up his banking app and, with thick sausage fingers, punched in an amount. He then scanned his arm with his smartphone and somewhere under the counter, a printer spat out a receipt.

'It's not much,' he said, holding out the piece of paper, 'but I'll pay you to the end of this month.'

Jasmine gathered her coat and started to slip it over her shoulders. She strung her bag over her opposite shoulder, so the strap hung across her chest. Still holding onto the counter, she launched herself swiftly through the café towards the door. The taste of blood was now diluted with saliva as she felt the bubble of nausea stirring in her stomach. She just had to get past Paolo.

'Are you okay, Jas?' Paolo asked, having excused himself from his fans.

Jasmine stopped abruptly. She hadn't heard his voice in three months. For a moment, she contemplated her shoes, her sensible Fly by Night Café shoes which she probably wouldn't wear again. An image shot through her head of the old film that she couldn't quite remember the name of where the girl in a gingham dress and pigtails clicks the heels of her ruby red shoes and repeats to herself the words, "There's no place like home". Then the girl in the gingham dress and pigtails wakes up. *God what was the name of that film,* she thought to herself.

She spun around on her Fly by Night shoes, pulling in her fingers on her right hand to form a fist, and connected it with the side of Paolo's temple.

Even before he hit the ground, she was leaning over him. He came crashing down, spreading tables like a brick in a pond. The two women he had been courting gasped in unison.

'No one knows what I'm going through with my mother more than you. And you will stand there and not say anything,' she spat as she looked down at him.

Paolo writhed on the tiled floor between the upset chairs and an upturned bowl of sauce sachets. Holding the side of his head and clamouring to get to his feet, he reached out for the gingham tablecloth and managed to pull it and its contents onto himself. Now covered in ketchup, butter and tea leaves and grease, Paolo briefly resigned himself to staying put. In those few moments he afforded himself, he managed to offer,

'I'm sorry, Jas. I didn't know.'

The cafe turned into a thick, heady blur; she could only see Paolo in front of her, dripping with condiments. Jasmine dropped to her knees.

'You didn't know. Which bit?' She asked. 'Me still working here, our sodding baby, or mum?'

Jasmine felt lighter as two hands pulled her to her feet. Martin reached around her, pushing her out of the way and towards his son. He straightened up the collar of Paolo's open-necked shirt and finally got to use the tea towel that was still faithfully perched on his shoulder to wipe down his son's suit jacket.

'Don't worry, your precious boy will be fine,' She turned to leave the café as she continued, 'and I think your business will survive with this poster boy wiping your tables.' As an afterthought, she stopped and said to the Paolo Lovell fan club of two,

'What do you say, ladies? I bet you wouldn't object to him keeping your condiments topped up.' The two ladies rustled together in raincoats and laughed lightly, awkwardly.

'Okay that's enough,' Martin snapped. 'Believe it or not, Jasmine but I am sorry for this,'

'Don't worry, we're all sorry for something, it will pass. Betty, come with me.'

Unmoved throughout the commotion, Betty gladly lifted herself in response to Jasmine's call. Her movements were painfully slow, and Jasmine, Martin and Paolo all stood silently in a triangle, drips of pancake syrup and tomato ketchup falling to the floor, as they watched the old woman shuffle across the tiled floor.

Outside, Jasmine put Betty's arm into hers, and they walked to the footbridge. Neither of them uttered a word for a good amount of time. Just as they stepped off the bridge and through the gates of the park, Betty finally said,

'So, Paolo. That's the boy you like is it?'

Jasmine didn't think she would ever stop laughing.

*

Jasmine tucked her arm under the folds of Betty's coat to keep warm. They sat together on a park bench under a familiar oak tree and watched the same piece of litter, a Snickers bar wrapper, dance. For a long time, nobody said a word. The furtive winter crept and discoloured the bordering trees and the highest grass white with an afternoon frost.

A man wearing a dark suit appeared in the distance following the path cut into the field. With their attention now split between the litter and the man in range, it was enough to cause Betty to stir.

'I'm not stupid,' she said rather unexpectedly, sending out plumes of condensation. Jasmine looked at her friend. 'I know he's gone. No, I know he's dead. Dead is the word. I know that. But I know there's a part of my brain that takes over and wants to tell me that any minute now he'll walk through this door or that door, or he's even this fella.'

She pointed to the man in the dark suit slowly but confidently walking towards them.

'And that's the cruellest part, Jas. My mind is forcing me to live a life that isn't real, and the outcome is always the same; he's gone, dead.'

Betty's grandson Freddie had always frightened Jasmine in the best possible way. He was older than her and had an unforgettable presence. He'd lived with his Grandmother since Jasmine could remember and had the same steely blue eyes as Betty. He'd worn leather, even when it was summer, and always seemed to be destroying something, or finding someone to destroy.

Jasmine would watch Betty's house sometimes; she lived just on the round of the estate, so the front bedroom gave a perfect view to the driveway. Girls would come in laughing, Freddie's jacket slung over their shoulders, and then a few days later she'd see the same girl's face, marked with mascara and swearing at Freddie who would shrug his shoulders with a smug smile. The only woman he didn't try to destroy was Betty, and it seemed like he'd done that now anyway.

He also had a penchant for stealing cars and, on his nineteenth birthday decided he would gift himself a Mercedes C-Class he'd stumbled upon, unlocked and still running. Unable to control the big vehicle, he'd burst through a farmer's wall, dropping some thirty feet and impacting a tree, folding the car almost entirely around the trunk. He had been pronounced dead at the scene.

'Have you seen the doctor, Betty? Perhaps there's something she can give you.' Jasmine couldn't think of anything to say other than that. It felt cheap, like a stock answer.

'You're not the first to say that.' Jasmine noticed the slow and deliberate way she turned her attention to the man in the dark suit. 'But honestly Jas,' she continued in a low whisper, 'I'm afraid of their drugs. What if they get rid of the wrong side of things, the bit that does know what's real? Where does that leave me?' Betty felt Jasmine's fingers squeeze tighter around her arm.

'Listen to me. These aren't a young girl's problems. You've got other things to think about. Like this 'ere fella coming to talk to you.'

Jasmine flicked back to the man in the dark suit who couldn't have been more than fifty metres away. She squinted but couldn't see anything that would suggest he was coming to talk to her.

'How do you know he's coming to see me?' Just then, the man raised his arm and offered the shortest and most efficient wave she had ever seen.

'Jasmine Wilson?' the man in the dark suit shouted, his step quickened, and his distance shortened. 'I'd like to talk to you.'

Chapter 4

'Will you be killing her in broad daylight?'

Jasmine dug two of her fingers into the bridge of her nose as though to support a heavy head. Her eyes were tightly closed, wishing that when she opened them, the man in the dark suit wouldn't still be standing there.

Betty, distracted by Jasmine's sudden recoil, said to her, 'It's a fair question.' She turned quickly back to the man in the dark suit; suspicious eyes followed the contour of his stiff, efficiently wrapped body. 'Because if not,' she continued, 'then I've got a bus to catch and I'll be off. I can't be sat here all day in the park. My arse on this 'ere bench you see.'

At the sound of the man's soft laughter, Jasmine opened her eyes. Still not making eye contact with the visitor, she pulled her arm from under Betty's. 'Perhaps we had better go.'

The man in the dark suit took a less than confident half step forward. 'Actually, I was hoping to have a word with you, Jasmine.' His voice was as soft as his laugh, and his words were long and drawn out, carried upon the faintest Irish accent detectable only at the tips of each sound.

The momentum lost; the women slipped back onto the bench. Jasmine took in the stranger. He had straight lines defined by what she guessed was a made to measure suit. His slender shape compromised none of it. He seemed to melt into a state of relaxation as he recognised

The Room

that he had his audience captive for a moment or two. His black hair, speckled with grey, seemed to leap from just off centre and gather in waves over his ears. His green eyes rested behind a narrow expression.

'It is a fair question,' he directed towards Betty. 'I'm sorry, I don't know your name. I'm Daniel.' He stood, unmoved by the November chill, waiting for Betty to answer.

'Betty, if you must know,' she said flashing a wink before continuing, 'I don't shake hands and, before you ask Daniel, the answer is yes, I am too old for you.'

Jasmine laughed out loud. A smile spread across Daniel's face, instantly warming his features.

'Well, Betty, to answer your question, I don't plan on killing anyone in broad daylight.' He plunged his hands into his trouser pockets and looked up at the oak tree behind them. 'That would be foolish,' he said. He brought his stare down upon them. 'That's more of a nocturnal pursuit, don't you think?'

Betty looked at Jasmine. 'Sense of humour as well,' Betty noted.

Jasmine looked back at Daniel. 'You're the "tea for one" man at the café.'

'My friends call me Daniel.'

'Listen - before you two get started, I'm getting off home,' Betty interrupted.

'But, I'll make sure you get home okay.' Jasmine let her hand rest lightly on Betty's arm as she started to move.

Unhindered by Jasmine's hand, Betty started to get to her feet. 'Today has been a shitty day for both of us, but at least yours might get a little better,' Betty's expression flicked towards Daniel, 'unless he does murder you.' She smiled and patted Jasmine's hand away and then kissed her softly on the cheek. She stood and stretched to her full height, adjusting herself on uncertain legs.

'Daniel,' she said and made an "I'm watching you" gesture with two fingers against her eyes, directing them towards Daniel before starting towards the park gates.

'I'll call you,' Jasmine called after her, but Betty didn't respond. She watched as her friend slowly moved down the path. Occasionally, Betty looked around as she reached the park border, and Jasmine wondered if she was still looking for Freddie.

'May I sit next to you?' Daniel asked.

'What do you want, "tea for one" man?'

'I told you, my friends call me Daniel.'

'Is that what you do? Go into parks in search of *friends*?'

'I was sorry about what happened; the thing with the job.'

Jasmine forced her attention to the trees in the distance and the errant litter tangled up in the branches. 'How do you know my name?' she asked.

Daniel lent back on the bench, his hands back in his pockets and his legs outstretched as though it were a textbook method for getting more warmth into the body. 'I used to love coming here.' he

The Room

said in a slow, methodical tone. 'But not now; I haven't been here in years.'

Jasmine watched him as he spoke. She joined him in scanning the park from one end to the other. The long path that weaved its way from the main gates passed the cricket pavilion on one side and the ice cream parlour and children's play park on the other. Eventually it took you past the park's crowning glory; the boating lake with a miniature train that ran around it. Two pounds for two circuits as Jasmine remembered. The last time she had been on it anyway. *It's been years,* she thought. And that word, *years*, the word that Daniel lost out of his mouth, seemed to fade away for Jasmine, too.

'They used to have fairs here,' she said out loud, surprising herself. 'And this is where the old-time carousel used to be.' She listened to the sounds whipped up by the wind against the oak. The distance traffic was gearing up, getting ready for rush hour. 'I guess parks aren't for everyone anymore, with chips and apps and everything in between.'

Jasmine slid along the bench, turning more to address him. 'What do you want? And how do you know my name?'

'I was in the café, and I saw-'

'Yes, I know what you saw' Jasmine interrupted, 'and I couldn't help that. It got out of hand and became a little bit public. I expect it gave you all something to talk about. A little story to leave with. But it's still my business and nobody else's, just remember that.'

'I wanted to offer some help,' he said.

'What the hell does that mean?' Jasmine got to her feet. She looked around and saw that they were the only two people left in the park. 'You followed us out of the café? You waited for us to leave and you followed me to the park because...because, what?'

Daniel slipped two fingers under his jacket and pulled out what looked like a business card. 'I wanted to offer you a job.' He motioned for her to take it.

Jasmine snatched it away from him, 'What is this?' she asked, turning it over in her fingers, the heat rising to her cheeks as she heard the hysteria, sharp and embarrassing, in her voice. The card was black, matte and thick. There were three lines of gold writing on it.

THE ROOM

Daniel Burton

The Architect

'Okay Daniel Burton. This doesn't tell me anything except that maybe you're in the construction business.' She spun it around her fingers again. 'There aren't even any contact details on here, Einstein. How would anyone know how to get in touch, unless this park bench is your office and that walks straight into my original assumption that you're some sort of sex pest that follows women into parks?'

Daniel laughed out loud, and as she watched him shake with laughter, Jasmine couldn't help but smile as she played back what she'd said. She studied the card again as she sat back down on the park bench.

'It's not a construction company. It's more like software meets therapy type of deal. And I need someone to keep it upright from an admin point of view while I deal with clients.' Daniel paused, rolling his eyes and then correcting himself, 'while Will and I process the clients. He'd kill me if I forgot to mention his contribution.'

'Who's Will?' Jasmine asked. 'Don't tell me; he's in the bushes now watching us?'

Daniel laughed again. 'I wouldn't put it past him.'

'This is all very interesting, Daniel. I'll call you Daniel, but I don't think we qualify as friends.'

'Soon, maybe.'

Jasmine swallowed. There was something about this man that seemed familiar, almost warming, like drinking whiskey in front of a fire. But the chill of the wind shook her out of her thoughts.

'Well that's just it, isn't it? Look, as you already know I've had a pretty shitty day, and in all likelihood, I'll never see you again, so if you're genuinely not a sex pest, then I apologise. But I'm not into playing games today.' Jasmine got to her feet and slipped the card into the back of her jeans. She started to walk away. As she did, she thought about telling her best friend Sammy about the man in the dark suit. She knew Sammy would love the story of a handsome older man offering her a job.

'It pays well,' Daniel said after her, 'the job.' Jasmine slowed her step to an almost stop. 'It would help with your mother.'

Jasmine stopped abruptly. She turned to see Daniel still sat on the bench where she had left him. 'How the hell-'. She paused, took a couple of calming breaths and pointed a finger towards him.

'You heard in the café, right?'

'Right.'

'My business.'

'Your business.'

She set her compass once again towards the gate. She was aware that Daniel had stood up and was now standing in the middle of the path, watching her. She knew he was going to say something else and, despite her eagerness to leave the park, she slowed her step.

His voice came clear down the path. 'The contact details. The card I've given you is dedicated to your chip. I'll activate it at six o'clock tonight, and if you're interested, all you have to do is scan it.'

Jasmine brought the fingers of her right hand and traced them across her left forearm. Somewhere beneath her skin, the LE chip silently waited, connected. She walked out of the park without an answer to her question.

How did he know my name?

She understood how he knew her first name, which was a no brainer. Anyone who was in the Fly by Night could decode that little mystery. Perhaps he stuck around and asked Martin for her last name and a few more bits of information. Martin would have given it all if he thought that she could land a job out of it, a welcome balm for a guilty conscience. But to have the business card dedicated to her LE chip was something else. That took some work.

On the threshold of the park, she turned towards the bench and the oak tree. Daniel had gone. A cold shiver racked Jasmine's body, and a crazy thought flashed across her mind. What if he was never there, and it was like those crappy horror movies that she and Paolo used to watch?

Jasmine smirked to herself; she was too old to believe in ghosts. She followed the edge of the park, rounding a corner and then towards an empty bus shelter. Betty had gone. Jasmine hoped she was well on her way home by now, and she made a mental note to make good on her promise and call her later.

She never did call Betty. She forgot.

Jasmine forgot a lot of things that night. It would only be in a fit of cold desperation that she would eventually scramble for her discarded jeans, reach inside the pocket and rip free the business card from Daniel.

Chapter 5

Claire Abbot wore too much makeup. She always did. And as she peered at her reflection in the bedroom mirror, her nose almost touching the glass and her breath fogging up the image of the woman looking back, she caught the outline of her smeared concealer, just around the bottom of the left eye.

'Not fooling anybody,' a fractured voice sounded from behind her.

The rasped noise in the quiet bedroom startled Claire, despite her knowing full well that there was another woman in the room. Myriam was swathed in bed linen on the king-sized bed, a mass of pillows, blankets and tissues.

'I thought you were asleep,' Claire responded, turning away from the mirror, unsatisfied with the reflection.

'Asleep or dead?' Myriam replied sharply.

Claire crossed the room that was set in evening darkness. She reached to turn on the bedside light.

'You know, some in the hospital would say that the two are one and the same.'

'Rubbish. If you're dead, you're dead.'

'If you feel that way, that's your prerogative. But I don't think that kind of thinking is going to help your daughter.' Claire reached

The Room

across and brushed aside a ribbon of hair that hid Myriam's sunken eyes. Heavy dark rings underscored her once beautiful features, and no matter how many times Claire laid eyes on her patient, the sight of Mrs. Wilson sinking into the abyss always made her stop. Myriam flinched as Claire's fingers brushed against her forehead.

Claire had grown fond of Myriam from the outset, and although it was never verbally reciprocated, she knew deep down there was a mutual respect between them. That fondness for Myriam was the reason why Claire had stuck around for so long, despite not being paid for over almost two months. After six weeks of excuses, the bruises around Claire's eyes were starting to appear and Myriam, even in her sombre condition, had noticed.

'You need to tell someone,' Myriam said, struggling with each word.

'You need to rest,' Claire replied. Her hand moved again across Myriam's face to straighten out her pillow but was met by Myriam's unusually firm grip. Claire shook her arm free, desperate not to be touched.

'It's OK,' she said as she slid Myriam's arm under the cover. Claire took a long, steadying breath and sat down in the chair next to the bed under Myriam's fierce gaze. 'We're both under a lot of pressure.'

'So, how's Sid's face?'

'Money's tight. Everyone's struggling. It will be okay.'

'Listen to you,' the woman rasped. 'You bring home more than him.' She took a deep intake of breath. 'And he does this.' That took it out of Myriam. She closed her eyes for a long time, only opening them once her breath settled back to a slow, stunted rhythm.

Claire watched Myriam descend into partial sleep and whispered, 'Not right now, I don't.' She reached to smooth Myriam's pillow again, this time unhindered.

The sound of a key in the front door rattled through the house and caused Claire to look at her watch. Only Jasmine had another key, so she wasn't surprised to hear her voice drifting up the stairs after the door clicked shut. Claire took one last look at Myriam and then swiftly got to her feet and crossed the bedroom to leave. She threaded her small frame through the half-opened door and onto the landing. Jasmine was pulling herself up the thin staircase with the help of the railing.

'You look shattered, duckie,' Claire said.

'Strange day. How's mum?'

'The same. Still trying to boss me around from her bed.'

'I'll just pop in.' Claire was sure she saw Jasmine try to smile politely, but instead, she looked pained, exhausted.

'I'll be downstairs if you need me. You're early, Jas. Is that you in for the night?'

'Yes'

'OK. But I do need to have a word with you before I go.'

Jasmine pushed through into the bedroom, turning to face Claire as she started to close the door.

'I'll be down in five.' This time the smile she offered was bittersweet. She knew what Claire wanted to talk about and right now, she hadn't got an answer for her. As she softly clicked the door shut, she pressed an ear to it to catch Claire's footsteps on the stairs and then let out a long breath as though she was trying to get the day out of her lungs.

Jasmine knelt beside her mum's bed, her hands resting neatly across the duvet where the shape of her mother began. She counted her breaths, comparing each one to the one before, trying to imagine them deep and crisp and even. But they weren't. Each one was different, a weak rattle then a wheeze and then most painfully, sometimes there was no sound at all, just a silent opening and closing of a once bright mouth and lips that could stop traffic.

At least she is sleeping, she thought.

Jasmine traced her mum's unseen hand under the covers with her fingers.

'Remember, mum,' she said in a whisper, wiping away stray tears with her arm, 'when we used to tell each other secrets?' She reached over and brushed her mum's hair back from her sleeping eyes. Jasmine counted off four ragged breaths before saying, 'I tried to kill myself today.'

Outside the short sharp impatient sound of a car horn cut through the early evening. Through the aches of a long day, Jasmine stood up sharply, walking towards the window. She peered through the curtains. It was Sid. Jasmine knew he wouldn't get out of the car; he never did. She turned towards her mother. Myriam was just a shadowy lump in the gloom from where Jasmine stood. She could have been mistaken for an unmade bed.

Skilfully, Jasmine crossed the darkened room towards the door and the guiding light of the landing peeking through the cracks. She held onto the door handle for a few extra beats before stepping out.

Claire was neatly wrapped in her winter coat and sitting on the edge of the sofa, adjusting her thick-knit hat over her ears. She was lit by the thin muted TV in the corner, the only light in the room. Despite the poorly lit room, Jasmine could see in Claire's fixed shape that she carefully cradled the blue folder in her arms.

"*I know you haven't been looking through it Jasmine,*" Claire had said after another occasion when Claire struggled to find it buried behind a pile of forgotten paperbacks. "*But it's important. When that time comes, then arrangements will have to be made for the final phase.*"

It was the way she'd phrased it that cut into Jasmine. "The final phase" made it sound beyond clinical. It made it feel more like a process; an efficiently manicured process from the NHS, and a blue folder that made your journey into the unknown as effortless as humanly possible. And there she was, sitting in an uncomfortable gloom having wrestled the folder from the paperbacks. But Jasmine knew Claire was right about the blue folder. She just couldn't bring herself to take it down and open it. It would have been easier to throw it away, but she couldn't do that either. Claire *was* right, it was important, but it wasn't something Jasmine wanted to deal with. It would have felt like giving up - and she didn't need the blue folder to figure out how to give up. That was her specialist subject.

Jasmine drifted towards the front window and the small table sitting underneath. It was cluttered; a thin tablet glowed with unopened messages, surrounded by half-opened letters, not quite stimulating enough to be freed entirely from their envelopes. Jasmine pushed the letters to one side to see a house key fob that belonged to her mother, and a cigarette lighter she thought she'd lost the last time Sammy was round and was convinced her friend had slipped out of the house with it.

More and more since Myriam had *transitioned phases* as Claire might have said it, Jasmine had lent on Sammy for friendship. Friendship, no, that wasn't quite right, Jasmine thought. *Distraction* was a better turn of phrase. She'd answer Jasmine's call and come round to Jasmine's house, hugging two bottles of wine, and they would both settle in for the night. With Jasmine's mother sleeping in the next room, they would pass the time watching reruns of dating reality programs. Sammy would pick out the ones she fancied, then find them on Instagram, and initiate an elaborate plan of cyberstalking and then *sliding into the DMs*.

But Sammy's presence in the house was a rarity now. It wasn't fun to consume unnecessary calories with someone who didn't want to dance them off afterwards. Jasmine guessed that Sammy was struggling to find excuses these days, choosing to let her call ring out. It seems that she favoured real-life encounters in the city over nights in with her failing friend.

Jasmine picked up the lighter and then fumbled on the table until she found a narrow silver box. Its cardboard lid was creased all the way back and revealed a cigarette that had been left behind. She picked it up and shook the box free, neatly inserting the cigarette between her lips. Jasmine thumbed the lighter until a flame jumped from it and as she pulled on the cigarette with grateful breaths, she saw a car idling outside under a harsh white streetlight. Two sets of fingers curled around the steering wheel, just visible under the splash of light.

'Sid's waiting for you, Claire,' Jasmine said on an out-breath, fingering the cigarette free from her lips.

'It's okay, Jas,' Claire said. 'I've squared it with him. He knows I have to talk some things through with you.' She stepped out of the glow of the flickering TV and closer to Jasmine. 'Jas you must be the last person on earth who still smokes those things. Don't you know…?'

Jasmine could see Claire physically stop herself. The woman swallowed hard and continued, 'Of course you know. I sound like your mother.'

Jasmine turned from the window and reached across to pull on the weighted chain that turned on the lamp. Before she had descended the stairs and entered the living room, she imagined Claire would want to talk to her about the money that was owed, but then she saw the blue folder on her lap. A matter of two and a half thousand pounds and a Welcome to Your Final Phase folder. Those were certainly *some things*.

This may be the perfect end to a perfect day, she thought to herself. She took another drag on her cigarette as she looked intently at the excess of makeup around the bottom of Claire's eye.

'Did he do that to you?'

Almost as the words fell from her lips, Jasmine regretted them. But she couldn't draw them back. Jasmine saw Claire's expression melt into a helpless shame as her eyes fell to the blue folder she held under her arm.

'I'm sorry, Claire. That was…' Jasmine hesitated. She wanted to say *insensitive* and *none of her business*, but she couldn't help but wonder if it *was* her business. The fact that she couldn't come up with Claire's wages may have been the kindling under Sid that set his fists into Claire's face.

'That's not important. I'm fine.' Claire managed a thin smile. 'Right now, I'm here for you and your mum, and this.' She pulled the folder from under her arm and handed it to Jasmine.

Jasmine took the longest drag on her cigarette before pushing it dead back into its empty box. They both pulled up a chair and sat on either side of the lamp. The flat of Jasmine's hand pressed the folder shut, spreading her fingers across it.

'You know I've put this off for a long time,' Jasmine admitted.

'I know you have.'

'And I've fought you every turn about this.'

'Quite a ride.' Claire idly played with the lamp pull.

'But everything has to come to an end, doesn't it? And I tried my best to put this thing out of my mind. I even hid it in the back of the bookcase.'

'It's one of the first things they teach you as Visiting Nurse,' Claire said, 'to check the back of the bookshelf or under the bed for the blue folder.' They laughed again, Claire a little longer than Jasmine this time. 'Jas, I'm going to recommend to the oncologist team that we open up the last phase.'

'Claire—'

'I'm pretty sure that she won't be able to breathe unassisted, so she'll need to be in the General where she can be made to feel as comfortable as possible.'

'Wait a minute,' Jasmine said sharply, slapping her hand on the blue folder. 'I know I haven't read this thing, but I remember early on you said we could choose to have her at home when the time came. What's all this about the hospital?'

'The hospital can't support home care in the final phase. If you wanted that, it's usually done with private money and-'

'I can hardly pay for that if I can't even pay you what I owe,' Jasmine finished. With one hand she batted the table clean of all its contents, sending it all crashing. The lamp bulb smashed boldly, and the room was thrown to the mercy of the twitching TV glow once again. Jasmine folded her hands between her thighs and bowed her head.

She became slowly aware of Claire picking up the forgotten bills, and finally, the blue folder.

'Jesus Claire, just stop,' Jasmine snapped. 'I'll get you your money. I'm not going to bullshit you. I don't know how - but I will get you what I owe.'

Claire felt for the light switch on the wall and flipped it on. Ignoring Jasmine's outburst, she said gently, 'that's better isn't it,' she paused. 'Come on Jas, see me out.'

They both walked into the narrow hallway and stood with their backs against the walls either side of the front door. A few moments passed as they looked at each other, startled only by Sid's car horn outside.

'I've let mum down,' Jasmine whispered.

'You haven't let anyone down. You've got a lot on your shoulders, but you'll come through, I know it.'

Jasmine hadn't mentioned losing her job, and she felt the weight of that memory pushing down on her, and in that moment, she was glad of the support from the wall.

'And you, Claire,' she said, 'Mum needs you. I don't think she could bear not having you around and I know if she goes to the hospital, you won't be there.'

'You try and stop me,' Claire responded. 'Your mum needs us both, and you see if she doesn't get what she wants. She always has, hasn't she?' Claire noticed the car outside with its flashing beams. She turned to Jasmine and said, 'Look, I didn't expect to walk out of here with two and a half thousand pounds. I believe in miracles an' all, but some miracles you have to wait a bit longer for whereas others,' she paused, 'well, you looking through that folder will be miracle enough for now. Deal?'

Jasmine nodded and offered her a weak smile. 'Deal.'

Claire pulled her close and wrapped her arms around her. She whispered, 'I'll see you tomorrow.' She pulled open the door and started to leave.

'What about him? Will you be alright? If you want, I'll go and smack him in the eye for you?'

Claire laughed too loudly, enough that Sid might have heard. 'It's OK, my lovely,' she said.

Jasmine pushed the door shut and watched the daydream shape of Claire through the bubble-glass panel on the door. She waited until the colours had faded to the familiar black and white of the street before she slid down the wall and leant her head against the door.

Pressing her hands into her back pocket, she pulled out the business card. It was as she expected, black with gold lettering. The Room, Daniel Burton, the Architect. Slowly gliding it across her arm, she continued to hold it. A third line of gold print silently and softly appeared across the bottom of the card.

thearchitectiswaiting/7540872

Jasmines breath caught in her throat. 'What are you up to, tea for one?' She held the card so close that her nose almost touched it.

*

Jasmine bathed in the glow of her laptop as she sat with her knees to her chest, two sets of fingers wrapped around a mug of tea. She hypnotically blew steam from her cup to obscure the words she had typed into the search engine. Stretching out her limbs, she sat upright and placed the mug beside the keyboard. Her finger hovered above the return key for a few moments and then she pressed return on:

thearchitectiswaiting/7540872

The screen on the laptop went black; completely black as though the power itself had been ripped from it. Jasmine arched forward and started pressing keys, any keys.

'You got to be kidding me,' she said aloud. 'I knew it. That sex pest of a man has given me a virus.'

A cursor flashed in the top corner of the screen, then raced across the top trailing a message.

DB: You got my message, then.

Jasmine froze. She'd never seen computers do this except in old Hollywood movies. Her hands hung in mid-air over the keyboard. 'OK, this is weird,' she said as she lowered her hands.

JA: Is that you, Daniel?

DB: Depends.

JA: On what?

DB: Only my friends call me Daniel. Does this mean you're my friend?

JA: Not yet. But I'm curious.

DB: I may have answers for the curious.

JA: I'm curious about the job offer. I'm curious how you knew my name. I'm curious as to why you chose me, and I'm curious about what on earth you've done to my laptop.

DB: Is that all?

Jasmine sank into her chair and thought about what he'd said. She picked up the business card, bending its corners and tracing the words. She resumed typing.

JA: What is The Room?

DB: The Room is just the start.

DB: Get some sleep. I'll be in touch

The dark screen was replaced with the bright, inviting search engine screen and the question: *Where do you want to go now?* Jasmine stretched out for a blanket that had been kicked off the bed earlier and wrapped herself up against the chill of the early morning. A thought wafted away from her, disappearing into the darkness.

The Room is just the start.

Jasmine slept uninterrupted. The screen on the laptop flickered dark then returned to a resting glow.

DB: Sleep well.

Chapter 6

Now

Michael Powers slapped down hard on the lid of his laptop when he heard the door swing open. The blinds rattled as they flexed unnaturally on their hinges. The instant he looked across his office and saw Harriet standing there, he quickly turned back to the machine, filled with regret as he began to fumble with the lid without any success.

'You'll end up breaking it if you keep on like that,' Harriet said. She watched from the doorway as he played with the overhanging laptop lid and its tricky release button. He feigned a smile that was more frustrated than courteous. It was enough to make Harriet smile for real, however.

'Do you want me to have a go?' Harriet stepped into the office and was met instantly by Michael. He launched himself from around his desk and eased her out again by her elbow.

'Not now, Harriet. Got a shit-tonne of work to get through.'

'But...what? What are you on abo-'

Ignoring her, he pressed the door closed, struggling with the last few inches as he pushed her back out into the busy newsroom, a little too aggressively. But she was gone, and he needed to focus.

He sidestepped to the window that looked out across the crowded news space. Bodies flew in all directions like ants from a churned-up hill. But these ants were purposeful in their world, carrying tablets and thin laptops, speaking loudly into invisible earpieces. He spun the blind's long string between his fingers, snapping them shut before crossing the front of his desk on his way back to the difficult laptop.

Silence - now, he could focus.

The door was unceremoniously pushed open with some force again, as Harriet strode back into Michael's office.

'You do that to me again, and I will force-feed you that fucking laptop,' she said as she calmly walked behind his desk and sat down. 'Then see how you get on with that lid.' She motioned to the sleeping laptop in front of her. 'Besides, you're bullshitting me. What work have you got to get through? We got shut down last night, remember?'

'I think I preferred it when you were in my ear, at least then I could switch you off.'

Michael's mouth was wide open as he watched his assistant brush the front of the laptop with a gentle ease and the lid sprang up a few centimetres. He half stepped forward; his hand raised as if to stop her looking at the screen.

'Don't worry,' she said, 'I'm not a nosey bitch, and I'm not going to look at what you're 'working on'. But you do need to work on your interpersonal skills. That's for certain.'

Michael had liked Harriet from the moment he'd first seen her gamble through the newsroom two years before; a slender wisp of a girl with blonde hair. She'd always have it fixed in a ponytail that would bounce along with her aggressive, potty-mouthed words when she was angry; Michael would often find it hypnotic and amusing in equal parts. Back when she started at the newsroom, she tore through the office, making her 'mark.' She had managed to talk her way through the door by offering to work for nothing - and Jennifer was blinded by her confidence.

Everyone thought they had a measure of Harriet and, as Michael was quick to realise, that was her little trick. Eventually, she reached the dizzying heights of Assistant to the Jennifer Munroe, Executive Producer. But the problem with letting off a firecracker indoors is that the sparks will find every corner, every floor and ceiling.

Jennifer overheard that this foul-mouthed bombshell wanted to dethrone her, so in Munroe's eyes, she had reached her roof, and had to be contained. To dampen her spark, Jennifer made her Michael's Field Assistant and Ground Level Producer. It was a clever way of keeping both firecrackers in check. They'd both been tied up with local news and traffic-related politics for the past year. But sometimes, very occasionally, even the mediocre local news can rise above its stature.

'Yeah. I'll try and be a better boss,' he said as he walked behind his desk. He ushered Harriet from the seat with a light tap on her shoulder and sat down. 'That was a bit shitty of me, Harriet. I'll buy you lunch sometime; you know, to make up for it?'

'Nah, I can think of another way.' Harriet had walked to the office door, pressed it shut and turned to face Michael. 'Tell me what you're working on, Michael Powers.'

'Thought you said you weren't a nosy bitch?'

He looked up from the computer; his face lit from the screen. He leaned back in his chair and passed both sets of fingers through his thick black hair.

'You know what Harriet; I wasn't bullshitting you; I have got a shit tonne of work to do-'

'Well, please yourself,' Harriet interrupted and turned to open the door, just managing to place a hand on the handle before Michael continued.

'But I'm not sure what it is I have to do.'

Harriet turned with her back to the closed door. 'What do you mean?'

'It's about that shit-show last night.'

'Yeah, tell me about it. And why all that fuss over a couple of D.O.P's?

'D.O.P?'

'Yeah D.O.P. Dead on pavement.'

Michael took a few moments, screwed his eyes tight and said, 'You just made that up, didn't you?'

'Yeah, what do you think?' Harriet sprang forward from the door and with an outstretched hand; she feigned setting out a newspaper headline. 'Local Beauty thinks fast on her feet.'

'How about 'Local Beauty lets Legendary Newscaster get back to work'?'

'You think I'm a beauty, Michael? Seriously though, 'Legendary Newscaster'?' Harriet smiled, thrusting her upturned palms out in front of her, waiting for a response. None came. 'But what went down last night? There was a lock-in at the Castle after, and it was wall-to-wall with angry Paps. Some of them lost a good load of equipment, either taken or outright destroyed. Surely, they can't do that, can they?'

'Look, all I know is that I was down there with Zach in the thick of it and I still haven't got a clue what went on. And on top of that, I've got Jennifer Fucking Pinstripe calling me in for a meeting any minute, wanting a full run down.'

'Well, I'd start by trying to find out who the two bodies were, if I were you.'

Michael shifted awkwardly. 'It's a media lockdown, Harriet. What's the point?'

'Okay, fine. Tell her you went home early and got laid. I don't care. You're still seeing Carlos, aren't you?'

'It's Karl and no; I'm not seeing him.' His eyes were fixed on the screen.

'Karl, right,' she said, moving to leave the office. 'You got anything on the bodies so that I can do some digging - height, weight, colour, gender?'

'It was hardly the time to get my measuring tape out.'

'Suit yourself.' Harriet rolled her eyes and went to open the door. She had barely opened the door a few inches before she turned back, mouthing Jennifer's name. She retreated to Michael's desk.

He rose quickly from his desk and moved towards the blinds, separating them slightly with two fingers. It was just enough for him to view Jennifer as she moved swiftly through the newsroom, toward his office. She carried a pregnant old leather satchel in one hand, and a bulging concertina file under her arm. He waited until she was feet away before he opened the door and met her on the threshold.

'Can I help you with that, Jennifer?'

Jennifer dropped the file onto one of the hot desks opposite Michael's office, then swung the satchel on its handle, crashing it down. She didn't wait for him to move as she strode in, pushing him aside. Michael followed her, and noticed over Jennifer's shoulder that Harriet had pushed down the lid of his laptop.

'What are you doing here?' Jennifer asked Harriet. 'Never mind. Disappear - I need to talk to him.'

Harriet had already sat down at Michael's desk. 'Michael…Mr. Powers is having trouble opening his laptop, as usual.'

Jennifer slowly turned to Michael.

'Are you special or something? Should we allow you to be unsupervised?' She shook her head, not waiting for a response. Instead she turned back to Harriet. 'Just get out.'

Harriet brushed past Michael and whispered, 'You're fucked. But about that lunch, I'll get back to you.'

Jennifer sat back in his chair; her fire-red nails drummed out an unknown rhythm on the back of his laptop. He was glad Harriet had closed it, but it did lead his thoughts in a curious direction. He

The Room

wondered if Harriet had seen what he had been working on. Whether it was the hypnotic tip-tapping of Jennifer's nails, or the sudden silence in the office, Michael found himself staring hard at the laptop. He shook his head, as though to clear his thoughts, and looked directly at his boss.

'Alone at last, Jennifer,' he said, reaching for a chair that was wedged under a groaning bookshelf.

'Don't be smart, Michael,' she replied, leaning forward, shifting the sleeping laptop to one side, and planting her pinstriped elbows on the desk.

Michael was glad the finger drumming had stopped, at least. 'Well, at least we've gravitated to using my Christian name.'

Jennifer wound her long fingers together in a clasp like a dying spider. Her thumbs rubbed hard into the bridge of her nose as she composed herself, eventually releasing her spidery fingers and spreading them flat on the desk. She took in deep breaths, lifting her chest against her blouse and suit jacket. Her dark hair, with shots of ruby highlights, weaved around her shoulders and across her lightly tanned chest. She was beautiful, and Michael knew it. He didn't want to screw her. But he had to admit; she was quite something.

'I've just come from a meeting with Marty Hindle and the rest of the Editorial team for all the networks countrywide about last night. They'll be gathering everything concerning the events of last night for review.'

For review and an early burial, Michael thought.

'But this is a local incident, isn't it?' Michael knew it was more than that; he needed to get more information. 'Why are the nationals getting involved?'

'That,' said Jennifer, 'is not a question we're being encouraged to ask. Any further investigation will be met with prosecution. It's as simple as that. I've told them that you would give over any sundries and make a thorough report of the events as they unfolded. I've already briefed Zach, and he's transferred the raw footage across to the BNT Cloud. I'm going to be spending the next few days putting together a dossier for the networks total and complete involvement of the events. I expect you to be forthcoming with the information.'

And tell them that the whole thing shouldn't have happened? That I was there, with him - and her? Michael froze. Telling the authorities everything meant telling them what he hated most about himself; he had to stall this.

'And that's it? We just stop reporting the news? We just roll over, not knowing why we are rolling over?'

Jennifer sprung to her feet. 'Now, we've had a,' she paused, 'satisfactory working relationship for a long time, Michael. Why would you want to spoil it by getting yourself and this network into a fight?'

'I just think it's worth us - as Journalists - doing some of our own digging.'

Jennifer frowned. 'Do I need to remind you that I know where all your bodies are buried? Are we on the same page Michael?'

Michael got up and replaced the chair. *She had no idea about the two jumpers last night. She doesn't know who they are and how they are connected to me.* 'I'll make a start on the report,' Michael said.

'Yes, you will,' she said, her hand was on the door handle for a few beats. Without turning said, 'I'm not an idiot. I know this goes against the code or whatever they call it these days - and it grates on me and, frankly, stinks of a cover-up. But everyone's hands are tied here.' She pulled open the door and looked out across the newsroom.

'Don't forget the Princess who was in your ear. I want her report along with yours.'

Before returning to his desk, Michael flipped the latch on the door and fingered the blinds so he could watch Jennifer struggle with her bag and oversized file. Then, he sat in front of the closed laptop, trying to remember what Harriet had done to release it. Bent forward like an experienced mechanic sucking his teeth, he lifted the computer above his head to see how it was put together.

The office door started heaving with fits of rattling, and the blinds swung against it. 'Michael, you locked it. It's me, Harriet.'

The crashing of the blinds startled Michael causing him to nearly drop the laptop. He carefully replaced the machine on the desk. 'Of course it is,' he whispered to himself as he leaned back in his chair, and shouted across the office, 'Just need to get on the top side of a report. We'll sort that lunch later if you like.'

The rattling stopped. 'What about Jennifer? I mean, how much trouble are you in?' she paused before continuing, 'How much trouble are *we* in?'

'Oh, don't worry I'm not in any trouble,' he said as he squeezed the front of his laptop, his nose almost touching the edge of the lid. 'Your name was mentioned though. I'm afraid you're fucked. I'd clear your desk if I were you. I'd lend you a box for your things, but I never cared for you that much.' Michael smiled as Harriet gave the door one final shove.

'Prick.' Harriet pulled away from the door, and Michael could hear her stomping into the newsroom.

I am a shitty boss. He thought to himself before the laptop suddenly popped open. *Special? You're damn right, I'm special.* That made him smile again.

His smile didn't last long as the black screen flickered with a picture of a girl, twelve years old and wearing a short strappy dress with socks up to her knees. Her image was set alongside a more recent photo of her as a young woman with the same dreamy golden waves but cut short just below her ears and a definition to her face that looked, frankly, perfect. The young woman's smile, like most peoples, had lost its innocence but, in her case, Michael knew it hid something far worse than the natural loss of a childhood. He reached out and touched the screen where the little girl was staring out at him.

As he passed over to the older picture, he pulled his fingers back as though he had been holding a flame. *You didn't look like that last night*, he thought to himself. He continued to look at the pictures; he traced his eye over the name that appeared under both photographs.

Stephanie Milner

With shaky hands, he reached into his pocket and pulled out his phone. He sifted through his pictures until he found the image of the tall man he had discovered leaving the building, the same building where the jumpers had originated. Everything hung on this man's promise to get in touch. Michael heard the words the tall man had said to him, and they wouldn't stop going around like a marble in a bottle. *Because I know who you are, and I know what you did.*

'Your move, fella,' he said in a low tone as he studied the picture.

None of what he knew about last night, his chance meeting with the tall man or his previous with the jumpers, would make it to the report, and it was clear that Jennifer hadn't put two and two together. But there was something worth chasing, some part of the past that Michael had thought buried and tucked nicely away, but it was now reaching out to him. He saw it in Stephanie Milner's smile.

*

The report for Jennifer was easy to write. As he looked through the sanitised piece, Michael barely remembered tapping out the words. He'd laid out Harriet's version of events too and sent it over the email with instructions to erase any backlinks to him and, when she was happy, to send it on to Jennifer. He pressed the send button on his report.

He found Harriet at her desk. She was reclined in her chair, swaying from left to right. She was absently twiddling with the stir stick from her overpriced coffee; her staple afternoon treat from her favourite place down the street. He always warned Harriet about that place; if you want brown water and bubbles the toilets in the BNT offices are just as good and a hell of a lot cheaper, he'd say. Harriet hardly noticed him standing over her. Her attention was on the screen and the report that had just been emailed to her.

'Harriet,' Michael said as he crouched until they were at the same height, their heads locked in concentration over the report and the need for privacy.

'Shhhhh! I'm just getting to the good bit,' she said, sarcasm spilt over every word. 'Only I'm not, am I? Why have you written this? I'm capable of writing my own reports. I know because they taught me that in college, I remember that. What I don't remember is writing this tosh.'

'Listen, Harriet, something's going on, and something is coming our way. I can just feel it. It has to do with what happened last night. I need your help, and it doesn't involve reports for Jennifer fucking Pinstripe.'

Harriet planted the coffee in front of Michael. He turned up his nose at the smell coming from it and moved the cup further across the desk.

'But what did happen last night? What aren't you telling me?' Harriet asked.

'I'm not sure yet, but what I do know is that if we become part of this lock-down like Jennifer has then we'll never find out the truth. So, I need your help.'

'Should I be scared?'

'I'm not sure, but what this lock-down is going to do is make it almost impossible to move freely with any - let's say 'unauthorised' - investigation.'

'Hmmm. Sounds like *sexy spy* shit.'

'Jesus Harriet, take this seriously please.'

'OK, OK. I'm in. I don't think I've ever seen you so bothered by a story.'

'Somebody on a national level doesn't want us to ask questions about last night, and that makes me nervous, so if you're in, then you have to be prepared that this isn't any old local story. What I'm guessing is that the lock-down will affect us in the office. So here, keep hold of this.' Michael took a piece of paper from behind his phone case and slid it to Harriet.

'What is it?'

'It's the address to my Cloud. Anything you find, send it there, and I'll be able to access it on my home laptop. That should be secure enough, for now.'

'You can't open a laptop but finding a backdoor to evade cyber detection, you can do?'

'Okay, Harriet, a couple of words you used there I didn't understand. Will you help me, or not?'

'Shit yeah, anything under Pinstripe's radar, and I'm in.'

'Good. First things first, then. Read that report and send it. Then I want you to check up on a name for me.'

'Stephanie Milner?' Harriet said the name, catching her breath after.

Michael reeled at the sound of the name from someone else's lips. He'd not even spoken the name himself for nearly ten years.

'Yes, how-'

'Newsflash Mr Powers, turns out I am a nosey bitch after all.' Harriet waited a few moments, savouring the confusion spreading across his face. 'Oh, relax. When Pinstripe came into your office, I saw the pictures on your laptop, and I had to wonder, if Michael Powers didn't want me to see them then as sure as shit, he wouldn't want her to see them. Am I right?'

Michael pointed a finger at her, 'You got me,' he said, stretching to his full height. 'I can leave this with you?'

'Course.' She scrolled through the report asking, 'so, what are you going to do?'

'I'm heading off to Pinstripe's office to smooth things over, kind of fill in the gaps of these reports. She won't be happy with the fag packet edition of last night's events.' Michael took a few steps before Harriet stopped him cold with her next question.

'This 'Stephanie', is she our jumper?'

Michael heard the words but saw the crimson lady spread across the pavement under a cold yellow streetlight. He felt his stomach pull tight. He didn't answer Harriet and, after a few moments, he knew he didn't have to.

'What about the other one?' she asked.

You get one, and you have the other.

Michael wouldn't say his name. He wouldn't even close the gap between them and whisper his name in Harriet's ear. There was something chilling about softly whispering the name of a monster. It would be like saying *good night* to your child and finishing with "Watch out for the monster under the bed."

The two of them looked at each other, eventually reaching an unspoken understanding. Michael pulled in a laboured breath. 'You dig deep enough, Harriet, the other one will appear.'

Chapter 7

Now

A kaleidoscope of gold was thrown off by the crystal lattice glass generously adorned with Proper Twelve Irish. As Michael turned the glass slowly, held within his fingers, it reflected seductively, but then glared as it caught too much of the blue-white light from the monitor for his tired eyes. The fire he'd built popped and spat in the background and cast light that shifted nervously around the living room. Eventually, he lowered the glass into his lap, his attention falling and getting lost between the caressing flames, but not without the delicious burn from the whisky rising in his chest.

Michael had always enjoyed how small the room made him feel. It had a satisfyingly high ceiling that looked to be held in place by the two cluttered bookshelves either side of the fireplace. He particularly liked the way each structure seemed to hold onto the books and loose papers, caught in the act of trying to reach the peak.

Michael reluctantly pushed himself from the couch, raised his glass to the fire and turned to face the monitors in the corner. Still clutching his glass, he wouldn't sit down at first. He tried the monitors from every angle, eyeing them suspiciously as he paced in front of them, even though he was familiar with the pictures of Stephanie and the copy that was only *half right*. Earlier that evening, he had wrestled with downloading the materials gathered by Harriet, and his finger had hovered above the button that would prize them from the cloud and, for all he knew, forever print them on his hard drive. After a double click, all three screens filled with Stephanie's face, young and old and

The Room

headlines that Michael hadn't seen in ten years; unable even to recall writing some of them. That's when he'd pushed back on his chair and reached for the Proper Twelve, the only sturdy and Michael thought, sure thing on those herculean bookshelves.

He realised straight away that the articles weren't in any order. He knew this because when it all started, the name of the girl wasn't known; she wasn't even a missing child case, she was just a twelve-year-old body on a country lane, spat out from the woods on a beautiful Sunday afternoon. Until the police had contacted her parents, they hadn't realised that she'd been taken. But Harriet wasn't to know that, and the cloud spewed them out with complete and utter digital indifference. He'd pulled the articles from a folder marked "Media" and noticed another marked "Misc.". He'd decided to leave this until he'd exhausted the news articles and a part of him kept hold of a little Christmas morning excitement as he contemplated its contents. He cringed at the inappropriateness of a childhood Christmas memory alongside the details of how there came to be a bloodied and battered body of a twelve-year-old girl laid neatly across a lane, waiting to be discovered by a young couple and their young daughter.

With his whiskey nearly drained, Michael stroked the pad on his laptop, dragging down the words in front of him, allowing the familiar reports and sanitised images to wash over. He'd seen all this before. There was nothing new here, except a splitting open of bloody memories and a splintering of decency that returned him to wonder as he once did it all those years ago, how one human being can treat another with such disdain. As far as Michael was concerned, his wounds had begun to stretch the moment he first saw Stephanie Milner's body, coloured red in a sodden suburban street.

BEATEN GIRL, 12, DISCOVERED IN LICKEYS

Residents found a beaten young girl on Forest Road, Darwin Woods in the Lickey Hills Country Park this Sunday. A local family came upon the young girl lying across the road. The witnesses claim that the girl had been badly beaten and most of her clothes torn away.

Emergency services on the scene managed to resuscitate the yet unknown girl, and she was taken to St Luke's Hospital for further treatment and to be reunited with her family. It is understood that the girl who can't be named for legal reasons is yet unable to help the police with their inquiries.

Mr and Mrs Ableworth first reported seeing the young girl. They were able to tell us that an arrest of a local man was made at the scene. The police, who are appealing for any other witness to come forward, are not forthcoming with any further comments concerning the arrest of the male.

Despite the confident arrest, the police are still urging the public to maintain caution in and around the woods. For the foreseeable future, a large section of the park has been closed off while the police conduct a thorough search of the woods.

Michael absently slid a finger across the laptop pad.

MAN QUESTIONED OVER BRUTAL RAPE OF A MINOR

Alex Pevestone (pictured) has been named as the only suspect in the attack of a young girl in the

Darwin Wood area of Lickey Hills Country Park last week and is said to be cooperating with the police in their investigation.

Pevestone, former supermarket manager and neighbourhood watch liaison for Leamington South village, was reportedly found at the scene with traces of blood on his clothes.

In a statement made by the police, Mr. Pevestone was said to be acting suspiciously and was detained for questioning concerning the incident.

Meanwhile, the victim, unnamed, is being cared for by a particular unit of social services. They work closely with the local constabulary to determine the victim's wellbeing, and to garner any information regarding the terrible events that led to the discovery of the young girl of twelve in the popular family spot last Sunday afternoon.

Michael stopped reading and let his eyes fall to the keyboard, feeling the heavy pull of the whisky on his face. He slowly raised his eyes as though he was fighting for the last bit of strength to look at the grey low-resolution picture of Pevestone. Michael instinctively fingered the empty glass and got up to refill it, taking Pevestone's image with him.

Pevestone's face hung on the screen, his lifeless eyes hidden in dark recesses caused by strong overhanging brows. Short, snowy cropped hair started far back on his head. All of this surrounded a smile that revealed oddly placed teeth that spread unevenly flat and sharp. He had a white goatee that looked permanently unkempt around his crooked jaw.

As Michael returned to his seat, he didn't look at the screen again until Pevestone had disappeared, slid out of sight as Michael blindly hit the pad.

PEVESTONE: 'I DID IT. NO REGRETS AND I'D DO IT AGAIN'

> *These were the words spoken by evil local man, Mr Alex Pevestone as he was charged with the rape and attempted murder of a twelve-year-old girl early last week in the picturesque Lickey Hills Country Park.*
>
> *In a shock revelation, he told the police that "attacking the girl was like I was in a dream, and it was meant to be." He was also reported to say that the victim "was only the start," and that, "there would be more."*
>
> *As Pevestone delivered his confession in full, it was later confirmed that he was smiling throughout, and showed no remorse for his actions.*

Michael stroked the pad fervently over the old reports, content that there was nothing new for him here, except torn memories that bit down hard into his mind. Thankfully, the screens reflected the whites of a blank page and the end of his scrolling. He shut down the page and contemplated the second file marked "Misc.". He hesitated as he nudged the arrow across it, a sudden realisation of what might be at the other side of the click.

Henshall.

There was just one document in the folder with the name "Henshall".

Michael picked up his glass and threw its contents down his throat. He lingered with the crystal raised to his mouth and saw the name on the screen through its bottom, more evident as the amber smear slipped to the side of the glass.

'Jesus, I need another bottle for this.' His voice echoed around the living room.

He pulled himself to his feet, ready to refill his glass, but headed for the window instead. Weaving his fingers into the drapes, he created a gap in the curtains and a view of the quiet light-dappled street below; perfect circles of light and shade unaltered by pedestrians. *The quiet before the storm*, he thought.

Michael crossed the room, again avoiding the screens, he lifted the Proper Irish from the shelf and sloshed the whiskey into his glass. Recapping the bottle, he placed the tumbler on the fireplace. On the mantelpiece, there was only one picture. It was a framed cover of Rebecca by Daphne du Maurer. It had been his favourite book, way back when people cared to ask.

'If only there could be an invention that bottled up a memory, like scent. And it never faded, and it never got stale.' He recited from memory, pitching his voice higher in mockery of a woman's voice. 'Fuck you Rebecca' he spat, seeing his breath fog the glass, 'some memories need to go stale and die.'

He looked at the frame and the book cover inside. Carefully fingering the edges as though he was expecting it to fall from its hook, he gripped the frame and lifted it down, turning it around and leant it on the fireplace next to the glass.

The thing that was taped to the back of the frame was a small black lump, wrapped in white tape and dust, wedged in the corner. He peeled back the still sticky tape, leaving grey marks all over the device, and freed it from its hiding place.

He held it close and studied the USB stick, wondering if the damn thing still worked after all this time. He felt like dropping it in his glass. It had caused him so much trouble, so much pain all these years; it was a wonder he still held onto it. But, instead Michael placed it carefully next to the laptop - but not in it. He wasn't there yet. With one hand, he gripped his glass while the other clicked on the document marked "Henshall".

REPORTER SLAIN OVER RELEASE OF VICTIM'S NAME

Promising Reporter for the Birmingham Echo, Ben Henshall, finally lost his fight for life last night, as the decision to turn off his life support was made by his girlfriend and Ben's mother and father.

The young reporter of twenty-two had recently taken up an internship at the paper when he was brutally beaten and left for dead by Harry Milner, father of Stephanie Milner, the twelve-year-old victim of rapist Alex Pevestone.

It was revealed in the days leading up to the attack that Henshall had illegally received a piece of

> *evidence from an unnamed police officer who was under investigation for his dealings in the interview process for the Pevestone case.*
>
> *When pressed, the rogue officer named the paper and, very quickly, Henshall was ousted as the courier of the crucial evidence and the source of the leak.*
>
> *The police at this time are not forthcoming as to the nature of all the evidence that may have been compromised, but would like to assure the public and the families of those involved that all is being done to see that the proper procedures are followed and that even officers are not beyond reproach, and will meet the full impact of their actions.*
>
> *Harry Milner is currently in custody and is likely to face charges of manslaughter.*

Before closing the document, Michael re-read the line "the nature of all the evidence that may have been compromised." As he did, he slid the USB stick from the desk and held it tight in his fist. He drew in deep breaths, closed the application on the laptop and fed the stick into the side of the machine. The computer readied itself to play an audio file. He turned up the volume of the two external speakers and waited. What he was waiting for, he didn't know. Maybe it was for his hands to stop shaking, or his breathing to slow. But, to Michael, it felt like waiting for a hand to come out of the darkness and grab his throat.

He pressed the triangular play icon and drifted towards the sofa. The fire glowed red now, and the night slowly began to swallow the room. Michael hoped he wouldn't drift off as he heard *that man's* voice float around the space from his computer. It started with one of the officers setting up and establishing the interview conditions, the legal stuff. Michael was almost deaf to it.

He waited.

Alex Pevestone's voice was eager and childlike. It was as though he had waited a long time for his moment.

Chapter 8

Now

'You look like shit.'

A voice out of the darkness shook Michael awake. He pulled at the damp folds around his crotch, a creeping chill that made him want to piss. His eyes tried to adjust as he struggled to find the voice in a room that he hardly recognised, except for the suggestion of furniture.

There was a figure stood at the window. 'You look like shit.' The voice again. A man's voice.

Michael fumbled with the wet trousers gathered in his lap, and realised he was no longer holding his whisky glass.

'How did you get in here?'

'MICHAEL!' The figure shouted his name, cutting through the room. The room seemed to crash about him, furniture lost in a blur as the figure of the man rushed to him until their faces were almost touching. Ben Henshall shouted his name again. Michael could feel his breath on his cheek. His face was bloodied and contorted and his mouth wide, spilling out a blackened tongue that glistened with fresh blood.

'You look like shit.' This time, it was a woman's voice.

Michael screamed. His arms flew out in front, sending his whisky glass bouncing across his living room floor, which was now flooded with lemon sunlight. Harriet pressed the toe of her shoe downwards, neatly stopping the crystal.

'Bad dream was it?' she asked, turning from the fireplace and pointing to the dinner-plate size stain on his trousers.

He glanced at the laptop, silently glowing with a screensaver and saw the USB stick where he'd left it. 'Something like that,' he said.

'You okay?'

'Yeah. Just got a head like a nun's chewed chuff.'

'Lovely,' Harriet said. 'Where's the kitchen, through here? Tell me you have coffee. That, and a shower, should straighten you out.'

'Fine,' Michael replied as he watched her leave the room. 'I think I might need something a little stronger than coffee, though,' he shouted after her.

'How about yesterday's coffee?'

Michael felt the attack of the wet trousers finding new areas around the tops of his legs. He walked over to the computer. Michael's eyes fell to the USB stick flickering red as it waited for its next command. He snatched it away as he heard Harriet's footsteps from the kitchen.

'Goodbye, Pevestone.'

He bent in front of the fire and inserted the stick between two fighting embers. With very little fuss, the stick withered to a skeleton of metallic threads.

The Room

'Oh, you're up. You should get out of those wet trousers,' Harriet said as she entered the room. She held two steaming cups in front of her by the tips of her fingers, forcing one on him. She paused, waited for his response. 'Not even a bite at that comment? Nothing about an in-your-endo? Christ, you must be really hung-over.'

Michael watched her half commit to sitting down at the desk, caught in the act of forgetting something then, like an electric charge through the body, she remembered. She marched to the living room door and picked up her backpack, and on returning, she slunk the bag over the chair and began to cradle her cup of coffee.

'Harriet, as much as this is thoroughly joyous - you in my house uninvited - what the hell are you doing here?'

She peered over the rim of her coffee. 'I came because…well, first of all, did you know your door was unlocked? That's a no-no, even if you do live in some village in the middle of nowhere.'

'What do you mean unlocked? Was it open?' Michael's head pounded; anyone could have come in.

'I mean, I guess it wasn't exactly *open-open*. But I banged a few times. I thought you might have topped yourself due to Pinstripe, so I tried a few numbers on your keypad. Seeing as you're pretty ancient, I figured you'd have the same pin for your front door as you do your office.'

His eyes widened. 'So, you broke in? For Christ's sake Harriet.'

'Correction, I found a flaw in your security system. You really should be thanking me. If you're going to have a smart door lock, then at least try and be *smart* about it.'

'Well, seeing as I'd rather not have your face greeting me in the morning, I will be changing that sodding pin.'

Harriet feigned a sad expression and then continued. 'But the reason I came was to give you this.' She put her coffee down and pulled out a clipped bundle of printed sheets from her bag. She stretched across and handed it to him. 'It's the rest of the stuff on Ben Henshall. I couldn't complete the miscellaneous file in time, so I hand-carried it.'

Michael took the file and set it in his lap. He looked up at Harriet as she tested out her drink. 'What makes you think I'd be interested in Ben Henshall?'

'Don't be an arse, Michael,' she said. Pausing, her gaze switched between her coffee and Michael. 'Two reasons. First, you had me dig up anything that had the slightest connection with the jumpers, and secondly, right before you screamed yourself awake in a pool of what looks like your own piss, you called out 'Ben Henshall', so yes, I'm thinking he figures largely in this narrative.'

Michael lingered a little too long on her, watching her eyes brighten as her lips finally met with the coffee. Eventually, he spoke.

'It's not piss,' he said, looking at her with a renewed clarity, 'only, I wish it was. Must have fallen asleep with a tumbler of the good stuff. What a waste.' He reached for his coffee. 'What did you mean you couldn't finish the miscellaneous file in time?'

She drew in a breath that Michael thought too dramatic. 'It came down the unofficial line that they were going to replace the floor's laptops. I mean, *everyone's machine*. No reason, all unscheduled. I figured that with everything you told me and this lock-down, there's something they don't want shared or found out.' She motioned towards the papers perched on his lap, 'I emailed everything I could to myself and printed it off at home. It's not very *eco*, but I couldn't risk sending them to you, plus a hard copy seemed to make sense.' She paused. 'I'm guessing now, after finding you fresh from a nightmare starring our friend Henshall, that I did the right thing.'

Michael slowly released the papers from the clip. 'Is this everything?' he asked.

'Pretty sure. I mean I covered my tracks. Went over it a few times.'

'Did you read it?'

'Yes. Usual roundups of the investigation into corruption in the force and Ben's heroic fight for life, blah, blah.'

Michael tossed the clip to the side and squared the papers neatly between his fingers. He rose to his feet and strode to the fireplace. He fed the wad to the sleeping embers, violently waking them with each intrusive poke.

'What the fuck are you doing?' Harriet pushed her chair out and restlessly hung behind Michael. They watched the papers contort to the new flames. 'Do you realise how many different places I sweated on my body to get that shit?'

'You have a lovely turn of phrase Harriet.'

'Yeah, I get it from you. So, what gives?'

'There's nothing in here that I haven't seen before, and by the sounds of it, it's hardly worth the hassle of anyone finding this stuff on you.'

'But that's not all of it, is it? What about the stuff that's in your head? There's stuff that's shaking you out of sleep. That's something that won't appear in any old news articles for you to burn.'

Michael wiped down the knees of his trousers as he stood upright and stretched his back. He felt his head clearing as he joined Harriet back at the desk; he rattled his cup.

'Could do with another one of these, if you're staying.' Michael could feel the wave of her stare against him.

She got to her feet and gathered the cups. 'You don't appreciate me. I'm not asking for a marriage, just a bit of professional courtesy - and maybe some respect.'

'Harriet, I do appreciate you and everything I ask you to do for me.'

'Should I get some tissues? Fuck this, Michael. I'm gone, you're on your own with Cruella now.'

'Harriet…' He started. He had to give her what she wanted; any information that would keep her on his side. He needed to tell her something —something personal. He was going to need her help eventually. 'Do you still want to know what Jennifer has over me?'

Harriet's breath caught in her chest, and she swallowed hard. With eyes wide, she nodded and fumbled in her pack, eventually pulling out a pen.

'Don't fucking write this down,' he said on a long drawn out-breath.

She laughed. 'Sorry - old habits.'

The Room

'It's not something I ever want to see written down.'

'Understood. I'll…' Harriet flicked the pen across the table, sending it over the far edge. It bounced noisily across the floor and spun out until it hit the skirting under the window. She moved to get up.

'Just leave it,' he said. He looked at his coffee and felt the urgent heat coming from the sides of the cup. He closed in on it with his fingers, chasing every bit of warmth he could. He was waiting for Harriet to settle back in her seat.

'She knows my real name.'

'Huh?'

'Yup, she bullies me about it; says she's going to tell everyone.'

'Huh?' Harriet said again, frowning. 'All this is about your sodding name?'

'Well, I-'

'So you're telling me 'Powers' isn't your real name, well blow me down with a feather.' She rolled her eyes. 'Even you're not good enough to have been blessed with the name of 'Powers'.

'So, you knew? You knew it was a stage name?'

'Well, I kind of figured, Austin. So, go on then, what's the big secret, what's your real name?'

He coughed. He had to tell her now. 'Michael Piddle'

'Sorry, say that again?' The corners of her lips were curling.

'You heard, Harriet.'

'As in 'to piss'?'

He nodded and then waited for her to stop laughing, her fist hitting the arms of the chair.

'I'm so pleased my childhood trauma is funny to you, Harriet.'

She regained composure and held her stomach, puffing her cheeks out. 'That's honestly the best thing I've heard for a while. Piddle! Jesus, your school days must have been interesting.'

'Yes, it didn't go down particularly well at a boy's grammar.'

She laughed again, but this time when she finished, she narrowed her stare, 'but it still doesn't explain why you're screaming Ben's name in the middle of the night.'

'Harriet, I-'

'No more lies, Piddle, I'm warning you.' She lifted her arms into a shrug, 'don't tell me now, whatever, fine. But I'll find out what you're hiding. You mark my words.'

Michael's stomach clenched as he watched Harriet leave the room and heard the slam of the front door. He needed to think, but all he could see when he closed his eyes was Ben's screaming face.

Part 2

Chapter 9

Jasmine sat neatly on the edge of her mother's crumpled bed. In her hands, she played with Daniel Burton's business card. The cardboard felt weak in her fingers, just like any other business card that had passed her way. The unique identifier, unique to Jasmine, had disappeared and could no longer be roused by her sleeping chip. She picked up a piece of paper that lay on the bed and unfolded it for what seemed like the millionth time. She'd found it sitting in the output tray of her printer, waiting for her when she woke, but she had no recollection of printing anything out.

She poured over the paper, and the message that simply said, "When you wake, come to The Room for 9 am sharp. Don't be late; it's your first day." Then it gave an address.

'What's that, Jasmine?' Myriam struggled to raise herself, digging her elbows in the soft bedding.

'Wait, let me help you, mum.' Jasmine reached around to lift her, but Myriam patted her hands away.

'I'm alright,' she snapped, 'You're doing it wrong anyway. We'll leave it to Claire when she gets here; if she ever gets here.' Myriam looked across to the bedside table towards the digital clock. The green numbers flickered at 8.02 am. Jasmine returned to her paper, her back to her mother. Myriam slowly raised her hand and found Jasmine was just out of reach. She longed to play with her *mad curls* as she used to call them, but she let her hand fall back onto the bed.

Jasmine hadn't noticed her mother reach for her. Instead, she got up and opened the window, allowing a streak of sharp sunlight to come in from the slit in the curtains, distorting the lemon glow with ice white light. She felt her hair, sat messily on her shoulders, lift from the breeze.

'I used to love watching your curls in the wind,' her mother said.

Jasmine turned and smiled thinly. From this viewpoint, she could see her mum in the unforgiving morning light. *Was she changing every day?* Jasmine thought. She folded the paper once more and set it down on the dressing table. She sat in front of the worn mirror and, using a hairband that sat loosely around her wrist, pulled her hair up into a ponytail, flattening the curls against her head.

'Dad used to say that.' Jasmine felt the coldness between them at the mention of him. She watched as her mother pulled the duvet up closer to her chest and rechecked the clock.

'She's late.'

'It's just after eight,' Jasmine replied.

'That's it; take her side.'

There was a pause. 'Mother-'

'Jasmine, *darling*, don't,' she interrupted.

'Do you ever think of him?' she asked. 'I think of him all the time.'

'And does it do you any good?'

Jasmine saw her mum's eyes soften. It was a small piece of her that Jasmine could recognise still. 'I don't know. I guess I'm still processing that at the moment.'

Myriam found the energy to straighten up and press her back firmly against her pillows. 'Well, while you're processing, remember this, he went off to Dubai when you were very young after the-'

'The what, mother?'

'He left us both when he got a sniff of my health problems, and I wasn't as useful to him. But we managed. We lived without him.' Myriam stopped abruptly to take on painful breaths that rattled stubborn in her chest.

Jasmine waited for her mother's breathing to settle.

'What was it you nearly said, mother? He left after what?'

Jasmine didn't remember her father leaving. The last memory of her father involved a merry-go-round and a horse with a purple rear. But she remembered the aftermath clearly; the vodka on the kitchen table, the weeks where her mother wouldn't wake up to take her to school, Betty cooking her meals, and walking to Sammy's for a lift to school every day.

Myriam closed her eyes and let her head fall back into the soft pillows. 'Let me be. Can't you see I'm ill and tired?' She said nothing for a while, only stirring when she heard the front door rattle open. She opened her eyes and seemed surprised to see Jasmine still sat there. 'Why are you dressed like that, darling, all posh? A bit overdressed for the café, no?'

Jasmine looked down at her trouser suit and brushed both arms to the cuffs. She hadn't worn it in the longest time, struggling even to remember why she had bought it in the first place. She was just glad it still fit.

'I have a new job. Today is my first day.' Jasmine waited for a reaction, and when one didn't come, she turned to look at Myriam. She caught her mum sneaking a look at the clock, and she knew that she was making a mental note of the time; to throw it in Claire's face when she eventually popped her head around the bedroom door with her mother's morning porridge.

'That's nice,' Myriam uttered, sounding like an afterthought.

'Mother, it's a better job with more money, and god knows we could do with the money,' Jasmine said. That last bit she wished she'd bitten her lip. As far as she knew, her mum had no clue as to the financial mire that was pulling at them.

A bright but muffled tune drifted up through the house as Claire rattled around in the kitchen singing. Any other time Jasmine could have made a game of trying to pick out the song currently being butchered, but as she sat there on the edge of the bed, her thoughts drearily danced from her. The annoyingly cheerful sounds from the kitchen were enough for Jasmine and her mum to share a moment. A few seconds existed between them, a few seconds of focus, stretched out and painful until Myriam eventually spoke.

'My God, her voice makes my ears hurt.'

Jasmine smiled to herself. 'I better get going. You have a restful day, mother.' She leaned over and kissed her on the forehead. She

The Room

made it to the door, feeling her mum's eyes on her, before her mum spoke.

'If you remember, ask Martin if he can keep back a few of those tiger buns I like.'

Jasmine opened her mouth, but nothing came out, only an empty breath and a forced smile. From a distance, her mother looked featureless, sinking into a hungry bed. She couldn't tell if she was smiling or just wearing a plain, flat-lined expression.

'Yes, mum. I'll see what I can do.' She thought she saw her mum smile and sink a little deeper and that was good enough for her. She stepped out of the room and clicked the door shut

Downstairs, Jasmine rested her hand lightly on the kitchen door handle, waiting for some mysterious strength to rise from deep inside her, enough to 'make nice' with Claire and come up with an excuse as to why she hadn't read through the blue folder. In her mind, she reasoned that it wouldn't make for *good bedtime reading*, and she wasn't ready for the inspired nightmares it would throw up. She had enough with her uninvited dreams, where a dead child's hand reaches from under the bed.

Jasmine stepped into the kitchen, slipping her letter from Daniel into her pocket before Claire could see it. Claire was hunched over the sink; the winged marigolds were busy foraging in the full bowl. Claire's singing had been replaced by the hum of the microwave as it spun her mum's porridge under the spotlight.

The microwave pinged. Claire, like a scrubbed surgeon, lifted her marigolds into the air and made her way to the tray and the neatly set out bowl and spoon. She let out a thin, bright scream when she saw

Jasmine standing just inside the kitchen. The sound she made was enough to make them both laugh.

'Jeez Louise, Jas! You scared the living rot out of me,' she said, still on the tail of laughter, 'You ought to be careful. I could've walloped you with a bowl of baking hot porridge.'

Claire peeled the gloves off like a second skin, setting them down on the drainer. 'I didn't know you were still here. Running late, aren't you? You'll have missed the morning coffee run.'

'Erm yes, well - no, not really.' Without thinking, Jasmine checked her pocket for the letter. It was still there.

'Not making much sense, Jasmine dear,' Claire remarked, a sliver of a smile spreading across her face.

'The thing is, I'm starting a new job today; a bit of an admin thing and I haven't got my hours sorted yet.'

'New job, eh? Sounds exciting. You will let me know the hours as soon as you can?' Claire punched the big door release button on the microwave and pulled the bowl of porridge clear.

'Yeah, sure, I will do.' Jasmine swallowed hard. 'I'm hoping to make good on one of those miracles I promised and pay you.'

'One of the miracles?' she asked as she finished spooning the porridge into a chilled bowl and began stirring. 'Do I take it then that you didn't read through the infamous blue folder?'

'It's on my list.'

'How is her ladyship?' Claire asked, changing the subject. 'Is there anything I need to know before I go into *No-Man's Land?*'

Jasmine dried off her hands and walked into the hall, feeling for her keys in a pocket that didn't hold Daniel's letter. 'She's clocked you were a couple of minutes late,' she said from the front door, 'oh, she hates porridge today. She'll probably spill it all over you. I'd keep your marigolds on, if I were you.'

Jasmine stepped out into the chill of the morning and slowly closed the door so she could enjoy the sound of Claire laughing from the kitchen.

*

Share Street felt cold and neglected in appearance as Jasmine rounded the corner. A wet mist descended thickly like grey soup, enveloping the buildings either side of the broad street. She slowed to check the numbers on the nearest doors to get her bearings. Even; she was on the right side of the road.

The road, filled with cobbled terrace houses and pockets of front garden, was a strange choice for a business and Jasmine had to re-type in the address on her phone, and even sync with her chip, to see if she was going in the right direction. She'd gotten off the bus on Halesowen High Street, cluttered with shops selling sad-looking carpet rolls and plastic containers. But Share Street was perpendicular to this main shopping street, pivoting Jasmine away from the public high street and into a residential road.

Daniel had asked her to switch off her GPS when she reached the lane, and she did this with uncertainty. She gripped the letter she'd found in her printer and, although the address was memorised, she kept looking down at it and checking the numbers off with the doors. When she would discover a string of houses without numbers; in those moments she would pick up the pace, her heart pulling at her chest, convinced she had gone past number sixty-two.

Share Street was on a hill, and Jasmine faced the decline on her journey. On both sides, the road was lined with red brick terrace houses, touching the sky with apex roofs, stacked with thin chimneys and tired satellite dishes. She moved into the street, splashing her trousers slightly when she stood in a puddle, to let a family walk past. The adults, panting but still talking loudly, were led by a little girl bundled in a pink shell suit. She stuck her tongue out in concentration as she peddled her tricycle up the incline. Jasmine could hear the adults talking simultaneously, both using their chip-sync to contact someone else. They did not thank Jasmine for moving out of the way and continued to speak into the space before them, eyes focused on the incline ahead. Jasmine looked down at her trousers. They were ruined with brown splatters that seemed as bright as neon paint on the clean black.

The weather was unnervingly cold for November, and Jasmine's hair that she had tweaked and adjusted into a ponytail was being pulled apart by the bracing winter wind, her curls falling across her face. The terrace houses, with their painted doors like bright lollypops in winter, were giving seldom shelter from the elements and the wind curled up the street in a make-shift tunnel.

Either side of the road was littered with unevenly parked cars, mostly petrol cars that had been abandoned in various modes of undress. Overgrown gardens hid collapsed trampolines beneath dense grass, almost a meter high. She stopped outside number sixty-two and looked back down the street. It looked like a war zone. The mood of the road was affected by the November brace, but she imagined that in summer it would be alive; kids racing up and down on their bikes and sneaking in and out of gardens retrieving balls, the smell of BBQ arresting the air.

But Daniel Burton walking down this street, hair slick with wax and dressed in a pressed suit? Jasmine felt cold; something wasn't quite right.

'I think I've gone mad.' She thought out loud, the words expelling a cool mist into the empty road. She turned to face number sixty-two. The windows were covered with brown cage wire and showed all the signs of abandonment, and the door was hidden behind two metal plates of the same colour as the cages. The short path was guarded on both sides by overreaching privet that lay heavy and threatening; Jasmine couldn't help but brush against them as she slid past. She felt the sharp cold of the wet on her thigh as she raised her hands clear of the bush and waded through to the door.

The metal door itself was set back under a little arched recess. It had no handle. She searched the dark corners of the porch for security cameras, but there were none. She took a deep breath and pushed on the door with the spreading palm of her right hand.

Nothing.

She took a few steps back as though to get a fuller look at the door. Thinking of the business card, she breathed in sharply as an idea crossed her mind. The fingers of her left hand squeezed then stretched like a waking spider. She pressed her left hand against the door until an electronic beep filled the little porch, and the door jumped a few centimetres from her hand. She could see the gap the door had made as it lurched, a hole big enough to slide her fingers through, but still, she had to lean her whole body against the thick metal door for it to move. It scraped loudly across a concrete floor.

As she pushed, the door jerked again as though someone on the other side had pulled at it with two hands. It swung wide open and ground to a stop on the uneven floor. Her senses were consumed with the room where she now found herself.

This wasn't like any terrace house home she had seen before. It was bright and expansive. There were no dividing walls, and therefore, no separate rooms. The walls had been stripped back to brick and were painted white. They stretched to the far end of Jasmine's sight, where a counter was positioned across the width of the room and flanked by four chrome barstools with bright red vinyl seats. Against either wall were fixed tables and chairs. A dishevelled man with wild white hair sat at one of them and looked up briefly from his tablet and smiled. Then he turned his head in the direction of the counter and shouted,

'Will, you got a customer.' He then turned back to Jasmine, 'You better step in; that door's got a mean kick.'

No sooner had he said it that Jasmine heard the door straining to free itself from its jam. It swung shut and let out a last determined click.

'Told you,' the man said.

Jasmine took a few steps closer. 'I'm here for Daniel, Mr Burton? I'm Jasmine.'

The Room

The man gently put his tablet on the table next to a cup. He raised a bony hand as if to stop something. 'I don't know if I should know your name. Unless Will or that other bloke tells me so.'

She nodded her head. 'I understand, I think,' she said, still looking around, waiting for someone called Will to show his face. 'I'm not even sure I'm supposed to be here.'

'Oh, you're supposed to be here, alright. That door wouldn't have budged if you weren't supposed to be here,' he said with a knowing smile.

Jasmine spun around and could hardly make out the door now sitting white against the far wall. The old man stretched out his left arm and tapped the inside with his right fingers. Jasmine lifted her arm and understood.

'My LE chip.'

The old man winked.

'You must be Jasmine, 'ello. I'm Will.' A very tall man strode towards her, jet black hair bouncing on his forehead. He stretched out one of his long thin arms, ready to take her hand.

Jasmine was taken aback by his enthusiasm as he bound toward her like a giant, lank dog in anticipation of a long-overdue walk. His smile was wide as he yanked on her hand, a firm hold for such slender arms. His almond eyes were bright behind large, oversized glasses and, she thought, *soft* in comparison to the sharp and defined bones of his face.

Will broke away from Jasmine and looked over to the man trying to get back to his tablet.

'I see you've met Derek. If he's bin bothering ya' I can 'ave him thrown out. In fact, that will probably be ya first job.' He flipped back to Derek. 'Derek, this is Jasmine. She's gonna be workin' the Hub for us.'

Jasmine turned to the man seated at the table and said, 'I guess it's okay for you to know my name, then.' Derek nodded at Will and then smiled.

'The Hub?' Jasmine asked.

'We'll get to tha' soon enough. I'm Will by the way.' He grabbed her hand again and shook it. His accent was warm and soft, like his eyes, with a subtle London twang.

'We've done that bit, Will. But it's nice to meet you. I've come because Daniel Burton offered me the job. You're expecting me?'

Will gathered himself, pulling on his camel coloured suede jacket as though Jasmine were a mirror.

'Of course, I've got me mornin' brain on. An' yeah, we've bin expecting you.' He ushered Jasmine over to the counter and offered her one of the red-topped bar stools. He whirled around, and from across the long white room, he called to Derek,

'Another tea, Derek?'

Jasmine and Will both watched Derek raise his cup triumphantly, signalling for another. Will placed his hand gently across Jasmine's arm, 'Wha' about you?'

The Room

Jasmine, briefly taken aback by Will's familiarity, took a second to look behind the counter and over his shoulder. All she could see was a metal sink supported on two rods and fixed into the wall. Next to that, an unassuming door as white as the washed walls. A kettle was permanently throbbing almost out of sight under the counter, but she could feel the warmth from it through the acrylic top.

'Have you got a coffee machine back there?' she asked. This was a cafe in the making, she thought, relief spreading through her bones. Maybe Daniel had pursued her so dramatically, in her mind, for the sole purpose of operating his catering business; a start-up cafe, by the looks of things.

'Sorry, house rules,' Will said. 'No coffee 'ere. The clients' experience is inhibited by coffee, so we limit it to good old-fashioned tea, black or white - no sugar. An', of course, you can 'av water, that's my recommendation.'

'Experience?'

'Yeah experience…sorry I'm jumping the gun a little. I should let Daniel fill ya in.'

'Sounds like Daniel likes his rules.'

'Well, the rules about the contaminants, as I call 'em, are mine. I'm a Chemist by day, an' the contaminants can affect our client's experiences.' He narrowed his eyes and looked at Jasmine.

'I'm doing it again, jumping-'

'The gun,' Jasmine finished. She watched Will pour water from the kettle over a tea bag into a fresh cup. She made a mental note that he didn't belong behind a counter, serving, because of the way he carefully poured the boiling water, perhaps afraid to mark what looked to be an expensive jacket.

'So, this is the Hub, is it?' Jasmine finally asked.

Will laughed, almost tipping his milk serving elbow beyond a dangerous angle. 'Nah, this is more like the waiting room. The Hub is upstairs an' is infinitely cooler than down 'ere. I'll take you up. Just got to get Derek 'is second, or is it his third? He does like his tea.'

'I'll take it. I've done this kind of thing before.' Will gave her a knowing smile, and she wondered then how much of her life, and her previous job with its humiliating finale, had been relayed to the tall, awkward Barista.

'Are you going to throw me out, Jasmine?' Derek wondered aloud as he watched her approach with the tea.

Derek must have been in his seventies, a shock of white hair forming into an ice cream moustache that wiggled when he spoke. It was near hypnotic, and Jasmine had to pull her attention away from it.

'I wouldn't dare, Derek. Already you are my favourite,' she said.

Derek pushed the empty cup towards Jasmine and brought the full cup closer in readiness. He smiled. 'I'm meeting my wife today,' he said, looking up into Jasmine's eyes.

Jasmine felt the intensity with which he held her gaze, weakened only by a sense of hope he'd attached. She shuddered as his interest dropped back to his tablet.

'That's great, Derek. I hope I get to meet her,' she said, a vain attempt to re-engage his attention. He smiled quickly, almost cautiously, but said nothing.

'Come on,' he said, 'It's time to meet the great an' mighty Daniel Burton in his natural 'abitat.' Will motioned for Jasmine to follow him behind the counter.

She followed Will through the door behind the counter and into a corridor. The bricks either side were natural and dark, thick with moss and glistening with cool damp from a pressing winter that was just getting started.

'What about Derek, Will? I mean shouldn't someone be looking after the,' she paused, 'waiting room?'

'No. Watch your clothes on these walls, here; you got to go up 'ere.'

Will pulled at another industrial looking metal door at the end of the corridor. Jasmine saw that it led to an old concrete staircase, lit by a neon strip that flickered incessantly.

'He's just upstairs. Good luck.'

'Are you not coming up?' Jasmine looked at the flickering light and the enclosed concrete stairs.

'Nah.' Will rubbed his free hand through his coarse stubble. 'Nothin' up there for me just yet.' He paused. 'Now off ya go, don't want to be late for the big man.' He grinned, showing thin, slightly spiked teeth. His eye twitched in a half-wink before he let go of the door. The slam reverberated up the concrete stairway, and Jasmine felt it run through her bones.

Her breathing sounded coarse and dry in the thin stairwell. She put one foot on the first concrete stair, her black boot looking bluish under the fluorescent strip light. She began to walk up the first few stairs, forcing her eyes to focus regardless of the constant flickering.

At the top of the stairs, she stopped, taking a step back like a drunk and surveying a large, heavy black door with a round door handle. She twisted it gently and pushed; she could feel a drip of sweat snaking down her back.

'What do I have to lose?' she muttered softly, as she pushed harder on the door.

The door opened into the room; smooth, graceful and silent. Jasmine squinted at the harsh, pure light. The brightness of this room seemed more intense than the waiting room, and for a few moments, it proved too much for Jasmine. She stepped in and felt the door close behind her. She knew instantly why this space was called the Hub.

A sizeable kidney shaped desk with a black glass top commanded the area from the rooms' centre just like the hub of a wheel. Around the edges of the perfectly round space were brightly lit billboards with messages that Jasmine guessed celebrated the services offered by The Room. She slowly traced the inside edge of the walls, visiting the boards and passing over the words thrown up to inspire. "Believing is Seeing" was one, "Creation is Within us all" was another. Beneath the words were stock photos of embracing families; beautiful people kissing, hugging. Forgettable stuff. Nothing new. It felt like Jasmine had been fed all this most of her life.

Towards the edge, a white leather sofa blended neatly into the white wall and floor. An empty coffee table gleamed under recessed spotlights. Behind the kidney shaped desk was a plain white door without a handle. There were two other doors either side of the desk; the door on the left was marked with a small plaque brandishing "Changing Room", and the door on the right was labelled "The Room". Jasmine was drawn to the door boasting "The Room", and she stroked the words, then pressed her ear to the door; silence. She looked around to see that she was alone before pulling on the sleeve of her left hand, then she quietly, but firmly, pushed against it.

No movement, nothing.

The desk, just like the coffee table, sparkled under the spotlights. The glass top was thick and black. Jasmine pulled the high-backed chair from underneath it and moved closer to see her reflection staring up at her. Absently she lowered her left hand onto the desk, and the area around it reflected blue, following the contour of her hand.

The desk surface transformed, and two monitors rose elegantly out of it as a keyboard appeared in light form in front of her. Startled, she brushed the glass surface sending the keyboard off the side of the desk and into nothing. The two monitors finished their ascent, and the one that would face Jasmine if she were seated blinked "Good morning, Jasmine".

'Good morning, Jasmine.'

The soft, familiar voice filled the room and made her jump like breath on the back of her neck.

She turned to see Daniel strolling towards her. He must have come from the unnamed door, she thought. The relaxed figure drifted in a suit that defined his strong shape, and his open-necked shirt announced tanned skin. He held out his arm and guided her closer to the desk.

'I see you've figured out the workings of your new desk,' he said, finding a seat for himself on the edge of the glass table. He motioned for her to take her place and then looked quizzically at the glass top desk in front of them. He tapped the glass twice with one finger, and the keyboard floated to the surface. 'That's better.'

'Yes, I wondered where that was,' Jasmine remarked, avoiding any eye contact.

'So, by now, you must have met Will. How did you find him?'

'He's perfectly nice. Tall, and he likes shaking hands. Not very forthcoming about the finer details of what goes on around here though, oh and he could use a bit of training when it comes to pouring a good cuppa.'

Daniel laughed. 'Well, he's under instruction not to be too forthcoming about what we offer around here and about the other thing, the cuppa? I guess that's your department. Perhaps you can give him a few pointers.' He frowned. 'I'm sorry I just heard that back, and it did sound a bit sexist. Of course, it's not expected of you, it's just that-'

'I get it, Daniel,' Jasmine said. 'But the whole thing does sound a little cloak and dagger. I mean, fifteen minutes ago I was resigned to the idea that I would be doing café duties downstairs.'

'Yes, I can see how you'd get there. But your duties are much more than that.'

'OK, I imagine they are, but until someone tells me what they are and what this place is, I'm going to be at a distinct disadvantage. I mean to say that if I don't fancy being stuck behind this desk doing admin, you'll have gone to a lot of trouble for nothing,' she said, raising her chipped arm.

'I'll get to it.' Daniel slid off the desk and slowly walked around the room, taking in the billboards. 'Although I haven't yet known anyone turn down a starting bonus of eight thousand pounds and a monthly salary that I'm confident is three times what you were earning at the Fly by Night.'

Jasmine nearly sent the virtual keyboard flying again. She swiped it back to the centre of the desk just in time and held a tight breath until the sound of her heartbeat no longer thrummed in her ears. She allowed herself to imagine what that would mean. The bonus alone would go a long way to pay for her mum's care.

'Are you ready to hold the keys to the world, Jasmine?' Daniel asked.

Chapter 10

Now

'Right, that's a wrap. Zach, send the footage to HQ.'

Michael walked back to the team, waiting by the channel's van. Another story complete; another menial member of the public happy with their five seconds of fame. This one, a school Head Teacher who was now climbing Everest for charity.

Harriet had a clipboard folded to her chest, and her eyes fixed on Michael. 'I need to talk to you.' She said.

'Can't this wait? I have a bottle of whiskey at home with my name on it.'

'Oh,' she said, licking her lips, 'so you don't want to know about Stephanie Milner's blog? Well then that's fine, smart arse, I'll just keep it to myself.'

Michael pulled Harriet into the van. Zach was too busy correctly placing the camera back into the case to notice anything, so he sat down and ushered Harriet into a make-shift seat on top of the cable spools.

'Jesus, Harriet, do you want to give me a heart attack? Zach could have-'

'I'll tell you what I know' she said, interrupting him and looking at her pink fingertips, her nose turned slightly up. 'But you have to tell me what Pinstripe has on you. Right now. Else, I'm telling the whole bloody station *your piddly little secret.*'

Michael groaned into his hands. 'So, it's come to this. I thought we were friends?'

'We can be. You just have to prove you trust me.'

'And you know something – something more about Stephanie - this isn't some bluff?'

Harriet shrugged, now biting at her nails as if they were a sandwich. 'Decide if you can trust me. Then, you'll find out.'

'Jesus. Fine.'

Harriet let go of her poor pink nails. 'Fine? You're going to tell me?'

Michael checked that Zach was out of earshot and then turned to Harriet.

'Yes but Harriet this is the only time I say this, OK?'

Harriet nodded eagerly.

'Years ago, I was working on the Echo with Jennifer. Can you believe it, I was still working under Pinstripe?'

'No rest for the wicked' she quipped.

'Let me tell you the story, yeah?' He paused as Harriet feigned zipping her mouth shut. 'Right. Back then, we were just farting around with local feel-good stories to fill some pages and bolster the local community. In those days, it wasn't a case of no news is good news; it was more a case of no news is a reason to think someone is hiding something: what aren't they telling us? That type of thing. Occasionally, on a quiet news day, we had a thing with a few of the coppers where we called them up, and they would drop a few storylines our way. It was mostly made up crap, but with enough credence, so we could fill in the gaps in the way our English teacher taught us, and everyone would sleep easily. And that's how it went. It was all deemed in the public interest. Nothing to get too excited about.

'And then the little twelve-year-old girl was snatched, and the community we served seemed to implode. I remember Jennifer pushing me hard to get my nose in the story and when she wasn't happy, she brought in one of the interns out from the copy room to be my extra pair of legs, arms, hands, eyes, whatever. His name was Ben Henshall.'

Harriet's eyes widened. 'Ben, he worked under you?'

Michael nodded. 'If you've read your research bits, then you'll know that when the police detained Pevestone at the scene, they began a lengthy investigation, mostly behind closed doors. Everyone was stuck. Nothing new was coming through the wire, no new information; it was starting to level off. It felt like people were forgetting it and going back to the summer fairs on the green and the two for one offer at the bowling alleys. We needed to pull on our coppers, see what would fall from the tree. I put Ben on it. Ben seemed eager, and I was a coward. Business as usual.

'Ben made the call to our copper network, and it hit first time; a fifty-year old man, a little bitter because they wouldn't let him have a bite of the big cases so near to retirement. Coleman was his name, but you already know that.' Harriet nodded, her face cold, ponytail still for once.

'It was unusual that Coleman insisted on meeting with Ben because, in Coleman's own words, it was *way bigger than anything he'd ever handled.*'

'What was it?' Harriet whispered.

Michael looked out of the van doors. 'It was a recording of the Pevestone interview, interview and confession, the whole fucking profile of a fiend.' Michael turned back to Harriet; her mouth was wide open.

'They had CCTV of Coleman lifting the USB stick. They took a gamble and waited for it to be used somehow. It found its way into the hands of an unpaid junior reporter. Then, me. Ben passed it across my desk, and I used it. There was a shit tonne on there, but I only used the name – the victim's name.'

'So, you were the one who spread Stephanie's name?'

Michael nodded. 'I didn't care about anything back then. To me, she wasn't real – she wasn't human. She was a story, and I needed something sensational. And trust me, Harriet, I've paid for my own stupidity. I figured I'd drip feed what was needed in a timely manner. The thing is, it wasn't an easy listen, so I never went back to it. It was too hard. But not only that, when the blue lights came for Coleman, he named Henshall.

'The boy needed my help, but it would have been the end of me. He was young; he could take the fall. So, I stood back. And Stephanie's father bumped into Ben when he was on bail, after months of being hounded now her identity was known. And well, he beat him to the point where he couldn't breathe anymore.'

Harriet took a sharp intake of breath.

'But you know that, and the rest you know from the articles you found, except, of course, the bit where Jennifer has her own CCTV footage of me accepting the audio file from Ben. That's her Ace. That's what Jennifer has on me.'

The van was silent. Both of them listened to Zach outside, talking loudly to HQ on his earpiece about sending the footage from the shoot.

'So you used to be more of a wanker than you are now?' Harriet said.

'Yeah, I suppose.' Michael bore into Harriet, seeing how uneasy she'd become. 'Look Harriet, there's nothing anyone can say to me that I haven't said to myself over the last ten years of bathroom mirror therapy sessions every morning. So, get Zach and skedaddle home.'

'Skedaddle? Who says that anymore?' Harriet pulled the van's laptop close to her. She brushed the keys until the screen flickered bright.

'What are you doing?' he asked.

'You've told me yours, and now you get to see mine.'

Michael tried to keep up with each mouse click as she brought up Google and started typing into the search bar. 'What, you didn't print this one out? I can't burn this one?'

His attention was caught by the little black letters appearing as she typed—*Stephanie Milner's Blog*.

'She had a blog?' he asked. 'That's kind of old technology, isn't it? I didn't know people went in for that sort of thing these days.'

The page seemed to waft into view, filling the whole screen. 'She had a blog,' Harriet whispered, leaning closer to the screen 'but not a good one, just one post. Like most newbs, she couldn't find it in her to commit.'

A Room with a Better View

You can probably tell from the title that I've never written a blog post before. But here I am. My name is Stephanie. That's something else that's changed dramatically in my life. I can't remember the last time I could confidently tell anyone my name without me worrying about somebody somewhere wondering about me, whether they'd make some connection to a past that should remain forgotten.

The Room changed all that for me.

It gave me (and still does) a life that is rich and full. Is that too cliché? I must admit, but probably shouldn't, that I'm addicted to The Room.

I know I'm not supposed to talk about The Room, so I will honour that; it's the least I can do for Jasmine. But for anyone who can find it then it will give you anything you want. More than that it will give you the thing you need the most. You just have to give over to it.

I went to a party, me a party, hosted by the founder of The Room, Jasmine Wilson and finally got to meet her. I had this image of a grand wizard behind a curtain, but it turned out she's just like me. We got on straight away. She has shown me so much of what is trapped inside my mind and that through The Room I can shed all my insecurities and live a life exactly how I imagine it to be.

Right, that's it, I feel like I've said too much.

I'll probably write another post soon. But If it gets taken down, then so what. It was the writing of it that I needed.

I can finally live again.

S.

Michael sat back. 'And this is all there is?'

'It's all I could find. It's strange, though. Something about this blog doesn't sit right.'

'How do you mean?' Michael asked.

'Well, I turned over the whole internet for you the other day, spent so long on it, and this blog; I don't know, it seems to have just landed in my lap last night.'

CHAPTER 11

Daniel's suit puckered open as he sank into the white sofa. His one arm was stretched across the back of the seat, and he used his other hand to brush out creases that had formed at the top of his knee. He seemed far away from Jasmine as he relaxed, speaking to her intently, methodically, about her role.

Jasmine was focused only on him, picking up every word and piecing it together to determine once and for all that this wasn't some sort of human trafficking outfit, drug den or prostitute ring. She held back a smile at the thought of her being the star of any attraction, especially something as scandalous. Daniel's voice flowed through her ears gently. It was soothing; a restful power lay concealed behind every word, and the faint Irish accent flooded every syllable.

'The Room, Jasmine,' he started, switching his attention to her, 'was something I developed alongside Will Cline a few years ago. My field is software development, and Will is a human behavioural scientist and chemistry major, as well as a first-rate tea maker.'

'I'm yet to sample that,' Jasmine remarked.

'Shame on him.' Daniel smiled and waited for her to do the same before continuing. 'With our combined expertise, we create experiences for our clients.'

'Experiences?'

'Yes. Experiences that they conjure, and through a combination of carefully administered medication from Will and the building tools that I provide through my software, we create an experience that is as real as it gets.'

'So, a bit like The Matrix?' Jasmine recalled the old, hazy movie Paolo had made her watch. She had sat in his t-shirt, legs curled up underneath her, cringing at the graphics and old technology.

'No, not really. I would say it's entirely the opposite of 'The Matrix'.'

'I don't understand.'

'Because the power lies in the subject to create their world, just for one hour. But, to the subject, it can feel like days have passed, even weeks in some cases.' He continued. 'I realise that this is far from a technical explanation but, if you can, try to imagine it, Jasmine. Imagine anything you want to experience - and all you have to do is think it up, and we'll do the rest.' He sat back further in the couch, shifting to look directly at Jasmine.

'Anything?' Jasmine frowned.

'Anything,' Daniel affirmed. 'I know what you're thinking.'

'What am I thinking?'

'You're thinking what everyone thinks when I first give them the basic spiel about The Room. You're thinking about what you would use it for.'

'Actually, my first thought was, is it legal?'

Daniel let out a short laugh. 'Yes, it's legal. Well, Will tells me it's legal. I just get to play with buttons and such.' He stood and

The Room

brushed down his suit. 'By the way, what would you use it for, if you ever could?'

Jasmine's eyes fell to the desk in front of her. She preferred scanning the opaque glass to looking Daniel in the eye. She didn't have an answer for him because she didn't have an answer for herself. Her thoughts had drifted while he'd been talking, and as she followed them, she found her father still at home. She thought about her mother taking in deep breaths as she swam like she used to when she was younger, and about her lost baby; the life she could have had.

'I'm not sure. I don't think I'd want to live in fantasy-land.' she said eventually, raising herself from the darkness of her thoughts. She eyed him suspiciously and then took in the whole space. 'You know, there's a pub in the city that puts on a hypnotist every so often. Isn't that just the same as what you're offering?'

'Jasmine, we're not in the business of making people cluck like chickens.' He started to walk toward her slowly. 'Within the confines of The Room, we can assist in creating experiences that are fully charged and powered by one's imagination. We're not tricking anyone. The client creates everything. Imagine, if you will, a dream you could conjure and exist inside and direct as *you* want.'

Jasmine watched him closely as he rounded the room and moved out of sight behind her. Eventually, he perched himself on the end of the glass desk.

'You said it's the basic spiel,' she said, looking up into his green eyes again. 'Does that mean there's more to it than meets the eye?'

Daniel raised an eyebrow. He folded his arms across his chest and nodded his head. 'Yes, that's about right. Some of it is on a 'need to know' basis; you needn't be hindered by that.'

The door that led from the Waiting Room opened, and Will stepped through. He winked at Jasmine as he made his way to the door marked "The Room".

'How's it going here?' Will asked.

Daniel swung round off the end of the desk. 'The usual,' he said, a smirk spreading across his face, 'just trying to convince her that we're not an *end of the pier* curiosity.'

'Good luck wiv' that,' Will said. He was backed up to the door marked The Room and Jasmine sensed he was about to use his chip. 'Don't forget we've got Derek downstairs for his appointment. He's pretty much drinkin' us out of tea.'

Will swung his arm behind him, and the door pinged and jumped from its frame. 'I'll get his doses prepped.' He opened the door and disappeared into a dark room.

'We can start with Mr Grace,' Daniel said as he turned to Jasmine. He towered over her, his hand slid gracefully over the blue keyboard, and she felt the shape of his forearm through his suit and shirt as it brushed against her shoulder.

'Mr Grace. Will that be Derek then?'

'I don't approve of the familiarity that Will proffers with the clients.'

'Yes, you're are probably right, Mr Burton.'

The Room

Daniel smiled at Jasmine's confident mocking tone. 'I like to keep a professional distance from our clients.'

'Wow! You make dream casting and wish-granting sound appealing. But please, on my count, let's not keep Mr Grace waiting any longer,' she said.

'Before we go any further, I should ask you the all-important question.'

'What's that, Mr Burton?'

'Daniel. Please.' He said, raising his eyebrow.

'Daniel,' she repeated.

'Do you want the job?'

Jasmine's eyes drifted from him and followed the room, once again taking in the backlit billboards and the precise white sofa and coffee table. The screen in front her, the one with the *Good Morning* greeting still glowing as though it were breathing in and out, started to change. A folder with Daniel's name on it, also marked confidential seemed to float into existence. From over her shoulder, Daniel's hand reached for the virtual keyboard and with fingers splayed they danced a particular dance, too fast and intricate for Jasmine to follow.

From the glass desk just above where the keyboard hung, and the screens stood to attention, two large buttons appeared. The green one was marked YES, and the red one marked NO. It was clear what was required of her, and as Jasmine's fingers hovered above the red button. She thought once again of the Matrix, that old movie Paolo had once forced her to watch, only these weren't pills as they were in the film, they were light projections.

The only certainty presented to her at that moment was that the life she knew was waiting for her on the outside of those walls. She pressed gently on the glass. It was like she could feel the electricity as her finger pressed down; it was like she could feel the change.

'Yes? Excellent. Excuse me, may I? It's easier if I guide you.' Daniel brought his hand down and rested it gently on Jasmine's. She took in a sudden breath at the touch of his hand on hers. He pulled her arm to a dark area of the desk to the left of the keyboard.

'Just two more steps, and we are good to go,' he smiled again. The area around her arm illuminated blue, causing a document to fly from the confidential folder. Daniel started around the desk and headed towards the sofa. 'This is just an NDA that I require you to sign.'

'NDA?' Jasmine looked up from the screen, flushing from the heat of his hand on hers.

'Non-Disclosure Agreement, amongst other things. I require something official that says you won't discuss what goes on in and around The Room. Standard stuff. Also, there's a *few dos and don'ts* for your benefit.'

Jasmine started to skim the document. Her fingers scrolled on the mouse pad, pushing the pages upwards

> *Do not discuss the client's activity/motivation/opinions in and around The Room. They may proffer the above, but wherever possible, you must remain attentive but overall indifferent.*

At no point is The Room to be used by a member of staff.

As she read, she wondered if Will had already broken some of the rules when he had told her about Derek and his dancing wife. She felt a sharp pain pulling at her insides, making her feel heavy in her seat. *Derek's wife wouldn't be coming to meet him really*, she thought.

There was a space at the bottom to sign her name electrically. She cautiously typed it out using the blue keyboard. The last instruction was to have it confirmed by Daniel Burton. He must have sensed she was ready. He was already rounding the table. 'All good?' he asked.

'All good.'

Daniel typed his name under hers. The keyboard disappeared, leaving a black space.

'Okay,' he said, 'we're ready. The desk is now yours and is in constant communication with your chip as you hover above it. That way, the system doesn't require your permissions all the time and is constantly updated with your levels of clearance. And so, to the last step in the process. The next time you place your chip across the desk, your starting bonus will be deposited in your account.'

Jasmine looked nervously up at him as if to ask permission to place her left arm across the desk. He smiled and nodded. Her arm glided silently across the counter. Nothing happened. Except her phone whistled in her pocket.

'It's in the rules that you aren't permitted electronic devices on the premises,' he said with a knowing smile.

'I'll just turn it off.' She freed the phone from her pocket and pressed the button that allowed the screen to illuminate. The light through the cracked glass screen was jagged and irritating. Just before the light died and the phone gave in to its prolonged death, she saw the preview of a message from her banking app. Eight thousand pounds had been deposited into her account.

At first, she couldn't comprehend the numbers, they looked wrong shining up at her from her phone, and she knew it wasn't because they were distorted through the prism of the shattered fragments; she was used to seeing everything like that through her old phone. It took a few moments, but eventually she understood her silent bewilderment. There wasn't a negative sign preceding the numbers.

The message from her banking app concluded: "Please proceed with caution in addressing this anomaly." *Anomaly, you got that right*, she thought.

Jasmine struggled to return the phone to her pocket.

'Leave it out if it's easier,' he said, reaching for it for a closer look at the screen. 'If you want, I could probably fix this for you.'

Jasmine took the phone slowly back from him as though she were asking permission. 'That's okay, Daniel. Seems like now's the best time to replace it.' She placed the phone to the left of the emerging blue keyboard and noticed the same blue light that had traced her chipped arm earlier was now drawing a contour around the device. The phone itself coughed and spluttered into life briefly to let anyone that cared know that it was charging.

Without any prompting, one of the monitors spread out a file, and a list of names appeared across the screen. Jasmine noticed that Derek's name was at the top. Next to his name, there were four buttons in a row. Two of the buttons were green, and the remaining two were red. Five other names also had one green button followed by three red buttons. The rest were all red. Jasmine was silent for a moment as she looked down the names and wondered about them and the hidden histories that nurtured such a need for something like The Room.

'This screen is the work that has to be completed today,' he said. 'What we will do, with Mr Grace's permission, is process him together; I will start you in the middle of the client's induction. But very quickly,' he said, indicating with his finger towards the screen and the open file, 'we have a list of thirteen names. The topmost are the more relevant and need our attention. The four lights next to each name are milestones.' Daniel stroked the desk at the side of the keyboard as though it were a mouse. He hovered over each button for a brief dropdown description of its function and then clicked through to the first one. 'This is the appointments screen as well as the master record. It's constantly updated with current information regarding the client; feedback and medical performances during each session.'

Jasmine recognised Derek's picture sitting neatly in the top left-hand corner of the screen. He was smiling and slightly out of focus, and she could tell that it had been taken by himself in the waiting room across the dingy hallway. His smile was full and hopeful. Below his picture were some of his vitals. Height, weight, chest size, amongst others.

'We try and keep this as full and as up to date as possible. As you can see from the dates and times, his is the next appointment.

Your job will be to put out a robe for them and prepare an empty locker for their things, prior to their arrival. They can all be found through that door. I've already done that for Mr Grace.' Daniel leaned further across her and pointed to the door marked "Changing Room". He flipped out of Derek's screen and back to the list of names. 'All the ones with the first button green will have their session today because their appointments have been made.'

'What was the section of writing on the far right? Can we go back to the appointment screen?'

Daniel obliged, and with a swift stroke of his fingers, they were back on the main screen. 'You'll have plenty of time during a session to familiarise yourself with this screen.' Jasmine noticed the fleck of irritation in his voice. 'These are our notes and observations about the client and their experiences.'

'This is a note about his wife and dancing. I thought we weren't permitted to discuss the sessions with the clients?' She wasn't going to tell Daniel that she had already known about Derek and his wife from their chance meeting downstairs.

'We aren't, but we can't stop them telling us about it, and if they do, then it is worth putting it on file. Sometimes, Jasmine, it's hard for our clients to leave the process behind. They're only permitted ten sessions per year so, depending on what they choose to use, The Room can determine a struggle or not in walking away. We have a program in place where a portion of the fee is withheld for counselling should they need it. The Room is good, it's powerful, but we need to remind our clients that what's beyond these walls is more real.

'Also, while we are on this screen, there are contact details and should you have to contact them to set an appointment which you will be doing today, then just click on this button and depending on the number of sessions they've had determines which script pops up on this other screen.' As he spoke, Daniel clicked on the button, and a short script appeared on the second screen.

'Stick to the script when confirming the appointment, please. They will have been waiting for your call, so they'll be excited, perhaps a little agitated, so we must keep control of the conversation. When the date and time is agreed, hit the book button, and the appointment will go straight into the system. They'll receive a notification on their phone which will direct them to scan their LE chip which will give them access to the waiting area only on that specific date and within twenty minutes of their time.' He noticed Jasmine nodding slowly.

'I see you're getting this. That's good. Now, let's get back to our Mr Grace.'

'Wait,' she said quickly, 'what are these numbers?' she pointed but was afraid to touch the screen as though it was as elusive as her shimmering blue keyboard, 'are these money values?' She traced a line across the screen.

'Yes, Mr Grace is on his ninth session today. Yes, that's right.' Daniel paused and watched Jasmine take in a deep breath and let it out as she leaned back into her chair. Her face seemed to contort as she tossed numbers around her head.

Daniel smiled. 'Yes, Jasmine, that's forty thousand per session.'

She looked him squarely in the face. She had held her own, she thought admirably, over the eight thousand that had dropped into her bank account, now she had to do the same over the insane pricing structure of The Room.

'I knew that,' she said with a small shake of her head.

'A little bit more than the Hypnotist charges, I imagine.'

'Yes,' she replied, 'but at least you get a cup of tea.'

He smiled. 'Back to business. You'll notice that his second light is green.' Daniel hovered over the button, and the small dropdown flickered "Payment".

'This button and the next are fully dependent on the client. Mr Grace has just made payment using our tablet downstairs and is now waiting for us to invite him into the Hub. Shall we?'

Jasmine took over and brought back Derek's profile screen. She noticed a prominent button had appeared which bore the word "INVITE". She dragged the arrow across it and clicked. The screen now showed a two-way split-screen CCTV image of the corridor and stairs between the Hub and the waiting area. A shadowy grey figure with unmistakable wild white hair glided like a ghost from one screen to the next.

The ping seemed louder and more enthusiastic than when Will had slipped through. At the same time, as the sound echoed around the sparse hub, the CCTV images disappeared.

'Mr. Grace,' Daniel said, 'Welcome back. Nice to see you as always. I know you have met Jasmine, who is going to be working at our Hub.'

'It's nice to see you again... Mr Grace.'

'What happened to Derek?'

Jasmine flicked her head in Daniel's direction. 'Boss's orders.'

'Mr. Grace, would it be okay if the two of us saw you into The Room today, so that I can show Jasmine the ropes?' Daniel interjected.

'I'd rather it be just Jasmine.' He winked at her. 'But I suppose it will do this time.' He motioned to the door marked "Changing Room" and waited for Daniel's nod.

'Sure,' Daniel said, 'it's all waiting for you.'

'Grand.' Derek leaned over the desk toward Jasmine, his deeply tanned cheeks bunched up in a grin. 'We'll be dancing tonight, Serina and me, just like always.' He half danced; half walked towards the changing room. Jasmine smiled nervously, catching Daniel's stare. He nodded. She fought the urge to respond and instead made a mental note to go back to Derek's profile and add the name Serina to his records.

'He'll be a couple of minutes,' Daniel said, leaning over Jasmine's shoulder again. His fingers curled around the edge of the nearest monitor and unplugged what looked like a plastic peg. 'When he does make sure he's wearing this on the tip of his left index finger.'

'You're not staying?' she asked.

'No, I have to be on the other side of that door to bring him into The Room. Don't worry; he'll know what to do.'

'Okay,' she said, uncertainty in her voice, 'what is it?'

'It'll measure his heart rate. Will is in communication with this little device. When Mr Grace enters that door there,' he pointed, 'he will be in a little glass anteroom that will build up a profile of his vitals. When Will decides he is stable, then he can enter The Room and his third light,' he hovered the icon over the third button, the drop-down read "Medical", 'will turn green.'

'And that just leaves the fourth light,' Jasmine herself had hovered above that one. 'Wipe Codes'

'Ah, yes. This is important to remember because often the client is so preoccupied with their session that they sometimes forget. With their profile screen open, invite them to place their chip arm on the desk, and that will wipe all the dead security access signals from their LE's. You'll know this has worked when you see the fourth light turn green. They'll no longer need them as the exit is provided for them at the far end of the changing room. A more traditional exit if you like.'

'Sounds very efficient; it's a wonder you need me.'

'The Room will always need a face that our clients can relate to, other than mine and Will's, of course.'

'Looks like you're having fun,' Derek said as he approached in his white towel robe, his beard and moustache flickering as he laughed.

'Derek, you made me jump.'

He smiled and held out his finger. He knew the drill.

Jasmine picked up the peg and placed it gently onto his finger. The light on the device jumped between its two colours.

'How's it going so far with the job? Do you think you'll like it? I hope you'll stay. It would be nice to see your face around here.'

Derek's sentiment softened jasmine. She managed a look at his profile screen and saw that this was his penultimate session and wondered if he had remembered. She smiled, 'I'll get through this first day and let you know.' There were a few moments of silence, and she thought she had forgotten something. 'Well you better get in Derek. They're waiting for you.'

'Yes, yes; mustn't keep her waiting,' he responded, 'See you on the other side.'

CHAPTER 12

A long wooden bench stretched along the length of the changing room and reminded Jasmine of the boy's locker rooms at school, the ones her and her friend Sammy used to sneak into so they could confirm rumours about what went on under those gleaming tiled walls. Of course, the only thing they came away with was the urgent smell of piss and a faint whiff of deodorant. The conclusion? Boys were gross.

But this changing room gleamed under sunken spotlights that bounced from every wall. The dark wood slats that made up the bench were polished like glass and held the reflection of the room from every angle. In the centre was an island, and in the middle of that, a wooden box with a hinged lid. Jasmine had set out the valuables box for the first client of The Room the following day and left the tall standing locker set against the far wall open with the correct sized dressing robe hanging inside. With the door to the Hub still ajar, she stepped through the changing room, enjoying the clipping of her shoes on the ceramic floor.

She opened the laundry basket and counted off the robes for the day. Then she pushed on the door to the outside world next to the basket. This was the only way out as far as she knew for her and the clients. The back of the buildings was clumped together and held no discernible shape as far as Jasmine could make out. They seemed taller than she expected. She found herself halfway up, clutching the metal rail of a fire escape with two sets of skeletal steps either side of her. One set leading out to Share Street, and the other, Jasmine imagined, to the roof. As she looked out across Hagley, over the dual carriageway and to the edge of where the city was starting to rise, the wind pulled her hair away from her face. She stared down the city defiantly.

Far behind her, through the changing room and into the Hub, one of the screens rose from the desk and flickered into life with the split-screen CCTV pictures. The images shook nervously, the sepia tones wobbled and contorted, dealing the figure of a man passing through the brick corridor and towards the steps leading to the client's entrance to the Hub. The desk made a gentle 'pinging' sound that cut across the Hub and volleyed through the changing room.

Jasmine turned at the noise and, seeing her screen active and rising from the desk, she marched back in, closing the external door behind her. She could see the smudge of a figure making his way across.

'Oh shit, oh shit. You're not on the list!'

She hadn't pressed the invite button, and there were no more scheduled appointments for the day. She sat down at her desk and pressed buttons, any buttons that presented themselves.

'Daniel?' she called in the empty space, 'Will?'

Jasmine curled her fingers around the edge of the desk, smoothing the underside of it for some sort of security alert button. Nothing.

The door opened. The man that stepped through into the Hub was dressed heavily, fit for the season. He carried himself awkwardly, as though his pockets in his long winter coat were laden. At first, he seemed surprised to see Jasmine sitting at her desk. He smiled at her. It was an uneven smile, full of toppled tombstone teeth. He pulled at his gloves and stuffed them in his pocket. A hand shot out as he bounded, childlike towards the kidney shaped desk and Jasmine.

'My dear, what a pleasant surprise,' he almost spat. 'Never, never in all my times coming here have I been treated to such a delightful sight as you.' He still held his hand out to Jasmine. His fingers twitched impatiently waiting for her to take them. When she did, he raised dark eyes slowly as though he were following the contour of her arm and then shoulder. He swallowed hard.

Jasmine stood up to meet him, at the same time pulling her hand in a jerking fashion from his.

'I'm sorry sir, I didn't realise there was another appointment today. You haven't shown on the system. Mister?'

'Ah well, Mr Burton and I have what you might call a *special arrangement*.'

At that moment, Jasmine's eyes fell to the desktop on the monitor and Daniel's confidential folder.

'Special arrangement? Sounds intriguing.' Jasmine managed a smile.

'Yes, quite.' The man lingered a little too long in the ghost of her smile. 'And it's Mr Pevestone, Alex Pevestone.'

'Mr. Smith.' Daniel emerged silently from the door behind Jasmine's chair.

Jasmine let out her breath. Alex stepped away from the desk, his eyes still on Jasmine.

The Room

'Oh yes, silly me, it's Mr Smith. Daniel, it's come round again,' he said, extending the same hand this time to Daniel, who didn't take it.

Daniel looked pale and agitated. He took Alex's arm and led him to the entrance of The Room. 'Are you early or am I late?' he asked, eventually smiling. He didn't wait for a reply.

'Just give me a second, will you?' he said to Alex.

'I was just getting the changing room ready,' Jasmine said as he drew closer, anticipating his question 'You know, first-day eagerness and all that.'

'Well your time to leave is five, Jasmine. I need you to respect that.'

'Ah. OK' Jasmine felt the heat rise on her cheeks. 'Do you want me to help you with Mr Smith?'

'No, I got this one,' he said. 'I'll see you tomorrow.'

'Goodbye, Jasmine,' Alex bellowed, 'It was nice meeting you. See you again soon. I hope.'

Daniel took Alex's arm and put it to the door. 'A lovely girl that Daniel,' Alex said, his smile broad and overwhelming. 'Do you think I'll see her again?'

Daniel's reply was resolute. 'I don't think so, do you?'

CHAPTER 13

NOW

Michael lent over the table, his hands neatly spread between the tightly wrapped cutlery and the ketchup dispenser, to take a closer look at the photograph hanging from the tiled wall. It was of a man with thick black hair and an oversized chef's hat, a plump face with a welcoming grin, despite the distracting slug of a moustache, and a faithful tea towel draped over his right shoulder, lovingly held in place between thick sausage-like fingers. Michael's gaze dropped to the name, pressed black against a gold rectangular background.

Martin Lovell.

The name washed over him, failing to register in his tired mind. A flicker of light in the glass frame caught his attention, and he turned to see that his toast was being carried towards him by a young man.

'He looks like you, or is it maybe you look like him, that's probably the right way to phrase it.' Michael stumbled awkwardly over his point as he directed it to the young man delivering his toast. He had a familiar tea towel draped over his shoulder.

Paolo Lovell looked over at his father's picture then back at Michael. He smiled.

'Yeah, I suppose I do. I've never noticed it before myself, but if enough people tell me, then it must be true.'

The Room

Michael sensed the unwillingness of the man to continue the conversation. He changed tactics. 'It's a nice place. Was it your father's?'

Paolo's green eyes widened as he looked around as if it was the first time doing so.

'Been in the family for years, this has.' He smiled, revealing a row of clean, white teeth. 'And it's still Dad's. I really should put a few more words under that picture.' Paolo drew his fingers apart as though it were an imaginary plaque. 'Not dead, yet.'

'Sorry,' Michael sputtered. It was an awkward laugh. 'I see a picture like that, and my mind goes…'

Paolo raised a hand. 'Like I said or at least implied, it happens all the time. Dad had a stroke about six months ago, so he had to take a few steps back. I stayed for my placement year at Uni, and here we are,' Paolo dropped his gaze at the table and the round of toast still sitting in front of Michael, 'except you haven't got your tea yet. Be right back.' Paolo disappeared around the large column in the middle of The Fly by Night, his father's towel flapping in his wake.

Michael had waited until he was out of sight before pulling out a piece of paper from his pocket. It had Harriet's scrawl all over it. Markings that mostly made sense and had brought him to the café. According to Jasmine's chip history, her traffic pattern was solid and had centred at the Fly by Night Café for the past three years and then suddenly stopped about twelve months ago. As Michael poured over the piece of paper and the drunken scrawl, he recalled his conversation with Harriet that day he'd first heard Jasmine's name and wondered about "The Room" and the double suicides.

'Are you sure this is legal?' Michael had asked.

'Fuck no. Does it look legal to you? A back door to any LE chip on the planet through a disguised computer terminal?' Harriet snorted. Her fingers danced across the keyboard, throwing up screen after screen of code that made no sense to Michael.

'So, it can't be traced back to this machine?'

'Not if I can help it.'

'How do you know about this stuff?'

'I'm a woman of many talents. Why does this surprise you?'

'You're joking, right?'

She'd smiled and rolled her eyes. *'A boyfriend from way back has a family who work for the government. They use this little greasy technique to monitor habits of its little sheep, that being us. It used to be effective with the smartphones only in cases where the user had enabled their location setting. But now, with the LE chip, that setting is hardwired and enabled permanently.'*

'Serious? I think they left that little gem out of the brochure.'

She had nodded. *'Something else that isn't in the curriculum is the location of the backdoor where you can access a shitload of saved data. So, all I had to do was cross-reference the name in Stephanie's blog with Birmingham residents, and low and behold, we found someone who we think is our Jasmine. Standard gov issued chip, nothing fancy. Not something you'd expect from the 'owner' of this Room place that was grossing so much money every year.'*

'Tax fraud? Identity fraud? What's it saying?'

'Maybe. We'll have to find out.'

Harriet stopped typing. Her face became stern and determined as though to find the thing that was missing.

'What is it?' Michael pressed.

'Not sure.' Her words were slow and thoughtful. *'Hand me a piece of paper and something to write with.'*

'Paper and pen? That's old technology, almost as rare as cash in a wallet,' he had said as he handed them to her

'What? Oh yeah. Well we can't be too careful, can we?' She had taken the paper and started writing. *'This can't be right.'* She stopped writing, brought her elbows to the table and with cupped hands, she bounced her thumbs on her lips.

'There's very little information here, and to be honest, you'd usually find that if the pattern is pretty solid, which it is. A lot of her traffic is centred around this shitty café by the train station, the Fly by Night Café, which we can probably assume is where she worked, but as we know from Stephanie's blog she was associated, or even owned, "The Room".' Harriet leaned back in her chair. *'Have we a date on that Blog post she threw up?'* Harriet hadn't waited for a reply. She clicked on a static tab, and Stephanie's blog appeared. She traced a finger across the top of the screen. *'The seventeenth. What's that - two weeks ago?'*

Michael rounded her and looked over her shoulder at the glowing screen. *'So, what does it all mean, Detective?'*

'It means that something happened to her chip...' Harriet's lips danced silently as her eyes found a corner of the room, *'...a year or so ago. Either*

it stopped working, which is unlikely given the dependency level for these things, or someone has successfully disabled its location feature. Even my ex-boyfriend said that's impossible. And of course, that brings us to the blog. Remember I said it felt like the blog had come out of the blue?'

'As though someone knew we'd be looking for it so there it was,' Michael had replied.

'That's a very good way of putting it, Michael. How come the LE chip, as advanced as it is, has lost Jasmine twelve months ago and the blog, which might as well be a throwback to a digital stone age, has her in charge of some weird kind of experience theatre only two weeks ago?'

'Weird theatre? You just make that up?'

'Roger that.'

'Do you think the blog is fake?' he asked.

'It's possible, but I don't get it. Assuming it is fake then we know that the trail for Jasmine still went cold about a year ago and, why go to the trouble of dropping a name in a fake post unless-'

'Unless you want to draw attention away from another. That "Room". It's all tied up with that, and I still haven't a clue what it is. What's the name of the place she worked at before her going silent?'

'The Fly by Night Café,' she had said. *'I know it, never been in mind, it's on the ring road opposite the train station.'*

Michael, still hanging over Harriet's shoulder, noticed a flashing over another tab hidden behind the current screen. He reached over and pointed at it. *'What's that?'*

Harriet slapped his finger away just before he touched the screen. *'Careful. Smudges.'*

'It is my laptop.'

'So it is,' she had offered. She opened the tab.

Michael pulled up a chair and watched the screen bleed red then turn white as it announced its search was over with just one matching result.

'This is the Capital City Archive site. It's not as black hat as the other methods I've used, and someone somewhere will know we used it.'

'Yes, but what have we used it for?' Michael asked.

'Look,' she said, smudging Michael's screen. *'It turned up a result for Wilson.'*

The screen was so sparse under the red Capital City Archive banner that Michael wondered why he hadn't seen it. He leaned in, drawing his eyes tight to read the headline and the fragment of a line from an article with the name Wilson highlighted.

Tragedy Strikes at Pilsley Park

"...there was nothing we could do. It all happened so fast," said Aryan Wilson, who had been previously enjoying the fair with his seven-year-old daughter Jasmine...

'Is this an article? Can you click on it?'

'Michael, you know I can't. You'll have to apply for a copy from Birmingham House.'

'And this is the only mention of that name?'

'It's what it says.'

'Look at the date,' Michael had said abruptly. 'This article is twenty years old.'

Harriet nodded her head and shook a finger at the screen, struggling to get her words out. 'Yeah, her chip history goes back twenty-seven years. As they're usually put in in the first year or so, it's pretty safe to assume she's had it her whole life. So, this Aryan Wilson, technically, could be Jasmine's father, and the seven-year-old-girl is Jasmine herself.'

Michael weaved his fingers together behind his head and buried them in his thick black hair. He leaned fully back in his chair and heard the soft click in his back.

Harriet scribbled the details of the search onto the piece of paper and slid it in front of him. 'So, what now?'

'I need to visit the café where she worked but first, I think I'd like to read the rest of that article.'

*

Michael finished reading Harriet's notes and set them aside. Reaching into another pocket, he pulled out a carefully folded piece of paper. He opened it, carefully pressing along its folds with one finger. The letterhead gave it as once being the property of Birmingham House and below that was the faded copy of an old article.

The disjointed cries of a young baby jostled with the music pulsing across the café, caused Michael to look up. He thought it strange that he couldn't see a baby amongst the customers scattered like ashes across the space. Two older men sat opposite each other, each reading their own newspapers and a smartly dressed woman intent on her laptop, furiously typing, *the next great novel,* Michael had thought. He saw Paolo squeeze from behind the counter with a mug of tea and head his way.

'There you go,' he said, putting the mug down next to the photocopied news article, his face fixed on the full but discarded plate. 'Was there a problem with the toast?' he asked.

'No, not at all. Just enjoy a mug of tea chaser.'

'Well, let me know if there's anything else.' Paolo started to move away to one of the other tables.

'Actually, there might be something you can help me with,' he said sharply. 'Some information about someone who once worked here.'

Paolo had returned to the table, letting out a short burst of surprised laughter. 'Whenever somebody is after information in the movies, they are usually with the police - or a newspaper.'

They both laughed.

'So, which is it?' Paolo asked. His attention was slightly taken by the slow build-up of a baby's cry.

'Does it matter?'

'Depends.'

'I'm trying to get in touch with someone called Jasmine Wilson. I believe she used to work here.'

Paolo took in a long-drawn breath and let it out just as slowly. 'I haven't seen her in six months or so, not since the funeral.'

'The funeral?'

'Yeah, her mum Myriam died. Cancer.' Paolo seemed to be lost in his own thoughts. He started to taper off. 'We went to the funeral, and that was the last I saw of her.'

'But you didn't wonder where she was in those six months?'

Paolo started straightening nearby chairs and tidying condiments. 'Not really. I had my own stuff to deal with, and we left on bad terms.'

'Bad terms?'

'Yeah. She turned a bit crazy, in the end.' Paolo frowned. 'You sound more like a newspaper man.'

'As it happens, I'm here to straighten out Myriam's will, and we've noticed Jasmine's absence over the past few months.' Michael was impressed with his quick lie. He made a mental note to gloat about it to Harriet later.

'Well, whatever. As I said, she turned into a massive bunny boiler. She's got a new job, and I guess she thinks she's better than us. That's why we don't see her around here anymore.'

'New job? Is that at "The Room"?'

'Room?' Paolo asked. 'Never heard of it. All I know is she amazingly found money to pay for her mother's care which by all accounts was crippling her.'

The baby's cry intensified, and both men looked over toward the counter. 'Look I got to get back.'

'Do you have an address for her, even an old one I can chase up?'

The lines around Paolo's eyes gathered as he chased a memory. 'I suppose you could try their old family home.'

Michael reached into his inside jacket pocket and pulled out a pen. He placed it on the article that had been sitting on the table the whole time. He slowly slid them toward Paolo.

When Paolo returned it to him, Michael carefully folded the piece of paper and put it in his pocket as he followed Paolo to the counter. As he offered his chip for payment, he saw the baby, pink and wrapped tight in a pram.

'Precious,' he offered with very little sincerity. 'You do well to manage on your own Mr Lovell.'

Paolo seemed taken aback that Michael had used his surname. 'Her mum has taken off to have her hair cut. She'll be back soon,' he said.

'How old?'

Paolo reached for the answer, looking the baby up and down as though taking a measurement. 'Six, almost seven months.'

'Six months, you say? Things were certainly busy around here six months ago.' Michael patted his pocket just above where the papers were stored. 'Thanks for your help. Bye now.' Paolo nodded, and as Michael made his way across the café and to the door, he could feel

Paolo still looking at him, following him with his eyes. With the door half-open, Michael felt for the papers in his pocket before turning back into the café.

'Something else?' Paolo asked, both hands pressed on the counter.

'Maybe. Did Jasmine ever mention a man by the name of Daniel Burton?'

CHAPTER 14

Sammy Check brought her glass close to her full red lips, opening them just enough for the clear liquid to trickle in.

Jasmine hadn't touched her cocktail, busy instead watching her friend make a glass of water look like liquid gold. She sighed, feeling the usual heat of jealousy and admiration, all mixed into one.

'Holy fuck – you know what this means, right?' Sammy said.

'What does this mean?'

'You're finally rich. I mean, I thought you'd always be piss poor. No offence.'

Jasmine covered a smile and feigned offence at her remark. Her friend's striking looks were no match for her Birmingham accent and ability to swear in every sentence. Even still, Jasmine thought Sammy was cripplingly beautiful. She was pale, whereas Jasmine was ashy, even grey in some lights she thought, and Sammy's face was perfectly heart-shaped with a pointed chin and a thin, long nose. Sammy could make drinking water look...Jasmine tried to think of another word, but the only one she could muster was *sexy*. It was no surprise that men wanted her with something close to desperation. And Sammy loved men as equally as they loved her.

'I wouldn't go that far as to say 'rich'. Just enough to pay off some of my mountainous debts. They're looking more Snowdon than Everest right now, which is one relief.'

'Whatever, still much better than the sorry state you were before. Barman, get a shot here for a *wealthy as fuck* friend.'

The barman, who had been cutting up lemons, while shooting occasional looks at Sammy's perfectly proportioned face, jumped to attention and began filling up a shot glass with tequila.

'No, ignore her - I don't want a shot.'

The barman flushed and narrowed his eyes at Jasmine, slamming the tequila bottle back into the ice bucket.

Jasmine played with the little straw in her drink. She already regretted telling Sammy anything at all. But, after her app had informed her of her positive bank balance for the first time in three years, she'd called Sammy to celebrate straight after work. She'd never seen so much money. She'd felt like she was floating, filled with a warmth that seemed to sparkle and pop inside her like an endless firecracker. There was so much heat inside her that she'd almost forgotten the feeling of the biting wind on top of the Radisson Blu hotel, or the icy stare of Mr.Pevestone. The idea of going home and letting the bubbles pop slowly one by one as they rested on her mother's medicines scattered around the lounge, and the blue folder in the bookshelf, had felt so wrong. So, she insisted that Sammy meet her at Jesters Bar, to prolong the feeling as much as possible.

'I just do admin; it's nothing mind-blowing. And Jesus, Sammy, stop shouting about my bloody bank balance - do you want me to get mugged?'

Sammy's questions were bound to start, so Jasmine decided to keep her lie simple. It wasn't a 'lie' as such, but she bent the truth just enough so that she could keep within her NDA.

'That's it? Just admin?'

'Yeah. For this guy. He owns his own business. He's really cool, actually. He gave me a starting bonus. And now I can pay off Claire.'

'Well lardy-dah Jas. I'm impressed. Jealous as fuck, but impressed.'

'I'm hardly rolling in it, but I need this job, Sammy. I have five maxed-out credit cards to pay off, in mine and mum's name.'

Sammy put her manicured hand in her bag and pulled out an e-cigarette. She puffed on it proudly, ignoring the irritation of the table next to them, who were covered in a cloud of sweet vapour.

'So, let me get this right, yeah, you just have to work for this guy, doing admin and you get bonuses and stuff?'

'Yeah, that's it.' Jasmine pushed the thoughts of the white, vapid room and Mr.Pevestone out of her brain. It *was* admin in a way; that was the truth.

'I'm so fucking jealous right now. If you weren't my best friend, I would hate you. Do you know how hard I work for minimum wage?'

'I wouldn't exactly say you have the best work ethic, Sammy. Didn't you say you took the afternoon off last week to get a tattoo, and told your work you had come down with the flu?'

'It was 'women's problems' actually, and who are you, fucking HR?' Sammy squeezed her eyes together, and puffed on the e-cigarette slower. 'Anyway, your new job means you don't have to work with Paolo the Prick anymore.'

Jasmine flinched. She remembered the crack as her fist hit Paolo's head in the cafe. It felt like another lifetime ago. 'I guess so,' she responded.

'Has he spoken to you since his Dad sacked you in front of everyone?'

'No, not a peep.'

Sammy smiled thinly. 'Well, that's at least one silver lining. It would be shit if he were still trying to contact you, and make you feel even worse.'

Jasmine felt her stomach pull and contract. She remembered the last text message she'd received from Paolo, a few days after she'd gone into hospital. She'd read it at least a hundred times. It merely said: 'I'm sorry it's like this'. She'd guessed he was talking about not wanting a baby, or not coming with her to the hospital after her miscarriage. But the truth was - she didn't know what those five words had meant. Maybe he was sorry, honestly sorry that she had lost her baby. Or, perhaps he was sorry he had to feel guilty about it.

'Your new boss, though. 'Nice' did you say?' Sammy went on.

'Yes, he's nice.'

'Fuckable, nice?'

'Jesus, Sammy!'

Sammy shrugged. 'Well, all I'm saying is you could give him a 'starting bonus' too.'

The Room

'Way to pull feminism back a few decades.' Jasmine rolled her eyes exaggeratedly. 'He's cool. Let's just leave it at that, shall we? Now, that cocktail - are you gonna play with that all night, or drink it?' Jasmine tried to tease her, but Sammy's face grew stern, preoccupied.

Sammy put her hands over her eyes. 'I've meant to talk to you about something, so when you called, I thought...sod it, now is as good a time as ever.'

'Spit it out, girl.' Jasmine prodded her friend's arm.

'I've got something serious to tell you, Jasmine.'

Jasmine's mouth twitched. She hated that sentence. She hated the suspense, the impending doom. Claire's voice echoed in her mind, *'I've got something serious to tell you, Jasmine'*. She'd said that way back when she told her that her mother wouldn't be getting better, the first time her mother had crawled into bed and didn't get back out.

'OK?' Jasmine swallowed hard.

'I'm pregnant.

Jasmine felt like she was underwater. The pressure in her ears tightened, and everything around them felt blurred, clouded. She could hear Sammy's voice piercing through the cloud

'Shit, I know this is crap timing, what with, you know.' Sammy was looking at her, her round blue eyes traced in a soft brown powder. 'And I really didn't want to tell you, babe. I've waited it out; I'm three months gone now, they say more like 15 weeks. And I wanted to be sure, like really sure before I told you.'

A pain began in Jasmine's forehead over her left eye

'Jasmine seriously, get a grip. I need you.'

Jasmine, through dry lips, managed just one sentence. 'How did this happen?'

Sammy smiled with one corner of her mouth and lifted her glass to her lips again, sipping lightly.

'Well, I did the sex thing and everything. And since then I've been craving pickles and throwing up every morning.'

She swallowed and continued. 'I haven't had a period in like, three months. At first, I just figured I was having problems with my implant again. I felt fine; I feel fine. Christ, I'd been bloody drinking and smoking like a chimney.'

'Well...are you-'

'Yes, I'm gonna keep it. Mom's gonna have a fit, but I have to keep it. I'm not a child anymore; I have a job. I have my own place, and it'll work out.' She took another drag, blowing the vapour out slowly. 'It'll work out. Right?'

Jasmine squinted. There was too much light in the room for her, too much noise and banging and talking.

'Babe? What the fuck?'

'What?'

'I ask you if everything's gonna be fine and you go all freeze-frame on me.'

Jasmine sat up. She felt like she was going to be sick. 'I just, I can't believe it'.

'Well' Sammy drew in her vapour cigarette again. 'Believe it. It's happening, and I need you to tell me everything's OK.'

She stared at her friend, who was looking at her expectantly. Sammy's red lipstick had rubbed off a little, leaving her with a pink flush on her lips. She looked so young.

'Course. Course you'll be fine.' Jasmine rubbed her forehead. 'Sorry, I guess I was just taken back.' She took Sammy's hand. The tears were coming now, thick and fast. *She thinks I'm crying for her,* Jasmine thought.

She wiped her face. 'Who's is it though, Sammy?'

'Fucked if I know.'

Her mouth creased into a smile, and the two women both started to laugh. The tears fell down Jasmine's face freely. Out of the corner of her eye, she saw the sweet couple on the barstools next to the pair edging further away. She envied them in that moment, and their sense of normality.

Jasmine grabbed her friend into a hug and regretted it instantly. It felt like there was something alien between them, a vacuum of air filled with a *thing* that wasn't right, wasn't fair. They pulled apart from each other almost as quickly as they had embraced.

'I'm having a fucking baby.' Sammy picked up the e-cigarette and started to puff again. 'A real-life ruining, body destroying baby.' Jasmine wanted to snap that e-cigarette in two. When she had been pregnant, she had taken the vitamins; she'd stopped drinking. She'd done everything *right*.

Sammy traced the grain in the table with her long, orange fingernail. 'I guess whoever the dad is, he wouldn't want anything to do with it anyway, or me.'

Jasmine didn't respond. She simply watched as her friend's face went from thoughtfulness to disgust.

Sammy rolled her eyes emphatically. 'Fucking hell, I swear this city is getting smaller.' Jasmine went to turn, following the gaze of her friend.

'Don't look. P the P is here.'

Paolo the prick? Jasmine's heart was in her throat. Paolo, *here*? This was her and Sammy's drinking spot. He knew that. She could feel the bile lifting through her oesophagus. This was all too much.

'For god's sake, don't turn around Jasmine. He's got a girl with him.'

Jasmine lifted her hands to her throat. She was going to be sick; she was sure of it.

'Oh, for fuck's sake.'

Sammy pretended to drink her cocktail, lips pursed around the straw, eyes on the bar, as Jasmine felt a hand, warm and strong, on her shoulder. Paolo tapped her once.

He smiled at her, half-cocked. He'd shaved off his beard, showing fresh olive skin, bright with only one mole in the centre of his cheek. She remembered kissing that mole only a few months ago.

'Oh, hey.' Jasmine tried to make her voice sound as casual as possible.

'Hey… err… I heard the full story about what happened the other day. Dad told me. Just thought I'd see how you were? And, figured I'd show you the result of your impressive punch the other day.'

Paolo pointed towards a faint green-purple bruise shadowing his left eye. It hadn't done anything to change the attractiveness of his face; in fact it made him that little edgier.

He leaned against the bar. He sounded so calm, as if he was talking to a stranger about the football, not to an ex-girlfriend; a woman he'd repeatedly told that he loved. It was true, wasn't it? Jasmine thought. He had kissed her after rugby practice and lifted her in the air, shouting to all the lads; 'This is my girl.' He'd bathed in her ability to be beautiful when she tried. He had run his hands through her curls and kissed her face. And now he was at the bar, another woman on a table around the corner, wearing a t-shirt he had bought while they were going out.

Jasmine swallowed the bile, still septic in her mouth and felt the flush of heat rising to her cheeks. All she wanted to do was grab his arms, firm and smooth, and shake him, shake him with all her might, until the raw emotions fizzled their way to the top like a bottle of Coke; until they burst through the lid.

'Yeah, it's all fine. I have a new job, a perfect one at that; we're celebrating.' Jasmine tried to brighten her voice, flicking her hair out of her eyes.

Paolo smiled back, thinly. 'Celebrating! Wow' His eyes widened, Jasmine thought she could see something in his eyes, surprise and something else - what was it - pity?

'Yeah, I mean...I can see it! Cocktails' His eyebrows lifted. 'What's that you're having? And, Sammy?'

His gaze lifted to Sammy, who ignored him, shrugging her arched shoulders and scrolling absentmindedly through her phone. He smiled coolly. 'Good to see you as always, Sam. Anyway, I have to go; someone's waiting for me. And I don't want to interrupt your evening.'

Jasmine's heartbeat faster. She hadn't been this close to him in ages and his smell, that soft musk mixed with washing powder, was intoxicating.

'Stay,' She said, far louder than she'd intended to. She faltered. 'I mean, do you want to have a drink? On me, of course. I guess I owe you, especially after that right-hander the other day. And we are celebrating after all.' She got up on her feet and waved at the barman.

'No, I best not.'

'I won't take no for an answer,' Jasmine responded. She formed a fist and lightly punched him, hitting his chest. She felt him flinch.

'Maybe no more punching, Jasmine?'

'Yeah, course, just miss you.' Her tongue felt dry. She felt like she had no control over what she was saying.

'Yeah, that's great and all, but I don't think that's a good idea.' He looked at her, taking his time to roll his eyes over her white shirt, greying from the day's use, her mud-flecked trousers, her limp curls.

'See you soon, though. Bye, Sammy.'

Sammy waved at him without moving her head to face him, arching her hand ever so slightly, so her middle finger stood prominent.

'Yes? You sure you want a drink this time?' The barman looked at Jasmine, a flicker of a sarcastic smile on his face.

'Make it a large Long Island.'

The bar was vibrating; Sammy was shaking next to her. Jasmine looked down and saw her in fits of laughter.

'Now babe, when I think about how crap my life is, I'll remember you talking to Paolo the Prick, begging him to stay, and I'll feel like it's not so bad after all.'

Jasmine didn't respond.

'*Oh, stay, sire.*' Sammy mocked. 'Leave your new girl around the corner and grace us with your company. I'll even buy you a drink for your troubles.'

'Fuck off, Sammy.'

Sammy whistled. 'Jesus, I was only joking. Bite my head off, much?'

Jasmine tipped her head back and poured Sammy's untouched cocktail down her throat.

*

In the dream Jasmine had that night, she called out for the boy. She made no petition for his name, just to see the hand she had been holding and longed to hold again. There were no scratches as she looked down through the clearing blur of stirring images and stretched out her small fingers. She saw her white knee socks against her brown skin and her red shoes tapping lightly on a pavement. They were light steps because she felt like she was supported as though she was holding someone's hand. In the dream, she daren't turn to see who it was, even though she suspected it would be her father's hand tightening around hers as they went along. She wasn't ready to see him; she wasn't prepared for the questions that would have poured out uncontrollably.

Then, her steps became heavy, and she was quickly moving towards a woman with hardly any features. The shape of the woman seemed to be engulfed in a wispy fog that swirled and kept her hidden, but Jasmine knew she was struggling, animated, her arms twitching high and low and round and round, desperately trying to control the small boy. Tears started forming in her eyes as she realised that all she had to do was to hold out her hand, and she could save the boy.

'Jasmine.'

Then, nothing.

Jasmine looked down and saw the small hand, small but the same size as hers, clutching hopefully around her fingers. She followed the arm as it disappeared under a green t-shirt. The fog was lifting to reveal a mop of black wavy hair, his head was low and his face unseen, fixed on the ground. Jasmine called out to him. The boy's head turned up in response to her call, and he looked into her face with brown eyes, flecked with gold.

Don't let her take me. Another rush to her ears.

As Jasmine struggled to separate the poor boy's face from the familiar dream that would inevitably be consumed by the screams of those left behind, she felt his nails digging into her hands. She hadn't noticed the featureless woman rise behind the boy and snatch him with both arms and hold him tightly as though she were holding a pillow to her breast. Jasmine's blood-striped hand was still extended, and her fingers stretched when the woman, still clutching the boy in the green t-shirt, took one step back and the fog folded around them.

Jasmine woke panting. She pulled her hand out from under the duvet and saw there were crescent moon shapes in her palm. She must have dug into her hand. The darkness was empty all around her. With some precision, she swung out of bed and walked silently to the bedroom door. She opened it, crossed the landing and pressed her ear to her mother's room. It's what she did; it was a habit. She listened for her mother's laboured breath, persistent and cruel. Her mother's breathing was heavy and regular. She was asleep.

She walked back towards her bedroom and clicked the door shut behind her, all the while trying to understand why her brain was showing her a little boy in a green top. She pulled her covers close to her neck. Her thoughts focused on one person: Sammy. Maybe Sammy was the woman in the fog, stealing away her child, stealing away her happiness. But when Jasmine had miscarried, she already knew the sex of the baby that Paolo didn't want. It was a girl.

CHAPTER 15

Now

Michael pressed the phone tightly to his ear to combat the rush of the biting wind and the intermittent traffic noise. With his free hand, he pushed the garden gate into the ground until it lent unnaturally. He eventually brought his leg up against it and used his whole body to create a big enough gap for him to pass through.

'No, he didn't bite,' he said into the phone, puffing with the effort of opening the gate, 'and he didn't react to Daniel Burton. So, he's either an outstanding actor, and he's keeping something from me, or he genuinely hasn't a clue as to Jasmine's whereabouts.'

He stopped at the front door with bubble glass panels and peered through into the distorted darkness. 'I'm inclined to believe it's the latter. I mean, he did give me her last known address.' Michael stepped back to check the upstairs windows. The curtains were drawn. 'Yes, Harriet, I'm at her house now, but he did say he thought it was abandoned. So, I guess I'll find out if that's true. I'll call you later.' Michael slipped his phone into his pocket and knocked on the door.

With cupped hands he peered once again through the long-panelled window. 'Hello,' he shouted. His fingers found the letterbox and pushed it open. 'Miss Wilson?'

There was no response.

He noticed the edge of the door was splintered with blonde coloured wood. He stretched to his full height and checked all around him; the street seemed to be empty. Unlike the garden gate, the front door swung open as Michael pressed a hand to it and light spilt into the hallway from the street.

Michael cast a shadow that stretched the full length of the hall as he stepped in. What little furniture had serviced this part of the house was now upended and cast about the floor. Sheets of wine-red wallpaper hung limply, and the smell of cat piss filled the hall. He stepped to the foot of the stairs and glanced up as far as the natural light would allow. Thankfully, the house was silent and settled except for his heavy footsteps on the lightly covered floors. The door opposite the stairs was ajar, and a red glow from the light pushing against the curtains filled the whole room.

Michael assumed this was the living room. The sofa had been gutted and partially skinned and spewed snowy white feathers that dressed every surface. The floor was littered with books from the shelves and splintered fragments of wood that may have been a coffee table at one time. He crouched amidst torn papers and a smashed television, turning over anything that might be useful to give a clue as to Jasmine's whereabouts, but all he found were sheets of fiction ripped from paperbacks and broken china.

Michael picked up a blue folder that was empty and, as he threw it down, something caught his eye. He noticed a slight discolouration on the walls, patterns and shapes. He stood up and went to the window and opened the cherry red curtains. Light flooded the room, and immediately he saw what those shapes were.

It didn't take him long to kick through the debris and find what he was looking for. Each picture frame he discovered was empty. The

The Room

pictures had been stripped out. Judging from the broken glass shards still wedged in the frames, the photos had been freed in a hurry.

You took the pictures, Jasmine. Was it you that wrecked the house? Thoughts raced through his mind.

The stairs groaned loudly with every step as Michael disappeared into the gloom of the windowless landing. He reached for the light switch; nothing happened. He pushed another door and stepped in. The windows were featured with light around thick dark curtains that hung heavy on brass rails. It was enough light to guide him through the room until he could fling apart the curtains and reveal the bedroom.

The upturned theme continued in this room. The mattress was stripped, and balanced half on-half off the bed frame. Clothes were torn and spread about the floor. Michael noticed a computer table on its side and a laptop that had been snapped from its screen. He righted the table and scooped up the two pieces of the computer, quickly discarding the screen with its spider web fracture across its face. Settling it on the desk, he noticed the picture of a woman staring up at him from the floor. Groaning, he bent to pick it up, turning it in his fingers and read the words beneath the picture of a woman, perhaps in her fifties, with milky brown eyes, light brown skin and glossy black hair that cradled her face. She was laughing and looking away from the camera.

In Loving Memory of

Myriam Wilson

Forever with Us

He placed the card on the desk and sank onto the edge of the bed frame. The sunlight streamed in; its rays burst with dust rising from the newfound warmth. Something up against the far skirting board caught the sun and sparkled for a moment with a bright flash, enough to catch his attention.

He moved across the littered room to the grey and silver lump on the floor. It looked like a handheld shaver. The shaft under the round head cradled the contours of his hand, his index finger naturally finding a trigger like button. It was plagued with clumps of dust and hair, and it wasn't until he wiped a thick grey paste from the rounded top that he realised it was a small video camera.

Michael turned the camera over and over in his hand, looking for any sign of life. He found the small rubber 'ON' button for the camera and pressed it. Nothing happened. Michael wasn't sure it was working at all or that it needed charging. Despite the condition of the laptop and the lack of any connecting leads, Michael vainly looked for the USB ports. It wouldn't have been any use. As he turned the laptop over, a rectangular chunk was missing from the back which Michael guessed was once the computer's hard drive.

He flipped the laptop over and ran a finger across the caved-in keyboard. A large centre portion of it had been mashed. *Someone was determined that the computer would never be used again,* Michael thought as he let the computer drop to the desk and picked up the camera. He tried holding it in both hands and found that it was comfortable in either. While his attention was around the room again his fingers found another button that clicked and split the handle. Carefully, he pulled a part of the handle that was secured by a hinge and twisted it until a small charcoal grey screen faced him. He instinctively tried the rubber

'ON' button again. It turned a brilliant blue under his thumb, vibrated and pinged.

'Yes!' he said aloud, imagining Harriet's face when he told her he could use technology, *thank you very much.*

Michael saw that the screen had hidden a series of buttons in the handle. They were set out like compass points with a round button in the middle. Scrolling through a series of menu options, he found one raw video file. He pressed the middle button.

The screen collapsed in on itself then expanded to reveal a woman sitting on an upright chair. She wore jeans and a green fitted t-shirt which had a faded image of three daisy heads all in a row. Her hair was black and hung with curls to her shoulders, and when she looked directly into the camera, Michael got goosebumps; it was as though the woman from the funeral card was staring back at him.

But it wasn't her. Michael knew it. The video woman's face was blistered with tears. Every breath was laboured in-between her sobs. It was like she was crying from somewhere else, somewhere deeper.

Hello Jasmine, Michael silently uttered, his hands tightened around the camera. He quickly checked the room once more and then waited for the lady in the chair to speak.

'I've seen her again today. It's getting that I can't go out of the house without seeing her. But I know it's not real.' Jasmine's hands pounded her thighs and then ran her fingers through her black curls. She leaned into the camera, clearing away fresh tears, shouting the words,

'It's not what you think it is, The Room! It's a big nasty lie. Stay away, or it will get inside you. It will mess with your head. They used to teach you that salvation comes from being at one with yourself, being present in the moment, going inside yourself and all that shit. But the thing is, we're all a bunch of greedy bastards. It's never enough; we always want more. There are dark places within us all, and The Room can find them and take you there, but it takes something from you and sends you back into the real world.'

Jasmine rocked back and forth, finding a creaking rhythm to the chair which distracted her for a few moments. Blood appeared from her nose. She caught it with her wrist and smeared it across her cheek.

'I saw her again today, and every time I do, I have to leave her again. She's smiling as she plays, laughing actually, just as she did when I first...' she tapered off.

'They know about it. They've got hold of The Room and, the fucked-up thing is, they're pulling strings. Oh god, they're creating monsters. No, that's not right. They're giving the monsters somewhere to hide.'

Jasmine was pulling on her shirt unnaturally, trying unsuccessfully to stretch it over her knees. She slowly looked about her, and it wasn't until then that Michael realised; she had filmed it in the very room he was sitting.

Her eyes rested on the camera. With soothing breaths rising and falling in her chest, she almost whispered, 'I saw her again today. There's only so many times a heart can break, isn't there?' For a few moments, Jasmine and Michael held each other in a silent, desperate stare. Maybe half a minute passed and then he watched as her face slowly transformed into a chilling wide-mouthed scream. She leapt forward from her chair and swiped at the camera. The screen careered in Michael's hands before returning to charcoal grey.

Michael sat on the edge of the broken bed for a long time after the camera gave up in his hands. The echoes of Jasmine's scream still lingered, as did the way she seemed to reach him through the camera.

CHAPTER 16

Jasmine stretched out her back while remaining seated in her desk chair. The Hub was unearthly silent, but to her, it sounded like heaven.

Mr Damson was in his first ten minutes of his Room use. She would be alone for a while. In quiet moments, sitting at her desk, she would often find herself consumed by the blank, clean space. It seemed so different, so far removed from the clutter, the mess and the noise of the Fly By Night Cafe. It was the only place where the cleanliness meant she didn't think about her nightmare, and the little boy in the green t-shirt. There was too much brightness, too much clarity for him to seep in.

The days had drifted into weeks and months in the Hub, where Jasmine shared short moments with The Room's clients as they travelled through from the waiting area to her charge. Often, when the clients had to wait for Will to open the changing room and administer the medication, Jasmine would find herself sitting opposite one. They'd be flushed and agitated in a soft, white robe. She had tried to find some comparison in the people who drifted through, but the only thing that was consistent about them was they were, for want of a better word, *happy*. They would often talk animatedly with Jasmine, bounding words falling out of their mouths like gumballs. She had seen seventy-year-old men squeal at the sight of a door opening; teenagers turn into children with broad, unstoppable smiles. It was mesmerising.

Jasmine had realised that, by being in The Room, she was surrounded by *happiness*. It had struck her a few weeks back that she'd never really seen this much contentment, this much overwhelming joy, and it was far superior to any drug or liquor that had passed her lips. She left every night, consistently at 5 p.m. sharp, with a balloon of pride in her chest. *She was making people's lives better*, she was getting paid obscenely well, and because of that she was better, too. She wondered whether this was what happiness was meant to feel like, because it was the closest she'd ever been.

She began typing notes on her afternoon client list; reminding herself to gather payment from Mr Derr, to change the robe size for Mr Sears. She cast her eyes down to her hands, her manicured fingertips, slick with shiny red gloss. She had tipped the manicurist £25. She smiled to herself and shook her head; £25! She'd done the same with the hairdresser who had tended to her curls, softening her starched black hair with auburn highlights. The hairdresser had kissed her on the cheek like they'd been best friends forever. She'd even given Jasmine her brother's number, telling her she must go out for coffee with him, if her busy schedule allowed, as she thought they'd be a *match made in heaven*. Jasmine found the man on Instagram later that day, his feed filled with stark black and white photos from a modelling portfolio. She'd laughed to the point where she had to stop for fear of being sick.

But occasionally, when she came in some mornings, she could smell the tinge of sweat, dank and overpowering, in the beautiful, white Hub. She'd pull on gloves, swallowing down spit that formed in her mouth, and spray the counters, the kidney-shaped sofa, the walls, until the smell was replaced with vapid freshness. Daniel had told her that every client should feel like the only one; there was to be no stray hairs on the floor, no bent and misshaped clothes hangers in the changing room. Each experience was unique, and therefore could not be contaminated by others. But whoever used The Room after dark left something that Jasmine could *feel*. And she had to clean it away.

It was in these moments, when the balloon of pride in her chest deflated just a little, that the questions would start forming on her lips. She had seen a file on the computer that was inaccessible to her; it was just named 'Private' and she hated herself for clicking on it, hoping it would open, most days when she was sat at her desk. It was curious to her that although she was employed there, and had been for nearly four months, she still had no clue as to what The Room could genuinely do. When she was as sure as she could be that she was alone, Jasmine would sometimes let her ear rest against the door marked The Room. But she heard nothing but the wood grain moving with her breath.

Every time her finger hovered over Daniel's confidential file, she cast uncomfortable thoughts back to her meeting with Mr Pevestone and Daniel's inept dealing with a man he clearly disliked. She thought it strange as to why Daniel, who by all accounts was so proud and protective of his precious Room, would go out of his way and offer his exclusive service to someone like that.

The Room was supposed to help people, *wasn't it?*

And it was true. The smiles, the excitement. Everyone who entered The Hub looked happier for being there, of course. She nodded to herself and wrote a further note on Mr.Derr's appointment.

She had barely seen Daniel and Will in those few months, apart from for the first few days; the pinging sound of doors would have her look up from her screens to see a blurring body whisk from one door to the next. She always caught a smile and maybe a 'Good Morning' from Will, but hardly anything from Daniel. But still, in the quietude of the Hub between visiting clients she thought about him leaning over her and the sweet lavender smell creeping up from behind his collar and the opening of his shirt.

Sammy had become distant, too. With the extra care for Jasmine's mother, paid for months in advance now, thanks to her new salary, Jasmine had imagined that they would spend more time together. But instead, without any warning, Sammy's texts tapered to almost nothing and replies were stunted with excuses of being too busy or "The Bump" was kicking the hell out of her. Jasmine had offered to help all she could with the baby, but she was met with the same answer every time. *This is all me, and I need to do it myself.*

Jasmine decided long ago that her confidence in public was due, in part, to Sammy and every time they ventured out, she silently sought her best friend's protection. Jasmine always was the quiet one; the one who held the drinks while Sammy shook her hair free and chatted to other bar-goers. She'd thought that she was content in that life, being the understudy for the main attraction. But now, Jasmine wondered boldly if Sammy was in fact - could she be - jealous? Was she jealous of her new job, her new spending habits, her new look? Sammy had been used to Jasmine's ability to be sub-par in every respect, and it was a change indeed to be better, to be *happy*. Jasmine smiled to herself; no one had ever been jealous of her before. She allowed herself to imagine Sammy's perfect face, distorted with crude sadness, a green tinge to her skin. *That must be it*, she thought.

A week ago, Sammy asked if Jasmine still had the spare key to her flat, because she needed it back. She hadn't responded to her other texts. So, she had started carrying the key around with her, feeling for it in her pocket, passing it through her fingers; all on the off chance of running into Sammy.

And that time had come that same morning. Jasmine was walking towards the high street, and she could see a figure, a proud 'b' shape forming on her belly. Jasmine's fingers automatically went to the silver key in her suit jacket pocket, and she played with it, tracing the raw edge down her thumb. But she never gave any thought to returning it. Instead, she watched her friend step onto a bus, one hand reaching for the rail and the other cradled delicately under the contour of her bump.

Jasmine's breath had caught in her chest. She touched her own belly, flat and tucked into her suit trousers. She didn't call out or to try and reach her friend. She just stood there, watching the bus as it indicated out into the traffic, orange lights glowing in the mist. She had felt like she was underwater, staring at the lights as they turned into a street off the High Street.

'Move it!' A woman walked past her, grazing her elbow by Jasmine's side. The noise of the city traffic popped through and burst into her eardrums, as if someone had turned up the volume. Jasmine had shaken her head and lifted her hand that had been rubbing the key out of her trouser pocket. Blood. She made a promise to herself that she would return the key at the end of the day.

At 5 p.m. sharp, as she always did, she left the Hub and Share Street behind and turned towards the city. As soon as she folded her fingers around Sammy's key, still warm in her pocket, she looked up and found she had landed outside Jester's Wine Bar. She teetered on the edge of the gloom cast by the overreaching doorway. The early evening light moved on, and the colours from inside Jester's were deep red formed by thick velvet curtains that hung from walls and framed sepia vineyards with blossoming mood lights. The noise from inside washed over her, a mess of chatter, clinks, shuffles.

The Room

The picture window dressed in plastic hanging vines under dark warm filtered lights framed Daniel Burton and William Cline perfectly. They were sat at a low table. Daniel perched himself on the edge of his chair to take up a glass containing blood-red wine. Will sat back, relaxed. Through dark fingers joined in a steeple to his lips, he was gently nodding his head in agreement to words only he could hear.

Jasmine was satisfied that neither of them had seen her and, taking two steady steps backwards, out of sight, she prepared to walk unseen past Jester's busy picture window and the two men.

More than one person faltered and stopped when Will rapped enthusiastically on the window. As Jasmine turned, her rehearsed smile melted seamlessly into a genuine expression of delight. His arms, long and wild, were signalling for Jasmine to come in. Behind Will on the other side of the glass, Jasmine noticed Daniel was shaking his head, a thin smile on his face.

'I can't believe you were just gonna walk on by and not say 'ello,' Will said, fighting for breath as he wrestled a third leather chair up to the table. Two dark bottles towered above two resting glasses.

'Jasmine,' Daniel said, pushing himself out of the overly soft chair, 'Please forgive Will's eagerness. He doesn't get much of an opportunity to interact with other humans, but when he does, it sometimes turns into a bit of a show.'

'You can piss off for a start,' Will said, turning to face the table and hiking his trousers to an acceptable height after he struggled with the Jester's furniture.

Daniel turned to Jasmine. 'How are you enjoying the show so far? I think he's doing well, don't you?'

Jasmine smiled. 'Excellent, very entertaining.'

'I'll get you a glass. You've got to try this red,' Will remarked.

Jasmine pushed forward in her seat. 'No, I really shouldn't.'

'Why? Got somewhere else to be?' Will replied. 'Somewhere more important than with me an' the international man of mystery over 'ere?'

Will hadn't waited for an answer, instead he launched his full, lank body up and directed it towards the bar.

Jasmine stared at the grain on the table as the silence between herself and Daniel in Will's absence, grew palpable. She looked up quickly to see that he was, in fact, looking at her, relaxed back in his seat again, his eyebrows knitted together in concentration.

Jasmine tucked her hair behind her ear, which felt hot to the touch.

'I used to come here all the time with...' she felt like she paused as the memory of seeing Sammy earlier that day came into her mind. She resisted moving to her pocket for the feel of Sammy's key and instead picked at a tiny sliver of wood on the table's edge,

'...a friend of mine. I've never been in this place without her.'

Daniel nodded slowly. 'Yes. Will and I often frequent this place. It's busy, loud and narcissistic, so there's the anonymity that-' he paused, 'is pertinent in our lives.'

Will reached over and placed the new wine glass in front of Jasmine before falling into his chair. 'You should have seen the look on the bar tender's face when I asked for another glass. Rude bastard; I was interrupting his chat-up lines.'

Jasmine smiled and turned to see that it was the same bartender who had glared at her when she had refused a shot of tequila with Sammy, before she embarrassingly begged Paolo to stay.

'Seriously,' Daniel said, directing his gaze to Jasmine, 'I cannot take him anywhere.'

Will tipped one of the bottles towards Jasmine's glass, crashing red liquid against its sides. She lifted the glass as though she were looking deep into it.

'A toast,' she announced.

'Very posh,' Will said, mimicking Daniel, who had already picked up his glass.

'What's the toast?' Daniel asked.

'To the barman,' she said, eyeing both, slowly turning her head from side to side, 'fuck him.'

Daniel and Will responded, 'fuck him.'

After the delicate sound of their clinking glasses had died and the first mouthful was swallowed in honour of the rude barman, the small group settled into a silence nestled awkwardly between the cacophony of bad days, inane gossip and spilt secrets that fluttered around the bar.

Jasmine took another sip on her glass and settled back cautiously into her chair.

'So, how come I don't see you guys much at work?'

Daniel placed his glass carefully on the table. 'Are there any problems, Jasmine?'

'No… no I don't mean that. It's just that for the last few weeks maybe, it's just been the clients and me in and out. Press my buttons, and the machine keeps rolling.' Jasmine felt the taste of the wine linger in her mouth. She swallowed hard and placed her glass on the table. 'It would be nice to talk to someone, you know, someone I'm allowed to talk to.'

Will was nodding his head. 'Well, I 'fink we can do something about that. Maybe the occasional high five between visitors. Somethin' like that?'

'Yeah, something like that,' Jasmine smiled.

Daniel had rescued his glass and took a heavy mouthful; his eyes fixed on the street outside. He replaced the glass on the table then became preoccupied with the straightening of his collar.

Jasmine noticed Daniel's sudden disconnect. 'Have I said something I shouldn't?'

'Daniel,' Will said, waiting for him to look up from his cuffs now. Daniel looked at Will, wide-eyed. 'Jasmine wants to know if she has said something wrong.'

'No, Jasmine, you haven't said anything you shouldn't. Forgive me; I'm a little distracted. A week in The Room takes its toll sometimes.'

'All the time,' Will replied. 'And it's not getting any better.'

'Not now, Will.'

'*Not now Will.* That's your answer for everything. You should really change it up a little.'

'Will, not now,' Daniel said. 'How's that for mixing it up?'

'Aces.' Will replied, presenting his middle finger.

'Okay,' Jasmine said, reaching for the nearest bottle and pouring the red into her glass. She noticed Will and Daniel watching her. 'Sounds like a can of worms right there. Doesn't bode well for my next question.'

'Okay, Jasmine. I'm game,' Daniel replied.

'What's it like in The Room? I know what it says in e-brochure - and I know what you're selling - but what is it really like?' She looked from one to the other.

Will stretched to an impressive height, even in his seat and beamed across at Daniel before turning to Jasmine.

'Well, don't look at me. I've never been in The Room,' he said.

Jasmine frowned, 'But-'

Will reached to replenish his glass, perching himself on the edge of the chair. 'The room in Share Street and The Room are two very different things, Jasmine.'

'Will,' Daniel interrupted. 'Need to know-'

'Oh, Dan aren't ya jus' a little fed up with this pretend spy shit?' Will took a deep breath and turned back to Jasmine. 'Listen. It's no secret tha' I'm not a big fan of The Room experience. Personally, the life out 'ere is the one worth livin'.' He gestured with a quarter full glass and splashed the window with wine.

'Hey!' The barman shouted across the noisy bar.

Will flipped round in his seat and raised a now empty glass towards the barman. 'Sorry,' he shouted. 'A toast to you, sir.' He grinned, showing his sharp teeth again, then carefully returned his glass to the table. He lowered his voice and leaned in so she could hear.

'Truth is, I don't need the kind of distractions we're offerin'.'

Daniel rubbed the arch of his nose. 'We're merely providing the means to realise the distractions that you alone create.'

'So, depending on the person, then an experience can be a bad one?' she asked.

'Every dream left behind is a bad experience,' Will said with a loud snort.

'So, why are you a part of this?' Jasmine looked at Will.

'Someone has to look after them while they're in there.'

'Let's talk about something else,' Daniel said abruptly.

'Have you ever used it, Daniel?' Jasmine asked.

Daniel clenched his jaw, and she could see the muscles contracting in his cheeks. He looked at Jasmine with heavy eyelids. Will was silent.

'Yes, of course. The Room is my creation. It helped me, and I wanted to develop it so others would benefit.'

'Why did you go in?' Jasmine asked. The wine, and Daniel's short, but precise answers to her questions had made her far more confident than her reality. Her stomach contracted as she saw Daniel's face close, the warmth that had been massaged out of it through wine and small talk gone.

Will upended the nearest bottle of wine. 'Chasing ghosts.'

'That's enough,' Daniel snapped. 'Thank you both for your time, I must leave.'

'Mate, I didn't mean it.'

Daniel waved a hand in Will's direction, nodded to Jasmine and then left the bar.

'Sheeeesh. Someone's in a bad mood.' Will looked at Jasmine. 'Sorry you had to see that.'

'It was my fault. I asked too many questions.' Jasmine could feel the bubble bursting in her chest. She wanted to push out of the confines of the ridiculous, large chair and run after Daniel.

'So, what about you, Jasmine,' Will said as he slowly peeled his gaze from the door. 'What's ya story?'

'Story? I have no story,' Jasmine replied with a small shrug. She wanted Will to stop talking so she could excuse herself and go after Daniel. She needed this job; she needed that feeling of *happiness*. But, most importantly, she also hated the idea that she had upset the man who smelled like lavender.

'Oh, I dunno if I believe that. Everyone's gotta story.'

'Story,' she repeated, trying to re-focus on the conversation. 'You're right, I guess, Will. Everyone does have a story. But, mine is so complicated I wouldn't know where to start, and it certainly would bring the evening crashing down - even more so.'

'Oh no, we wouldn't want that,' Will said, a big smile spreading across his face. He drank deep and heavy, emptying another glass. 'But there must be somethin' interesting about ya for our Daniel to hunt you down in the park like 'e did.'

'He told you he 'hunted me down'?'

'A matta' of speaking only. He said he saw something in you that day.' Will slapped his hands on his legs and bounced in the chair, like a petulant child. 'You know what, when Mardy-arse 'as got his gear together, you 'ave to come to his promotional night.'

'Sounds thrilling,' Jasmine said. 'I'm not much of *promotional night* girl though. Besides, if I haven't been invited by Daniel it's probably a sign-.'

'It's a party, Jas,' Will interrupted. 'There's free alcohol an' you get to dress up. It's tomorrow.' He waved off her excuses as she started to protest. 'It's somethin' that happens every two years an' it's a right laugh. Plus, I could do with a mate there. What d'ya say?'

Jasmine's hand sank to her side, and she felt for the key in her pocket. She'd already made her mind up to go to Sammy's under the pretence of returning her key and figured the wine she'd drunk would give her the courage she needed to ask some difficult questions about why she's been avoiding her.

She had to leave.

'If Daniel wants me there, I guess I can come.'

Later that evening, she pressed her head against the cold bus window, hypnotised by the lights of the wakening city outside. At the same time, she felt her phone vibrate. She lifted it into the pale light of the bus. It was a text message from Daniel.

Will is right. But don't tell him that. You will be needed at the party. Black tie. I'll text you the rest.

Jasmine didn't reply. She replaced her phone in her pocket and returned her head to the window. A wide smile stretched across her face as she wondered if she had anything suitable in her wardrobe. Probably not. But that wouldn't be a problem.

CHAPTER 17

The softness of Jasmine's brown eyes lay heavy with the wine. They glistened with the night and the delicately subdued light of the leafy suburban street. As she sat on the wall outside Sammy's apartment block, she cupped her phone in her hand and swiped across with her thumb. Daniel's text message was still there, and she had read it correctly. It *was* real.

She swapped the phone for Sammy's key and for the hundredth time that day she played with it through her fingers, thinking back to when she saw her earlier. *Was it just today?* She thought. It seemed like weeks. She couldn't remember when she'd made the decision to visit her friend, but she knew it was the wine that had sealed the deal and given her the courage to make it as far as number 34 Clement Avenue.

And even then, she'd only made it as far as the wall. As she sat there, kicking her heels against the crumbling brick that had survived world wars and teenagers alike, including her and Sammy, she had no idea what she was going to say to her, if anything at all. At that moment Jasmine wished for a cigarette, and she knew that if Sammy were there, kicking her feet next to her, then she'd be rolling her one from a tin she'd always kept in a pocket.

It was supposed to be a happy memory, but it turned grey and weighted in her stomach. She realised how little she knew her friend now; the newly formed mother-to-be. In those last few months, her life had turned a corner and, when she tried to look back over her shoulder, she had found that the people who were supposed to be there, weren't.

She shook the dark thoughts free and used her arms to push herself off the wall. She turned and looked up at the townhouse in front of her. Lights flickered red against the curtains of the uppermost window. Sammy had taken the first floor flat and a shadow moved across the glow. Jasmine's attention was caught by Mrs Harley blundering out of the lobby door with two tightly wound Labradors. She looked straight at Jasmine as she held the door and the two spirited beasts.

'You coming in, Jas?' Mrs Harley asked. Her tone was thin and tired. 'You might guess from the racket that she's in.'

'Yes, Mrs. Harley. Sorry, miles away.'

'You alright there, Jas? You look a bit tired; you do.' Her thick Birmingham accent lifted with concern. Jasmine had always liked Mrs Harley despite Sammy's reports of the "nosey old cow downstairs".

As Jasmine stepped in, the music drifting from upstairs became like a heartbeat in her ears. She glanced up the stairwell as if to see it in physical form. Turning back to see Mrs Harley and her desperate dogs pulling her back towards the street she said,

'Yes, I'm fine. Just a little early evening drink with some friends, that's all.'

Friends. She'd used the word, and it seemed alien to her. She'd awarded Will and Daniel the title of *friends* and enjoyed how it felt. It may have been the last remnants of the wine chased by the bus ride over to Sammy's and the night breeze that she clung to, but she hoped it would last.

The music reached a terrible crescendo that landed between them both. Briefly, Jasmine looked back into the house and then back at Mrs Harley. 'I'll have a word about that.'

'Yep, see what you can do. Can't be good for that child she's carrying.'

As the sprung door clunked heavily behind her, Jasmine realised that she hadn't buzzed up to Sammy's flat. The strain of the old stairs creaked loudly with every one of her steps but was lost to anyone else in the house, swallowed up in the dulled, intrusive beat. A faint strip of pink jittered at Jasmine's feet from under the door as she raised a hand to knock. She curled her fingers realising immediately that a conventional knock on the door wouldn't rise above the music. She pulled out her phone and clicked to dial Sammy's number. The rings continued until her voice filled Jasmine's ear.

'Hey gorgeous people. Drop me a Whatsapp, don't you dare leave a message, I ain't gonna listen.'

The key slid effortlessly into the lock and turned. The door, as though it were leaning, jumped from its latch a few centimetres into the flat.

'Sammy!' she shouted down the long hall, waiting for one of the doors to open and for her friend to appear. The same shadows she had seen in Sammy's bedroom window were now dancing under the door at the far end of the hall. Jasmine moved along and dropped the key into an unused ashtray, perched on a table and under the "Last Chance Mirror" as Sammy and Jasmine had dubbed it.

She only managed a few steps before she stopped dead. She walked back to the table and stirred the keys in the ashtray with her outstretched finger. Other than the single key she had returned, there were two more sets. She recognised both sets of keys from the key rings attached. Sammy's was a glittering Prosecco bottle with the insignia "Prosecco. How Classy People Get Shitfaced," and the other? She knew the other key ring because she had bought it for him two years previously when he found out he'd got a place at University. She wanted to give it to him to show she was okay with him going away, but they both knew she wasn't.

A cold wind arrested Jasmine's body and rose through her legs to the pit of her tensed stomach. She held her breath as the feeling continued up her arms and rose to her neck. As she finally let out a breath, her temples were being stabbed like pincushions. It was easier if she didn't move - but she couldn't stop, she moved anyway, closer to the door at the far end of the hall.

But she hated him? She called him Paolo the Prick.

Jasmine's hand trembled as her fingers glanced at the doorknob and then pressed in and turned. The door opened without any further help from Jasmine and the pinkish hue darted with oranges and reds, and the music filled her ears.

The shadows on the walls played their part, smooth and reaching across every corner of the room, casting familiar shapes of two bodies. Jasmine stood in the doorway frozen but indifferent to the joke she was the last to get. Sammy straddled Paolo; her long blonde hair dressed her naked shoulders and swayed with the motion of her body. Entirely naked, Sammy cradled the child inside her. There was something primordial and devastatingly beautiful about the way she offered herself to Paolo. Jasmine watched in her own silence as Sammy reached for Paolo's hand and with them still together, fingers entwined they both traced the arc of her swollen belly.

Jasmine took a half step out of the room, but her back came to rest against the door jamb. Slowly, her legs folded beneath her.

Sammy screamed and sat up, clawing for the sheets to cover her breasts. Paolo had to follow her gaze to see Jasmine crouched in the doorway, staring across at them. He mouthed something under the noise and struggled with the sheets to get out of bed. Sammy laid a hand on his chest for him to stay. He looked like someone helpless, caught in the middle of something so inconceivably bigger than himself. In the silence that they shared, they looked from one to the other.

Sammy had been caught in a lie of sorts and lacked the empathy to react accordingly. She drew her lips tight, raised her eyebrows and shrugged her shoulders.

It was enough for Jasmine. As she left the house and stepped out onto Clement Avenue, the phone in her pocket buzzed, and for a moment she thought it would be a follow-up text from Daniel. She pulled out the phone and held it, disappointed. She brushed her finger across Sammy's name to bring up her message.

Yes, it's his.

Jasmine looked at the screen for a few seconds, trying to process what she was reading. She was aware she had dropped her phone, but she didn't try to rescue it straight away.

Jasmine screamed.

Her phone came into focus at her feet, and she bent down to pick it up, pressing it into her pocket and then started walking towards the bus stop. In her mind, all she could see was Sammy, looking like a perfect woman, her full belly rounded and soft, and Paolo, his eyes fixed on her.

She tried to think of anything, everything to remove the permeating image of her best friend and her ex-boyfriend. Right then, she would have given anything to drill that out of her brain. She wished she would have stayed with Will drinking instead of going to see Sammy. She wished she hadn't become friends with Sammy all those years ago. She was desperate for another reality, one where that little girl walked straight past her and didn't play with her in the cul-de-sac; one where she was free from the woman who would go on to steal her future.

The Room must be like that, she thought as she walked toward the bus shelter. As the bus rounded the corner and headed towards her, she remembered something Daniel had said to her.

"If you could create anything, then what would it be?"

For the first time, Jasmine set her mind seriously to that question.

CHAPTER 18

The crisscrosses of metal that formed the only doors on both sides of the freight elevator was easier to close than Jasmine first thought. She'd girded herself against the eight-foot structure and pulled hard. The door gave a prehistoric yawn as it glided shut, making the last meter unaided. It caused Jasmine to lose her footing and almost hit into the wall. It wasn't a good look in her swaying black dress and heels, so she was relieved she was alone still. She stood in the middle of the crate, gathering her dress from the wood and brick around her and tried to compose herself.

Daniel had given her specific instructions on how to get to his apartment, and how to work the freight elevator. She found the wheel with its crank handle to her right and leaned across, not wanting to move from the spot in case her heels got caught in the worn panelled floor. She pushed the crank a quarter turn forwards towards a small metal plate that simply said "Up".

Under a single bulb, surrounded by its own cage, Jasmine gently swayed with the ragged movement of the elevator. She straightened out her dress, enjoying the cool smoothness of the lace across her palms. She felt…well, there was no other word for it than *beautiful*. The dress was from one of the designer boutiques in town, and once she had composed herself from the view at Sammy's apartment, she'd decided to spend some of her hard-earned Room money. The black dress pulled in tight to her slender waist and flowed outwards to the floor. She slid her hands across the 'v' cut over her chest and tugged at her necklace, another new edition to her wardrobe she'd dared to buy herself.

She opened her new clutch and pulled out a pocket mirror, realising for the first time in a long time that she was not upset with what was looking back at her. Her hair fell wildly over her bare shoulders, set in loose curls by the vivacious hairdresser earlier that day. Her skin looked golden brown, not ashy like usual and the makeup artist had highlighted her cheekbones and smoked her eyes to the point where she wasn't sure her mother would recognise her now. Jasmine breathed in. *Time for change*, she murmured under her breath. *I bloody deserve this.*

Voices which seemed distant drew closer and filled the empty spaces between creaks and groans of the lift around her.

The stopping of the elevator was more graceful, feeling it only rise briefly in her stomach. She stopped next to a brick wall and put her hand out. She stroked the bricks, wondering what she was meant to do now. She frowned. Were the voices behind the wall? She knew Daniel was smart, but she hadn't expected a secret entrance to his own house. Was this another Hub in the middle of Birmingham?

She heard a cough behind her, and her stomach clenched.

'Madam, the lift opening is this way.'

Jasmine turned, her dress catching in her heels. She stumbled and caught the open arm of the man in a waistcoat that had slid the lift door open, packing it neatly to one side.

'Are you OK, madam?' The man arched his eyebrow, looking at Jasmine's fingers, gripping his white shirt for balance.

The crimson on Jasmine's face was radiating as she flushed with heat. 'Yes, just err, just admiring the brickwork. Exposed brick is my thing – I'm thinking of having my place done just like that.'

Jasmine could see the man stifling a smile. 'Quite. Mr Burton is happy you are attending his soiree. Let me take your coat, and my colleague will offer you a welcome drink.'

Good start Jasmine

The same man who had opened the elevator door wore a sparkling fifty pound an hour smile. Jasmine stepped into the room, and he presented her with a silver tray filled with slender flutes, each one a pale yellow with sliver flecks racing to the top.

'Prosecco, Madame?' Waistcoat man offered.

How classy people get shitfaced, Jasmine thought, trying not to laugh as she thought about Sammy's keyring. *Oh my. I have come a long way.* She smiled and took the glass, then looked across the room.

It was a vast space. Pockets of light from lamps spilt pools all over the oaken floor and in them gathered clutches of dark suits clinging to glasses and bottles and hugging plates half full of overly minuscule, pretentious foods. Jasmine imagined that in the daylight hours, the six picture windows that lined the loft apartment would submerge it with refreshing light and, she was sure from the glittering street lights outside, breathtaking views of the city and the canals threading their way to the centre.

Everywhere Jasmine looked there were faces gathered together, only some she recognised from her work. Three couches full of faces she didn't know surrounded a coffee table that rested on the only carpet she could see on the wooden floor. An animated discussion at the far end of the room centred around a dining table and occasionally rose above piano sounds.

'If you like, Madame,' a voice whispered from just over her shoulder, 'Mr Burton has provided a bar offering a large selection of cocktails.'

Just as Jasmine turned, she saw the waistcoat man lean back into his station. He pointed to an unseen part of the room.

'You think I need them?' she said, offering a smile.

'Err…no Madame…I just-'

Jasmine heard the unease in his stunted words. 'Because I do.' She smiled sweetly at him then emptied her glass in one go. She handed the glass to waistcoat man, saying, 'I feel a little out of place here. I don't feel like I'm doing too well so far. Any tips?'

He relaxed and returned the smile. 'I think you are doing fine, madam. I would advise against stroking the walls, however.'

Jasmine smiled. 'Too much?'

He nodded coyly. 'It's still early, and …well, I've seen worse.' He paused to quickly scan the room then leaned closer and said, 'Oh yes. Don't eat the prawn cocktails. Our seafood prep man is going through a nasty divorce.'

Jasmine laughed out loud, turning a few heads as she started to walk into the apartment. Her dress swayed and lashed at legs that got too close. She turned back to waistcoat man and mouthed 'Bar?' and pointed to somewhere in the space. He returned the gesture and nodded. Just then, a familiar voice cut through the noise.

'Well, I've just won a bet,' Will beamed as he reached for Jasmine.

Jasmine wasn't quite ready for his embrace. She was glad when he pulled away; he was so much taller than her that she'd found herself clutched to the bottom of his ribcage. She wondered if the picture of the two of them looked as awkward as it felt.

'Good odds I hope,' she said, straightening out her dress for the second time that night.

Will was dressed in a fitted tuxedo. He looked good. Careful lines drew the eyes down, complimenting his slender, tall shape.

'They were fa' me,' he said in answer to her question.

Will reached behind her and grabbed two flutes off the tray. He thrust one towards Jasmine who, caught off guard, flung her hands up to her face in a half-hearted attempt at defending herself, taking the glass as a passing courtesy.

'Daniel, you remember Dan, yeah? He's tha' moody one out of the double act,' Will didn't have to wait for Jasmine's smile. He returned it proudly, 'he bet ya wouldn't turn up an' I said you wouldn't turn down a free drink and 'ere you are.'

'Here I am' she said, raising her glass, the confidence from her reflection in the lift slowly fading. She swallowed another mouthful, feeling the vinegary bite of the liquid on her tongue.

The Room

'So, what have we got here, Will? Are all these Roomers?' she asked.

'Roomers?' he laughed. 'Did ya just come up wi' that?'

'I'm working on some way to make sense of all this, so I just decided to call them all Roomers.'

'Well, it's a good word. It's about right. Just don't let Daniel 'ear you call 'em that. As you know, he's a bit sensitive, about loads of things.' He waved his half-empty glass at the scattered bodies in clumps around the loft space. 'Those that you will recognise are ones that are still in the programme. All the others are past users of The Room an' this is our chance to see if we can get them to sign up for some more sessions. It's bloody easy in my mind as we don't have to earn their trust. They've been 'down the rabbit hole' an' know what The Room is about, an' what it's done for them.'

'Down the rabbit hole? You make it sound sinister like a conspiracy.' She said that last word slowly, careful not to trip over the ill-placed syllables with the warmth of the alcohol in her chest.

'Well I'm try'na keep it street. You know for the kids, mate. But, truth be told ya must see how happy everyone, thanks to The Room.'

Jasmine felt the warmth rise inside her. Yes, she'd noticed. The place that had brought her so much seemed to also bring so much to its customers. She was standing in a room full of perfectly happy, perfectly dressed people, in a dress that she wouldn't have afforded, or even looked at, a few months ago. She had decided to waiver the bus for tonight, brushing off the icy roads and January weather in her slender heels, for a taxi. This was something she hadn't done in… well, she couldn't remember when she'd last splurged and held her chip out for a taxi driver to scan. She was, by all accounts, better for The Room, and it seemed like everyone else was too.

'See that guy 'ere?' Will pointed at a man in his late thirties, kissing the cheek of a very handsome man, with a smattering of silver stubble. 'Yeah, he hadn't been with a bloke until The Room. Catholic family. He was on the verge of...let's just say things weren't lookin' good for him. Now, he and his husband have been together for three years. They're adopting a baby girl. But for Christ sake Jas-'

'Don't tell Daniel,' Jasmine finished. They both laughed like two kids at the back of a Sex Education class. 'Where is the moody one by the way? And, has he got a better tux than you?'

'He wishes.'

Jasmine threaded her gaze through the crowd. She amused herself with thoughts of a cinematic drawing away of the people, like the pulling back of large velvet curtains to reveal the star of the show. But this wasn't Hollywood. This was a penthouse loft space skewered in the heart of Birmingham city. Moments of busy blurred bodies flickered in front of a scene of two elegantly dressed people; a man and a woman so close they could have been in a Jack Vettriano painting, as though they were the only two in the room.

The woman clung to the man with almost every contour of her body and swayed to a mixture of piano and chatter, both too loud and uncomplimentary. Her dress tugged seductively at her figure every time she moved, pressed and hung from milky shoulders below a thick rope of diamonds. Jasmine was too far away, and the angle was too awkward to see, but she had already decided that the woman's featureless face was beautiful and striking.

The man, she did know. It was Daniel. He *had* got a better tux than Will, but she would never tell. He stood faithfully pressed against the woman, moved slightly by the music, but defined by classic lines from the slicked-back hair to the tips of his black leather shoes. The dance they did together was one that Jasmine thought looked just like one of lovers; a dance established in social gatherings that protected each other from outsiders. She imagined her whispering in his ear, 'Don't leave me alone here, darling'. And it made her stomach lurch.

The elegant lady who was pressed so tightly against Daniel threw her head back at something he had said, and draped a slender arm across his chest, her fingers resting on his shoulder. She leaned in and kissed him on the cheek allowing her foot to flick back.

Who does that? Jasmine thought, nearly out loud, but managed to clamp down on her lip. She wondered if the smell of Daniel was on her, the lavender and musk entwined on that soft, white as powder skin. Jasmine watched as the lady from the painting turned her gaze from him to scan the party. Yes, she could see now, her face, from the sharply pointed nose to the high cheekbones, was utterly perfect.

'That's Emma by the way.'

Jasmine heard the voice over her shoulder. She'd forgotten Will had been standing with her. 'Emma?' She had been distracted as Daniel had caught her eye from across the room. He smiled at her, thin and encouraging, and it held her for a few moments. Daniel motioned with both glasses, now his hands were free from Emma, who was chattering to a couple next to them, and made circles with both.

Jasmine raised her glass in response then, realising it was empty, she shrugged her shoulders and smiled back.

'I think he wants you to mingle.' Will said.

'Mingle? Of course, what else is there to do at a party?' Jasmine found a little table for her glass and set it down. 'I think I need a better drink than this, though. I hear there's a bar?'

'Yeah, just around the corner.'

'You coming? Maybe you can tell me all about the clingy Emma.' She felt the bite in her word and winced at how harsh they sounded out loud. She hooked Will's outstretched arm and pulled him deep into the party.

Just then, someone cried out Will's name. Out from a tangle of arms and torsos, a short, balding man tugged at him.

'Will, you're up. You've got to knock Simon of his perch he's becoming insufferable,' the man said.

Will wrestled his arm free. He laughed and brought the man in close. 'Ken, this little stunner 'ere is Jasmine. Jasmine works the Hub for us now. Jasmine, this is Ken; he's one of our old-timers.'

'I hate it when you put it like that,' Ken said, 'it makes me sound so old.'

'But you…' Will felt a pinch on the arm that Jasmine still held.

'Nice to meet you, Ken. Do you want to take Will away from me?' she asked, a smile spreading across her face.

Ken started to redden in his face as he fumbled for his next words, falling upon them as though he'd been struck with an idea. 'You can come, too. Will's going to need a little support if he's to break any ground with Simon.'

Jasmine looked over and saw the black and white squares spread across the coffee table and the chess pieces waiting on opposite edges.

'Chess?' She looked up at Will; a comical eyebrow stretched as high as it would go.

Will shrugged his massive shoulders and smiled. 'Some people 'ave drugs, Jasmine, I 'ave chess. But you should come and see. It might be good for my image to have a lovely lady on my arm.'

'Charming you are, and a little sexist.'

'Sorry, it's the smell of chess in the air. It's got me all giddy.'

Jasmine released his arm. 'I do appreciate the offer, but I think I'll pass. A black-tie event, a mythical bar and a chess tournament? That's a little too much action for me.'

Will had to bend some to plant a kiss on her cheek. 'You're a doll,' he said, pulling away from her and folding himself neatly into the gathering crowd.

Jasmine watched him disappear into a blanket of black and white and then realised she was alone again in the busiest room in the city. Daniel was gone too; blended into the living space that had been stripped of charm by the well-meaning party goers.

Five minutes later, another man wearing a waistcoat slid a gin and tonic across the counter towards her. She cupped the large round glass in her palm and for a moment enjoyed the prickly feel of the cold and the swirling of ice and cucumber racing around as she gently moved her hand in small circles.

She savoured the cool numbing on her lips and swallowed a mouthful of her drink. It caught her off guard, snapping at the back of her throat, bringing on a coughing fit. Her chest expanded in the too-tight dress as the gin clung to her oesophagus, spluttering out awkward coughs.

'Here, darling, have my water.'

Emma's wide eyes were bright steel, an icy blue that cut through anything they settled on. But Jasmine noticed how the rest of her features, her slight nose almost lost in pure snowy skin and dominating smile flanked by a subtly toned pout, made you forget the harshness of those eyes and even gave them an intoxicating softness. Jasmine, still embarrassed by her unexpected coughing fit, returned Emma's smile and found she couldn't find any words. She quickly scanned over Emma's shoulder for Daniel, but he had not reappeared.

'Joules, you know how to give good measures!' The barman smiled at Emma and bowed his head. She turned her whole body, facing Jasmine with crossed legs.

'Are you okay?' Emma lightly touched Jasmine's arm as she asked. Unlike Jasmine's fingers, cold and clammy from her mothering her glass, Emma's fingers were warm and soothing.

Jasmine looked from the long slender fingers, tipped with jewels on a bright varnished bed to those crystal blue eyes, now turned with concern. She was beautiful. Why wouldn't Daniel be with her? Jasmine felt a tingle in her arm that lasted a few moments after Emma pulled her fingers away and brushed a yellow strand of hair back behind her ear.

Eventually, Jasmine's words came. 'Yes, I'm fine. I've had worse coughing fits. There are probably worse ways to induce a coughing fit than a heavy-handed barman.'

'I like the sound of that, "A heavy-handed barman".'

Jasmine looked at her sideways, light laughter building between them.

'Wait. You're Jasmine, aren't you?' Emma asked. 'Oh my God, you are, aren't you?'

Jasmine was taken aback by Emma's sudden fandom. More so since she'd never considered herself to be the subject of something or worthy of such attention. She had no time to respond before Emma spoke again.

'Daniel's told me so much about you. He said you are so good for The Room and all of us here.' Emma swung her glass round to motion for the whole room, spilling some of her drink. 'We saw you from over there, and I begged him for me to meet you.'

Jasmine noticed her soft voice was as soothing as her eyes. 'Beg? I'm sure you didn't have to beg.'

Emma laughed again. 'He wasn't too interested in us meeting straight away.'

Jasmine took another drink, pointing to Emma's empty glass and said, 'Talking of things a bit strong, you're out of liquor.'

'You're right,' Emma responded, sliding her glass dangerously close to the far edge of the bar. 'I'm Emma, by the way. Didn't I say that straight off? Rude of me if not.'

'I know. Will pointed you out.' Jasmine thought she'd said too much. 'He didn't tell me about you, just your name. He got side-tracked by the chess club or something.'

'Sounds like Will. He's adorable, don't you think? Very handsome. Gay, of course. Just my luck.'

Jasmine nodded as though she knew Will's sexual preference, but it was news to her. Uncomfortable with the moments of silence that rose between them, she feigned looking for Daniel.

'Has he slipped away?'

Emma turned to follow Jasmine's gaze; her slender neck flexed with even the smallest shift of her head. 'Slipped away? Who?'

'Daniel,' Jasmine answered, taking note of the smoothness of Emma's skin as she returned to her glass, 'I saw you both together earlier. You look well suited.'

'Jasmine, you think Daniel and me are a couple?' She threw back a porcelain neck and laughed. A few moments passed then she stopped abruptly. 'Of course you do,' she said as she spun awkwardly on her stool to face Jasmine.

'It's my fault, really. Let me tell you something you already know about Daniel Burton. That guy is an uptight, everything in its place, *right angle, wrong angle* kind of guy- especially when it comes to his precious Room. So, it was my way of trying to loosen him up a bit, having a dance. Plus, if you'll allow me, he is a bit of a looker too.'

Jasmine settled heavily on the bar. She smiled, silently agreeing with her. *He is a looker,* she thought. She could feel her heart racing as she sat, taking in what Emma had said. *They weren't a couple.* That meant Emma must be a client. The thought took Jasmine by surprise, and she wondered why it hadn't crossed her mind once since seeing her and Daniel together.

'He has done so much good for me,' Emma continued, 'that sometimes I wonder if he knows just how much. If he's done that much for me, he must have impacted everyone here in much the same way. And not just here. Daniel tells me that these are just a selection of handpicked clients, so there are countless more, don't you think? I mean, you must have seen it. All those people coming through the Hub.'

Jasmine sat quietly, taking it all in. She was attempting to finish a thought she'd had earlier. Emma had confirmed to Jasmine she was a client, but it left a gaping question in her mind.

'Yes, I have seen it. It's a very positive experience,' Jasmine answered. 'You must be excited to return to The Room then Emma if you are considering it.'

'Listen to you, Jasmine. You sound like Will and Daniel on a sales trip.' Emma held up her hand and smiled, 'I'm just kidding. Of course, I'm coming back; I'm still in my contract for ten sessions. I've completed four so far.' She lifted her head, extending her neck to pull the answer from the ether.

'Still in?' Jasmine asked. 'How come I haven't seen you?'

'Believe me, Jasmine, when I found out about you working there, I asked a similar question of Daniel, why hadn't I seen you? It would have been nice to see another woman about the place. But it seems I'm not on the books.'

Jasmine looked at the woman in front of her. Her perfect face, her relaxed charisma. Why would she be a secret?

'Private file?'

'Private file?' Emma asked in response.

'I'm sorry. You're just so…' She paused, flushing. 'You're just so pretty. I'm surprised you would want to use The Room. Your reality must be pretty good, anyway.'

'Darling, I don't think I have to tell you that appearances can be deceiving, especially when it comes to The Room.'

Jasmine smoothed down her expensive dress and nodded. 'Perhaps we shouldn't be talking about this, if you're meant to be a secret from me. You know, Daniel being Daniel.'

'Sod, the gorgeous dictator. It's a punishable crime to keep us apart this whole time. We'll have to think of a suitable way to punish him. But in the meantime, you've sparked my interest. What's the Private File?'

'Daniel has a private folder on the system that I can't access, well, because it's private.'

Emma had taken to chasing the lime around her gin with a straw. She smiled inwardly.

'That's probably where I live. I'm what you might call *government-funded*.' Emma saw the confusion light in Jasmine's face. 'Rehabilitation.'

'Daniel said that some use The Room as a therapy tool.'

'Yes, I guess they do. Mine's a little 'next level'' Emma broke the silence after a few moments. 'I'm not in that place anymore where I can dive into the details. Daniel's helping me to use The Room to *deconstruct the demons*.' Emma gave up on the lime and tossed back what was left in the glass. 'Goodness, darling, this conversation has taken a turn, has it not?'

'Emma, are there others in the private folder that you know of?' She coughed. 'I mean, are there more who are *government-funded*?'

Emma lifted her eyes up, as if reaching for a memory but came back with nothing. 'Look, darling, it's like Daniel is suggesting, it's best we don't know, or words to that effect, a little less dramatic perhaps.'

They fell into a comfortable silence. The music changed from piano tunes to some old-time Motown that even Jasmine recognised. Stevie Wonder's crashing harmonica and wailing soul cut right through the party and a natural dance floor rose up out of scattered bodies in the middle of the apartment.

Emma carefully and deliberately planted her glass down. She reached for Jasmine's hand.

'We're dancing.'

'What? No, I need to finish-' Jasmine stammered.

She felt an excited pull in her stomach as she realised, she wasn't resisting Emma's tugging grip. As they found a space on the make-shift dance floor, Jasmine saw Daniel leaning his back against the window and looking in at the party. He was looking straight at Jasmine, and she could feel the intensity of his stare. He smiled and nodded his head. She returned the smile, nodding her head awkwardly to the music as Emma swayed incautiously in front of her.

The flow of Emma's body and her icy white smile, grinning, shining, sparked a memory and a name she had been struggling to recall; Alex Pevestone.

So, now there were two in the folder. She had to understand why.

CHAPTER 19

———•❖•———

Jasmine's hair had always been a thick nest of curls. As a child, it was quite often the first thing anyone said to her. *Such a lovely head of hair* or *I would die for your curls*. Even at that age, she hated it, not the hair itself, but being defined by her hair that brushed her shoulders and tickled her ears with every breeze it caught. She tolerated her hair because her father loved it. That was all.

Her eyes pulled focus from the reflection in the bathroom mirror and to the thick curls that now hung heavy and lifeless. The pencil line was thick under her eyes, but she'd managed to find a stack of cotton pads in Daniel's bathroom cabinet. Thankfully, Emma had an old liner pencil amongst the tipped out bag in the middle of the tiled floor. She imagined that Emma wouldn't mind her borrowing it.

Emma groaned and spat into the toilet. Her dress was pulled up to her waist so she could spread her legs across the cool bathroom floor. Jasmine had managed to wedge her between the toilet bowl and the radiator for extra support.

A knock came at the door, and Daniel's muffled concern fell short just behind it. Jasmine looked at Emma as she managed to pull her head from the bowl. 'Occupied,' she groaned, but the word involved too much movement for her mouth, and her body stiffened at the invitation and sent more bile and gin down the toilet. Jasmine went to open the door, just a little, so she could tell him Emma was unwell.

Daniel was standing just outside the door. He shouldered the jamb as though he was waiting for a bus, his hair no longer slicked back, but flopping from side to side as he tried to see in.

'Listen, Daniel, I know this is your place but I'm going to have to say the bathroom is off-limits to you and anyone else until I restore some dignity to that woman in there.'

Daniel's dimples rose high on his cheeks as he smiled. 'But she's alright, Jasmine?'

'Emma? Yes, she's in good hands. Fortunately I have a friend,' Jasmine stopped herself, 'had a friend,' she corrected, 'who lived her life staring down a toilet and I saved her from drowning a couple of times so I have *previous* you might say.'

'Previous,' he repeated. There was a moment where he'd somehow commanded silence between them and seemed to be searching her face. His eyes tightened as though he'd found something and then he asked,

'Are you alright?'

Oh God, what does he see? Have I completely lost it with the eyeliner? She took her hands up to her face, covering her cheek and wiping her eyes self consciously.

'I'm fine. Bit of a mess but...Just all partied out, I guess.'

Daniel nodded; concern lifted from his green eyes. 'That can happen when Will starts the Chess games,' he said, a little pleased with himself. Jasmine noticed and returned a small laugh.

'Well, if there's nothing I can do I'll…' He gestured down the hall where the party was continuing without them.

As he moved past her, Jasmine caught the familiar scent she had committed to memory, and in a moment where she was certain no one could see, she breathed deeply through her nose contented. 'Oh! There may be something you can do.'

Daniel had stopped short of the door and turned back towards the bathroom and looked at Jasmine leaning against the door. Jasmine could tell he was looking at her, really looking at her, the shape of her and the cut of her dress as she pressed lightly against the frame.

'What is it?' he asked softly.

'Emma's not going to make the rest of the party. I think I need to take her home. Could you arrange a taxi?' They became distracted by the violent retching sounds, which seemed more energetic and furious. Jasmine turned back to Daniel, saying, 'Let's give her ten minutes, shall we?'

Daniel smiled. 'Leave it with me, Jasmine.' He let his hand rest on the door handle before turning back to say, 'and thanks for looking after my guest.'

*

The old MI5 building in Birmingham had been converted into apartments, and the uppermost space where Daniel had thrown his party was now empty. Jasmine walked barefoot into the open space. It was as though she'd woken from a deep sleep, as though days had passed instead of the hour, maybe more, since Daniel knocked on his bathroom door.

She cautiously stepped inside, stepping over empty bottles and half-drained glasses. A discarded napkin stuck to her foot and the struggle to free it nearly landed her on the floor. Mercifully, the piped piano had stopped; even the soul music that was so welcome earlier had no place in this ghost town of a room. And as her hands fell to her dress, she instantly felt she was far too overdressed for this room.

She saw Emma curled up like a child on the sofa in front of the open fire. 'Emma?' Jasmine's dress billowed behind her. She crouched by Emma's head and whispered her name. Emma's lips pursed with a forced breath followed by the rattle of a snore. Jasmine arched her back and found the coffee table with her bum and sat down. She shook her head. She couldn't help but smile. Another snore, this time louder.

'She's fine. Did you enjoy your snooze on the bathroom floor?' Daniel said from behind the kitchen bar. He rounded towards the sofa, where the chessboard lay abandoned in the middle of the table. In his hands, he had two tall glasses of water, and he offered one to Jasmine as he took his place on an empty sofa opposite Emma's resting body. He looked up at Jasmine, still standing, holding her glass. 'Oh, its water, not, you know.' He smiled and motioned for her to sit with him.

'What happened here?' Jasmine asked, cautiously smelling the glass then tipping it gratefully in her mouth.

Daniel shrugged his shoulders. 'She just came out of the bathroom right as rain, said she would wait for you to come out, she found the sofa and the rest is, well, horizontal and nasal.'

Jasmine looked at Daniel. She'd never seen him so relaxed. His tux was partially removed, only a white shirt and black trousers now.

He had a jovial, childish way about him that before only seemed to work for Will. His lips curled into a guilty, almost naughty smile as Emma let out another snore.

'Yes, I do see that. But what happened here? What happened to the party and all your guests? Where's Will? I'm sure all I asked for was a taxi.'

'Yes, the taxi. I made an executive decision on that and decided to hold off. At least until I was sure she'd be able to walk. I imagine it would be a nightmare at the other end if you found she couldn't stand on her own two feet. Rather sleep it off on the sofa than on the streets.'

Daniel slipped out of his seat and went over to the bar. He returned with a glass jug full of water.

'Oh, yes, the party. Well, I didn't see any point since Emma was out of it, so I thanked them all and sent them home.' His faint Irish accent dipped in and out and, despite the questions gathering around Jasmine's busy mind, she couldn't help being soothed by the sound of his voice.

'If I didn't feel so ropey, I'd insist this is gin because I'm a little confused. No offence to Emma, she's a lovely girl, and I've just met her, but I'm sure the party would have survived a few more hours without her.'

They both watched Emma's body rise and fall with deep intoxicated sleep. 'You're right of course,' Daniel said, 'but that wasn't the point.'

'Wasn't the point? Not following.' Jasmine reached for the jug and sloshed water into her glass, splashing the table partially.

'The party was for Emma's benefit, part of a course of therapy along with her sessions. To bring her back into society.'

'You mean, it was a fake party?' Jasmine asked.

'No, the party was real. Just Will and I and now you were in the know. To be honest, I hadn't expected her to latch onto anyone, but when she did, and I saw it was you, I knew she'd be fine, I mean not exactly this fine,' he said, gesturing to Emma sleeping on the couch, 'that's why I thanked you earlier for what you did. It meant something different to us.'

Jasmine sat back deeper against the leather, feeling its cold touch on her shoulders. She watched Emma for the longest time and fell in with her steady breathing. She could have fallen asleep there and then.

'Do you have a blanket?' she asked. 'I want to cover her.'

Emma moved slowly under her blanket as though her body welcomed the touch and the growing warmth. Jasmine settled back on the sofa and wondered if she would sleep.

'How damaged is she?' She felt the words forming in the air before she'd even considered their effect.

Daniel seemed un-phased by the question; it was as though he were waiting for it, Jasmine thought.

'I wouldn't use that word to describe her.'

'No, sorry. Does seem a little bit brutal when I play it back.' A moment of silence was shared between them. 'She told me she was government-funded.'

'I'm afraid that would be the drink talking,' he replied.

Jasmine reached for her glass, disappointed again at the lack of answers. She had thought Daniel was relaxing, easing into her knowing more.

'Oh, I see.'

'What I mean is: yes, she is funded by a government project. Not that, indeed, she needs the funding, she has paved her way in banking exceptionally well. She just shouldn't have told you. That's the drink for you. Loosens tongues. By the way, how are you feeling?'

Jasmine stiffened at the words "government project". It sounded like aliens in fish tanks, spies and James Bond. Not The Room on Share Street.

'Sorry, what?'

'How are you feeling?' Daniel repeated.

'Oh, I'm fine, I think. A bit of pounding in my head and a decent wobble when I walk but apart from that, I'm practically perfect.'

'Yes, indeed you are,' Daniel said, looking directly at her. Her head, filled with cloudy alcohol, seemed to clear for just a moment. He averted his eyes after a few seconds and pulled himself up. He disappeared around the bar and came back with a strip of pills. 'Here, take one of these,' he said.

'What are they?' Jasmine asked, taking the small diamond-shaped pill between her fingers.

'One of Will's specialities. We give them to the client before they go into The Room. We can't exactly trust that they haven't had a reassuring drink, or indeed a stimulant, before each session, so one of these power pills cleans them up very quickly.'

Jasmine looked into Daniel's green eyes, seeing for the first time his worn expression. The party and the evening lay heavy in his face, but it didn't detract from his beauty. A strand of black hair fell away and cut across a tanned forehead heavy with light lines.

'You realise I've got to be mad to take a pill in a bloke's apartment while her friend is passed out only feet away.'

'Absolutely,' he replied. 'Just take the pill, or not. It's of no benefit to me – only to you. I don't care.'

'Maybe just a little, I think. I think you care just a little.' Jasmine smiled and licked her lips again. She placed the pill into her mouth and chased it down with some water.

'Yes, perhaps that's true.'

She could feel the heat of his stare, but nothing from the pill. She waited for something magical to happen. Nothing. Her eyes rested again on Emma, drawn by the bubbling noises she made from her mouth.

'So is Emma some kind of experiment that the world doesn't know about? Or is that too much of a "Hollywood" dramatic way of putting it?'

Daniel rolled his eyes and smiled. 'This, still?'

'Listen to me, Daniel Burton,' Jasmine said, rounding on him, 'I just swallowed a pill that may or may not mean I'll be face-planting some gutter before the nights over. I think I'm owed a bit of trust, don't you? I'm all for selling your precious Room because I see what it does for people - but for me not to ask a few questions doesn't sit right, don't you think?'

'I'm well aware of your predicament, Jasmine. You want to know.' He paused, taking in the form of Emma on the sofa.

'A part of the government that exists just below the surface, out of sight if you will, is showing a little interest in The Room. They want to investigate the health benefits of using it or a version of it for the rehabilitation of victims who have suffered extensive trauma in their lives.'

'That sounds like a good thing, doesn't it?'

'It feels like it, Jasmine. I see great results with Emma, but I know that's because I have control. The Room is a powerful tool, and I'm wary that my grip will loosen if others have control. I can't let that happen. A lot of years of my life have been put into it.'

'But I don't understand,' Jasmine interrupted. She could feel her head clearing for the first time since taking the pill. 'You've already allowed access to The Room. Our doors are open, and I have a list of clients on our database-'

'And they're all carefully chosen, monitored and schooled about the exclusivity of the service we offer.' Daniel took a deep breath, slowly letting it out. 'I used everything I had, time as well as money, to kick-start The Room. To prevent the work grinding to a halt, I had to bring Will onboard and develop a commercial edge to it and sell the experience to a small, carefully controlled number of investors. I believed that worked-'

'Until the "evil" government got involved.'

'Something like that,' he muttered.

'But Daniel, you must have seen this coming? Eventually, you must have known that the bubble would eventually burst.'

'Now you sound like Will,' Daniel said.

Jasmine stretched a gowned leg and kicked the black king into white territory. They both watched the piece roll from the board and disappear silently off the table.

The apartment seemed even more vast now, with all the guests gone. She imagined a battalion of cleaners sweeping through in the morning, restoring each gleam and reflection to every surface. Someone would pick up Daniel's suit and return it that same day, and he would brighten their day by scanning over a generous tip.

A question formed in Jasmine's mind as she looked around the apartment, eventually coming to rest on Daniel.

'What am I doing here?' she asked.

'You're my guest,' Daniel replied.

'No, I mean - why me? Why did you come to the cafe that day? A greasy spoon like Fly by Night and you and this place, they just don't go.' Jasmine hung her elbow over the back of the sofa and cradled the side of her head. She could feel the dull ache starting to fade. As she watched Daniel, she witnessed him go within himself. He seemed to fidget, no longer able to look at her for more than a few seconds at a time.

'Daniel?' she pressed, 'are you embarrassed about something?'

Daniel swung his elbow over the back, a perfect mirror of Jasmine. 'Promise me you won't think less of me?'

Jasmine laughed out loud. It caused Emma to stir. She threw her hand up to her mouth, then whispered through open fingers, 'I promise.'

'I followed you.' He waited for Jasmine to close her mouth before he continued.

'I was walking in the park that day, and I saw you standing on the footbridge, the one that arcs over the market. You'd stopped as though you were admiring the view, or the padlocks fastened there. I thought you were interesting so I-'

'You followed me? Daniel I'm really trying not to judge you but, you *followed* me?'

'I knew I shouldn't have said anything. Don't get me wrong; it wasn't personal - I do it to lots of different people.' He allowed the silence to fall between them until Emma conducted them both with her steady breathing. 'Okay, that sounded better in my head before I said it.'

'Do you think?' Jasmine asked.

'It's just a... little game I play. Walking in other people's footsteps. My father taught it to me. You pick someone who looks interesting, and you walk a mile in their footsteps, then you move on to someone else. It sounds petulant, but my life is fairly...intense. Sometimes I use it as an escape. I ended up in the café that day and saw what went on with your boss, and I wanted to help. Serendipitous, if you'd agree. It's a very positive exercise, if indeed a little weird.'

'On that we agree. That's my only judgement.' Jasmine shook her head and let out a laugh.

He coughed lightly. 'I consider myself actively interested in the human form. Doing this 'game', as you will,' he paused. 'It's a little like research. There are so many distractions these days that prevent us from simply focusing on one another.'

Jasmine remembered the little girl on the tricycle, on her first day going to Share Street. Her mother hadn't even looked at her, talking openly to someone else via her connected chip. It made sense, in a way, to do something that was so wholly anti-technological to try and connect with someone else.

'Do you think Emma will be okay; I mean not tomorrow; she's screwed on that score. Do you think she'll make it through her sessions? What was it you called it, *next level trauma*?' she asked.

Daniel rubbed a hand through his hair. 'Yes, it is certainly 'next level'. I can't tell you about that, of course, but yes, I do believe she'll be fine. She's miraculously strong, and we're focusing on that strength in her sessions.'

With the rush of clarity and escape that the pill had given her coursing through her body, Jasmine thought about her own trauma and the months leading up to her getting her new job. She thought about the promises she'd made to herself to end her own life. She thought about the darkness that pressed in some nights and smothered her mind, and the dreams of the little boy who wanted so much to hold her hand. She could feel her breath catching and rising, but she didn't want it to turn to tears.

'I want to use The Room.' Her voice shook so hard it splintered.

Daniel looked right into Jasmine's eyes. 'I know you do,' he said—his voice, thick and warm with concern.

Jasmine reached for his arm, resting her fingers there. 'This could be another thing you could do for me; just like your footstep game.' She wiped tears away from her eyes, allowing a breath out that felt like she'd held for the longest time.

'I have a dream that won't go away, and I feel like it will stay as long as I don't understand it.'

'Jasmine, I'd rather you didn't share this, not now,' he said softly.

She looked at him and saw a hardness form on his face. The colours of the room changed with her blinking eyes, thick with frustrating tears.

'Why, it's just a dream isn't it?'

'Jasmine, The Room isn't designed to sort out our dreams. It's there as an expression of your creativity. You won't find the monster under your bed.'

'You make it sound like magic.'

'Will and I would agree that it comes close.'

She took in a slow, confident breath before she spoke. 'In my dream, I'm a young girl, and I'm outside the park with my dad. I mean he's there at the beginning and then he's not. And there's a small boy, smaller than me; I think he wants to hold my hand.'

'Jasmine, please stop, I can't help you with your dreams,' Daniel pressed.

'But there's this woman who won't let him. She snatches him away, scratching-'

'Stop!' Daniel jumped to his feet. His hands went to his greying temples, rubbing. For a few moments, it was like he'd just woken up and didn't know where he was.

'I'm sorry,' he managed.

Emma made some incoherent mumbling and Jasmine slid to her head, lightly brushing through her hair with her fingers. In response to seeing movement from the sleeping guest, Daniel pulled himself up, and started towards a door at the other side of the kitchen.

'I'll see about that taxi.'

Jasmine was curled up at Emma's feet, numb to Daniel's sudden outburst. She played over and over what she had said to make him react the way he did. For her part, it was the first time she'd told anyone about her dream, and she could feel the comfort in it, like the comfort of Emma's blanket in the chilling room.

CHAPTER 20

Now

'What do you think he wants?' Jasmine didn't look at Will as she spoke. Instead, she scanned the tree line in the distance and noted every clutch of activity in the park. The sounds too were filed into her mind as *everyday family noises* and, in the distance, the ever-present hum of traffic.

'What they all want- a story. I don't know too much about this Michael Powers bloke, but I do know 'e has a past, a past that he'd rather keep on the low, if ya know what I mean? Maybe that's something we could use.'

'Use?' She lifted her head to enjoy the spots of sunlight, pushing through the branches and leaves of the oak tree. 'Do you think he'll come after us?'

'All this – all this mess because of Dan an' his fucking machine.' Will sighed deeply. 'Sorry. Jesus, I never thought this would be the end. I never thought I'd be doing this without Dan. He's well an' truly screwed us, Jas.'

Jasmine blinked hard and fast to stop the tears from forming and pulled her cap closer to her eyes. She couldn't let the families think they were anything other than a couple sitting on a bench; her crying would only bring about unnecessary attention. She'd cut her hair short and straightened the curls to form a neat bob around her face. She could barely recognise herself, but she still felt so exposed.

'I just think, with what I know about the bloke, that if the wrong people come after us just for our association with it then I think someone like Michael Powers might be a good piece to 'ave in the game,' Will said.

'So, you trust him, then?'

'Nah. Not yet. I've only met 'im once.' He shifted uneasily on the park bench. 'I'm sorry I got caught leaving. It was a shit lottery of a chance. But he took my picture. He called it *his insurance*.'

Both of them sat quietly, letting the restrained calm of the park wash over them.

'What now?'

Jasmine didn't answer directly. Her mind had been on Daniel; she thought about his eyes on her, the soothing smell of his cologne, even the first time they had met and talked on this very bench.

'I was falling in love with him, you know,' she eventually let out. 'I don't know if I knew at the time, or if I'm only coming to terms with it now, after all this mess. But I hated him for what he did to me.' After a few moments she turned to Will. 'We still have to protect him. I don't know how, but we have to try. We want to be free of this and while Powers is snooping around it won't be safe - for either of us.'

She shook her head and took another look high up into the speckled canopy of the oak tree. 'When did my life start becoming some horrendous spy film? All this talk of *them* and *coming after us*. This is not the Room anymore; it's reality.'

'Amen to that,' Will replied.

Jasmine found it in her to smile. 'I didn't know you were a God guy?' She put a hand on Will's arm and squeezed. 'Get in touch with Powers, however you think necessary. We'll keep his appointment, but it will be on our terms.'

CHAPTER 21

Then

Jasmine saw the remaining pills that Daniel had given her on the table in the empty apartment. They were the type that you pop from a packet. She picked them up and turned them over in her fingers. The stiff plastic was dressed in silver foil on one side, but Jasmine couldn't find a name or description of any kind on them.

She looked across to the door that Daniel had gone through to book her a taxi. She kissed Emma's sleeping head lightly and lightly walked to the burgeoning light that peeked through the door frame.

Why would he have the pills here if they are exclusively for use with The Room?

Her dress seemed to flow as her body moved beneath it. It was as though the dress didn't know the party was over. Her hand touched the ornate doorknob; it was cold but not uncomfortably so; it felt like electric beneath her fingers, and she felt it in the pit of her stomach too.

The heavy brown panelled door moved silently when Jasmine pushed against it. The room inside was dark, except for soft pools of light from low lamps. The hazy warm glow directed her eyes to a black leather chair tilted back, and Daniel sat just behind the impressive chair at his little desk, half in shadow. Beyond that, Jasmine picked out a small silvery trolley that you might find in an operating theatre and on this one she could see, reflected against the spotlights, a syringe and a wadding of cotton wool.

The Room

The light from the kitchen spilt into the mysterious room. She instinctively knew the harsh light was intrusive, so without invitation, she stepped in and closed the door. Through portions of shadow, she heard Daniel's voice.

'I had a family once,' he said. The busy sound of fingers on keys fell like rain, soft and gentle. 'I lost them; I lost my boy first then my wife; she couldn't cope, so she made her own way out.'

Jasmine couldn't speak. She dared herself to move closer to the chair and the sound of his voice.

'Just you were talking about your dream reminded me of...what I'd lost. I'm sorry for-'

'You don't have to be, and I'm sorry about your family,' Jasmine whispered.

'Do you want to have a seat?'

Jasmine didn't move. 'Daniel, is this The Room?' she eventually asked.

The busy sounds of the keyboard stopped. 'It is a version of it. I like to keep it close so I can work on developing it still. Don't tell Will. He has no idea it exists outside the Share Street site, and he believes, mainly because I let him, that he's the only one that can administer his suppressants.'

Jasmine took a step closer until she shared the pool of light with the oversized leather chair. 'I thought you didn't want me to use the Room; you know the whole staff embargo?' She dared herself to touch the stiff leather arm. Her fingers dipped beneath the inside of it and suddenly turned blue with a soft blurred light set deep into the arm itself. She pulled her hand away, noting that the light reminded her of her desk at the Hub.

'I gave you the pill, didn't I?' Daniel responded.

Jasmine lowered herself into the chair and the light that washed it. She was aware of the sweet smell of sweat and lavender once again as Daniel emerged from the darkness. He stood to her left and gently directed her left arm to rest under the arm of the chair. From somewhere tucked beneath the seat, he produced a strap and began to secure her arm to the underside of the chair's arm.

'This will make sure your arm doesn't move. It's my way of keeping in touch with you while you're under. I'll will be in constant contact with your LE chip and keeping the part of your mind "fertile" if you like for whatever you bring to it. Do you understand?'

Jasmine nodded. She did understand, she thought, but in the subdued light of the space, she tried to hide the fear that prickled over her whole body, the fear of being stripped bare and coming face to face with her mind.

'I do understand,' she said. 'It's not how I imagined it, though.'

'So many people expect some big space they can run around in, but this isn't an episode of Star Trek. The place exists in your mind. You carry The Room inside you. We just trick you for a while into creating experiences that you require to fulfil your outside life. It's the only way you can experience the impossible.' Daniel disappeared into the blackness as he took his place at her right arm.

'Okay, Jasmine, how are you feeling?'

The Room

She closed her eyes tight. 'You're going to stick me with that needle now, aren't you?' she asked. Before he could answer, she felt the sting of the needle and the cold liquid filling her arm with ice. Her breaths became heavy in her chest; deep and long.

'It's okay, Jasmine. We're nearly ready to begin. I have contained the drug, and in a sense, I'm holding it back from doing its job. When I release it, the rest is up to you.'

'What if I don't know what to do?'

'Don't worry; you'll know what to do. Your body is doing fine, your heart rate is good, and you're breathing just right. You should be feeling well.'

Jasmine breathed in deeply. 'I feel relaxed. Like I could sleep, but I know something is keeping me from sleeping. This is…I've never been able to breathe like this before.'

'That's good, Jasmine, that's all I wanted to hear. Now I want you to say the words, "Big Red Lollipop" for me.'

'Big red lollipop,' she repeated, confused.

'That's great. When you say that or think it the software throws up a coded profile that I can instantly recognise if you need to exit your room early. It's kind of a safe word if you like. When I see that profile, I will ease you out. Do you understand, Jasmine?'

'Big red lollipop,' she repeated.

'I'll take that as a yes then.'

'Do you see my experience? Are you a spectator for it?'

'No, I just sit here and look after you. There's so much code passing through, it's all numbers and letters, but the distinction of our safe word is unique, and I'll be monitoring for that. It's all about your safety.' Daniel leaned further back into the dark and pressed the return key on his laptop.

'Okay Daniel, I think I'm ready,' she said into the darkness. She was only aware that her words were audible when Daniel replied.

'That's good, Jasmine, because I already released your drug. Welcome to The Room.'

The ice was still in her arm, but she didn't feel its bite. It moved across her chest and dripped through her entire body. Like water, it penetrated every inch of her and lifted her free of her real surroundings. She took in the distant smell of lavender in one deep breath.

*

There's a tree that I always liked in the park, ever since I can remember. My dad used to take me, and we'd always end up there sitting under it, an oak tree I think it was, and in my memory, it always used to be a dazzling day. The sun was so bright it seemed to bounce off the leaves like jewels. But with a crisp day, we used to enjoy it. It was easy to let your imagination run wild.

I'm going to take Mia to that tree tomorrow, I hope I can still find it, but that will surely be part of the fun. If it's anything like today, then those leaves are going to sparkle like drops of diamonds.

Mia is running around and around, trying to catch the little roundabout. She's laughing so hard I think she's going to lose her footing. And even though I'm her mother and that scares me to death, I can't resist her when she starts laughing like that. I once tried telling her that it's just as much fun to ride it than it is to push it and chase it, but then she would give me 'that look.' Her big brown eyes were soft with surprise, and her determination to scold was lost in them, despite her squashed up face and two chubby hands on her hips.

I stand at the edge of the playground watching her, and I try to remember what kinds of thoughts were running through my head at that age. Mia has caught up with the roundabout and hangs onto the side, catching the wind in her thick black curls and daring herself to let one hand go so as to wave to me as she sails round. It's funny that she waits until it almost stops before launching herself off in the most dramatic way, as if she imagines she would keep going and fly high into the sky.

I shout to her that we have to go, and that Daddy is waiting for us at home. Whether she hears or not, she bounds over to a patch of uncut grass and sits on her haunches, her face inches away from something that has her attention in the grass. I try to move towards her, to see what it is she has seen, but she spies me and tells me to stay where I am. It's a surprise you see. I don't have to wait long before she hurries toward me as well as she can in her summer wellies with her hands fixed behind her back and her curls bouncing on her bare shoulders. I bend down to touch her nose with mine and ask what nonsense she has got behind her back. One hand brings round a daisy, and she gives it to me. It's my favourite flower. I don't mean to, but I tear up. Mia reached for the tear that must have shone in this sun on my cheek and wiped it away. She told me not to be sad because she had one for Daddy too. And she had. She brought the other from behind her back.

On the way home I told her about her grandfather and how we had a special place and a unique tree with diamonds for leaves and would it be a good idea if tomorrow we should go and look for it.

She held my hand tightly as we walked along.

~

Jasmine hadn't noticed the scratches on the palm of her hands until she got home that evening. She stood in front of her dresser and looked at them, tracing them with her fingers. There was no pain, but as she brought her hands close to her face, she could smell Mia all over them. She gently touched one of the flowers resting in the miniature bottle on the dresser. Mia had been so excited that she insisted they fill it with water and with a surgeon's precision, had then transplanted the small flowers to the little vase. She wanted it *nice for Daddy,* she'd said. Jasmine smiled through the reflection of herself as she saw the bedroom door behind her open slightly.

'Do you want some help with that?' Daniel's voice carried over the softly lit room. Every line of his tuxedo was perfect; Jasmine noticed as he drifted closer. She imagined the lines under that suit, and her body tensed at the thought.

Jasmine didn't have to say anything. He was standing behind her, savouring every moment by not touching her with his hands just yet but with warm lips brushing against her naked shoulders. He felt her shiver beneath his kiss. He was frustrated because he would have to use his hands to lift her hair away so he could start on her neck. He knew his wife very well, and he knew that she longed for him to kiss her neck.

The Room

Jasmine watched him trace her hair with his fingers before plunging them deeper to get a handful. 'Nice flowers,' he murmured as his lips found her neck and brushed lightly towards her ear.

Through heavy breaths, Jasmine said, 'Mia picked them for us.'

'That's sweet,' he said. He worked her trembling neck with his lips, his hands pulling on the zipper of her dress. 'Would it make me a terrible father,' he said, hot breath on her skin, 'if I didn't look in just now, but instead, I stayed here?'

She absorbed every word in her body, and her dress floated past her skin. At the same time, she reached behind her and pulled him closer. She whipped herself around and started clawing at his trousers, but he was stronger. He turned her back around and held them both in their reflections. With gentle fingers, he held her throat while his other hand undid her bra.

He stepped back and started to unbutton his shirt.

A white, engrossing light bathed Jasmine in the ecstasy she enjoyed with Daniel. The light became so bright that it became all she could think of, and that's when she realised it was something out of her control.

Even thoughts of Daniel and Mia faded eventually, faded into the unbroken light.

*

'Jasmine. Can you hear me?' Daniel asked her. He was leaning close to her face. His hands were resting on the arms of the big leather chair. He'd already unstrapped her arm from the blue scanning light that still hummed and pulsed with an unnerving rhythm. She nodded her head but was scared to open her eyes.

'You take your time. The lights are still low.'

'It was real,' she said, 'it was real.' She opened her eyes to the dimly lit room. Daniel was somewhere behind her now pressing keys on his laptop. He stepped around to help her out of the chair. As he offered her his hand; she took it, unable to look him in the eyes.

'It wasn't real,' she said firmly.

'If it felt real, Jasmine, then we've done our jobs. How do you feel now?' He asked.

'I don't know.'

'Listen, don't worry about it. Now you know. Your experience is yours. It's personal to you, and that's how it should stay.'

Jasmine thought about his fingers around her neck. 'You aren't able to use your software to see in?'

'God, no. Like I said, the package is designed to recognise the structure of code for your specific safe word. That's all.' Daniel saw that Emma was starting to come around. He tugged on Jasmine's arm before they reached her. 'Are you okay, Jasmine? If there's anything specific, you feel you need to tell me then I will break my own rule if it comes to it.'

Jasmine shook her head. 'No, it…it's fine.'

'The first time is always a bit rocky. It's just as much of an exercise coming out of it as it is going in. Maybe you'll do it again since

The Room

I've already broken my "No Staff" embargo.' Daniel's inside pocket started to vibrate. He reached in and pulled out his phone. 'Your taxi's downstairs. I took the liberty of calling one.'

Emma spent the journey with her eyes closed against the dappled sun peeking around the city buildings. For Jasmine though, the light of the morning revealed empty streets that rested under a warming sun. She picked out a lone man with a fluorescent vest and an inadequate broom. He was pushing something against the feet of a man sleeping in a doorway.

*

Daniel turned from the large window that looked out over the waking city and slowly walked a circuit of the loft. He bent to pick up the chess piece that Jasmine had mischievously kicked to the ground and replaced it on its rightful square. He absently stroked the kitchen counter that had doubled as a bar as he walked toward the room where the big leather chair was still, disappearing into the room just long enough to retrieve his laptop. Looking about the living room, he reached for the light switch and pulled down on it. It gave a satisfying clunk. There was a spiral staircase in the corner, tucked neatly behind the kitchen. At the top of this were his own private office and bedroom. A perfect getaway for a party host, should he feel the need.

In his office, he loosened a couple of buttons on his shirt. He took up his position at the desk and flicked a switch to turn on his desk lamp that threw a triangle of light across the surface. Opening the laptop, he sent his mouse icon across the screen a few times. Eventually he landed on an open tab at the bottom. The name of the file flashed briefly as he hovered above it, preparing to close it down.

The Architect Enters The Room.

He clicked the mouse button, and the tab disappeared. Daniel waited for the USB stick to stop flashing before he pulled it clear. As he did, he accidentally knocked a photograph sitting under the desk lamp. He was expressionless as he straightened the picture of a woman holding a boy in her arms. The woman was beautiful with long straight hair and the sharpest blue eyes. The boy was captivated by her golden strands that hung to her slender waist. He had his father's green eyes and hair that was too long, flopping over his forehead and almost touching his eyelids, but they liked it like that. The woman was laughing as the boy played with his mother's hair. She may have been looking at her son with that loving expression that mothers have for their children, or she may have been looking at the big red lollipop the little boy held in his other hand.

CHAPTER 22

Now

The door of number sixty-two Share Street buckled at an angle, but it was just enough for Michael to squeeze himself through. His first instinct was to call out, but the last thing he wanted was to startle someone, someone else who shouldn't be there. The smell of both human and cat piss was thick in the air, causing him to reach inside his coat and pull his scarf over his nose and mouth. In the furthest corner of the space, there was a discarded blanket. Someone had been living here.

Piles of leaves had gathered from visiting winds through the gap created by the ruptured door, and Michael couldn't quite bring himself to walk through them, fearing that a hand would come out and grab him.

He tipped a syringe to the side with his brogues before stepping further in, and towards the counter. Red vinyl bar stools lay drunk next to each other. They sagged on stained chrome legs, leaning towards a dirty tiled floor and drooping like worn down candles. Somebody had slashed the vinyl tops, and foam guts fell and seemed to hang in mid-air. At the other side of the counter, the floor was a carpet of broken glass and china shards. Stepping over them made a satisfying crackle that reminded Michael of when his dad used to crack his own back.

He reached a door beyond the counter. It was unnaturally locked - like someone had gone out of their way to make sure it was never opened. Michael managed to feed his fingers behind a thick bar that crossed the door and terminated in a steel fist-like housing. He yanked it a couple of times, the echo of metal on metal dwindled into the room.

'I wouldn't do that if I were you.' A voice replaced the echo.

Will looked tired. His eyes were dark and lifeless, grey circles shaped them, and he looked like a man for whom it was an effort just to hold up his head. He stood in the middle of the decaying space; his hands thrust deep into his jacket pockets.

Michael turned towards him, moving around the counter as though it would act as a barrier between him and the thin, tall man.

'You said you'd get in touch,' Michael said, leaning against the counter.

'I weren't ever gonna deliver on that promise,' Will said, his voice was low, and his words were cracked and uneven.

'And yet, here you are.'

'I've bin following you.'

Michael pushed himself from the counter. 'Following me? I didn't think I was that important.'

'I knew you wouldn't be able to leave this place alone, and f'now that makes you important enough.'

'How so?'

'You know why,' Will said, the edge of his mouth turned up, mocking. 'Because of your connection with the two that jumped.'

Michael shifted awkwardly. 'Maybe I just got a hold of one of your pamphlets and wanted to book a few sessions of your Room experience.' Silence filled the space between the two men. Michael continued, 'how do you know I have a connection with the two jumpers? You said that to me the last time we saw each other.'

Will leant against a wall and paused as though he was straightening out what to say. 'We 'ave 'ad a very sophisticated computer system with very detailed records. There weren't much we didn't know about our clients.'

'Clients? Were Stephanie Milner and Alex Pevestone two of your clients?' Michael waited, but no answer came. 'And you'll know from your *detailed records* that Pevestone should still be serving a prison sentence. He's not even halfway through. You can imagine my surprise when I saw him doing his circus act without a net.'

'You also should know - from the way that shit show was shut down - that there are bigger forces at work than just a missing net.'

'That's true. So, is that what the Room is; a bells and whistles circus act?'

'Not even close,' Will replied, a mocking tone dressed each word.

'But it did go wrong, didn't it?'

'The Room has gone now. We dismantled it before they could get their 'ands on it.'

'Who's 'we'? Do you mean Jasmine Wilson?'

Will looked Michael straight in the eyes. 'Jasmine's dead.'

Michael took in a deep breath He looked down at his shoes and started shaking off wet leaves that clung to him. 'I'm sorry to hear that. I was looking forward to finding out about The Room. I'd heard so much about it. Maybe more accurate to say, I read about it. Stephanie kept a blog, did you know? Of course you know. You have, or shall I say had, *very detailed records.*'

'What do you want?'

'I want answers,' he said, his voice pitched higher and echoed around the room. 'I want to know why a couple of my loose ends find themselves on your roof in the middle of the night. I want to know what The Room has to do with it all, and now I want to know what you have against me going through that door.' He pointed to the door behind the counter, fixed and held to by a metal arm.

Will closed his tired eyes for a few moments. 'Before Jasmine died,' he managed on an outgoing strained breath, 'she made me promise to come an' find ya. I had told her about our first meeting and that I knew who you were.'

'Why did she want you to find me?' Michael asked.

'Funnily enough, mate, she wanted t'protect you.'

'From what?'

'From the people who signed off on the unofficial release of Pevestone. Those detailed records I keep talking about, they 'ave them now an' by the time they process the information from that security door over there, they will cross reference your profile with the background info we've held on all our clients.'

Michael's fingers went to his left forearm. 'Fucking LE chips.' His brow furrowed as a thought rose to the surface. 'But all they'll find is what went on the public record. I can go to any archive and pull up a copy of a newspaper.' He thought of the work that Harriet had already done and realised he didn't even have to do that. She'd worked tirelessly and pulled at every thread.

'Our spiders ran a little deeper than the tabloid toilet paper that you sell, Mr Powers. They even go as far as CCTV an' audio files.'

Michael's hands went to his temples, and with splayed fingers, he dragged them through thick clumps of his black hair. He scanned the room. 'Isn't there anywhere to sit down in this fucking place?' He swiped the counter with the sleeve of his jacket and hiked himself onto it with shaking arms. *Too old for this shit*, he thought. His mind now settled on what Will had said. *Of course*, there would be another copy of that audio file of the Pevestone interview, not to mention the CCTV Jennifer had claimed to have seen capturing the exchange with officer Coleman and who knows what else the tall man's detailed files held.

'Okay,' he paused waiting for the tall man to fill in the gap, 'I don't even know your name, and from the silence, I guess you're not going to give it to me. But it's my turn – what do you want?'

'I've already told ya'; drop whatever you think you know, and stay away.'

'But that's not good enough. There are still questions. Why, if they have everything, do they not have a 'product'?'

'Only me an' Jasmine can operate it. We made it that way, it's our security measure.'

'Convenient.' Michael smiled.

*

Will stepped out of the Share Street building that day into the brightness cast from the milky blue sky. The air was cooling, and it soothed as he pulled in as much as he could. It was a relief to leave number sixty-two, to escape the nausea of decay and also the understanding that he would never see it again. He walked swiftly away from the light buzz of children playing and cats idling, but mainly he walked swiftly because he'd left Michael Powers in the building and he was done with his questions. Will made good on his promise to Jasmine and told Michael the full story, the version that Daniel had told Jasmine.

Will played back the question that Michael had asked after hearing the story. It surprised him when he asked it, and he'd never formulated an answer until now.

'How did Jasmine die?'

Will was as truthful as he could be; only the names had changed.

'She was messed up. She took her own life when she couldn't use it anymore.'

'How?'

'The Room is hers. Nobody knows it like her. That's all.'

The Room

Before he cleared the end of Share Street, he took one last look over his shoulder. He couldn't see sixty-two. It was hidden behind overgrown privet, and he, more importantly, protected from Michael Powers' view.

The waiting car was idling. It was just another car in a line of end to end parked vehicles on the edge of the city. It trespassed beyond the allotted twenty minutes stay, but the person in the driver's seat didn't seem to be concerned with that. Will crossed the front of the car and opened the driver's door.

'Can you even drive? Slide over,' he said.

Jasmine arched her back and launched herself at an awkward angle into the passenger seat. By the time she'd straightened herself, Will was engaged with the car and ready to pull away. 'So how did it go?' she asked.

'Weirdly exactly how we expected it, except f' one thing.'

'One thing?'

'He knows ya still alive.' Will swung the front end of the car into the road, seconds later passing the end of Share Street. Neither of them paid it any attention.

CHAPTER 23

Jasmine didn't have to look down in her dream this night; she could already feel the little boy's hand in hers, and the eagerness of his fingers' movements, like a fluttering sparrow clasped in her palm, as they walked along. The dream was crisp and warm. And, more than anything, *real*. Two shadows cast long across the pavement that ran along the edge of the park as they made their way towards the chattering and clunking far ahead.

The summer fair sounded close enough to touch, and the smell of hotdogs and onions was thick in the air. But the park was empty. Jasmine knew that if she looked across and through the spindly railings that there would be no fair and there wouldn't be any people. She knew that people would only pop up when necessary. *Necessary,* Jasmine thought to herself. She had no idea what, or who, drove her dream and the people who visited her, but it always felt like she was the passenger.

In the distance, the fog crept along the grass towards them. Jasmine watched as it slid on its white belly. The fingers in her palm squeezed, a firm grip for such a small hand. She stopped. She could see the fog, but she could feel it more, even before it was upon them. Cold snaked around her body and down her arm. The little boy flexed his fingers again. She looked down at him and realised that he was only perhaps half a metre shorter than her.

'What's your name?' she asked, not recognising her own voice, the bright high notes.

The Room

The little boy looked up at her through thick tufts of black hair that fell over his forehead and swept over his bright eyes; his free hand crept like the fog up to his mouth. He extended his small index finger and pressed it against his lips.

'Shhhhhh.'

The fog was almost upon them. It swirled and moved as the shadowy figure of a woman, dark like a silhouette, appeared. Jasmine felt the little boy's fingers flex once more.

'You can't save me,' the little boy said in a voice that didn't belong to his lips.

'Only my daddy can save me.'

Jasmine felt the ripping of skin on the palm of her hand. The featureless woman, still partially woven into the fog, said something. Maybe it was the little boy's name, but Jasmine struggled to make it out. Behind, the featureless woman's dark shape moved ferociously in the fog as though something had already happened. Jasmine knew this dream. She knew how it ended the last time, so she waited and watched.

She fought to keep hold of the little boy and free him from the featureless woman. She wanted to scream as the scratches on her hand were made again when she lost the fight. As the featureless woman finally yanked the little boy into the mist, Jasmine fell onto her knees. The stinging of her hand was almost too much to bear. The moment she decided to raise her hand and check the fresh scars was the moment she knew she was holding something.

She spread her fingers; the big red lollipop fell to the ground. It fell to the soundtrack of tyres being ripped apart against the hard road and the heavy thud of bodies against steel and glass.

Shattered pieces of the little boy's lollipop lay at Jasmine's feet on a beautiful bright summer's day. There was no fog, and if she cared to raise her head, she would be assured of a view for miles across the empty park. But instead, she looked down at the shattered remains of the lollipop, resigned to what came next. Jasmine knew this dream. She waited for the screams, not knowing if one of them would be hers.

*

She had hardly enough time to process the dream before her new laptop, which she'd bought with some of the surplus from her wages, fired up and asked for her thumbprint.

Hello, Jasmine.

The computer greeted her with its Welcome screen. In the centre of the screen, Jasmine was smiling, outdoors with her arm around someone but she realised she couldn't remember the picture being taken. The circle had conveniently cropped the other person out, and Jasmine was relieved to not recall who it was at that moment. She was fresh from her nightmare, and she had only one thing on her mind.

Daniel Burton and the boy he lost.

The search engine was less polite. It only flashed: *I'm waiting*…She appreciated it. She searched for the government website Capital City Archive and navigated to the media section. Before it asked for her login details, it boasted nearly four hundred years of history told.

'Shit!' Jasmine's login details could only access set secure data from when she was a student. And, she could not create an account, not now, now that she knew Daniel was – she didn't know what he was – but that he was involved with the government and far more powerful than her. These days, there was a tight leash on anyone accessing the national databases, and it was heavily supervised, even at one in the morning. Jasmine groaned. She'd heard stories of people who had hacked logins, or accessed information, and subsequently found their LE chips severely inhibited for travel and spending. She looked at the wall of her bedroom, behind which her mother slept soundly, thanks to the new drugs and care. She couldn't go back to being poor. She refused.

She leant back in her chair; the cold light of the computer screen lit a side of her face. She stretched her arms far back behind her and used the chair to crack her back. Not knowing what her next move was, she thought about her dream. Questions formed in her mind. Why had she thought of the safe word that Daniel had told her, and why was it relevant in her dream? Did it have a place? Had it worked? Was she in control of the dream just like in the Room? In just the same way she had imagined Daniel as the father of her child and not Paolo, had she tried to use the safe word to take control and at least save herself from the terrible events that continued to scar her sleep?

In the stillness of the dimly lit room a chill ran up her back, and she longed for the blanket that used to hang on the end of her bed, but she now remembered she had put it in her walk-in cupboard.

A new thought occurred to her as she shivered in the gloom. *What if the lollipop was already there, and I hadn't seen it until now*?

All she needed now was to confirm whether the dream was a dream or not. But it would mean trawling through the archives for a local report of a missing - or worse - dead child during a summer when Jasmine was in her younger years. She wondered if it was the time of the fair as she remembered the tinny music and the smells of cooking meat wafting in the air. But she couldn't access the archives, could she? She continued to stare at the screen.

Jasmine's legs were stiff with the cold and fought with her as she crossed the room to the cupboard. She swung the door open and was distracted by the whipping of five or six of her old lanyards and work badges that had found themselves abandoned and hung on the inside of the door. She reached for the blanket that was folded on the shelf at the rear of the cupboard and wasted no time pulling it across her shoulders. As she turned back into the room, she almost allowed the door to close. The ID badges were like a hidden history of Jasmine's jobs she'd held. She fingered through them, turning them and looking into the various faces that smiled back at her. They were all versions of Jasmine at differing times in her life - from sixth form to Sales assistant at Corona Fashions on the high street.

But the last badge she turned over hadn't belonged to her. It was Paolo's old ID badge he'd got for Uni. Jasmine remembered that it wasn't that old because he'd complained he lost it and had to get a new one, just before he stopped responding to her messages.

I guess it wasn't lost, after all, she thought.

She drew Paolo's badge closer to her face and looked past the black hair and a smile that was far too beautiful for his ugly personality. His eyes were dark and brilliant. She felt a twang in her stomach. Even after all the mess, she missed her version of Paolo. Perhaps though, she wondered, it had always been a lie. Frankly, it was best not knowing. Jasmine still held the badge close, but she was done with the picture of Paolo. She traced a twelve-digit number under the photograph, running it to the last number then back to the description which read. "Student Number".

She still held the badge in her hand when she'd returned to the computer. She moved the arrow across the screen and traced the instruction to enter a Username or Identifying Number. Her hand was shaking as she began entering the number from Paolo's badge. Paolo had told her that all students above college level are required to request an account with the Capital City Archive to, as they put it "facilitate studies." When it came to the password, that was easy. Paolo used the same password for everything, just simple but obvious tweaks with numbers and capitals should do it. She typed the password in blindly while holding her breath.

Pau0d1z

Her finger hovered over the enter key, and sure she had typed it correctly with all the variations.

Hello, Paolo.

She sighed in relief and fell back into her chair. The cup in Jasmine's left hand had been empty for a while now and had turned cold. Her other hand worked the mouse pad, skimming through page after page of headlines, waiting for a spark of something that would cause her a second look.

Jasmine's mouse hand jumped from the laptop as though she'd received an electric shock. She caught the pages spiralling off the screen and started to scroll back up just a few articles, slowing to stop at a headline that caught her eye. The cold tea cup thudded onto the carpet. Jasmine didn't notice.

Tragedy Strikes at Pilsley Park

Jasmine tightened the blanket around her shoulders again. It was as though the opened article was a crack in a window, spewing out icy air. There was a picture further down, and it told her everything she needed to know. It was the picture of the scene of an accident. It was the picture, no – the reality - she saw immediately after her nightmare left her thick with chilling sweat.

And it was that picture she reached out to touch, her blanket falling from her shoulders. The child version of herself, black curls pushed clear of her face, in the back of the photograph. Jasmine, the younger Jasmine was holding a man's hand, and despite the man standing too far out to be included in the picture, she knew it was her father. But the centre of the image, the focal point, that was what Jasmine touched with her fingertips, as if her eyes were not enough confirmation.

In the centre of the photograph, a man and woman sat on the edge of the pavement, each covered by a police-issued red blanket. Their faces were smudged with terror, and the woman was in the throes of a scream. They were young, perhaps early twenties, but Jasmine could recognise the clean contours of the man's face. Her eyes dropped to the caption beneath the photograph.

Parents of tragic toddler. Daniel and Patricia Burton left to grieve by the roadside.

She burst into the bathroom and emptied the day down the toilet.

Later that night, Jasmine stepped out into the rain. She'd felt so much tonight, but now her hands, her limbs, were numb. There was nothing left to feel as the droplets pecked at her and pressed heavy clothes against her skin. In the house, she had left the computer glowing in the bedroom.

Tragedy Strikes at Pilsley Park

The local community of Pilsley were today rocked when a woman, unknown to the police, who was said to be behaving suspiciously, attempted to snatch a little boy from the pavement just outside Pilsley Park in full view of his parents.

Witnesses close to the scene watched helplessly as a brave young girl attempted to rescue the little boy from the woman who seemed to come from nowhere.

"...there was nothing we could do. It all happened so fast,"

said Aryan Wilson, who had been previously enjoying the fair with his seven-year-old daughter.

The woman was described as manic as she lifted the boy clear and fled into the road and into the path of a bus before it had a chance to stop. Emergency services on the scene had determined that death for the two victims was instant.

It is difficult at this early stage to determine a motive for snatching the young boy but the police, as well as councillors on the scene, are working hard to shed some light on today's events. The parents of the toddler who is currently unnamed at this time are Daniel Burton and his wife Patricia Burton. They are said to be understandably inconsolable.

Stricken Mother Found Dead in Pilsley Home

A local woman and community liaison for Pilsley was found dead in the early part of yesterday evening. Patricia Burton, a local figure and force for good in the area as well as devoted wife of successful businessman Daniel Burton was discovered at approximately six thirty yesterday evening with what the police have termed, self-inflicted wounds. They are not considering her death as suspicious.

This tragedy is the latest for the Burton family, it being just nine months since their own three-year-old son was murdered in front of them.

Mr Burton, who discovered his wife, is not available for comment and the police have asked at this time that all such petitions should be held in respect of his privacy.

CHAPTER 24

Daniel balanced the mug of tea on top of the old round-arched sideboard. He stood flexing his toes on the hardwood floor and looked out over the city, as much as the distorting rain would allow. Water bounced off rooftops, and pipe guttering threw arches of white frothing water into the streets.

Behind him, the elevator rattled loudly into life and started creeping towards the apartment. Daniel checked his watch as a matter of routine. It took the elevator twenty-seven seconds top to bottom, so he padded over to the breakfast counter and set his mug next to Jasmine's. At almost three in the morning, out of this weather, he assumed she'd welcome a hot drink.

When he'd answered the intercom, she sounded hysterical. But Daniel knew who it was, in fact, he'd been expecting her to call at some point. *Dreams just don't go away,* he thought.

He pulled the cage door open and took a few steps back. Jasmine stood still even though her body arrested with shakes from the icy chill of her clinging clothes. Her hair was almost straight and painted to her face, and its ends glistened with falling drops of rain. Her jacket, once camel coloured, was stained a muddy, sodden brown. Her eyes were wet with blackened mascara smudges, but they were wide, alive and intent on Daniel.

'I was there,' she said.

'I know,' he replied.

'Why didn't you tell me?'

Daniel held out his arms to her. 'Come inside, Jasmine. You need to get dry.'

'I said, why didn't you tell me?' She held his gaze. He turned away from her with his hands on his hips, looking to the ceiling before swinging around. Despite her anger, she noticed how beautiful he was, how his hair had become dishevelled from his disrupted sleep. His pyjama bottoms hung lightly from his hips and a white t-shirt fitted around his chest and arms. He lifted his arm to his hair, his muscles contracting into the white cotton.

'Jasmine, I-'

'Stop it!' she shouted at him. She squeezed her eyes shut to stop her looking at him, to stop her thinking about what they did, or what she dreamed they did, in The Room. 'You're getting ready to lie to me. Stop!' She ran to him with pounding fists that connected with his chest.

'The truth,' she sputtered then, 'what happened? I was young, but not too young to forget this. Why couldn't I remember, Daniel? Did you do something to me? Some 'Room' shit?'

Daniel grabbed at her wrists. 'You went through something, something terrifying. Of course you couldn't remember clearly. It's classic dissociative amnesia, Jasmine.'

'Stop, stop trying to get into my head!' She squeezed her eyes shut. Her movements slowed as she gave way to the shivering, and before she knew it, she found her forehead pressed into his chest.

'What is this all about, Daniel? Why, why did you choose me?' she whispered.

Her voice was muffled against his t-shirt. He rested his cheek on her head and continued to hold her close. The cold and wet seeped on to his vest, and soon they were both shaking. He felt her sinking in his arms and pulling him closer.

'To keep you safe, Jasmine, to keep you safe.'

*

Jasmine let her hands fall to her sides and the hot water run down her face. It found the shape of her slender neck and then every curve of her naked body. The shower was throwing up steam and hid her in her little glass cubicle. The dinner plate spout poured water over her face and pressed her hair away down her back. It left her breathless, but she felt refreshed. With a finger extended, she drew an M on the glass. It squeaked then bled almost immediately, and just as quickly she couldn't bear to look at it. With the rest of the fingers, she wiped it clear.

On the other side of the glass, the lights played tricks. Smudges of colour flickered and moved across the bathroom and then behind her. She heard the shower cubicle door open then close. She felt the shape of Daniel behind her, but she wasn't ready to turn around. She enjoyed how his wet body found hers, and each contour of their bodies seemed to compliment the other.

He brushed her hair away from her shoulders and touched them with his lips, slowly moving up her neck. Her body softened in his arms as she felt him close against her backside. Daniel turned her around, forcing her to let him go so he could look into her eyes.

It was almost too much as she looked deep into his green eyes. They were soft and strained, and for the briefest moment, Jasmine wondered if he'd been crying. They were eyes that searched for something – maybe, she wondered, for someone to care about, or even *love*.

Daniel kissed her hard. The water continued to soothe them, and their kisses slowed, deep and full, until their bodies were silent, and the rage of the shower persisted. Jasmine held his face in her hands and searched his eyes. She still knew nothing about him, but she wanted this beautiful man, more than anything.

She felt tears rising within her. Daniel caught them as they overflowed and mixed with the water down her cheeks. She saw his concern and that he was about to speak. She didn't let him ask his question. 'I want to see Mia again,' she whispered.

Daniel looked at her, and she wondered if anyone had ever looked at her like that before. Wholly, wide-eyed and unabashed. It was as if they understood the same loss, the same fears. When his eyes couldn't take her all in, he dared to touch her skin with his fingers, tracing the shape of her face and the soft lips he'd kissed.

'Put your arms around my neck.'

She did, and he cradled her in his arms.

*

The bedroom was softly lit with warm yellows, but in the shadow of the unmade bed, Jasmine and Daniel sat on the floor facing each other. Jasmine was naked under the warm duvet she had wrapped around her. She was breathless as she looked at Daniel. He sat opposite her with his back to the side of the bed, a towel covering his lower body.

After a long silence between them, Jasmine spoke,

'You never asked me who Mia was.' She noticed Daniel's smile faded, but it wasn't sudden. It straightened out as he stole away from her for a moment, and she wondered if he was thinking up a lie to tell her.

'I didn't ask because you've never spoken of her and I guessed it was because she was part of your Room experience and-'

'You never ask about the sessions,' she interrupted.

'I avoid it if I can.' He smiled.

'I want to tell you about Mia, I do, but I need to know about my dream and what happened in the real world.'

'Jasmine I don't-'

'What was his name?'

'What?'

'It's the only question I ask the little boy in my dream, and I think he'll almost tell me but then,' she stopped, thinking of the woman coming out of the mist intent on snatching the little boy.

'Jasmine-' Daniel said.

'I should have spotted it earlier. He looked like you. You looked so young when you had him.'

Daniel's one hand went to his mouth and stifled a desperate noise, like an animal, while the other stretched out towards Jasmine. He sensed she was unravelling from her duvet to come to him, but he stopped her. 'No, don't.' He paused. 'His name is Seth.'

Jasmine went to her dream in her head and inserted the name in the little boy's mouth. 'I went to the archive,' she said softly, 'I had to know if my dream was real or not.'

'What was it that made you ask the question?'

She raised her eyes and met his. 'You told me the safe word.'

'Big red lollipop.' It was a whisper, but Jasmine heard it clearly enough.

'The little…Seth had one in my dream, and I saw it again in the archive.'

'He did. Seth loves them. I remember getting him one from the fair that day. Oh God, we were so young, Pat and me. We got married at seventeen. Maybe we were too young for kids.'

'Daniel, you talk about Seth in the present tense. It's the second time now.'

'Do I?' Daniel asked, the energy seemed to leave his face all at once.

'Are Seth and Patricia in your sessions?' Jasmine felt a pang in her stomach at mentioning Patricia's name.

Daniel frowned. His eyes became dark under the thinning light and Jasmine felt them press heavily against her. 'She's not there. She's never in our sessions.' He raised a knee and perched his elbow on it so he could cradle his head on his open fingers.

'She left. She made her choice,' he continued.

Jasmine hated herself for finding satisfaction in his resentment. She swallowed hard and pulled the blankets closer to her neck, feeling very naked.

'She took her own life?' she asked.

'I did all I can. I gave her our son back, but it wasn't enough.'

Daniel breathed out. 'I was an heir to my father's business; one I had worked in and grew since I was sixteen years old. He died when I was eighteen and all of a sudden, I had three hundred staff looking to me for the next move. We got married a few months later, and Seth was born when we turned twenty. It was like life was on fast forward, but it was the best years of my life.

'But, when Seth...when what happened, happened, I sold it all. Nothing mattered to me anymore. I knew what I could do, what I could create, so I made The Room for us, for Pat and me. But she didn't see it like that.'

Jasmine thought about what he'd said. He couldn't bring Seth back from the dead but what he had done was create the next best thing. She winced as she remembered the craving inside her to see Mia again, the gentle touch of her fingers, the way she looked at her - like Jasmine was her entire world.

Every day, she fought the separation between the two worlds, the real and the created. When she'd left Mia after her first session, she was instantly desperate for the next time she would be able to see her again. She'd felt like she'd won the top prize, and she needed to keep her winning streak. That raw understanding with this man, although with so much more life experience, felt so intense. He was almost old enough to be her father, and yet it felt like their souls, their frailty, connected them more than she'd ever felt with Paulo.

'Myself, Will, and now you, are the only ones who will know why I truly created the Room. Jasmine, I can't let him go. I know you understand, and I know you have only had your first session, but I know you feel the pull that a parent feels.'

'You're right about that,' Jasmine admitted. 'I never felt it until that moment, and I was in the Room with Mia. I created her then and tricked myself into believing I'd already had three years with her. I honestly felt like I'd already had memories, backed up in my brain. It was so complete; there were no holes.'

'And you want to go back to her,' Daniel pointed out.

'I do, and that scares me a little. It means I'm choosing the Room over real life.'

'No! It's real.' He cupped both his hands against his mouth and held Jasmine in an intense stare.

'Daniel, the feelings are real. That thing inside you, that yearning is real. But there also must be a yearning to grieve. That's what Patricia needed, surely? I know you didn't mean to, but she was denied her grief every time she went to the Room. You must see that.'

He was shaking his head, but a smile emerged from behind his gathered hands. 'Jasmine, what are you really scared of?'

She glanced down at her busy fingers, as though the answer was hidden beneath the folds of the duvet. 'I'm scared of losing this understanding of what it is you've created. Of being so far down a well that I can't scramble back out.'

'You have nothing to fear. You create that reality. You're the architect in your Room.'

'I'm not scared of the things I create in The Room. I'm scared of what's left for me in the real world when I close the door.'

Daniel was silent. And in that silence, Jasmine knew there was very little for him in this world. Even what they had shared together, and the way they looked at each other wouldn't be enough. His world, his meaning rested in the cold memory of a child long gone.

Jasmine felt sick at the thought. Was she close to ending up like that? What was it that separated her from Daniel or from the others who yearned for the Room? The pull she felt to see Mia again was far-reaching and suffocating to her senses, but it was pure in her mind. She didn't have to think of anything. It was like a dreamless sleep where she didn't have to think about the world she was leaving. With the Room gone maybe the only promise of purity and peace from what was real was the other side of The Radisson Hotel rooftop.

'I made a promise that you should never be scared again,' Daniel said. His voice was shaky and unsure.

'A promise? To who?' Jasmine asked.

'To Seth. After, when I saw him the first time in The Room. I made it to Seth to watch over you.'

The Room

'Daniel, I don't-'

'You tried to save him. You Jasmine, you were the only one of us who saw what that woman was trying to do, and you tried. You had cuts on your hand where he had held onto you, and you to him.' He held out his palm towards her. 'They were little crescent moons, of his tiny fingernails, all over your palms.'

Still looking at his hands, he said, 'To my eternal shame we were his parents, we were supposed to look after him, and we failed him. But you, you did all you could.'

A spark of realisation rose through her body. 'Your father didn't teach you that game, did he?'

'What game?'

'The footsteps game. That day you came into the café was for real. You weren't playing any game, and it wasn't random. You came in for a reason.'

'Jasmine, the...' Daniel fell over his own words, reluctant to let them go. He took a deep breath. 'I made a promise.'

'To look after me? Daniel, you made that promise years ago. You're...you're almost fifteen years older than me, and I feel like I'm explaining this to a child. I'm trying to get my head around this. All this time you've been watching me?'

Jasmine took a deep breath and then continued, 'And now I find you in my life. You're more than a fucking guardian, watching out for me. We did...the thing in the shower, the way you've been with me. It hasn't felt like watching over me, it's felt like-'

'Love?' Daniel looked up from his hands. Jasmine breathed in sharply. He continued. 'Because that's what it feels like for me. I have looked after you for years, at a distance. I want to look after you now. Completely.'

'But this...this isn't fair,' she stuttered. 'It isn't right. You've done me so much good, you've helped me so much, but you also lied to me, Daniel. I don't know how to think, how to feel.' She paused. 'Why did you come into the café that day?'

The warmth of the duvet seemed to leave her body as she spent a few moments with the question and started to form her answer. As the idea percolated in her mind, she felt bile rising in her mouth and through tears formed, the whole room seemed to reflect wild kaleidoscope lights that stabbed at her irises. She pulled her knees up and struggled to free herself from the duvet and get to her feet. Naked, she ran to the other side of the bed and pulled on her top. Daniel was already behind her; his arms stretched to steady her, the towel still twisted around his middle.

'It was you,' she gasped, fighting against his grip. 'Let me go. I need to get out of here.'

'No, you don't,' he replied. 'Right here and right now is the only place you need to be. We love each other, Jasmine, and I take care of you. And that's all that we need to be the best parents to Seth and Mia.'

Jasmine turned around in his hold and felt him loosen his arms. She looked up at him. They were both struggling with tears. Daniel gently wiped hers from her cheek. 'It was you, wasn't it? Tell me!' she pleaded.

His silence was enough for her to comprehend without the burden of saying the words.

You were the man in the window. You were watching me.

'How did you know I wouldn't jump?'

'I didn't.' He reached out for her arm. 'But I knew when you stepped back from the ledge that I had to do something. I had to try. It felt like a second chance for me.'

'I'm not Seth. I'm not your failed project.'

'It's okay,' he said, finally backing away. He stood across from her on the other side of the bed.

'So, you're here to watch over me? Liked some *fucked up pretend* God?'

'I've given you everything!' Daniel banged his hand against the wall. The sound reverberated around the high ceilings. 'Jesus, yes I may have kept some truth from you, but I've given you a job, a life. You have money for yourself now, for your mother.'

He sunk onto the bed and wiped his hand through his hair, raw and red from hitting the wall. His face was creased with concern. The lips she had kissed only a few moments ago were now thin and focused. He breathed in.

'I've given you me. And I've given you Mia.'

'You couldn't just be my friend? You couldn't just call out to me from that building, to tell me not to jump? You couldn't tell me that you'd been…stalking me for years. Why didn't you tell me the truth?'

'The truth. The whole truth and nothing but? That would have been quite an introduction, wouldn't it?' He paused. 'It was too soon for me, Jasmine. I'd have to relive some of what happened to Seth and Patricia. I'll be honest with you; I wasn't sure if you'd recognise me. That's why I gave you my business card that day in the park. If you had recognised me, and my name, I'm sure things would have been different, I would have been more honest. But you didn't and I…I didn't know what was best, but I knew that you needed me. It was my chance to be true to Seth, to look after you.'

'I still…I still don't understand.'

His face shifted from that thin, curious line of deep thought to raw and open, like a rabbit in headlights. He crawled towards her, and put his hands on her waist, staring up at her. He was almost at her shoulder height.

'Jasmine, think about, please. You can have everything you ever wanted. You can have it all. You'll never have to worry about money, about bills. You'll never have to work at a shitty cafe again. You can wear silk dresses and dance with me forever.' He squeezed her waist tighter. 'I give you me. I give you all of me. And I offer you Mia. Just…just stay. And I'll make your life perfect.'

Mia. She looked down at this broken, mature man and twirled the gentle curl that had formed on his forehead. She could leave him and return to her normal life that had sent her to the top of the Radisson Blu.

Or, she could have everything? She barely whispered the words, but Daniel heard them, and his thin lips curled into a smile.

'I want to see Mia again.'

CHAPTER 25

Mia flew from Jasmine's hands as soon as she got wind of the game, and she ran. The house was familiar to them both, but it was Mia who knew all the nooks where she could disappear, only to giggle and give herself away. Jasmine didn't let on about her daughter's signature slip up; if it weren't for laughter around every corner of the old house, she'd never find Mia at all.

'Okay,' Jasmine said, her voice echoing off the dark oak panels. 'Just one more time.'

If Mia was disappointed, she hid it well behind soft dark eyes and a smile that bubbled with spit. 'Turn around,' Mia said, 'and count the shoes of a millipede.'

'That's a lot of shoes,' Jasmine replied.

'You better get started,' Mia returned proudly. 'You'll never find me. Not this time.'

Jasmine turned away, and with hands over her eyes, she started counting. By the time she got to twenty, her voice had faded into the woodwork. Around every corner, Jasmine saw the pale sky-blue dress disappear, and heard the padded footfalls of slippers on thick carpet.

'I'm coming,' Jasmine called, said only to listen to her daughter shriek with excitement from around another corner. Jasmine slowed now, hearing the scramble of little feet up some stairs. She knew Mia was going for the Attic.

The Room

Nowhere else to go.

Jasmine pressed her ear to the old door and listened for the frantic scramble and indecision for the perfect hiding spot to cease. But there was no sound; it was as though someone had hit the mute button.

The door moved in its frame. Jasmine stood back. It looked like the door was flexing in its wooden structure, pulling at its hinges. 'Mia.' It came out as a whisper from Jasmine's lips. She threw herself against the door, and it burst open, helped by a fierce November wind.

Jasmine was outside, high up overlooking the city. The wind whipped as it always had, playing with her hair.

Mia stood motionless on the ledge of the Radisson Blu Hotel. Jasmine couldn't move. She opened her mouth to call for her daughter, but no sound came. Mia slowly turned her head. Her smile was the most beautiful thing Jasmine had ever seen, and it moved as she said, 'You'll never find me.' Just then, Jasmine saw the big red lollipop in her hand.

Mia didn't jump. She stepped lightly and silently off the edge.

CHAPTER 26

About the same time Jasmine had found sleep again in Daniel's arms that night, after she'd woken bathed in sweat due to the vision of Mia on top of the Radisson Blu, was the time that Emma's name appeared across the cracked screen of Jasmine's phone. The phone lay too close to her body as it vibrated and caused her to stir. Daniel caught it just in time before her eyes opened fully.

'What is it?' she managed, her face buried in his neck.

Daniel thumbed the cracked screen just to see if it would cut him. He made a mental note to get her a new one; not this mess of old technology and broken glass. This didn't suit *his* Jasmine. It suited the girl from the bad cafe.

He looked at the name on the phone and slid it off to the right. Then, he pressed the uppermost side button until the phone declared it would switch off.

He squeezed her; 'nothing. Not important.'

*

Wet, panicky tears on Emma's face were highlighted blue against the cold, unfriendly light of her phone. Just before the screen went dead, she held in her hand a picture of Jasmine, a raised glass in hand, smiling straight down the camera. She'd taken the photograph the night of Daniel's party. They had exchanged numbers and insisted, as instant best friends do, to keep in touch. Only now, when Emma needed her new best friend the most, was she left alone, her back pressed against a tree.

The street, her street, was wide and long. A buzz hung in the air; a sound that only existed in the absence of the busy bustle of daylight hours and the splutter of impatient traffic that scarred every day. And through that buzz, Emma heard the voice she'd run from; *his* voice.

She moved her head away from the tree trunk so she could see down the street to the car - and the man resting against it.

But this couldn't be, she thought. She slid down to a squat and pressed redial on her phone once again. No answer.

'Get up and run,' she said in a low voice to herself, 'and don't look back.' She struggled to her feet, sticking close to the tree and the cover it gave. With her hand spread against the thick tree bark, she tilted her head out to look back down the street in the direction of her house. The car stood still and quiet under a pool of yellow light, but there was no one leaning on it. He was *gone*.

Emma stepped out into the road to get a broader view of the street. It was a vision; a nightmare, in reality, Emma thought to herself as she counted off her steps and the click-click sound they made on the road. She'd had visions like that one, *of him,* all the time before she started her sessions with Daniel.

The air became still, and all sound seemed to be swallowed up and replaced by the heavy breathing of someone close behind her. Emma's eyes dropped and began to will her feet to move. *Faster, faster.* She looked back across the road and caught the silhouette of a figure blended with the tree she'd just been hiding behind.

The man in the shadow moved a hand into the streetlight and seemed to stroke the tree that Emma had used to conceal herself. His face became washed in the streetlight as he brought it closer to the tree. Emma couldn't move.

His hair was different; the greasy black strands were now flecked with charcoal grey, but the same disjointed chin was accentuated by his goatee and twitching smile. He took an exaggerated intake through his nose, arching his back as he threw back his head.

'Some things you just never forget.' Alex Pevestone flashed his teeth, bringing wet lips together as he watched her.

Emma hurled herself into the road and the path of a car. The screeching tyres cut through everything the night had to offer, causing Emma to cover her ears. As the car lurched and settled, Emma all but fell across the bonnet. With a mixture of exhaustion and relief, she found herself smiling at the wide-eyed driver staring out at her; the sign on the roof of the car said in shining black letters; 'TAXI.'.

Emma whirled around and levered the back door open.

'Are you off your fucking trolley?' the cab driver demanded, twisting round in his seat. 'I almost killed you.'

'Look, I'm grateful you didn't kill me, but do you see that man out there?' She pointed to Pevestone, the back of his coat visible in the distance. 'I'm pretty sure he *does* want to kill me.'

The driver looked behind him and saw Alex Pevestone's figure approaching; he had broken into a jog now. 'Alright, bab. Fasten your seatbelt.'

The Room

The car swerved in and out of the Birmingham streets.

'So that's your boyfriend, is it? Seems nice.' A glance through his mirror into the back showed that Emma wasn't in that kind of mood. Her face was painted with discoloured tears. 'Listen,' the driver said, slowing down to stop, 'do you want me to take you to the cop shop?'

Emma felt the car slow. 'No, don't stop,' she said. She twisted herself to look out of the back window. 'He could be following us. He has a car.'

'Oka, bab, but I've checked that mirror, and nobody is following us. I can guarantee that.' He watched as Emma fumbled in her coat for her phone. 'Look, when you jumped onto then into my car, I was just closing down my shift, so I'm on my way home, but before that I need a place to drop you off. I can see you've had a bad night and as long as you don't take the piss, I'll drop you, no charge. But I do need to know where you're going.'

She handed the driver her phone. 'Can you take me there, please?'

He took her phone and studied the address, 'yeah I can do that.' He handed the phone back to Emma, and she killed the light from it immediately and fell back into her seat, hoping that if she closed her eyes, she would catch a few minutes of sleep, quiet and unfettered by a past that had just shown up outside her own house.

*

Jasmine pushed against what was left of the gate. It buckled and scraped loudly against the path, scoring over the same arc pattern in the concrete.

She staggered along the path, more with tiredness than the half bottle of wine her and Daniel had taken on and the restlessness she felt over her latest Room session, and the dreams of Mia that followed. Eventually, unable to find any more comfort in his arms, she'd picked up her phone and discovered her missed calls. The latest call was from Claire; and that was enough to jar her from any fragments of sleep that remained.

With one hand negotiating the gate and the other pressing the phone to her ear, she spoke softly and reassuringly.

'Don't worry Claire. I'm here now, and I'll go up and check on her right away.' Jasmine fumbled at the door, searching for a key, eager to finish the call and tuck her phone away. 'You see to Sid and let me know how it turns out.' She hated the way that sounded. As much as she disliked Claire's husband, the way she said it seemed to trivialise Sid's sudden illness, brought on by emphysema, and more importantly, how it affected his wife.

`I'm on my way,' is what Jasmine had told her as she wrestled with her clothes in the quiet of Daniel's bedroom, 'Worst case, there'll be a thirty-minute gap where she'll be on her own, and she'll be most likely asleep through it. Mother won't even notice the shift change.' Jasmine could hear the relief in Claire's voice and the reluctance to agree.

Claire was now doing the night shifts with Myriam, and Jasmine had also recruited another carer - someone Claire trusted - to

The Room

look after her mother while they both rested or were at work. And Myriam had been doing well; the doctors were impressed, and although the care was palliative, they thought if she kept up her strength that she would increase her life expectancy. It seemed that money could buy you time. But there was something in the panic of receiving the call from Claire that blinkered her from the rest of the missed calls listed down her phone; the dozens of calls from her new friend, Emma.

Eventually the call ended, and the phone went dark, as did the porch outside the door. A smudge of orange bubbled through curved glass from the hall lamp that would continue through the night. With a free hand, she forced her fingers against her pocket, and the key pushed up and out.

'Shit!' The key flashed and tumbled gracefully out of her hand and disappeared into the early morning gloomy cast. 'Shit, shit, shit,' she said as she bent to search for it. From behind her, the shadows came alive and moved unnaturally, as another hand reached for the fallen key.

Jasmine screamed as her hand brushed an outreached arm. She jumped to her feet and slammed herself against the house, the wind knocked clean out of her. Out of the shadow and into the welcoming light of the hall lamp stepped Emma. She held the lost key out to Jasmine, and only half-smiled; her face quickly melting into a sorrow that looked so unnatural on the contours of her perfectly proportioned face.

Jasmine hadn't time to laugh or chastise her new friend for the scare she'd given her. She could see Emma was broken. Jasmine rushed to her and held her close. 'Emma. What on earth are you doing here?'

Emma sobbed against her. 'He's back; he's back.' Jasmine held her tight as she eased her into the house and sank with her to the floor. She knew it was pointless asking her the question of who she was talking about until she could find her a place to settle.

Jasmine sat back against the far wall of the narrow hallway and took her in. 'Emma, you are going to stay here tonight,' she said. She was close enough to reach over and raise Emma's chin with her fingers. 'Do you hear me? Stay with me.'

Emma nodded her head. 'I'm sorry for landing like this,' she said as she pushed herself to her feet. Her voice was raspy and weak. 'I just didn't know where else to go.'

Jasmine frowned; this beautiful woman didn't have anywhere to go? She didn't know if she was lying, but looking at her face, beaten by tears, she needed *someone.*

'Come on,' she said, linking arms with Emma and walking to the foot of the stairs. 'We'll talk - but first, we're going to run a bath. You look like you've run a couple of marathons.'

'It's been a tough night,' she hesitated before putting a foot on the first step,' but I…I don't-'

'I know you don't have to tell me anything.' Jasmine interrupted, 'but if it feels right, then you'll tell me. I'll ask - but then the rest is up to you. I'm not here to hurt you. You came here for help. Now, that's something.'

The Room

The two women climbed the stairs, holding onto each other.

*

Jasmine had stopped going into the living room ever since she'd given it over to Claire for her overnight stays. She fumbled with a bottle of wine and two glasses from the kitchen, managing to end a call with Claire and flip off the harsh kitchen light. She would get herself a connected chip next month; she said to herself as she saw her cracked phone, battered and bruised, on the side of the armchair. It seemed that it was the only thing she hadn't replaced since working at The Room, and Jasmine toughed the screen gently, fondly, as if it was an old friend.

The bottom half of the house fell into darkness except for the faithful hall lamp that never slept as Jasmine ascended the stairs. When Jasmine popped her head into her bedroom, she expected to see Emma already in the pyjamas she'd laid out for her, but the room was empty. The three lamps spread out and created a pool of warm, welcoming light for the bed, the desk and the easy chair under the window. She placed the bottle and two glasses on the desk and left the room. She padded over to her mother's bedroom, pushed the door and stepped in.

Emma was wrapped in Jasmine's oversized robe, the hood in place and the polar bear ears bent forward, attentive. She sat in a wicker chair next to Myriam; an unmoved mound on the bed, just as Jasmine had left her. She noticed Jasmine approaching and flicked her head around.

'I'm sorry,' she whispered, her hands gripped the arms of the chair getting ready to heave herself out of it.

Jasmine laid a gentle hand across her shoulder. 'It's okay.'

'She was calling your name. I heard it from the landing.' Emma turned back to the heaped sheets on the bed. 'Of course, I knew your mum wasn't well. I shouldn't have come. You have enough to deal with.'

Jasmine gave her a reassuring squeeze on her shoulder, and at the same time, wondered how she had known her mother was ill. She couldn't remember telling her. Or had Daniel and his penchant for background checks supplied Emma with this information? Whatever it was, it didn't seem important as they watched her mother sleep. She *did* seem peaceful. And as Jasmine thought it, Emma spoke,

'She looks at peace, doesn't she? You can almost feel it.' Emma hesitated, searching for the right words, words that were appropriate in front of a dying woman and a sick woman's daughter. 'It's like-'

'It's soothing. Yes, I can feel it,' Jasmine finished. She sat on the bed, no longer intent on her mother. She looked at Emma and saw some of her youth returning in the brightness of her eyes. With an outstretched hand, Jasmine caught the top of Emma's arm. 'I'm going to ask you. Who's back? You said he's back.'

Darkness appeared in Emma's eyes. It may have been the reflected gloom of the early morning and the gentle lights that rested the house, but it was there. Emma took up Jasmine's hand and held it. 'I want to tell you.' She turned to look at Myriam lying still in the bed as though it would be the last time. She eventually pulled away from Myriam, adding, 'and I'm going to.'

*

The Room

Emma tucked herself in the armchair by the window, occasionally peeking past the ill-dragged curtain to the thinning sky outside. She held the glass of wine tight in two hands and sipped it gratefully.

In the quiet of the early light, Jasmine thought about Mia, the Mia she had created and put on the rooftop of the hotel. Was it a version of torturous grief that deep down she deserved and had been denying herself? She needed to see her again – happy, strong, carefree. Not the girl in her dreams. She felt the pull of the Room getting stronger. Every moment was drowned in thoughts of seeing Mia again.

'His name is Alex Pevestone.' Emma swallowed hard.

Jasmine sat upright. *Mr Smith*, she thought; *the man in the private file.* Jasmine nodded slightly as if for her to continue.

'I used to love riding my bike when I was little. There was a wood near where I lived.' Emma paused. 'I was twelve, and that year was the last time I went back to the wood. After that, we moved, and I had to change my name for other reasons.'

'What was your name, before?'

'Stephanie. Stephanie Milner. But, to be honest, it doesn't sound like me anymore. I prefer Emma. Stephanie was just twelve years of my life.'

By the end of Emma, or Stephanie's story, Jasmine was frozen. No amount of warmth from the radiator in her bedroom could penetrate her skin. She pulled her knees in tight to her chest and found she could no longer look at Emma. She knew that would pass, but for now she couldn't approach her friend until the images of Pevestone hanging over the blooded little girl and the smell of his breath still so real from her description had dwindled.

And Daniel had known about this the whole time. Was this another government project like Emma's rehabilitation? Jasmine's breath caught in her chest as she realised just how close she'd come to tell her that Pevestone was unofficially on the books.

'I don't need your thoughts on what I've told you. I've had years of therapy and more than one well-meaning textbook spouting professional with all the answers. What I need is a friend - and a favour, actually.'

'What is it?' Jasmine finally asked.

Emma put her glass on the floor and thrust her fists into the deep pockets of her robe.

'My last session is coming up, and I'd like you to be there.'

'Me? But why?'

'My sessions are always about changing my past and having a better future. And I want to be sure that something good, something true, from my present. I think having you there will trigger me into ending my experience there positively.'

Jasmine shuffled in her seat. This woman, this beautiful woman, was befriending her to the point of...well, Jasmine didn't quite know. It felt good to feel wanted. She felt the familiar warm suffocation of Sammy, forcing her to drink that last glass of wine, pushing her to go home when she'd found a man to leave with.

'Whether or not Daniel will let you come into the session is something else, but I would like a familiar face around.'

Jasmine managed a smile. 'I'll see if I can sweet talk him.'

'I need you to be there.'

Jasmine's mouth twitched. The words hit her hard. She remembered Betty, smiling serenely in the cafe and Martin's text she received on the rooftop. She was *still needed*.

'I understand; I'll be there.'

'I know you will.' Emma went back to the window now and played with the edge of the curtain, letting the dawn light dance around the bedroom.

Chapter 27

Now

On Harborne's high street, Michael stirred two sugars into his latte; it was a fatal attempt to make it taste just a little bit better. He raised a single eyebrow as he watched Harriet, sat opposite to him, her nails tapping on the wooden table.

'You look ridiculous, Harriet.'

'What?' She faced him, her gigantic sunglasses reflecting his own face.

'Don't you think you look more suspicious with those bloody things on your mug?'

'No, I don't actually, it's part of being *undercover*, Michael.'

'Just take the damn things off.'

'Fine. But I was just trying to be inconspicuous.' She removed them slowly, peering over the tops like a cartoon villain and setting them down next to her cup of coffee.

'Yeah, great job you did at being coy, wearing huge sunglasses indoors, in winter.'

Harriet didn't respond. Instead, her eyes darted around the cafe, squinting at every table.

Michael knew that she was looking out for Mr Derr. Through an extraordinary amount of social media searching and some unspeakably shady research from an ex-boyfriend, Harriet had managed to track down one single Facebook status that mentioned The Room on Share Street. It had been deleted by the user no more than an hour later, but it's dirty great big stamp had still stuck over the internet, or cloud, or whatever it was. And Harriet's majesty had come into play. She'd called Mr Derr, and asked him for a meeting.

'You know he thinks this is all official, alright? So, we've got to act like we are in the police, or better yet government. Let's get our back story right before this bloke gets here.'

Michael sighed. 'What did you tell him?'

'I just put on my sternest voice and said,' she coughed and said in a very deep, raspy tone, 'Mr. Derr, you need to meet with us as a matter of urgency. This is official business concerning The Room. I know you were a client of Daniel Burton, and we need information immediately.'

'So apart from thinking he's meeting Rod Stewart, did you tell him anything else about us?'

Harriet rolled her eyes. 'No. I just said I would meet him here; I would be with my colleague, get ready to answer some questions, blah, blah, blah.' She took a sip of coffee. 'He'll open up like a can of worms. He sounded really scared on the phone. This Room place, Powers.' She looked at Michael. 'The more I look into it, the weirder it seems. Do you think it's some sort of sex thing?'

Michael winced. Pevestone, yes, he could imagine him in some lurid underground gig. But Stephanie? It didn't make any sense.

'Doubt it. But something's not right with that place, I agree.'

'Shit!' Harriet practically squealed. 'That's him! He looks about twenty years older than his latest Facebook profile pic, but that's bloody him.'

'Well call him over, Harriet. And calm down, for Christ's sake.'

Mr Derr certainly didn't look like a sex criminal; like Michael remembered Alex Pevestone's appearance, but he knew that appearances could be deceiving. He had a face that reminded Michael of a Labrador – open and hopeful, with dark round eyes and sandy blonde hair. He was wearing a sharp suit, maroon in colour, with a white shirt and maroon tie intricately placed with perfect symmetry down the centre of his buttons. Harriet called out to him, and he smiled, awkwardly, in their direction.

'Ms Detective, sorry, I don't know your full name.' Mr Derr's voice was soft, warm. He reached a hand out to Harriet.

'Call me Charlie.' She said, her voice deepening. Michael rolled his eyes. 'And this is my colleague, Detective…Piddle.'

'Piddle. Right. Yes, I'm sorry I am a few minutes late, the traffic was mad.' He pulled up a chair and joined their table. 'I'm not too sure what you want from me, but I will try my hardest to help.'

Michael had met many criminals in his time, and this man didn't seem to fit the bill. He was polite; there was almost a kindness about him. Something didn't seem right.

'Cutting to the chase, Mr Derr,' Michael started, 'we know a lot about The Room – about Daniel Burton – and about many of his clients. But what we don't know is what you were all going there for. We know from public accounts that the place turned over huge revenues. Be honest, Mr. Derr, was it-'

'Was it a sex thing?' Harriet butted in, her eyes wide.

Mr. Derr looked flustered. 'No, goodness no it wasn't a...a sex thing.' He swallowed. 'Let me get this right – you still don't know what The Room actually was?'

Michael looked at Harriet. *They'd shit it,* he thought. He frowned at her; they needed this man to talk, and for that, they needed to appear like they knew more than...nothing.

'We know enough. But we want to hear your side of the story.' He was bluffing, the heat rising to his cheeks.

'I got into a lot of trouble for that Facebook status, you know. They almost took me off the books after that. Daniel was very secretive about The Room and its powers.'

'Powers?' Michael questioned.

The man fidgeted and played with the packet of sugar resting on the table. 'Yes. I'm sure you already know this, but The Room was special. I don't know how, and it would be far too technical for the likes of me, but it gave you dreams – it gave you everything you wanted. And that' why people used it, like me, I suppose.'

Mr Derr shrugged and continued. 'I didn't use it for...as you put it 'sex things', but it helped me with my confidence. I had a lot of trouble keeping girlfriends before The Room. And I'd go in, every week, and it would give me a life that I had always dreamed of – a wife, confidence. After a while, your reality and The Room exist within each other. And I became,' he paused, searching for the words. 'I believe I became what I always was. It just nudged me along a bit.'

'What do you mean 'it gave you everything you wanted'? Harriet leaned forward, 'was it some sort of drug? Health plan?'

The man frowned. 'Are you sure you two know what The Room really was? It sounds-'

'Charlie is just probing you with questions. It's part of standard detective procedure. Please continue, Mr. Derr.' Michael interrupted.

'OK. I guess... I guess there's no harm now, now that it's all over. But no, it wasn't a health plan, or drugs. Daniel tapped into my subconscious, and I would be able to experience anything I wanted in a one-hour session.'

'Like playing a video game?'

'Not at all.' Mr. Derr's eyes widened. 'It was real – it was more real than life itself. You ate, drank, slept. Sometimes an hour of The Room would be over two weeks for me in my sub-conscious brain. So, when I left after my hour, I would feel different; spectacular. I walked out after my first session and asked my colleague out on a date.' He held up his hand, a wedding band on his fourth finger. 'I wouldn't have done that without The Room.'

Michael stared at this man – he wasn't anything like Alex Pevestone. But then, a sinking feeling pushed into his stomach, and one question scarred his thoughts; *what would Pevestone have used The Room for?*

Chapter 28

Jasmine stretched out her body, stiff and awkward in the hospital seat. It had been over an hour since she'd gotten there, and the nurse was still nowhere in sight.

She picked at her cashmere jumper, a vain attempt to stop that feeling from sinking in again – that feeling she felt when she looked at her mother on the hospital bed in front of her. The cashmere felt so soft under her manicured nails, but as she watched her mother breathing through the tube strapped to her face, she felt a tug. Her shiny gel polish had chipped, revealing a sore nail underneath and had pulled her jumper's thread. A line, thin and pink like a scar, now ran across her cuff.

She hadn't meant to miss the calls from Claire. But Daniel had pulled her into his office in the late afternoon.

'Jasmine, you know it's terribly distracting having you working here, looking as you do.'

'I'm sorry, I can always wear a bin over my head, if that would help.'

Daniel grinned. 'Yes, well, as your boss I could always order you to do that. But it would hardly be satisfactory for our customers.' He had kissed her once, on the cheek, 'I trust that you'd like to see Mia again, Wilson?'

Jasmine had grinned, flushing at his scent and the closeness. Her body tingled. Mia, again, this was perfection. 'I only saw her yesterday. Are you…are you sure? I mean I'd love to-'

'Come over, once you're finished in the Hub of course.'

'Could I…' she paused. 'Could I not use The Room here, maybe? I've never seen past the Changing Room and I-'

'It's too risky.' Daniel said. He checked that the door to his office was locked, then lowered his voice. 'As I've said, Will isn't exactly aware of my other set up. I'd rather keep it that way. You understand?'

Jasmine's head was already filled with Mia's voice, her giggles, and the touch of her skin. She didn't need Share Street, if Daniel could give her that in the privacy of his flat. What was the problem?

'I've set it up, for you and Mia. I have business meetings to attend to, but I'll administer your drugs – and leave you to it.'

As soon as 5 pm had shown on her laptop, she had got into a taxi and rode the freight elevator up to Daniel's apartment, the single light bulb swaying gently like it was dancing with her. He'd greeted her with a kiss; strong and warm. When he took her across the apartment and to the panelled door, he held both her arms and squeezed them gently.

'Jasmine, I'm so glad you've chosen us.'

Jasmine laughed lightly. 'Course, nothing better than a mysterious man who gives me drugs.'

The Room

He'd smiled. 'Imagine if we could be a proper family – me, you, Seth, Mia.'

Jasmine was startled. Could that happen; could he mix an experience like that? She looked at Daniel. At that moment, all she cared about was being with Mia again.

'I have never felt anything like what I feel when I go into…when I sit in that armchair, Daniel. It's like–'

'Heaven' he interrupted. 'Now, come with me. I can't stay long, as I said. But I'll get you tucked in nicely.'

The way he had said that; the act of *tucking her in* like a child, made Jasmine's hair prickle at the back of her neck and an icy pain start in her temple. It was a turn of phrase, she thought, nothing *odd,* as he sat her down in the black leather chair and started to prepare the medication.

Once he'd left, a bubble of joy filled her stomach; it was like Christmas morning. The fog cleared and Mia ran through it, as bright as daylight. She had Mia to herself; it was the longest she'd ever left her Room experience go on for – a whole ten days. She'd counted the nights.

They'd play and talk and bicker. Daniel would come home from work with flowers; roses for her and chrysanthemums for Mia. They went to the Cotswolds for a *whole weekend.* She felt the grass dew on her calves as she sat, her legs out in front of her, watching Mia play with Daniel on the fields. She'd tasted the roast he'd made them; his family recipe, he'd said. When the light eventually shone too brightly, only four hours of real time had passed. But on Jasmine's phone, sat idle in her jacket, sixteen missed calls sat patiently.

The nurse coughed lightly as she entered the cubicle, forcing Jasmine out of her stupor.

'Hiya, Miss Wilson, is it? You look just like your mum.' The nurse nodded her head at the thin, frail woman on the bed. Jasmine shuddered.

'We couldn't get hold of you earlier, but an ambulance had to come and collect your mum from your home.' She rattled on as Jasmine stared at her mother's chest, moving up and down mechanically. Her mother had woken briefly, according to the nurse, but Jasmine had been too busy watching Mia twirl in her flowery dress to be there.

'We've administered some pain relief, and she's slept. Darlin', she's not in any discomfort, I know it's hard to see, but it is for the best – given the state she was in when she came in.' The nurse with pink ringed lips said, barely looking up from the clipboard. 'And I'm afraid that's all we can do.'

She looked around briefly at the bed, void of flowers, and void of love. There was one soft blue card from Claire that simply said "Get better soon. Best wishes, Claire x", and a growing stack of magazines on the side table.

'That woman, the carer is it? She came in when your mother was awake earlier.'

Jasmine felt her cheeks burn. 'I was at work. No one has actually told me why she's here though. I'm paying for round the clock care-'

'It's been a long day for you,' the nurse interrupted, looking at her. 'I'm sorry, Miss Wilson, but your mother is very poorly. She can't breathe on her own anymore. It's far better that she's here. We can make her comfortable.'

'It doesn't exactly look comfortable. It looks like that *thing* is breathing for her.'

'It is, well – it's aiding her. I'm sorry, I know this must be very hard for you, Miss Wilson. But it's…it's a matter of hours I'm afraid.'

Her pager beeped, and she tutted loudly, one hand on her hip and the other reading the small message on the front. 'Sorry I've got to go. I'll be back soon. The carer – Claire was it? She said she'd left a few things in the cupboard there.'

Jasmine opened the small cupboard next to her. It spilt with magazines; old copies of Woman's Weekly and horse-riding magazines. Underneath them was a little notepad. The pages were ripped and turned at the edges. The front cover said two words, 'Mrs Wilson'.

Even in those two words, she knew this was Claire's pad. She carried it into the house most days, jotting notes about medication, or how her mother was doing. She opened the tartan cover, thin and cheap, like most of the things that Claire used, hardly daring to spend money on herself, and looked at the first pages.

Date: 12/06/2027

Details: Mrs Wilson was unresponsive and challenging today, called me a "B" for giving her medication twenty minutes late! I was washing up and hadn't noticed the time. She watched black and white movies all day until Jasmine came home. She didn't want to talk to her daughter, so she asked me to move her in her bedroom. I put the movies on for her and left.

There were more notes, detailing medication, and her moods. But Jasmine stopped as she saw the date in pen – the 23rd of August.

Date: 23/08/2027

Details: Mrs W smiled at me when I walked through the door. She had been crying, there were watermarks down her cheeks, and she seemed vulnerable. I fetched her some food, and we sat in silence as she picked her sandwich apart. It was only ham and cheese, but she made a real meal of it.

We were watching telly, Loose Women, and Fern Cotton was on, she had a new book out about parenting, I think. And Mrs W just started crying again. I switched it off and was quite stern with her, what was wrong, I said, what's going on? She looked at me with those eyes, all brown and smoky, and she said "I don't think I know how to love anymore."

I say, what do you mean? There're no blokes around, and her and J never really talk, but it's her daughter, she has to love her. And she says:

"I'm going to leave her alone. And it's best, because she doesn't need a mother like me." She starts to cry again, and it's not for effect. She's blubbering, I've never seen her like this. I don't say anything for a while. Then I say, and it sounds horrible when I think back, but I said it: "She needs you as a Mother, Mrs W. Whether you want to be her mother or not."

Then she stares at the blank TV screen. "I used to be good. We used to have so much fun, her, me, and him. But do you know how hard it is raising a child that hates you? That blames you for her father going away and for all the mistakes you've made along the way? You end up resenting them as much as they resent you. And I would do anything to not be alone with her. I would bring anyone home, she'd just stare at the men like they were orphans. It was like she pitied them half the time. And I didn't want to be a mother anymore. I couldn't even look after myself."

She's just staring at the TV, her eyes flickering from side to side like she's watching something on it, but there's nothing there.

"She's beautiful, isn't she?"

I nod, I can't think of anything to say.

"When I go" She's looking at me again, "When I go, can you tell her I'm sorry, tell her that I regret not being a mother to her?"

I nod again. Her eyes flicker back to the TV screen, and it's like she turns back into stone. I try and hand her a tissue, but she bats me away with strong hands, considering how thin she has gotten. I put the TV back on, and we watch the rest of *Loose Women* in silence.

When 5 pm comes, I'm waiting for J for ages. Sid keeps texting me, telling me to go home, but I can't. I can't leave Mrs W. J finally comes at 6.15, and her eyes are all wild like her head's gone crazy, she's got mascara all down her face. She looks at me like she'd forgotten I existed, and then thanks me, for nothing in particular, and she goes into the lounge, sees her mother is asleep then comes back into the hallway, goes into her bedroom and just slams her bedroom door shut.

I stand outside her bedroom door, listening to her music, blaring and I want to knock, my hands out waiting to knock, but then Sid rings, and I know he won't stop till I answer."

Jasmine used her cashmere sleeve cuff to stem the flow of tears. She remembered that day. It was when she'd told Paolo about her baby; their baby. He'd said he didn't want it, that he had a life to live and that they weren't part of it. She hadn't even realised she had kept Claire waiting, or that her mother had…she thought for the words. She hadn't realised her mother had cared. She looked at the woman on the bed and sighed deeply.

'All these years, not understanding each other, hey mum.'

The nurse had said *she had hours left*. Jasmine didn't want her mother to die here, and now their home didn't seem enough either. She knew what she had to do.

Fumbling her mother's thin body into the wheelchair that lay unused at the mouth of the ward wasn't as hard as driving the wheelchair through the hospital corridors. The strewn chair was abandoned for a reason; one of the wheels would occasionally stop, causing her mother's sleeping body to jolt harshly. The oxygen canister sat on her mother's lap, bobbing gently with the movement.

Jasmine bowed her head as they passed several doctors. But nothing. They were too busy with paperwork and life and death to worry about the woman taking her sleeping mother down the corridor. After passing the receptionist, Jasmine stood outside in the bracing cold. She took off her jacket and wrapped it over her mother.

'Right…now what?' she said to herself.

A taxi pulled in, and a young couple fall out, the woman resting her hand on her swollen belly. Jasmine pushed her mother closer.

'I ain't taking you two anywhere.' The taxi driver rested his eyes over Jasmine's mother's hospital bands, the blue bruises on her thin hands.

The Room

'It's three miles away, max. And I'll give you £50.'

The driver looks at his watch. 'Make it £100 and you've got a deal.'

'Fine. Just, help me in with her, will you?'

They pulled up outside Daniel's apartment block. A harsh blue light lit the modern front door, heading to the freight elevator.

'Can you...can you wait for us? We'll be an hour at the most. We just need to do something.'

The driver looked at his watch again. It was 9 p.m. on a Wednesday night, and a bubble of annoyance rose in Jasmine's chest. It was hardly prime time for taxis.

'Jesus, I don't have time for this. I'll give you another £50?'

He winced. 'Yeah, but y'know, getting that bird out of the back of the cab, and then in again, yeouch.' The driver put a hand on the bottom of his back and bent forward slightly. It was like watching a bad actor in a TV drama.

'Fine. Another £100.'

He smiled and straightened up. 'I'll be here, one hour, yeah?'

*

'You didn't see anyone outside, did you?' Daniel said,

'No, it was deserted. Why? Does it matter? I really need to get mum-'

'I'd have appreciated a call at least. Jesus, Jasmine, I was in the middle of some business. Luckily, my…my meetings have finished.'

Jasmine frowned. Daniel pulled at his tie, freeing it from his collar and setting it down on the work surface. The city glittered behind him in the windows, but he looked matte, sallow.

'I'm sorry, I… the nurse said she only had a matter of hours left, and I thought I'd take her here, I needed to bring her here so she can experience it.'

Daniel sighed, and piece by piece as the air expelled out of his lungs, he formed himself together again. His shoulder straightened, and a sharp smile spread across his lips.

'Of course. You know I would do anything for you, Jasmine. Let's get your mother into the chair. There's still time.'

They passed through the heavy panelled door, with Daniel holding her mother in his arms, followed by Jasmine and the oxygen tank. He folded her into the black leather chair and pressed her thin, pale arm onto the hard leather armrest. It glowed blue, gently, like the reflection from a swimming pool.

'It'll take a few moments for the medication to enter her bloodstream.' He looked at Jasmine, mascara marks down her cheeks and nodded. 'I've given her something else. It will mean she could – if her body allows – talk through her experience. It engaged a sort of 'sleep talking' experience if you will.'

'But, it's her experience, I don't want to intrude-'

'I think you'll want to hear it. If it's the last thing you two do together, it seems only fair that you are part of it.'

Jasmine looked at him. 'You can't hear my experiences, right?'

'No. I have only ever done this one other time. Please, Jasmine. Sit. I will be in my office if you need me.'

Jasmine heard the door click behind her. She pushed herself into the corner of the room, the hardwood panelling cold against her back and hugged her legs, her eyes fixed on her mother, breathing deeply from the oxygen mask.

'Is that you in the corner, Jasmine?'

Her face was so still, but her mouth was moving and her voice strong, stronger than it has been for months, even with it being covered by the mask and muffled. Jasmine jumped up, tiptoeing closer to her. Her eyes were moving quickly behind her pale eyelids.

'I know you're in there.' Her eyes moved faster, rapidly changing direction under the papery eyelids. 'It's just you and me now, and that's OK. Because we are going to look after one another, aren't we?'

Jasmine reached out and grabbed her mother's hand.

'I know he's gone, but it's OK. I won't leave you. We're Batman and Robin now.'

Jasmine gulped for air as her mother smiled beneath the mask. She was re-enacting the day Jasmine's father had left. At the time, Jasmine had crawled into the wardrobe. Her mother hadn't looked for her, instead she had left the house and not returned for two whole days. But this time, she stayed.

'I know, mum.' Jasmine whispered. 'I know you won't leave me.'

Chapter 29

The last time Jasmine was at The Sterling Park Cemetery, she was just a fifteen-year-old girl hanging onto Betty Aldhart's arm. It was a beautiful day when they put Freddie in the ground. That was one of the things she remembered most about that day. It wasn't the fits and starts with which the coffin was lowered into the regulation-sized hole, but it was how the sunlight bounced off the wooden box.

The other thing Jasmine remembered was the way Betty had dug her fingers into Jasmine's arm as the box was lowered into the ground. She remembered Betty looking up into the cloudless sky and saying, 'kids shouldn't be here on a day like this. They should be out playing'. It was then that Betty looked down into the grave and, as though she was seeing it for the first time, she shouted her boy's name.

Moments after, Betty held Jasmine close. It was as tender as ever her own mother had offered. It seemed right that Betty knew that her role as a mother, the instinct that all mothers share, wasn't to be put away after Freddie's passing. Jasmine needed her, just as much as she needed Jasmine.

It was the way that Betty held her close that raced through Jasmine's mind as she now stood in Sterling Park thirteen years later at her mother's graveside. Peering down at the white oak box, she tried to recall a time that she had been held by her mother in that way; the kind of clinch that held everything in and kept all the stuff safe from the naked world. Betty wasn't there, standing next to her this day. She hadn't been back to Sterling since they laid Freddie down. She wasn't one of those mothers who visited once a week; same time, rain or shine. Instead, Betty Aldhart had allowed herself, over time, to believe that it wasn't real; that her Freddie would be in for tea.

Without Betty by her side, Jasmine stood alone in her crowd of fellow mourners. There was a frost that hung and pressed heavy in the trees and the overhanging grass that reached down into Myriam's grave.

The sound of grass crunching under Father McGill's busy feet permeated his words for Myriam. Diamond drops of rain clung to his heavy coat holding all but the bottom of his cassock in from the bitter wind. Behind her, Jasmine sensed many eyes; there was a mixture of cold and warm stares and the sound of a baby crying. She turned to see Claire, who reached out a black leather gloved hand and squeezed her arm. Beyond, she saw the vacant stares of her past in the form of Sammy and her old boss Martin. The baby's cry came from the back of the thin line of mourners and was soft and threatening, building to something worthy of protest against the bite of the cold morning.

Paolo held the bundle tight against his body and pointed up into the sagging trees to distract his daughter. It didn't work. He shifted the towel from one shoulder to the other as the baby stretched and kicked against being held. Jasmine caught his eye, and they both seemed to exchange the same thin, useless smile. She hadn't seen Paolo or Sammy since that night she had gone to return Sammy's key, and in truth, hadn't given them much thought in the following months. It had surprised her how easily she had welcomed the closing of that particular chapter in her life. With renewed energy, she had embraced her new job and met new people. She'd found a lover in Daniel and a friendship in Will. She had her own daughter now, for one hour every week. And this time, Mia was hers only; she didn't have to share her with anyone.

A splash of red flitted between the collapsing gravestones somewhere beyond the mourners and up against the looming church. It was a little girl, skipping behind the aged stones which were weighted with moss and decorated with powdered frost. A little girl in a thick red coat with an attached hood pulled over her head, but not quite enough to cover the thick bouncing curls. In her hands, she was holding a small bunch of daisies.

She has come out of The Room and found me.

Jasmine's eyes met Mia's from a long distance, but she saw the unmistakable smile in her daughter's face. Through fresh tears, Jasmine couldn't help but let out a spluttering laugh which caused Father McGill to look up from his hymnal. But she didn't notice his glances; she didn't even flinch at the sound of Claire calling out to her, or the light brush of Claire's fingers as Jasmine moved away. She cut through the parting bodies and stepped lightly between the crooked stones towards Mia, still bobbing up and down quickly, picking her flowers. Mia let out another excited giggle at seeing her mother coming towards her.

Ashes to Ashes, dust to dust

In the distance, the awkward stuttering of the priest's voice faded into the rustle of the trees and the ripple of bewildered onlookers.

Jasmine picked up the pace. She called Mia's name around each corner and curve of the old building. She tried the main door, the side door; they were all locked. After a full circle of the church, she settled on the step by the central doorway. The stone was cold through her coat, but she hardly noticed nor cared. From this vantage point,

Jasmine could look down through the park. It was crowded with headstones; she could just about see the mourners clustered by her mother's own grave.

She moved against the cold step, steadying herself with her hands. As she did, her fingers touched something cold, and without realising what the small lump was, she recoiled and then drew closer. Her finger moved slowly over a small clump of frozen daisies. They were hard to the touch and fastened with the cold to the stone.

She shifted her attention back to the park before her and settled her breathing. She opened her ears to the sounds of the birds' songs. Jasmine was still smiling. She thought of Mia dancing mischievously amongst the stones. She spoke into the cold air on plumes of condensation, a message for Mia.

'Why did you go, little bear? I wanted to see you again.'

From somewhere behind the church, she heard a familiar voice. Only when Claire called her name did she realise who it was.

'Jasmine? What on earth are you doing here?' Claire's foundation on her forehead was thick and creased over her natural wrinkles.

'I thought I saw-'

'You were calling out someone's name, walking after something.' Claire shuddered. 'It was like you were chasing a ghost. Was it - did you think you saw your mum?'

'No.' Jasmine looked at the daisies again. 'I saw a little girl.'

The Room

'There was no little girl, Jas!' Claire lifted her palms and shrugged. 'What's gotten into you? I try to talk to you about Myriam, and you don't want to know. You've left everyone there, by her grave, all of your friends, to chase after nothing.'

Jasmine was still looking at the daisies. They *were real,* weren't they? She squinted at the churchyard; this was all real, too, right? Her heart started to beat faster.

'It's like you don't even care about your mum. I know that sounds terrible, but Jas you're not acting... you're not yourself.'

'There was a little girl here. I swear – she had a red coat on, and black hair like mine.' Jasmine said, ignoring Claire.

Claire sighed. 'I miss Myriam, y'know. But I also miss you. You're never around anymore since this new job, and something about it doesn't seem...it doesn't seem rational that you're suddenly earning so much and your head's in the clouds-'

'You don't think I can be successful?' Jasmine shot back at Claire.

'I didn't say that.' Claire paused. 'I just know you've been different. You had hardly seen your mum awake since you started that job, and she missed you dearly-'

'So I'm a terrible daughter – for paying for her care, for working too hard?'

'I didn't say that.'

'Well it's not like you'll be around anymore. Now mum's gone.'

'I'll still look out for you, Jas, you must know that.' Claire frowned. 'I just want you to come back to us – come back to reality.'

She didn't answer Claire. Instead, she rose to her feet and started down towards the main road, hearing Claire calling her name after her.

*

'Don't you like it?' Daniel sat opposite Jasmine.

Jasmine was staring hard at the green beans on her fork. She shifted her gaze to Daniel. 'Sorry, what?'

'Rough day so far,' he said. It wasn't a question; that would have been ridiculous.

Jasmine looked back down at her plate. 'Yes, you could say that. Look, I'm sorry, I'm just either not very hungry, or I'm not in the mood. I'm having a bit of trouble thinking straight.'

Daniel's hand covered hers, and she set her fork to rest on her plate. Her phone came to life, and a picture of Claire shook and rattled on the tabletop.

'Fourth time for Claire,' Daniel said. 'Do you want me to get it? She's probably worried.'

'No,' Jasmine said, 'I just need to know how to turn this damn thing off.'

Daniel took the phone from her and pressed the two buttons to put the phone into hiding. 'That should do it,' he said as he gathered the plates and wandered over to the counter.

She smiled thinly, visibly relaxing as she stretched her arms along the counter and watched Daniel; her eyes focussed intently on him as he went about clearing the kitchen work surfaces.

'You know, there is so much I don't know about you. For example, I didn't know you can cook.'

'Ah yes, now we're getting to my darkest secrets,' he teased. 'I have Will to thank for that. He's always been my fiercest critic with a mothering complex.' Daniel looked over and saw that Jasmine wasn't moved by what he'd said about Will. 'Any other things you didn't know about me?'

She watched him closely. 'I'm sure there are lots I still have to learn. But I do have a secret.' She breathed in sharply. 'I didn't invite you and Will to the funeral, because the people there, I think of them as part of my old life. I just wanted to keep it separate.'

Daniel turned and leaned against the counter. His smile was slight and understanding. It was just enough for Jasmine to pick up. 'I did wonder. So did Will. I get it. We're here now for you and if that's as much as you'll allow then so be it.'

'I'm afraid I haven't been very gracious towards those people at the funeral.'

'Jasmine, you're going through grief at the moment, and nothing is expected of you-'

'I walked away halfway through. I left them to it. I didn't see it through to the end.'

Daniel was back at the table. He sat down and tried to hold her hand, flinching when she pulled away. 'Can I ask why Jasmine, apart from the grief you were feeling? Was there something else?'

'Funny thing is Daniel; I can't even find the grief for my mother at the moment.' She reached for his hand. 'I feel like I'm drowning with the stuff in my head and the only lifeline that I have, that I feel might be the thread to unravel the mess I've got myself into, is in The Room.' She squeezed his hand before saying, 'all I think about is seeing her, seeing Mia again. She's even in my dreams, in my thoughts when I'm awake. But she's most real in The Room.'

'That's a good thing. It shows that your body is creating a secure connection to your experiences here.

Jasmine looked back down at her plate. 'It doesn't feel like a good thing.'

'Rubbish!' He laughed lightly. 'In there, you're the Queen of your own destiny. Do you ever feel like this – this sadness – when you're there? No, of course not; it's perfect.'

'But, my reality was never like this before. I didn't have these hideous dreams; I didn't walk off chasing after my imagination-'

'So, you want to go back to the girl on top of the Radisson Blu hotel?'

She stared at him, shocked. He reached for her hand, but she pulled away slowly. The truth was she had to know if seeing Mia today was part of something that was within her control. If her Room experience had somehow bled into her reality, then she needed to know that she could stop it - one way or another.

Jasmine paused to look across the space and out across the city. She guessed it was late now; the greys of that day coalesced behind the jagged landscape. She needed to ask Daniel about Emma; she had to know.

'You know about Alex Pevestone, don't you? And you know what he's done.' Jasmine met Daniel's stare.

'How do you know that name?' he asked, his eyes darted around the room as he bumped up against a forgotten memory. 'That day in the Hub,' he said slowly. 'Mr Smith.'

'Mr Smith,' Jasmine repeated.

'But, how?'

'The night before my mother passed away, Emma told me her story; the story of a man and a twelve-year-old girl in the woods.'

'Jasmine, I'm -'

'Did you know that he's found her? He's found out where she lives, and he's following her. This monster who should be in prison – but you knew about it, didn't you?'

Daniel dragged a stool closer to Jasmine and sat on it. His fingers combed through his hair. 'I didn't know that. Yes, there are things I did know about,' he paused, 'Alex. But I had no reason to tell.'

'No reason?'

'Jasmine, the whole thing is a little more complicated than you're imagining. But, like I said, I didn't know that he'd tried to contact her. But you see, it doesn't change things where The Room is concerned.'

She closed her eyes and shook her head, her curls falling down her back. 'You're not making any sense. Whatever's happening here, you must see that the police have to be told about Pevestone, even if it means having to answer questions about his connection to The Room.'

'No, Jasmine, you don't understand. They won't allow any investigation into The Room.'

'You're going to have to help me out here. Who are 'they'?'

Daniel walked over to the window and turned his back on the view. With folded arms, he leant against a supporting beam and directed his next words to Jasmine.

'You won't have heard of "The Nurturing Project"?' Jasmine frowned and shook her head. 'In fact, I'd put money on no one having heard of it except those in the shadows of the government that myself and Will are in contact with.

'Yes, Will and I know exactly who Pevestone is and what he did. The Nurturing Project is an experimental project developed to combat overcrowding in the prison system. It works by taking a subject, and through programmes, they are encouraged to establish dependency. They are re-inserted into society, monitored and manipulated based on their learned dependencies. They identified the work we were doing with The Room as a means of creating dependencies. So, to establish control over him, they allow him to live out his crimes, or his desires, without hurting anyone in reality.

The Room

'Emma is in the same project. Bottom line, Jasmine, is that if this doesn't work – if Pevestone is not rehabilitated and the public find out – they will hold The Room accountable before themselves. They'll eliminate any trace of The Room and anyone connected with it.'

'Anyone?' Jasmine asked.

'Anyone,' he paused, unfolded his arms and walked towards Jasmine. 'I won't give up The Room. Not while it's giving so many people happiness. I will deal with Pevestone, just keep this between us, yes?'

She pulled away as he reached for her. 'What do you think they'll do to you? This is real life, Daniel – they can hardly make all of us disappear because their plan messed up. That sorta stuff doesn't happen-'

Daniel laughed again lightly. 'The Room is barely on the radar - and their so-called Nurturing Project is nowhere to be found. Whatever they decide to do will be just as invisible and effortless. For them, it will be the path of least resistance if it saves their jobs and faces.'

'So, what is your contingency plan if all this goes south?'

'That's mine. I won't tell.'

Jasmine couldn't help but laugh. 'You sound like a petulant child.'

'I feel like this is all getting out of hand.' Daniel opened the fridge and pulled out a bottle of wine. He set out two glasses and poured without asking.

Jasmine ignored the glass offered by Daniel. 'This all can't be right, can it?' she pressed.

He sipped his wine, slowly, ignoring her agitation. 'I never said that The Room wasn't without its difficulties. Why did you think that the salary was so high?' He laughed again, a little louder. 'And besides, there's not much you can do for Emma. You signed away that right when you started.'

'The contract?'

Daniel nodded and took another sip of wine. 'That contract isn't just for my benefit Jasmine; it's for the Nurturing Project's HQ.'

'What?' Jasmine stood up. 'I thought…I thought you wanted to protect me?'

'I do!' He shouted. 'And I will. Just leave this to me – and it will all be fine.'

'After all you've told me, we still have a scared woman with a genuine stalker with what sounds like nothing to lose. We have to protect Emma.'

'I said I'll deal with it, Jasmine.'

'I don't believe you anymore. I wish you hadn't introduced me to that damn Room.'

'Why?'

'Because,' she paused, 'I'm starting to think Will's right. We're both chasing ghosts. Something's got to be done.'

Chapter 30

Maybe in the years that had passed since that day in the park with her father, Jasmine had aged the carousel in her memory. The paint peeled away at the slightest touch, and she couldn't help but think it creaked and groaned far more than she'd remembered. The feel of the horse beneath her felt colder somehow, despite the warmth of the clear day.

Amidst the sounds of churning metal and piped tunes, Mia's unmistakable giggles cut through. Her small fat fingers turned white as she clung to the pole that fixed the horse in place. Jasmine loved how her smile was as wide as her eyes; they took in everything. Her hair billowed with the air rushing through it.

Mia, in her excitement, tried to say something but the bump and rush in her tummy brought about more playful giggles. Every time Jasmine reached out for her, determined she was going to tip off the other side of her horse, she had to snap her arms back in quick, to prevent herself from falling. This only brought on more laughter from Mia. Jasmine thought they both might burst.

Mia must have decided that her words weren't going to come as she confidently thrust out her arm and pointed to the great oak tree as it passed. Just as all those years ago, the great tree hung impressively over the carousel, splashing it with sunlight so that it sparkled with light and shade. And when the tree was out of sight, Mia twisted herself with more confidence to see the figure standing, watching them.

When she saw a little girl in a red coat and black curls standing alone by the tree, her breath caught sharply in her chest. Everything seemed to freeze. The moment was preserved, and Jasmine couldn't speak. She couldn't even move to respond to Mia as she said, 'Mummy, that girl looks like you.' It was true, it did look like her, but deep down she knew it wasn't. Like an old photograph can blur the lines between mother and daughter and father and son, she knew that the little girl with her father's favourite curls standing against the trunk of the old tree wasn't her at all.

'Why are you doing that, darling?' Jasmine had opened her eyes and felt for where Mia should have been. The blanket had lost her daughter's shape. Across the room, the little silhouette of her daughter caught in the light of the television moved to kill the intrusive glow of the set but not before the wicked witch cackled to threaten Dorothy's little dog.

'I thought The Wizard of Oz was your favourite?'

'It is,' she said, coming back to Jasmine, her yawn wide and almost as big as her. There was another hesitation, this time to pull the next thought out of the air. 'But I know the black witch scares you, mummy.'

'Scares me?' Jasmine asked. She didn't wait for an answer. 'Yes, you're right and so kind to think of that.'

Mia's big round eyes were glassy against the remaining light of the fire. She couldn't stifle another yawn. This time it shook her. Jasmine emerged from the thick folds of the blanket and scooped her up. She felt her little girl sink into her neck and said,

'Time for bed, munchkin.'

'Mummy, are you crying?'

Jasmine hadn't realised she was. She touched her face; wet. 'I don't know why, Mia. It just feels like I should.'

Mia closed her eyes, her voice fading into sleep as she lay in her warm bed. 'That's silly,' she whispered dreamily.

Jasmine stayed in the warm glow of Mia's bedroom, looking at her while she slept. She stayed as long as she could; as long as the drugs would allow her and then it was time to go. Somewhat unexpectedly, Jasmine's last thought before she left The Room was of the frozen daisy on the step of the church in Sterling Park Cemetery.

Chapter 31

———•⟐•———

Jasmine had a glass of water cradled in her interwoven fingers as she sat, staring at the uneven covers where Daniel lay. There was a gentle popping sound, a light snore rumble on every breath. Jasmine thought it was quite soothing but couldn't find it within herself to smile. On the arm of the chair where she was sitting, Daniel's laptop lay open, the screen blank.

Earlier that night, Jasmine had managed to slip through his arms, unable to sleep and if pushed, not wanting. After her last session in The Room, she'd become afraid of her dreams, but more to the point, she'd become frightened of her creations. Each time she was in there, time felt *longer* somehow. The last session had felt like she was with Mia for at least a fortnight. Each time she went under, the longer it took her to face normality afterwards.

The fire was almost out in the living room, but there was enough light for her to take a tour with her fresh glass of water. She stopped briefly in front of the window and took a sip. The city held nothing for her, and a brief thought flashed across her mind which surprised her.

Perhaps we could leave this place.

She turned and headed quietly up the spiral staircase. At the top, she was distracted by a sliver of light from under Daniel's office door. She looked briefly across the landing, expecting to see signs that Daniel had woken up and drifted to his office. Jasmine pushed against

The Room

the door, and to her surprise, it was unlocked, and it gave in against her hand.

Inside the dimly lit room, the imposing desk held the only light which spilt across a sleeping laptop. Daniel wasn't here, and there was very little sign he had been. She followed the edge of the room, taking in the bookshelves that held captive some ancient books that Jasmine understood were already classics some thirty years ago. She stroked the gold lettering upon stitched faded covers. Treasure Island by Robert Louis Stevenson tucked neatly against Fitzgerald's The Great Gatsby and The Selected Poems of Philip Larkin.

She turned away and was caught by the pulsing light just under the laptop's screen. She set her glass down in a small area that was free of dust. Something had been picked up and not returned. Jasmine guessed from the two parallel lines, one shorter than the other that it had been a picture frame. Jasmine nudged the mouse pad as if to suggest to nobody but herself that it was an accident. The screen jumped and brought three files to the centre of a black screen. "Patches Archive" and "Subroutines in Development" were the names of two of the folders and bits of those words she knew referred to computing and all that stuff that she had decided was way over her head. The third read, "The Architect Enters The Room". She stood at the desk for what seemed like minutes staring down at the golden icon shaped like the old stationary folders. Then she dared herself to hover above as she found the chair and heaved it closer.

She double-clicked and waited.

The screen in front of her filled with lines of, as far as she knew, meaningless text and numbers. It went on and on in some kind of loop. She leaned back and continued to stare at the spiralling mass of information flash by her, and then she noticed a little flashing magnifying glass on the static bar across the base of the screen. She directed the mouse icon above it, hoping it would highlight. It did, and she clicked.

The search window asked for a surname. She started typing.

Wilson.

The frantic mess of characters disappeared, leaving a blank screen. Then, one line raced across it; one entry dated the seventeenth of January. It was the date of Jasmine's first session in The Room. She held her breath while she double-clicked the line.

A bunch of lines spread green across the black screen. The structure, or the shape of it, spread downwards like a Christmas tree and for a moment she recognised it as some sort of programmer's code. Scrolling through, she was able to pick out the English words that were programmer's notes. There was a subroutine dedicated to the Architect called "backdoor" and Jasmine knew from the first line that this chunk of code was given the value "BigRedLollipop=True".

'What are you up to Daniel Burton?' she whispered. She scrolled through the system, blinded by the unknown letters and numbers. She reached the bottom portion of the code ringed by hashtag symbols, and it read, "Designers notes:"

The subject, Jasmine Wilson (subject: 7438) has proven very competent and open to level two suggestion which as we know is unusual in such intense personalities displayed by the subject. She has shown very reactive to the Big Red Lollipop protocol, and this could be explained by the subject's history and my own, crossing paths in such a singular way.

The Room

It should also be apparent that given our history to which the subject is unaware that I would not have gone out of my way to include this subject in my ongoing development program for obvious reasons. The subject insisted or at the very least strongly desired time in The Room for which I succumbed to and indulged. I took the opportunity to initiate a study as per the directive agreed, but given my involvement with the subject, my subjectivity has been severely compromised. I am therefore discontinuing this study and this as a matter of record will be the only entry for subject 7438.

Jasmine was still. She looked at the screen as though she was searching for something else, something that wasn't there. Words kept flashing before her. "Architect in The Room" and "back door". Had Daniel somehow been a part of her experience? Had he visited her in her session and made love to her? Had he denied her time with Mia, coerced Jasmine into having sex, or was it something else?

The lines were blurring. She'd felt like it was her who'd wanted him; that it was her who initiated their connection. She had felt like she was in control. But was their relationship a suggestion implanted by the 'architect'? Jasmine reread the notes. He'd lied to her; he'd lied to them all. He had programmed himself into the lives of so many people, and for what? Jasmine slid the laptop under her arm, picked up her glass and left Daniel's office.

Jasmine continued to watch Daniel in bed as she turned over and over what she had learned. She took the last of the water, then examined the glass up against the soft bedroom light. She aimed the now empty glass into a dark corner of the room and hurled it against the wall. It exploded and showered the carpet with clear shards. Daniel jumped from his bed, half-naked and let out a confused moan.

'Good morning, man of my dreams,' she said. There should have been a smile on her face, but she couldn't muster it.

'Jasmine?' His arm swung naturally to the space next to him. 'What's wrong? I heard-'

'What is the "Big Red Lollipop Protocol" Daniel?' Jasmine's fingers went to the laptop to turn it around, but she didn't have to. Daniel had already heard the words, his eyes going straight to it.

'Where did you get that from?' he asked, kicking at the gathering bedsheets to sit up.

Jasmine's determined eyes bore into him, and she detected a tremor in his voice. 'I couldn't sleep. I needed a drink of water. That's now against that wall and finding its way into your carpet. I saw the light.'

'You mean you went into my office?'

'Yes. Like I said, I saw a light, and it caught my eye. It wasn't the only thing that caught my eye.' She motioned to the resting laptop.

'You had no right going in there, Jasmine. There are some sensitive-'

'Oh, come on Daniel,' she interrupted, 'you've been fucking me for what, a few weeks now? Don't you think I've earned some trust?' She paused to press some keys on the laptop before looking up at him. 'I found my file.'

'Jasmine, I can explain all this.'

'You've found a way into the sessions, haven't you? You lied. You said it was a safe word, but it's something else, isn't it?'

'I haven't found a way-'

'Just stop it. This will be one more lie, won't it? Do you know when I first met you, I allowed myself this creeping feeling that my life was taking some kind of turn - and any turn from where I'd been was surely a good thing? And I didn't realise it at the time, but you turned out to be someone who could appreciate that shit more than anyone I know, but you know what, now I'm beginning to doubt lots of things about you.' Jasmine's voice became louder. 'I know this may be a shit thing to say, but how do I know Seth was real and that somehow you and your fucking Room have been the cause of my dreams?'

'You're right. That was a shit thing to say.' He took a deep breath as he took in the stillness in the bedroom. 'Is there any point in trying to answer your questions if you go straight to me being a liar? Why don't you assume first off that I'm telling the truth? Then you can pick and choose what you want to believe. I really don't care.'

'You don't care because you're trapped. You have nowhere to go. You have been found out.'

'Aren't we all trapped, Jasmine? This thing we call life - it's a joke, isn't it? It takes hold of you and tears all the goodness off the bone and spits you back out. And then what?' His eyes were glistening as he finally met her stare.

'It's all we have. This is it,' Jasmine said in an almost whisper.

'No! This is not it!' He slammed his hand down onto the laptop. 'I have created more!'

Jasmine jerked her hand away from the laptop, startled by the outburst. She noticed Daniel's attention drop to it.

'I did lie to you. You are right, and the lollipop thing isn't a safe word; it is a silent trigger that I gave you in your first session. It was to summon me into your session - but not in the way you think. I can't go into the session, but I can be part of the client's session, an idea or a creation based on the keywords.'

'But why?' Jasmine asked. 'What do you gain from it?'

'Research. You see, what you imagined, what you went straight for in your thinking was that I could somehow jump in or connect to you and join you in the world you created and in some ways be a co-creator. And that Jasmine is a science fiction - but that could be just around the corner. At the moment, it's all about recognising patterns in the numbers and code turned out by each session.'

'And then what, you recognise a pattern, build on it, feed it back, rinse and repeat?' Jasmine asked.

'Something like that,' Daniel said. 'I'm trying to prove to the people who can just take it away from me with just a click of their fingers that it can be developed for something useful.'

Jasmine's tears flowed. 'All these people, all your clients, are they all your research projects?'

'Yes, but I made it so that The Room serves them. It is real for them.'

The Room

'But it's not real, is it? It always comes down to that. It can never be their creation because you're the influence that directs their movie. You're already in there, moving things along. Do they know?'

'Of course not, Jasmine. It may counter multiple human rights, but it's still not a patch on what they want to use it for.'

Jasmine thought about the Nurturing Project for building dependency amongst criminals like Pevestone. She felt sick; because of this initiative and The Room, a man like that was walking free.

'I want to ask you something, and I want you to tell me the truth. If you feel anything for me, then please make it the truth.' She waited but not for any response from Daniel. The question worked its way up from the pit of her stomach. 'Seth is real - as in he existed, he lived, I know that. But,' she paused. 'Is Mia real? Is she my creation, my little girl grown up?'

Daniel had paused too long to answer. She started to shake her head, her curls like thick silken ropes batted her face.

'No. No. No!'

Daniel slid to the end of the bed to take her in his arms, but she pulled sharply away.

'Jasmine,' he said, 'look at me.'

Her head was down, and her face buried in hair. Daniel spoke in low tones and leaned in close,

'When I found you, you were in trouble. You wanted to end your life, and I couldn't let that happen. It was my mission, remember, to look after you, as you tried to help my boy. But the dreams you had;

those dreams of that day, they never left you alone. You had the idea - remember - to use The Room, *you had the idea.* It was all you. So, I let you in.

'You thought your first session was about Mia, but it wasn't. I know the patterns. I've trained since Seth left to recognise them. It was your first session, and you went back to the roof of the hotel, the same one I watched you from before we met. I don't know why you chose that, but I couldn't just sit there and let it play out. So I gave you Mia.'

Daniel's breath seemed to leave his body all at once as he wrestled with the words, 'I made you believe that she was the baby you lost. I wanted you to have something to live for.'

'What the hell? None of it is real.'

'And what's so good about reality? Even in your Room experience, you were on top of the Raddison Blu.'

'You made me fall in love with something fake, something you made up.'

'I made a decision to help you, Jasmine.'

'So you came into my session, you changed my thoughts. You gave me something that I can never have?'

Jasmine screamed, then grabbed the laptop and brought it across Daniel's head, sending him across the bedroom. He brought his hands up to his face and felt the warming blood down his cheek.

Chapter 32

A light flickered somewhere towards the back of the bus, throwing a grey tone over Jasmine's black hair. There was calm in the streets as dawn descended, and the pavements came alive with commuters speaking loudly into the air and clasping sealed cups.

She knew she could afford a taxi, but the number 166 had been bumbling along outside Daniel's apartment when she had reached the pavement; the old bus her and Sammy would get on after school. *It hadn't changed a bit,* Jasmine thought, as she picked at the faded chair covers in front of her.

She had ridden on the bus since the early morning; since she had run from Daniel's apartment. She was still clad in her funeral clothes, and her face was speckled with bits of mascara, staining her cheeks. The rumble of the bus was hypnotic to Jasmine as she absently picked out the people standing, walking, running, on the streets passing by.

The bus creaked to halt on Broad Street. Out from behind a line of people waiting at the bus stop, stepped a little girl. Her black hair bounced over her red coat, just like it did on the carousel.

'Mia,' she whispered into the glass window. It was so slight that barely a circle of her breath appeared.

The little girl turned her full face towards the bus and held onto her mother's hand, frowning at the stranger staring at her on the bus.

It wasn't Mia. It was another little girl, dressed in a red parka, black hair over her shoulders.

'You're not there.' Jasmine whispered as the bus pulled away.

The bus jolted against a speed bump and delivered a wake-up knock to Jasmine's head still against the window. She heard a voice, and when she focused, she saw an old lady leaning over her.

'Are you okay?' She seemed to croak, like her voice was on the edge of a coughing fit.

Jasmine needed to get off the bus. She pushed past the concerned lady and ran with such force to the front that the driver instinctively slowed the bus to a stop.

'Let me out!' she screamed at the driver.

She almost fell from the bus and into the street. Thankfully, there wasn't a soul on the quiet slip road, leading to an industrial estate. It wouldn't have mattered either way. She could have been in the middle of the precinct for all she knew. Jasmine bent double and vomited with such force that she almost lost her balance. One of her hands shot out and met the ground mercifully, keeping her from falling into her puddle of sick.

When nothing else came out of her mouth, she eventually gathered the strength to stand. She walked the rest of the way. *There's no place like home*, Jasmine thought.

Inside the empty house, Jasmine enjoyed the stillness and the familiar creaks of every weathered wall and pipe. She could smell cleaning chemicals, stinging at the inside of her nostrils. Claire had

The Room

been and attacked the house from top to bottom, she imagined. Of course; Claire would have had to play host to her mother's wake, and by the time the last of the well-fed mourners had left, she would've gotten to work on cleaning the house. Jasmine could see straight through to the kitchen and a piece of paper waiting for her on the counter. She already had six missed calls from Claire, and probably as many voice mails. She hadn't listened to any of them, and as she strode through the hall into the kitchen, she picked up the note and turned it over without reading it.

She went to the cutlery draw and pulled it free of its mounting, sending metal implements across the kitchen surfaces and bouncing along the ceramic tiles. She studied the fallen pieces as though she were looking for some sort of pattern, and then found the biggest knife and scooped it from the floor.

She had the knife with her as she went into the living room. She pulled a thick throw off the back of the sofa and spread it on the floor. Placing the knife neatly under the lamp on the coffee table, she then followed the contour of the room and unhooked pictures from the walls and snatched ones standing to attention on the bookshelves. She threw them unceremoniously onto the middle of the blanket and then bundled them together, pulling the loot out into the hall. She caught a glimpse of one of the pictures and reached inside the folds to retrieve it.

It was a picture of her as a child; her unmistakable curls spread between her parents as they all beamed into the camera. Everyone was younger in the picture, which seemed obvious to her, but it was almost *unrecognisable*; an imagined life that Jasmine could have easily conjured up in The Room.

The knife hacked at the sofa and ripped cushions, spewing white foam across the room. It gouged at the bare walls, tearing strips away. When the blade had done its job, Jasmine took two attempts to turn over the haemorrhaging sofa and toppled the bookshelf that contained the blue folder; she'd never read that damn thing anyway.

She made it into her bedroom and found the edge of the bed. Reaching into her pocket, she pulled out the funeral notice. There was a picture of Myriam smiling out, just like the picture from the blanket. She looked younger; in fact as Jasmine lifted her head, she saw a reflection of herself in the mirror. It could have been her on that piece of paper. She let the image fall to the floor.

Noticing the computer on the desk, her eyes widened, and an idea came to her. She rummaged through the desk drawers with frantic determination.

'For fuck's sake!' She said out loud after searching the final drawer. She knocked the laptop to the floor, cracking the screen. 'Can't you give me a damn break?' She turned to the machine, panting.

'Can you still see me, Daniel? Are you watching me like some sicko?' Jasmine said at the computer, watching her spit hit the screen. The machine had been part of the very first communications she'd had with him. He'd spoken to her through it; he'd taken over the whole screen in order to force her to talk to him.

If he could do that, surely he was capable of taking over her thoughts, her happiness, her life. *Why did I let him?* Jasmine thought. She picked up the computer and brought it down against the corner of the desk. The top half, the screen, hung lifelessly on its own ribbon cables as she threw it back onto the table. She reached for a mug with

The Room

a thin residue of liquid still in the bottom. It must have once been tea. Dark green ink spots of mould formed on the cold liquid in the bottom of the mug. She used the cup against the keyboard like a hammer until she was satisfied, spraying the old tea into her face as she pounded it into the framework.

Eventually, when she'd given the last punch to the laptop, she turned towards the bed, heaving the mattress free of its frame. There - between the slats - was the thing she'd been looking for.

Jasmine positioned a chair for the camcorder and rested it on a few books until she was happy with the frame of herself. She paused in front of the camera and brushed her black trousers.

She examined her whole outfit. The funeral clothes felt stiff and unwelcoming on her skin and a reminder of yesterday. She would never wear them again, what would be the point? She jumped up and tore at them, ripping sounds and the ping of buttons reverberating around the room. She stood naked in front of her wardrobe, a chill spreading through her body. She didn't want to care, but it seemed important; the clothes she would wear for her "performance" needed to be just right. She reached in and slipped a green t-shirt from its hanger and pulled it over her head, straightening it to her shape. It had her favourite flowers on the front, daisies, and it reminded her of summer, and that too seemed a long time ago. She then pulled on a pair of ripped jeans.

The chill still worked her body as she settled on an upright chair in front of the camera. She leaned across and blindly found the record button and pressed.

I saw her again today…

She screamed. The camcorder flew from the chair and hit the skirting, its lights faded to nothing, and then the room was quiet again.

In the hours that followed, Jasmine simply sat and watched the light change in her bedroom. It formed patterns across the floor, folding around the upturned chairs and the shredded funeral clothes. It threatened to pass over Myriam's fixed smile, but every time it did, Jasmine reached out with her barefoot and slid the picture further back into the shadows. When the light outside faded, she stood up and righted the mattress until it fell neatly back in its wooden cradle. She strode across the bedroom and drew the curtains. The dark swallowed her bedroom, and she welcomed it. She couldn't see her mum's picture anymore.

Jasmine rummaged through the pile of discarded black material on the floor and found the hard edges of her phone. Like Claire's note on the kitchen counter, Jasmine disregarded the text messages, missed calls and voice mails, not even bothering to delete them. Instead, she found a number and hit the dial icon.

'Emma,' she said. Her pitch was high and hopeful. 'It's Jas,' she continued. 'Yes I'm fine…Yes, it's been an unusual day.'

'Listen, I'm calling to see if you're okay, first of all. I mean, any more trouble?' Jasmine waited again. 'That's good then. Maybe this will be the last of it. I also just wanted to remind you that I'll be there for your last session on Friday…'

'Yes, I know it's a late one, but if you think that's the best - then that's the way of it…' Jasmine pulled the phone away from her ear as Emma's shrill voice cut through into the space.

The Room

When she eventually ended the call, Jasmine searched for one more name in her contact list. She opened up a text window to Daniel Burton and began typing.

I'll be there for Emma's last session, but after that I'm done. If you have any feelings left for me, then you'll give me the security clearance to attend.

Chapter 33

Now

'Will you let me take you out sometime?'

'Maybe. I'm pretty busy, right now Br-.' Michael froze, was it Brad, Buck? He remembered the man's name as being something horrendously American, but now he couldn't figure out what the hell it was.

'-bro.' He winced.

'How about Tuesday? Dinner at Al Fredo's?'

'Busy, sorry. I'm looking into this story.'

'Anything juicy?' The man propped himself up on the pillows, showing his tanned chest.

'It's an old story. Something new has come up.' Michael couldn't help but think of Stephanie's eyes, glazed and lifeless, on Share Street's pavement when he said that. He shook his head as if to clear his thoughts.

'OK. Thursday, then?'

'Look, as I said, I've got a lot on right now. But I'll be in touch; you gave me your number last night, right?'

'Didn't need to, what with you bringing me straight here from the bar.' The man paused as he wrote down his number on Michael's

The Room

pad and paper on the bedside table. 'Hopefully I can fit in with your busy lifestyle soon though, *bro*.'

Michael could see the reflection of the man on his bed, and his presence was nothing short of *annoying*. He was desperate for him to leave, partially because he was tired of the conversation, but mainly so he could strip the bed sheets and replace with his new White Collection ones. But instead, the man – Brad, Buck or whatever he was called - lay topless, stroking Michael's £150 scatter cushions with his rough hands.

The phone rang, and Michael pressed his ear. He mouthed the words 'shower' to his unwanted guest and threw a towel at him. The man got up, stretching his muscular body and revealing more tanned skin in just a small pair of tight boxers. Michael heard the en-suite door click shut.

'Harriet, you're a bit of a slag, got any ideas as to how I get rid of an overnight guest?'

'Harriet, maybe, but I certainly am not. However, from memory I'd suggest take away coffee – and never for God's sake let them shower.'

'Jennifer,' Michael paused, controlling a groan. 'How nice to hear-'

'Do you not look at the caller ID before answering your phone? We're not still on landlines, Powers. I knew you were old fashioned, but please check in the future. It's hugely embarrassing for all.'

'Yes, I- what do you want, Jennifer? I'm halfway through dressing so I can come and see your delightful face in the office.'

'I'm calling about that.'

'About me dressing? Is this your way of asking me what I'm wearing right now?'

'I've had Marty in the office, telling me they've highlighted a few searches on your computer and Barbie's laptop that don't exactly fit in with keeping quiet about Share Street.'

'Must be some mistake.'

'Oh, there's been no mistake, Powers. Your LE chip has made for pretty good reading too recently.'

Michael remembered his trip to Share Street and Jasmine's home. He stared at his forearm; he wanted to rip out the bloody thing.

'You're causing me huge amounts of trouble at the moment. You've been twitchy and unusually sweaty all week, and frankly, it's more hassle than you're worth.'

'What are you saying?'

'I'm saying this is done, Michael. You're a liability. I can't have any more government officials looking into our journalism. It would cause a shit storm.'

'So I'm-'

'Fired, yes. I'm... I'm sorry. I'll get your things sent to your home. And if you know what's good for you, you'll leave this Room business alone. Otherwise it won't be just your job you're losing.'

The phone clicked. Michael's hand went out sharply and swiped his dressing cabinet clean, bottles of fragrance dropping and smashing onto the tiled floor.

'Shit, you OK?' Brad, or Buck came out of the shower, a towel hung around his waist.

Michael turned round to him, breathing heavily. 'Get dressed; we're going out for breakfast. I know this place, The Fly By Night Cafe.'

Chapter 34

The moment Will noticed her standing just inside The Hub, his nervousness seemed to melt away, chased by an oversized smile spreading across his face. He fumbled his way free of the Hub desk and strode towards her, his long arms ready to receive.

'It's really nice to see you,' Jasmine managed before being swallowed up in his outstretched arms.

'You too, Jas, it's bin' what - a week or two? What with your mum's funeral and stuff,' he mumbled from the pit of the giant hug. He stepped back to look at her. 'Daniel told me you're leavin'. I'm bloody sad about that. Serious.' With a guiding hand on her arm, he directed her to the big white sofa opposite the glass desk.

'Did Daniel tell you everything? Everything as to why I'm leaving, I mean?' Jasmine asked.

Will scanned the Hub as though searching the corners that weren't there for answers that were equally as elusive. 'Daniel knows betta' than to 'ide stuff from me and give me a trivial reason for ya leaving.' He took her hand and gently squeezed it. 'There's an... underbelly to The Room that I think you 'ave discovered and maybe you were never meant to. But then again, there is a reason for you being here. Wha' I mean is, Daniel chose you. He went in search *of you*.'

'A bit like a stalker,' she said.

'Well, I think our Dan is a bit more complex than that. But still, there's a reason for ya being here, Jas.'

'Complex is right.'

'I get it. The Room isn't fo' everyone, and if it were left to me, then I wouldn't have let ya ride.'

Will shifted awkwardly in his seat. 'There's a change coming Jasmine. I think you might 'ave guessed as much. Daniel is being squeezed in all the wrong places, and for a man, a father, I think it's a tightrope.'

'Why do you still support him? Why are you still here?'

'Daniel's allowed me to tap into my obsession, and that has so far been my life's work. Jas, I have free range to study an' develop these drugs with the backing - semi unofficially - from the government. That's huge.'

'You're right. A change is coming, and it's a dangerous one.'

Will relaxed and laughed lightly. 'That sounds a bit conspiratory for me, Jas.' He got up and walked over to the desk.

'Our client will only be a few minutes now,' he said. 'I hear Emma has asked for ya to be present for the session. Did Dan agree to it?'

'I don't know yet. His text was a bit elusive. But I'm here, like it or lump it.'

'True.'

'Is he around?' she asked, her heart beating in her throat.

'He's in The Room now - calibrating.'

'Can you tell him I'm here?'

'He already knows, Jas.' Will lifted his arm and circled a finger across where his chip lay. 'He's like the wizard behind the curtain, don't you know?' he laughed, and the sound seemed out of place to Jasmine's ears. 'I wonder if you could receive the client for me? I 'ave to check my levels. It's a whole chemical thing.'

'You make it sound so exciting,' she said and smiled thinly. 'Go on. Go and play with your chemicals. I'll bring Emma through when it's time.'

Will threw her a fake gun gesture and made a clicking sound behind his teeth as he engaged the door to The Room. It occurred to Jasmine that in all the time she'd worked there at Share Street, she'd never seen The Room as it was meant to be seen – as a client.

And today, of all days, was going to be her *first and last time*, she thought. She grimaced.

Her attention was swayed towards the big desk. It signalled that the door at the top of the staircase was about to open. Emma seemed to lumber through it and brightened when she saw Jasmine seated on the sofa. The two women almost ran at each other and embraced. Despite her shift in her demeanour at seeing Jasmine, Emma looked tired. Her eyes were swollen with lack of sleep and her blonde hair darkened as it clung to her cheeks and neck.

'Emma, are you-'

'I ran here.'

'You ran? Why? Is it him?'

Emma held onto Jasmine's forearms as she lowered herself onto the sofa.

'I don't know,' she said on a long tired breath. 'I think so. I just…' Her words drifted as though she'd finally found a moment for herself to relax and couldn't quite believe how good it felt.

'I haven't slept much, Jas. I'm convinced he's on every street corner, on every bus that passes.' She looked around at the Hub almost with wonder, and it reminded Jasmine of the first time she had walked into the place. Back then, she felt like this place had saved her life.

'I need this, Jas. God knows I need this. It's like an escape or something. This is the only certainty I have left in my life.'

'What do you mean?' Jasmine asked.

Emma turned to face her; her eyes shone with tears. 'Certain that there's a part of the world in there where I know he isn't.'

Jasmine put her arms around her and brought her close. But she couldn't help thinking about what was left for Emma after her last session. So far, it would always be a world with Alex Pevestone in it. They'd both needed The Room at some point, but Jasmine had to come to terms with the fact that she couldn't do it, not anymore.

They'd all been part of an experiment. But the difference between Jasmine and the rest was she knew it- she knew that she was a rat in a cage. It hurt her to think about Emma not knowing, not understanding. She wanted to tell her about The Room, about Daniel and the foundation that all their dreams were built upon. But she couldn't. Like Jasmine, Emma was an addict - and there had to be a process other than cold turkey.

She needs this, Jasmine thought as she took in Emma's gentle features.

The door to The Room clicked open, and Daniel stood on its threshold. Jasmine looked down at the floor briefly. She couldn't allow herself to look weak in front of him; to let her eyes look over his white shirt. When he saw Jasmine and Emma, he offered an uncertain smile.

'Emma,' he said, pausing long enough for her to register his presence, 'it's time.'

Emma stood up and padded herself with her open hands. She finished wiping her spent eyes as she approached Daniel. 'Jasmine is to come in with me, yes?'

Daniel glanced across and caught Jasmine's eye. 'It is what you wanted, wasn't it?' he asked Emma, eventually looking down at her. Without waiting for her to answer, he continued, 'come on. Let's get you settled.' He reached around and pressed the small of her back, and she moved towards the open door. Jasmine felt a heat rise up inside of her. He turned and motioned for Jasmine to follow and then followed Emma into the waiting darkness of The Room.

As far as Jasmine could tell, The Room was another circular shaped space, but not as big or as welcoming as the Hub. It was dark, except for small clusters of lights which softly lit the walls giving the impression of neat little alcoves equally spaced around the back wall. In the centre, three little downlights set into the ceiling picked out a large leather recliner and two computer stations. One set just behind the chair and the other to the side hooked up to three glass tubes full of Will's chemicals, and an IV hung lazily on a tall metal stand.

The Room

Jasmine felt for the wall just to the side of where Will was steadily helping Emma into the recliner. Emma, she noticed, was smiling and it was good to see. Will steadied her arm, rubbing the vital area with alcohol before situating the IV tap. Behind them, Daniel was sat at his laptop at a tiny little desk, swapping clusters of windows on his screen until he seemed happy. He looked up at Will and nodded his head. This seemed to be his cue to place Daniel's electrodes across Emma's temple.

He pressed a button on the laptop and sent the screen black. He then stood next to Jasmine, his own back against the wall. She could smell him – lavender and musk. But now, there was a tinge to his scent – acidic almost, overpowering.

'Thank you for doing this,' he said in low tones, his breath warm on her cheek. 'I think you're the friend she needs.'

Jasmine turned briefly to see him. His face was half in shadow as he watched Will adjust the taps on Emma's arm. 'I'm not much of a friend if all I'm doing is standing by while she's sucked further into this...this nightmare.'

Daniel turned towards Jasmine, the contour of his eye was coloured dark blue from the laptop she'd used against him, and it featured in a pool of light for her to see.

'It's Emma's choice, Jasmine.'

'How can you say that? Was it my choice to create a daughter that never was? You used me to get what you wanted.'

'I was, and still am, compelled to look after you.'

'Compelled?' Jasmine pitched it a little above the low tones, regretting it immediately.

'By the memory of my son. No, not the memory,' he corrected, 'in mine and Seth's conversations we talk about you all the time. In those years, both of us watched out for you. In fact, it was Seth who told me to follow you to the café that day.'

'No, Daniel. Stop it. It's not real.'

Daniel's smile was hidden in the gloom, but Jasmine could sense it. 'Well, we've been through this haven't we,' he said. 'Round and round like a merry go round.'

Jasmine watched the man she thought she knew in silhouette against the mediocre light. *Was he mad, broken in some way?* She turned her attention back to Emma.

'What about her? Will you be playing the Architect tonight?'

Daniel shook his head, and it was a few moments before he answered. 'As intriguing as Emma is, her sessions remain unknown to me. The truth is Jasmine, I fell for you. This Architect business, I didn't make it a habit. I tested my code out a few times, and I used it on you more than I should have and well, like most things in my life, it got out of hand.'

'Is any of this meant to make me feel better?' she asked. Another moment of silence passed between them before she said, 'I meant it, you know. After this, I'll walk away. I don't need looking after.'

The Room

From the shadow, once more, Daniel looked at her, but she couldn't see his face, except for the dark line around his eye. Will called over to Daniel, and he then stepped into a new light. Emma looked sleepy and reached out for Jasmine. The two women clasped hands.

Daniel's voice filled the room. 'How are you feeling, Emma?'

'Good, I mean, better than good.'

'That's the way, Stephanie. Remember your breathing and on behalf of me Will, and now Jasmine, we would wish you a very happy creation.'

'Stephanie?' Emma's voice sounded heightened, her chest racing even though her eyes were closed.

Jasmine looked around to Will and Daniel desperately, but they were now alone. *Why had he called her that? Why would he want to bring up a name she was desperate to forget?*

She felt the fingers of Emma's hand fall from hers. Emma, or Stephanie, was on her own now - and the thought of it made Jasmine sick to her stomach.

Chapter 35

At the back of number sixty-two Share Street, a man in a heavy raincoat sat patiently in the shadows by the fire escape. Blood poured down his wrist from his left arm and seeped through his coat. He was satisfied that he'd contained the flow, but the stabbing pain spread like electricity through his body. In his hand, he held a rusted metal stair rod he had worked loose from the staircase and used to dig out his LE chip. The chip lay in a pool of blood at his feet, its shape hidden by flesh and hair. *Human, after all*, he entertained.

Alex Pevestone cradled his arm as he leaned forward as far into the light cast by the streetlights as he could; his attention caught by the police patrol car circling the block. He imagined that it wouldn't have taken too long to dispatch, directly spilling out of the city after a call from some nosey resident reporting a woman running down Share Street, squealing that she was being followed.

Alex drew back and continued to watch from the shadows as one of the officers leaned out of his car with a handheld scanner.

'Oh, bollocks.' He said, under his breath. He realised that his trick with the stair rod was only *half of the job*. He pushed against the brick wall and heaved himself to his feet. He stepped onto the bloody mess in front of him and heard the snap of the chip under his foot and could only hope it was enough. He would soon find out.

The lone car edged along the road. The thick heavy voice on the police radio droned and split through the quiet suburban street until it drifted towards the city. Alex smiled and, still holding his arm,

The Room

sank down, finding a step and pressing his body against the building. He wondered if he would find the time to sleep halfway up this fire escape, or if he should put off the notion of sleep in case he missed his prize. He quietly lowered the rod and reached across to touch the door that would open out onto the landing. He knew this place like the *back of his hand*; the good part about being a secret guest was he always had to use the back doors.

He grinned to himself, closing his eyes and taking in deep contemplative breaths. There was no pain anymore; all he could think about was Stephanie, only a few feet away.

Chapter 36

'You've never asked me about my sessions, have you, Jasmine?' Emma seemed preoccupied with Jasmine's appearance. She flicked Jasmine's curls away to the side to reveal more of her face.

'No, I haven't, and I never will.'

'You have beautiful eyes, you know. They shouldn't be hidden away.'

'I didn't know I was hiding anything,' she replied. She flicked her eyes around the Hub. Daniel had gone. Jasmine felt the bubble of anger swell in her stomach again – the one that had calmed seeing Emma smiling, eyes closed, in The Room.

Emma took her by her shoulders. She looked around the Hub and saw they were alone. 'I appreciate you not asking.'

Jasmine shrugged. 'I didn't think you would tell if I did ask.'

'Yes, I think you're right. What about you, Jas? Would you tell me yours?' Emma whirled her round and threaded her arm through Jasmine's. They both walked towards the changing room.

'Not a chance,' she said. Their laughter bounced off the walls and by the time they reached the door onto the fire escape, there was very little left in either of them. Jasmine turned to Emma and, squeezing her arm, asked, 'You didn't have a bad time, in there, did you? You didn't think about something you'd rather not think about?'

Emma grinned. 'Darling, I don't think I've ever had such a good session. It was a whole week's worth of pure happiness. I've done well, in this weird life, all things considered. I have money, I have confidence, and some say I'm not terrible to look at. But in The Room, I feel like I am...' She flicked out her tongue, as if to taste the word, 'invincible.'

'Will you miss this?'

They both turned on their heels, their backs to the door and looked through to the Hub. Daniel and Will were nowhere to be found. 'Not now,' she said, 'maybe later. It depends, you know, on what life has in store. Besides, I'll get back here soon, when they say I can. Come on,' Emma said, 'let's have a walk into the city. We can have a drink while we wait for a taxi.' They both smiled, and Emma held Jasmine's stare. 'I'm glad you came out tonight for me.' She laughed. 'I hope I didn't squeeze your hand too hard.'

Jasmine smiled again, enjoying the relief of the moment and the new confidence in Emma. 'Just promise me one thing,' Jasmine asked. 'Promise me that I wasn't holding your hand while you were having some sort of sex session?'

The door opened onto the fire escape as their laughter spilt out into the night and then was cut short as the metal stair rod, still marked with Pevestone's blood came down across Jasmine's shoulders. Her own weight prized her from Stephanie as she fell across the landing, her face contorted and squashed against the ice-cold floor.

Everything seemed to happen in a single moment. Only the piecing together of what had just happened seemed to take the most time. Jasmine heard Emma's scream cut short and, through blurred kaleidoscopic vision, she saw Emma and him scuffling. She seemed to break away from the man with the metal bar and climb the staircase to the roof.

More sounds came. It was a man's voice, but not Pevestone. This was a distant voice that echoed and grew louder. Pevestone kicked the door shut to the changing room and wedged the handle with the bar. The blurred images started to fill Jasmine's vision as Pevestone leaned over her body, his distorted face close to hers, asking, 'Are you okay?'

Jasmine froze as his hands smoothed over her shape. Her eyes shifted to the wedged door - it was moving in the frame. *Please God, let that be Will behind it,* she thought as Pevestone's hands touched her face.

'You are pretty. Has anyone ever told you, you have beautiful eyes?' he asked. 'And your hair. My goodness,' he added. His fingers glanced her breasts through her layers before finding the deep forest of curls. 'Maybe I'll find a place for you in my dreams.' He smiled.

He stood up and took a step back. What he did next was clear, terribly clear. Jasmine felt as though she had been hit in the stomach by a lump of concrete. As Pevestone delivered his kick, he watched with disgust as Jasmine vomited across the landing. She tried to scream, but all means of doing so had left her body. She felt his hands again, but this time inside her clothes. She guessed he was looking for her phone and when he found it, tight against her leg in her jeans pocket, he was smiling that smile again.

Her focus slightly improved, and she couldn't move – she could only watch- as Pevestone took the steps two at a time to the roof, and to Emma.

'Emma!' Jasmine whispered, clutching her stomach.

The door rattled violently against the rod, causing it to bury its end further into the door. Jasmine used the handrail to pull herself to her feet. She reached for the bar that held the door in place, but it was jammed and getting worse with every bit of force applied to it.

It was Daniel. 'Jasmine, the door!'

'I can't!' her voice was stronger. 'It's jammed. You're going to have to push through it.'

Just then, Jasmine heard Emma's screams coming from the rooftop. She looked around at the empty street below and then the stairwell that hugged the building. 'Daniel,' she managed to shout in between hefty thumps against the door, 'call the police.'

She didn't wait for any response. She knew what she was asking of him.

The roof was a maze of chimney stacks and fallen aerials that played an eerie tune against the weaving wind. But the stacks weren't tall enough to hide Pevestone and Emma. Jasmine stepped over the narrow walkways between the pitched portions of the roof that seated the stacks. Emma was standing close to the edge of the roof with her back to the street below. She was trapped by Pevestone, who was sitting cross legged on a ventilation duct. He watched her through tendrils of smoke that rose into the night air. Emma's face was swollen with desperate tears, and when she saw Jasmine slowly emerge from the cluster of chimney vents, she gasped and tried to reach out to her.

'No!' Pevestone became unsettled. He thrust his cigarette hand out towards Jasmine and without taking his eyes from Emma, he said, 'You don't get a part in this. This is ours, mine and Stephanie's.'

Ours? Does he think he's in a session? Jasmine took a step forward. 'This isn't Stephanie anymore. Not since you took her away. Emma, come away from the edge.'

'I should have made you swallow your own teeth, you fucking bitch.'

'It's okay, Jas. Stay back,' Emma said.

'That's enough from you. Okay ladies, here are the rules. *You*,' he said, pointing to Emma, 'don't get to talk to her and *you* don't get to talk to her.' His cold eyes stayed on Jasmine. 'And further, if there is one more word directed at Stephanie or if you're brave enough or stupid enough to take one more step, then I'll pitch this jittery bitch off the edge, and then we'll really see what she's really made of.' He pulled a face, an exaggerated look of horror that only he found funny.

Emma, or Stephanie - the lines were beginning to blur even to Jasmine - started sobbing. Her body shook dangerously close to the ledge.

'Or perhaps I should do it anyway,' Pevestone said. 'My one true love. Oh, what has happened to you? Stephanie, I think I liked you better in the woods. You seemed to have a lot more fight in you. I mean, you were a screamer. I'll admit it, I'm a bit of a screamer too as it goes, but you already know that about me. You see Jasmine; we're both screamers. For my part, it's because *I love so much*, so intensely, the details of which I won't bore you but suffice to say I do love the young, it's still got some twitch about it, very responsive if I may be so vulgar.

But I think in Stephanie's case I probably reminded her of daddy a little bit.' His eyes widened, full of expectation at his latest joke.

'Or maybe I won't have to pitch you off. It looks like you're doing a good enough job of it yourself.' He leaned in as though speaking to a petulant child. 'Stand still, you miserable fuck.' Straightening up, he took a long soothing breath of the night air as though he were still enjoying a cigarette. 'Where was I?' he looked at Jasmine, reminded of the interruption. 'Oh. Yes. Jasmine, before your unwelcome visit, me and Stephanie were talking about old times. *Catching up,* if you like. I've got a dickens of a weekend planned for us, a kind of a jaunt down memory lane, culminating in a visit to my old stomping ground. I thought we'd make that a Sunday to remember.' He turned his wanton eyes back to Stephanie; a trembling breath warmed his slightly parted lips. 'I love Sunday's Stephanie. Do you still love Sundays?'

'Alex!' Jasmine shouted. 'I can talk to you. That's not breaking the rules, is it?'

He smiled at her. 'Seems you have me on a technicality. More fool me.'

Jasmine almost stepped forward and then she remembered. Pevestone noticed her mistake and felt himself amused by her correction. Jasmine nervously looked at Stephanie and then back at Pevestone. 'Alex,' she said, desperately trying to maintain an air of confidence in another wise broken tone, 'this isn't The Room, all this.' She motioned with her outstretched arms. 'After all this, whatever your intention, it *will* be over.'

He laughed. 'You've been in The Room haven't you?' he asked, knowingly. 'And it's got to you. That Daniel is some kind of genius, isn't he?'

'I know it isn't real. I know I can walk away from it. Like you now - you can put a stop to this and walk away.'

'How do you know it's not real? Who's in charge here, right now? If it were you, then we wouldn't be here having this delightful conversation, would we?' He started to roll up his sleeve; blood pooled around the hole where his LE chip had previously sat. 'You see these?' he raised his arm, 'Well not mine,' he said as an afterthought, 'I had a brief altercation with mine, but these things, this is just the start. Once they get a hold of Daniel's Room, they will be the directors of your movie. They're going to have you so tangled up that you're not going to know what's real and what's one big giant Room. Genius, actually.'

Jasmine couldn't help but stroke the inside of her left arm. 'But, what now? What happens next, Alex?' She noticed Stephanie looking out over the edge and inching ever closer.

'Ah, yes. Well, I thought we'd just shoot the breeze, Steph and me, find out a little about each other, share some experiences, you know.' He turned back to Stephanie. 'So tell me, Stephanie, what do you dream about in your Room?'

'Wha…what?'

'Whaaaat?' He replied, mocking her with fake tears and gasps. 'It's simple enough. You tell me yours, and I'll tell you mine. Mine's awesome. You're going to love it.'

'No.' She folded, her knees buckled beneath her and she almost toppled over the edge. Pevestone laughed.

He pointed to Jasmine as he settled back on the vent. He must have been unnerved to the point where he was sure she was going over too. 'I'm going to let you have that one Jasmine because, well, that was as funny as fuckery.' He still laughed as he turned back to Stephanie. His face switched, and Stephanie saw a familiar look wash over him. 'I mean it Steph, my love. This is only going to go one way, and it starts by you telling your piece of shit Room experience.' He pulled out a cigarette from a packet under his coat and then flipped open a Zippo from another pocket. By the time the first plume of smoke had risen, Stephanie had found the calm she needed to speak.

'I…I'm in New York and head of a fashion house, establishing offices for Louis Vuitton's reach across the America's. I am the CEO, and I have a family-'

'Oh my fucking god,' Pevestone interrupted. 'Boring! Jesus, Stephanie it's like you've just read it off a cornflakes packet. I mean, with all that technology and an offer of indulgence -and you go to the office.' Pevestone spun his Zippo in the palm of his hand and let it slide into his jacket pocket.

'It's not just about that,' Stephanie said, strength building in her voice. 'I've done good, even with…with what you did to me. The career thing - that's not important. But I walk down the street without worrying you're following me. I laugh freely without your face appearing in my mind.'

'Oh, darling Stephanie, so you think about me? You know I think about you.'

'You're *disgusting!*' Stephanie spat, moving closer to the edge.

Alex shrugged and took a drag at his cigarette. 'Okay, my turn.'

Jasmine bore into Alex as she watched him squirm on the vent. *That's what you wanted all along*, she thought. She shifted her gaze and gave Stephanie a reassuring nod.

'Stephanie. Stephanie!' The second time he called, she met his stare. 'You'll know this story. It will be familiar to both of us.'

'Please don't,' she said, her voice weak.

'It has a good ending. They always do. I remember a girl in a yellow dress out for a bike ride one sunny Sunday afternoon. I liked the way her dress rode up her leg and fell effortlessly across her smooth skin.'

Stephanie wept, moaning as she dared to look at Jasmine, who inched forward with her palm out to calm her from a distance.

'We became instant friends, you and I, remember? Yes, it was awkward at first, and I didn't like putting marks on you, but we soon got used to it. And now, because of The Room, I can feel you on me every week - and it is delicious. Sometimes you tell me it hurts, and I think that's your code for wanting it harder and faster. You tell me you like the blood and I sometimes wonder if you're trying to protect me. And, at the end, you tear a little piece of your dress for me to keep and you make me promise to bring you back to those woods.' Pevestone seemed to drift as he looked right through her. 'Don't cry my little girl,' he said. 'Can I touch you?'

The Room

Stephanie was screaming, she clawed her fists together and began punching the side of her face.

'No. No. No!'

She looked over to Jasmine. Then, she looked down into the street. Her eyes were wide as she took in the bright lights of the city in the distance. She looked back at Jasmine, a new calm rose in her, and she knew that Jasmine had seen it. Maybe that was enough.

Yes, enough.

She took deep breaths, slow at first, but they grew short and fast, and then abruptly, she stopped, and it was as though the whole world had ended with her.

Jasmine noticed that she didn't jump; it was more like a step, *a next step*. A thought passed through her mind as cruel as a false hope - it was the next logical step. Hadn't Jasmine seemed to live her life according to those next logical steps? Hadn't that thinking been the catalyst that had brought Jasmine to her own rooftop?

Jasmine had screamed Stephanie's name, and then the shock tightened around her so she could hardly breathe. It was cut short by the terrible thud and crack of her body hitting the ground. Jasmine ran to the edge, stopping short, fearful of seeing her new friend spread across the street.

She turned away from the scene down in the street. More screams on the street level started filtering up. Soon the patrol car would be called, if Daniel hadn't done it himself. She could hear loud voices below; the sounds of people opening their front doors to get an idea of the commotion outside their homes. This needed to end.

Jasmine watched Pevestone with hate-filled eyes. He stood on the edge, peering down through fresh tendrils of smoke. He turned to face Jasmine, distracted by the shifting gravel at Jasmine's feet.

'Oh, don't flatter yourself,' he said, the same mocking tone he'd used for Stephanie. 'You are not my type.'

'I'm too old, you mean?'

'Yes,' he said defiantly. 'You are too old. I like them a lot younger than you.' He looked down at the small, twisted figure, half on the pavement and half on the road and said, 'It's a shame. Even Stephanie was getting too old for me. It would have been the last time for us. And now here I am - all dressed up and nowhere to go.'

'You bastard!' Jasmine ran at him, her fists clenched and ready. But as soon as she was close, he lashed out with his fist and knocked her off her feet.

'Be careful, Jasmine. Any more nonsense like that and I might find that you *are* my type after all.'

She pulled herself noisily to her feet, and Pevestone watched from behind with a smug grin. Jasmine inched closer to the edge and peered over. A short growl of a police siren and the beating of blue lights started to sweep the buildings on Share Street.

'Aren't you afraid they'll catch you?' she asked.

'There's time.' His voice was calm and controlled, as though he were talking with a friend. He watched along with Jasmine the building activity in the street below. 'If you know anything about The Room and our noble host, to which I believe you do, then you'll know that the operation that we've so dedicated our thoughts and obsessions to is also under the watchful eye of some experimenters in the government.'

'You fucking love the sound of your own voice, don't you?'

Pevestone laughed, nodding his head. 'I do, Jasmine. I really do. It's a good job it's not a crime.' Pleased with himself, he took another drag on the cigarette between his fingers. She noticed the bloodstain still growing through his coat. 'So, as the media interest builds down below and someone high up gets flagged about this place in jeopardy - and a naughty man who is *meant* to be in prison is on the roof - then we will be looking at a bit of breathing space while they clear a little back door for me to run out. So there's time. Time at least to finish my cigarette.'

Jasmine looked around the empty rooftop for anything that wasn't fixed down; anything she could use as a weapon. She could have run back down the fire escape, but that would have meant Pevestone slipping away into the night. She didn't want to see his face on the news days, weeks, months from now because she didn't do all she could.

They both stood in silence for a while. Pevestone on his third cigarette as they watched some TV vans arrive and set up along the street. In the distance, Jasmine thought she heard the moan of a helicopter.

'Are you still in charge, Alex?' she asked him, breaking the crippling silence between them. 'This all part of your plan? Maybe it's not real at all. Perhaps we are just fantasies in your Room.'

He drew one last time on his cigarette and flicked it to the floor. With the heel of his boot, he flattened it in a shower of sparks. Through the clearing smoke, Jasmine could see he was smiling.

All of a sudden, he spun around and within two steps he had Jasmine by the throat. She couldn't scream because of how tight he squeezed. She stretched on the tips of her toes to find some relief, but it wasn't enough. She was choking as spit escaped the corners of her closed mouth and tears welled in her bulging eyes. Her arms flung widely, trying to fight the arm that held her. She managed to bring one hand down across his face and felt her fingers go into the softness of his eye.

Jasmine hung like a ragdoll on his outstretched arm. Her eyes bulged, but her head was clear; all she could think about was Stephanie, stepping off into the street, giving up. Pevestone knocked her hand away from his face, screwing his eye closed.

'Is this real enough, you little bitch?'

I'm not her.

Jasmine raised her left hand and grabbed the edge of his coat and pulled him closer, her teeth bared. It caught him off guard, enough for him to release the pressure from around her throat just enough for her to gather the breath to say, 'How is this for real?' With her right hand, she closed her fingers around his left forearm and the gaping hole underneath his coat where the LE chip had been cut away.

They screamed at each other. Pevestone for the pain of feeling her fingers digging into the hole, and Jasmine for the extra strength to not let go. Eventually, he dropped to his knees and cradled his arm. 'You fucking bitch,' he said, spit and blood spraying from his mouth.

The Room

Jasmine circled him slowly while she regulated her breathing. 'You know you should really work on your trash talk,' she said then lunged at him kicking him square in the stomach. 'That's for earlier on the stairs.' She watched him writhe on the floor.

I'm not her.

Jasmine took as big a handful of Pevestone's collar as she could and said, 'And this is for Emma.'

She dragged him to the edge of the roof, adrenaline and determination giving her the strength she needed. Maybe it was shock, but he went over silently. Seconds later, his body folded over a parked car, which seemed to receive him gratefully.

Jasmine backed away, unable to look; unable to process what she had just done. For now, she could only continue to watch the city as it pulsed with life.

CHAPTER 37

About the same time that Jasmine was introducing Alex Pevestone to the edge of the building on Share Street, Daniel Burton stood watching, open-mouthed at the things unfolding before him. Even the screams reverberating from down on the street and the muffled police sirens still approaching weren't enough to shake him free.

He felt a hand on his shoulder, and he knew it was Will.

Will struggled to get the words out, 'What…what's happened?'

Without taking his eyes from Jasmine, he said, 'She's killed it. She's killed it all.'

''It all?' What do you mean?' Will asked, his attention now firmly on Jasmine.

'It's over, Will,' he said with such solemnity, as though they were to be his last words on this earth. And then, his eyes widened with a terrible understanding. He reached for a fistful of Will's jacket and looked at him. Will must have noticed the hollowness in Daniel's eyes and a discolouring as tears started to gather. Daniel's chest heaved as he formed the word that wasn't a word as such, but a name - hardly ever spoken outside of The Room.

'Seth.' Daniel pushed Will aside and running to the far edge of the roof he leapt down the fire escape.

'Will!' Jasmine called.

The Room

Will ran to Jasmine and held her by the arms. 'Jasmine, what's happened?'

She wanted to answer, but the words seemed to take forever to come out. She felt him move to the edge and lean over, but she had to stop him.

'No, don't.' She pulled him back. She wanted to tell him that the shock of seeing Stephanie and Pevestone split open and spread across the pavement would be too much to bear. Still, the reality was that many eyes would be directed at the roof, and having them see a person peering over would bring questions. 'It's Stephanie, I mean - Emma - and Pevestone,' she eventually managed.

Realisation spread across his face as he turned his head and looked to the edge. His attention stayed there. He released her arms and stepped back. His eyes were now on Jasmine, fierce and dark. 'Daniel said you *killed it all*. Jasmine, what does that mean?'

Jasmine took a step backwards and looked at the landscape of the city. 'He used his words against her, Will. He twisted them to the point where she couldn't see a way out.'

'She jumped?'

'He did it. She jumped, but it was his fault.' Tears spilt down her cheeks. She mopped them with the heels of her palms.

'An' Pevestone.' It wasn't a question. He was already moralising what he knew.

'I saw an opportunity, and I took it. I dragged him like a dog to the edge and let him go.' She could see Will was agitated; the colour drained from his face as he looked across the now deserted roof. 'What is it?' Jasmine asked.

'It's not wha' Daniel meant when he said you killed it.'

Jasmine had followed his gaze. 'Will, what did Daniel mean? Where did he go?'

'This is about Seth.'

Jasmine's head filled with images of the boy she'd conjured in her dreams.

I won't give him up.

'Oh, fuck!'

Will was not far behind Jasmine by the time she'd reach the door of The Room in the Hub. She tried to scan her LE chip. 'Nothing's happening,'

'Here, let me,' he said, brandishing his left arm for scanning. Nothing. 'He's changed the code,' Will said, his brow creased as he walked over to the black desk. 'But he wouldn't have had time to batch a new code cluster.'

Jasmine drew her fist and banged against the door. 'Daniel, it's me. Please open the door.' There was no sound as she pressed her ear to it. 'It's okay,' she continued, 'there is a way back from this, but for now we have to get away from here.' After more silence, she gave the door a kick which thrust her back. She joined Will at the desk. He was busy with the desk's interface.

'What did you say about the codes?' Jasmine asked.

'He didn't have time to create a new set of updated codes so he must have reverted to the old ones or at least the ones before the current, before the ones we've got.' Wills fingers danced across the virtual keyboard as he spoke. 'That's why we can't get in.'

'Can't you reprogram your chip with the old code?'

'He's thought of that. Look,' he said, pointing to one of the screens. 'They have zero value; in other words, he's deleted them. That's why I'm sure he's reverted back to the old codes because there would be no other reason to delete the codes prematurely like this.'

'Shit, shit, shit!' Jasmine walked back over to The Room. She raised both hands and spread her fingers and leant on the door. Her eyes closed as she drew a gentle stream of air through her nose.

She looked across the Hub and beyond the dislodged door, where Pevestone had entered from.

'He was bleeding.' She said aloud. She remembered the blood on the landing and had thought it was Stephanie's- but that wasn't right. She ran past Will and towards the door.

Moments later, she came back into the Hub. Will reeled on the chair as he saw her arm covered in blood. She held a spongy lump that was deep red with flecks of white; fragments of bone. Out from the irregular shape of the spongy mass was a familiar shape; a consistent form that he recognised.

'His chip? But how-'

Jasmine grimaced, 'Doesn't matter how. But maybe he didn't decode the Nurturing Project arseholes. Hopefully, it's our key,' she said. She held out Pevestone's chip to the door.

Ping.

The door jumped from its retreating lock. Jasmine dropped Pevestone's chip to the floor.

'Wait,' Will said, rounding on Jasmine, 'let me go in first.'

They both stood on the threshold looking into the dark room, dark except for the empty chair that waited. At the side where Jasmine remembered sitting holding Stephanie's hand less than an hour ago, was Daniel's laptop. It flickered unknown codes against a black screen.

'Daniel.' Will called out his name as he stepped into The Room, shortly followed by Jasmine. 'Mate, this ain't right. They're comin.'

Jasmine followed closely behind, noticing again all the dark alcoves. One of these held Daniel, she could sense it. As they rounded the room, Will became distracted by the chair and moved swiftly toward it.

'Daniel,' Jasmine began, 'I know how you feel. I know what this means to you, and I know why you're doing this. But it's not real. The memories of Seth are real enough, and in time you'll be able to nurture them without all this. That's what most people have called 'living.' To those people who have lost - like you and me - living in the real world is enough. It's keeping them alive in our memory.'

'These doses,' Will said, bent over the glass canisters. 'Dan, mate, it's too much!'

'That's the idea,' she said and then raising her voice, 'isn't it Daniel?'

Stillness and silence persisted.

Will ushered for Jasmine to join him and then whispered, 'he's probably locked me out of the command software, but I think I can release these drugs manually. I've never 'ad a reason to use it, but there's a kinda drain valve underneath 'ere somewhere.' His fingers disappeared below one of the canisters. 'Wait, I think I have it.'

A raging cry came from the shadows behind them as Daniel sprung into the air and came down hard across Will's shoulders and neck with Pevestone's old weapon of choice. The force of Daniel's swing sent Will sprawling across the room, a crimson spray soaking through the collar of his shirt. Jasmine screamed and ran towards Will. He stood over her, brandishing the bar.

'You both have to leave now. Please.'

'Daniel, we can all leave together. You can hide,' she looked at Will. 'You can hide your test circuit in your apartment. They'll never know.'

'What? What test circuit?' Will squinted through the darkness, holding the side of his neck.

Daniel sighed. 'It's connected to the main server. They'll take it all.'

He turned to Will. Jasmine saw his eyes widen as the reflection of the blue lights from outside spread across his face. Putting down the weapon, he went over to Will and thrust his arms under him and started to drag him towards the door.

'You have to get him out of here, Jasmine. He's bleeding where I hit him.' Daniel pulled him out of the Hub, and onto the sofa.

'I'm not going to stand here and let you go through with this. You know how this is going to end.'

'You, Jasmine. You of all people are not going to stop me. I've watched you remember.'

The man from the window, Jasmine thought.

Jasmine followed Daniel as he rounded the chair and carefully lowered himself into it. She leaned over him, her face was close to his, and his familiar smell seemed to surround her.

'Daniel, if anything, it's you who saved my life,' she said softly. 'I might not have liked it, but you have been the secret in my life since…since Seth and you have been there to pull me from the edge. Bringing me here the way you did, giving me direction with the job and even,' she paused, 'Mia. I know you didn't intend it Daniel, but you've shown me how dangerous The Room can be, and it's made me realise that out there is what matters. What your mind does with the stuff out there is all that counts. Please let me be there for you. Let me pull you away from the edge.'

Daniel smiled. He reached up and held her close. 'It sounds like I've saved you for the last time. It sounds like you don't need me anymore.'

'No, I do,' she said, pulling away slightly.

Daniel lifted his finger to her lips, 'Shush!' His fingers fell against her cheek and stroked her skin, playing with her curls. His eyes went from clear and hazy; his smile was dreamlike, and his words were weighted and slow.

'Look after Will. Tell him I'm sorry.'

'Daniel?' She looked at the canisters; empty.

Daniel's eyes were already closed, and his chest went still.

Jasmine slowly stepped away, retreating into the shadows. She wasn't going to take him away from his son.

She was startled when she heard Will call her name. He was standing in the doorway, a cockeyed living shadow, backlit from the Hub. Will took a few moments to look at his friend lying peacefully in the chair.

'We have to go,' he said.

Jasmine left The Room. She closed the door behind her and went to the desk. Her hands were shaking as she fumbled with the virtual computer. Will stepped up beside her and took her hands and then embraced her whole shaking frame.

'Can we lock the door? I just want to give him as long as possible.'

Will reached around Jasmine and struck a combination of holographic buttons until the door made the now sickly sounding *ping*.

'Yes, we have to go. But, separately. Are you okay?'

Will reached for the side of his neck and felt the wet patch creeping at his collar. 'Yes, I'll be fine. I'll find a way out of here and head to the hospital. I'll make up some excuse. I mean they won't believe this, will they?' Will tried to smile but he winced through the pain.

'Be careful. You know if they decide it's important enough to them, they'll come for us.'

'Then we'll have to stay one step ahead of them.'

'I'll contact you. The next few days,' she said, pulling away towards the broken door.

She stepped out onto the fire escape and waited, picking out a route between the untouched streets and the wave of pulsing blue lights that animated the buildings. Clusters of people gathered where they could, and Jasmine decided that she would be one of them. She stood, her hood up over her hair, watching the news reporters talking into large microphones, and listened to second-hand reports of what may or may not have been the cause of the terrible double suicide on Share Street.

CHAPTER 38

Michael's favourite desk lamp was now laid across the rug. Its neck was broken, and a cable ran through its splintered porcelain spine.

He couldn't remember how the lamp had ended up on the floor. The space flickered from dark to light, to dark to light. An empty bottle of whisky lay on its side just behind the dark patch of carpet that held onto the sweet odour of his drink. Around him were scattered papers, some torn and some screwed into odd shapes. The laptop had survived the previous night, and glowed with an unfinished piece that Michael had been working on.

TheRoomtheroomTHEROOMtHERoOm, one line in thick black text ran across the screen. It was all he had managed before Michael had retreated into his own living room, and collapsed backwards onto the sofa.

In his other hand, he held a piece of paper. It looked to be an old copy of a news report, yellowed, and only part of the subheading was visible:*BritCub Reporter Ben Henshall Left for Dead*. The Americans had gotten hold of the shit storm story back then, and it appeared in a side column of The Post. How he'd have wanted that many years ago, Michael thought as he screwed up the old article. *Global fucking fame.*

Michael's phone lit up. Harriet, again. He waited for the phone to stop ringing and then pushed himself gingerly off the sofa and tossed the ball of copy clutched in his fist into the dead fireplace.

He had seventeen missed calls from Harriet. She'd been fired too, just yesterday like Michael. He'd spent the day drinking with a man who he now knew was named Brock – an American Accountant. The Fly By Night had been closed, a sign hung idle on the door, when they'd arrived, and doing anything other than shots with his new friend had seemed pointless.

He scrolled down to the only Jasmine he had in his contacts. The side of the phone screen assigned to Jasmine's replies was empty. Despite this, Michael smiled and let the phone fall to the table, his free hand went to his face and, with fingers still numb from sleep, he scraped the stubble on his chin.

'Just another day,' his morning-after voice rattled. Just then he spotted the black business card that had belonged to Daniel Burton. The only other words on the card were "The Room" and Burton, introduced as "The Architect". He picked it up as he had done a thousand times and turned it over, not expecting to find anything new. He'd spotted it in the disarray at Jasmine's family home, thinking it was a clue, but it was as useless as the card it was printed on.

The mobile phone sprang into life and made him jump. He laughed awkwardly and didn't even bother to check who it was. He pulled himself up and walked over to his laptop, flipping the lid closed.

'You're too old to believe in ghosts,' he said to an empty room and then moved towards the door without looking back.

Michael had carefully chosen the path to walk that morning. It was sufficiently set back from the park's entrance and gave an almost uninterrupted view of the oak tree in the middle of the untouched grass. It seemed a centrepiece of the park and an ideal place should

The Room

anyone want to meet. In fact, it was the first place you would think have when someone suggested meeting in the park. It was easy, no misunderstandings here and you could spot someone coming a mile off.

And he knew from his own research, with a little help from Harriet, that Jasmine had a past here. Her dad's name had popped up in a couple of searches concerning a child's unfortunate death, way back. That, and the little secret of Stephanie Milner were all over her files. And somewhere in the midst of it all of this carnage, was The Room at Share Street.

Michael recognised Will straight away. He seemed to come from behind the oak and join a woman who was already sitting on the bench. He watched as Will sat awkwardly next to her and handed her something. Whatever it was, she leaned over and slipped it into her back pocket and then gave him a kiss on the cheek. Michael found his own bench along the meandering path and sat, twisted at an angle so he could watch them.

Eventually, Will rose from the bench and started walking towards the park entrance, but the woman didn't follow. Michael got up and followed the path towards the woman sitting under the oak. Without speaking, he took up the space next to her and stared at the overhanging tree and the long shadows cast across the root torn path.

'Funny thing about favourite places,' Michael began, 'after a while, they become a little predictable. They're a lot like passwords. We tend to stick with the same old words because they're familiar to us, and a lot easier to conjure when put on the spot.'

Jasmine turned to see Michael still staring into the sky neatly framed by the reaching branches of the oak. 'Do you want some sort of medal for finding us, Mr Powers?'

Michael seemed taken by the answer, realising at once how his opening remarks may have been misconstrued. But he smiled anyway. 'No. No medals here. Not today. That's the last thing I want.'

'What do you want, Mr Powers?' Jasmine asked.

'Well, for a start it would be nice if you called me Michael.'

'And then what?'

'And then, maybe we can talk, Jasmine.' He watched her take out her phone. 'Are you expecting a call?'

'You never know,' she said.

They both watched Will as he reached the gate. He turned and saw them both seated under the tree. He reached to his ear and tapped.

'It's okay. No, you stay where you are. It's all good. I can see you, and you can see me.' Jasmine looked over at Michael, her phone still pressed to her ear. 'I expected a visit from Mr Powers.'

'He's a worrier,' Michael said with a faint smile.

'He needs to know if he has anything to worry about.'

'And what about you, Jasmine? Are you worried for the future?'

'You never answered my question. What do you want?' Jasmine asked again.

'What does any reporter want? The story, of course. I'm tangled up in so many loose ends, but I think you're the one that can set a few of them straight, and even tie up a few of them for me.'

'It's no good,' she said in almost hushed tones, as though she'd never meant the words to leave her lips.

'What's no good?' Michael craned to meet her eyes.

'The story.' She allowed some recognition to rise in his expression before she continued. 'Let's imagine you get all your loose ends neatly tied up and, by the way, I have a feeling about you, and it tells me you have enough to already do that with a modicum of intelligence and your hounds all pointing in the right direction. But then, having done all that, what have you got? A story that is no good to you. You're doomed to only ever tell your version. Eventually, someone will join the dots together. Someone who knew Ben Henshall, or Stephanie Milner. These are triggers that you can't afford anyone to squeeze.'

Michael hung his arm over the back of the bench and turned to face her. 'So, Jasmine, given that we both have pasts that we'd rather keep under the shade of this oak tree, let me ask you, what do *you* want?'

She swallowed hard. 'What do *I* want? I want to be left alone. *We* don't want to be looking over our shoulders every time our LE's beep.'

'Don't we all want that?' Michael said. He turned back on his seat and absently rubbed the underside of his left forearm. 'The truth is Jasmine, no one can guarantee you that.' He sighed. 'I'll tell you something else that is true. I like it here in the shade. Yes, I want the story. But if you say I have all my loose ends in one place, then let that be it.'

'You have all you need,' she said.

'Except for one thing-' Michael replied.

'No.'

'Won't you tell me about him? Even now after he's gone?'

'Who says he's gone?' Jasmine lifted her eyes to the sky anticipating the sting of tell-tale tears.

'I know one thing; they'll never give up a body. He disappeared a long time ago. I just wanted to know about the guy that created The Room.'

Jasmine remained silent. She stood up and made to move away.

'Are you leaving town?' Michael asked.

'Does it matter? We won't be seeing one another again.'

'I suppose not. But, I have one more question. Do you think something this big will ever be allowed to sleep indefinitely? Do you think there will be other Rooms?'

Jasmine looked at him carefully. He leaned forward with his forearms neatly on his thighs. In that moment, Jasmine could hardly see him for the big oak tree, where in the past children laughed and screamed for the sheer delight of being tossed about by the clunking mechanical carousel.

She felt a pain deep in her temples as she shifted focus to somewhere beyond the tree. She saw two girls playing catch with each other. They were too far away for Jasmine to make out – but she could see that one of the girls was dressed in a red coat, a hood peeking out under thick black hair, and the other wore a bright yellow summer dress.

'Goodbye, Michael.' She slowly turned away and started walking towards the park gates. She held her face to the sun and enjoyed the warmth, and the breeze that tickled and picked up her thick black curls, just as it had when she was a little girl.

[The End]

Printed in Great Britain
by Amazon